MAN ON THE RUN

LARRY STEWART

iUniverse®

MAN ON THE RUN

iUniverse books may be ordered through booksellers or by contacting:

iUniverse
1663 Liberty Drive
Bloomington, IN 47403
www.iuniverse.com
1-800-Authors (1-800-288-4677)

ISBN: 978-1-5320-3330-8 (sc)
ISBN: 978-1-5320-3329-2 (e)

Library of Congress Control Number: 2017916845

Print information available on the last page.

iUniverse rev. date: 11/06/2017

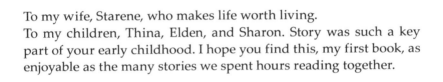

To my wife, Starene, who makes life worth living.
To my children, Thina, Elden, and Sharon. Story was such a key part of your early childhood. I hope you find this, my first book, as enjoyable as the many stories we spent hours reading together.

CONTENTS

CHAPTER 1

It was a typical Monday in late October. People had returned to their jobs at least as tired as when they had left for the weekend. But one man welcomed the new week. He was about to embark on an adventure unlike any in his forty or so years. Carrying a briefcase, the man entered a Citibank branch just after it opened. He briefly stopped at a kiosk and wrote on a card before approaching one of the three tellers. The man was about five ten with a hint of gray in his hair. People later described him as lean, but middle age spread was beginning to enlarge his profile. He wore blue jeans and a gray jacket. Nothing about him stood out; he appeared to be an ordinary customer.

His name was Lance Knight. He had toiled as a surveyor for close to twenty years but felt he had little to show for it. He earned a healthy salary but was saddled with the mortgage on his house and lived from paycheck to paycheck. The tax man would swoop in to claim any savings he managed to accumulate. In this he was no different from the other customers in the bank that day. Lance did not have extravagant tastes or expensive habits, yet at the end of each month his bank account was always empty.

Unlike the rest of the bank patrons, though, he was about to declare his independence from the rat race. He had been planning this move for two months, and within the next few minutes he would guarantee freedom for him and his wife for the rest of their lives.

Lance was attracted to this bank because it doubled as the regional office, making it a large distribution facility. After brief security checks, armored trucks moved to the rear compound for the transfer of funds to all the other Citibank branches in the lower mainland. In several prior visits to the bank, Lance had noticed that the wide double doors between the bank and the distribution center were often left open so that tellers and other employees could access the large walk-in safe about twenty feet past the doors. The safe was usually closed, but it was open early every Monday because this was the day when the majority of transfers took place.

As Lance approached the counter, the teller smiled.

"Good morning!" she said. "How can I help you today?"

Lance took a deep breath to calm himself. The moment had arrived.

"Yes, good morning, Sue," he said, observing her name tag. He swung his black briefcase onto the counter. "I would like to withdraw a hundred dollars."

"Very well. I'll need to see your bank card, please," Sue said as she began inputting preliminary information for the transaction on her computer.

Lance felt he had achieved the air of confidence he had repeatedly practiced. He slipped a plastic card across the desk to her and watched closely to study her reaction. Sue picked up the card and prepared to scan it to complete the transaction. A puzzled frown came across her face. Rather than the bank card she had expected, he had passed her a Tim Horton's gift card with a business card taped on the back. On this card Lance had written, "This is a robbery. I have a gun."

Lance saw the teller's eyes grow wide. She looked from the card back up at him. "A hundred dollars, sir? I don't understand."

A smile flickered across Lance's face. "Well, actually maybe a little more than a hundred if you wouldn't mind." With that he pulled a neatly folded cloth shopping bag from the briefcase and slid it across to her. "Please be discreet, if you know what I mean," he said in a voice designed to keep her calm. He motioned with his head toward her till. Sue's face turned pale. Without a word she opened the till and began emptying the contents into the bag, her hands shaking noticeably.

"If you wouldn't mind, could you ask the teller next to you to come over? Just ask her to help you with something. Keep your eyes on the computer screen. Do it now, please," Lance said.

"Jill, would you come here for a second?" Sue said, trying unsuccessfully to maintain a normal tone of voice.

The second teller came over quickly, a concerned frown on her face. Her eyes followed Sue's to the computer screen. "What's the problem, Sue?" she asked.

"If you wouldn't mind, just quickly read the note Sue has," Lance interjected calmly. "I'm making a withdrawal." He slid a second folded shopping bag to Jill. "Sue, if you're done with this till, would you please start on the one next to you?" Within a minute, Lance had the two tellers emptying four tills.

"Now ladies, we are going to walk through those doors to the back and pay a quick visit to the vault. Please stay calm. I'll be right behind you. If we meet anyone, simply smile and keep going. Are we clear on that?" he asked, looking hard into the eyes of the two women. The tellers stared back and nodded nervously. Satisfied, Lance said, "Very good. Let's start moving now. Please don't do anything foolish. We wouldn't want this situation to turn ugly, now would we?"

The young ladies walked stiffly to the end of the teller windows, carrying the shopping bags. Lance followed them with one hand in his jacket pocket and the other holding the briefcase. He glanced at the other bank employees and their customers. No one appeared to have noticed the drama that was being played out. *So far, so good*, he thought, *but let's not get cocky.* They proceeded through the double doors without encountering anyone. "No need to hurry, ladies," he said. Once in the open vault, the robber moved quickly. "Please fill the bags as quickly as you can, ladies," he ordered. Lance dropped the briefcase and opened it. He pulled out a third black shopping bag and began filling it with wads of money from the vault's shelves as the two women did the same with the bags he had handed them.

Several seconds later Lance was startled by a beeping noise. He glanced down at the briefcase on the floor. The sound was coming from the timer he had activated just before he had approached the first till. "I'm sorry, ladies, but my time's up. I'll take your bags," Lance said. He grabbed the bags, closed his briefcase, and took one last glance at the shelves, which still contained many packets of bills. He resisted the temptation to stay longer and left the women standing motionless inside the vault. It had been exactly one minute, thirty seconds from the time he had approached Sue.

Lance ignored the curious stares of a few patrons and left the bank toting three stuffed grocery bags and the briefcase. He walked a half block down the street, got into a white 1996 Chevy Impala, and drove away.

·····•••••◆•••••····

Detective Rob Passaglia sat shuffling papers into neat piles on his desk in one of the many cubicles on the third floor of the Vancouver police headquarters. Each pile represented one of the many tasks he would need to complete on another busy Monday. As he reached for the first stack of papers he would attack, Captain Russ Harding walked in.

"I've got something for you, Rob," Harding said. He strode to Rob's desk and placed a thin folder in front of him. Harding was dressed much like Rob, in a neat but casual long-sleeved shirt and tan khaki pants. Although officers in the investigative branch did not wear uniforms, the careful cut of their attire, their sharp appearance, and the shine on their shoes reflected the rigorous training they had received. Careful observation would lead many to conclude that they were indeed police officers.

"Aw, come on, Captain. Look at all this stuff I've got!" Passaglia protested, gesturing at the stacks of papers on his desk. "Can't Bill and Dave take this one? They just wrapped up that string of gas station heists."

Rob had moved from a patrol car to the investigative branch three years earlier. He had been the rookie in the office and as such had paid his dues that first year. He had taken the friendly gibes of the more experienced officers with patient humor and had been stuck with the files no one else wanted. In that first year, however, Rob had won the grudging admiration of the other detectives. He had solved case after case with his intelligence and dogged determination. Many found his approach unorthodox, but the scoffing gave way to respect as his successes mounted. And recently it was rumored that he was being watched by those upstairs for a promotion.

One case in particular had become legendary. When the detectives found time to meet after work at a local pub, witnesses would recount the story over beers. By now, nearly every member of the force knew the details of the case.

The unit had been called to an upscale apartment in downtown Vancouver. A woman had been murdered, and her husband had been badly beaten. The place had been ransacked, and most of the valuables were missing. Rob was a junior member of the investigative team. The senior detectives were sure this was a case of a break-in gone terribly wrong, but Rob insisted that this was an elaborate set-up and that the husband was guilty of murder. He pointed to the woman lying twisted and mangled on the living room floor. "That's a crime of passion," he stated flatly. Then he examined the scene, questioning every detail. "How could that vase in the corner have been broken?" he asked. "Why would a burglar have left the filing cabinet undisturbed and gone through all the board games in the closet to discover the wife's jewelry hidden in the Monopoly set?"

At first the other members of the team chuckled, but eventually they grew weary of Rob's observations, especially since they could come up with no logical answers to the questions he posed.

Finally the lead investigator pulled him aside. "You've made some very astute points, Detective Passaglia," he said, "but have you noticed the husband's leg?"

"Yes, of course," Rob replied.

"Well it's broken," the detective said. "I highly doubt that a man in his condition could have done what you seem to be implying he did."

That had quieted Rob, at least temporarily.

At headquarters the next day, Rob stood with other members of the team behind a one-way window and watched as the husband, wearing a large leg cast, was interviewed. "His demeanor just doesn't seem consistent with someone who's lost his wife," Rob said.

This brought groans from the other detectives. They told Rob he was being irrational. "Shut up and listen to the interview," one of them said. "Maybe you'll learn something."

The investigators asked the husband about his leg. He said he had been mountain climbing with friends about a week before when a rope had given way and he had fallen some twelve feet, breaking the leg. He said his friends had carried him to the car and had rushed him to the hospital in Whistler.

The interviewers asked him for the names of the friends, and he readily provided them.

Some of the detectives outside drew pocket notebooks and

wrote down the names, but Rob was uninterested. The investigators were about to move on to the circumstances of the break-in when he jumped up from his chair and knocked at the door to the interview room. He didn't wait for an answer but burst in.

"Excuse me, Mr. Wise," Rob said, "but could you tell me the name of the hospital where you were taken and the name of the physician who attended you?" The two interviewers swung around and frowned, clearly perturbed by the interruption.

"Well, I don't know," the man said. "I believe there's only one hospital there, but I'm not sure what it's called. As for the doctor, I don't remember his name. You can understand. I was in a great deal of pain."

"And that was on the twelfth, was it? About what time did you arrive at the hospital?"

"Yes, the twelfth. It must have been about two in the afternoon, I guess," the man replied, somewhat nonplussed.

"Thank you, sir. Excuse the interruption," Rob said, nodding at the interviewers. He didn't stay for the rest of the session.

When the interview was concluded the lead investigator stormed into the main office where Rob sat with dozens of other junior detectives.

"If you ever pull a stunt like that again, Passaglia, it'll be the last time you're ever on one of my investigations," the detective shouted.

"I'm sorry, Captain, but that guy's dirty," Rob said. "There are just too many things that don't add up.

"I think I explained to you yesterday, Passaglia, that it's impossible for him to have done what you seem to say he did."

"I know that, sir."

The captain stared at him and finally walked away, shaking his head without saying another word. Just before leaving, he stopped suddenly and turned back. "Hey Passaglia!" he shouted.

The din that was starting to resume ceased. "Yes, sir," Rob replied.

"If you want to pay for the X-ray, I'll have it arranged."

Rob beamed. "You're on, Captain. Thank you very much."

The captain shook his head once more before leaving the room.

The following afternoon a prowler was caught red-handed. He was well known to police and had a rap sheet that included break-ins with occasional violence. He was held on suspicion of murder in the Wise case.

As the lead investigator was tidying his desk, getting ready to leave for the night, Rob knocked on his door. "Excuse me, sir. Do you have a minute?"

"Passaglia, you are beyond a doubt one genuine fucking pain in the ass. What is it?" the captain asked.

"Well, sir, I just want to update you on my progress."

"I'm sure you're going to insist it can't wait, so I won't bother asking you to leave it until tomorrow," the captain said, sitting heavily back in his chair.

"Thank you, sir."

This part of the story always drew a laugh as the guys pictured Rob's meek attitude just moments before he dropped the bombshell that would crack the case. In the previous twenty-four hours, he had driven to Whistler and had interviewed the doctor who had treated Wise; he had returned to the crime scene, where the team continued to search for evidence, and he had consulted with an orthopedist about the X-ray of Wise's leg that had been done at the request of the police.

The doctor in Whistler had produced an X-ray showing a clear fracture but was scant on details or records of the case. Later that morning Rob had investigated the doctor and had learned that he was Wise's high school classmate.

At the crime scene, Rob had one of the men pull apart the bathtub drain. Rob poured the contents of the drainpipe into a container and screened out a fair amount of plaster, the material from which casts were made.

In his meeting with the orthopedic expert he ascertained two things. First, the X-ray he had obtained from the doctor in Whistler and the X-ray that had just been conducted at the request of the police were not X-rays of the same person. Second, the orthopedist insisted that the break his X-ray showed was fresh and could not possibly have happened a week earlier.

In the end, when the doctor in Whistler discovered that he could be facing accessory-to-murder charges, he came clean. Wise had put him up to it. Wise had been an accomplished gymnast in high school and was able to absorb the force of the fall from the mountain without injury. He had said he intended to play a practical joke on the other climbers, and the doctor had agreed to put the cast on his old friend.

Faced with the mounting evidence against him, Wise finally confessed. He had removed the cast, savagely beaten and murdered his wife, and then staged the break-in scene. The pièce de resistance was breaking his leg by using a rope to pull a set of heavy weights down on top of it. The pain must have been excruciating as he dragged himself to the bathroom and placed the cast around the leg before finally calling the police with the phony break-in report.

"Relax, Rob. I'm doing you a favor," Captain Harding said. Most of the cubicles were still empty. As usual, Rob had been one of the first detectives to arrive. He tentatively opened the file folder. "This is going to be the easiest case you've ever had," Harding said. "If it's not solved by the end of the day, I'll eat my shirt. Citibank was robbed half an hour ago. A lone gunman made off with a ton of cash. They're still counting, but they say it could be $500,000."

Rob whistled. "That's a lot of cash for a bank robbery. I've never heard of a take like that. Why so much?"

"The bank routinely doubles its cash for Monday. Besides that, with the end of the month and the long Remembrance Day weekend ahead, there were even more funds on hand than usual. The guy got into the safe and helped himself. But he didn't get greedy. He was gone in less than two minutes. The squad cars arrived forty seconds later, but he had vanished.

"It's obvious the perp chose his moment with care," Rob said. "He did his homework. You said this was an easy one. How come? It sounds to me like this guy was pretty thorough."

"The officers who responded to the call will fill you in, so get your ass down there right now. Forensics is already on its way."

You're being pretty coy, Captain. What's up?"

"You'll see when you get to the bank."

"Come on, Captain. I'm up to my ass in work."

"As far as I know, you haven't taken over my job yet, Passaglia. When you do, you can make all the assignment decisions you please. But for now that's my job, and I'm assigning you to this case." Harding pushed the folder toward the detective, smiled, did an about-face almost as if he were on the parade grounds, and marched away. Rob ran his fingers through his hair in frustration.

Half an hour later he walked into the downtown branch of

Citibank. Uniformed and plainclothes officers were busy with the investigation. Two members of the forensics team were dusting the counter where the perp had first approached the tellers. Three bank administrators, a police officer, and a female teller were clustered around a computer, while other officers were interviewing bank employees, notepads in hand. The bank had been closed to the public immediately after the robbery. Rob introduced himself to two uniformed officers conferring over a notepad. "What do you have?" he asked.

The officers looked up and exchanged a glance. Rob got that look a lot. Though he was thirty-seven years old, he appeared to be in his twenties, so people were often taken aback when he introduced himself as a detective.

The officers studied him quickly. At five nine, Rob was probably an inch or two shorter than average, but his frame exuded strength. He kept his thick black hair short. Rob ignored the look and gave the officers an encouraging smile.

"Right! Sorry, sir," said the more senior of the two. "The perp entered the bank about 10:05 a.m. I just watched the security tapes. He wasn't wearing a ball cap or anything, so we've got a pretty good look at him. Less than two minutes passed from the time he entered to the time he left with the cash. We have a witness who says she saw him speed away in a white sedan. She didn't get a plate number. Kevin's working with her to come up with make, model, and year." He pointed to where the woman sat peering at the young officer's sketch pad.

"Captain Harding seems to think this case is a slam dunk. What's that about?"

"Oh yeah," the officer said with a sly smile. "Hey Martin, you got the holdup note," he called to the officer huddled with the bank employees at the computer.

The officer straightened up and grinned like a Cheshire cat. He reached for a plastic evidence bag resting on the desk and strolled over. He handed Rob the bag containing the card.

"Have you heard the story about the bank robber who wrote the robbery note on the back of his business card?" the officer asked.

"Nooo! You're not telling me ..."

"Yup! Here it is," Martin said with a chuckle.

Rob pulled the card out of the bag. He read the note and flipped the card to the front. "True Line Surveyors. Lance Knight. You don't really suppose he used his own business card to write the note, do you?" Rob asked.

The two officers laughed. "That's what we were thinking," the senior officer said.

"Well, that's highly unlikely," Rob said. "This guy seemed pretty methodical during the robbery. I doubt he would make a mistake like that."

Rob moved over to where another officer was huddled with a balding man in a gray suit. "Detective Passaglia," he said, offering the older man his hand. The man shook hands and announced, "He got $737,280, all in bills."

Rob gave a low whistle. "Okay, we're going to need to take the security tapes. My team will be here another hour or so. I would ask that neither you nor your staff speak to the press about anything to do with this case. The police public relations bureau will handle all that. Simply tell them 'no comment' and refer them to the police department. We will be making a statement later this afternoon. Right now, I'd like to talk to the tellers the robber interacted with."

The manager assured Rob of the bank's cooperation and led him over to where Sue and Jill were being interviewed by a police officer.

"Excuse me," Rob said. "I'm Detective Passaglia. I'm heading the investigation. I realize this has been a very upsetting experience for both of you. Do you mind if I ask you a few questions?"

The two women looked at him and nodded. "That's fine, detective," Sue said, "but I'm sure the officer here has been very thorough."

"I'm sure he has been," Rob said with a smile, "but I like to get a feel for things myself. Is there anything else you can add to your statement?"

The tellers thought for a few seconds and shrugged their shoulders.

"The note said he had a gun. Did he?"

The two women looked at each other, and finally Jill replied, "Well, he never showed it, but there was definitely something in his jacket pocket. I believe it was a gun, but I can't be sure." Susan nodded in agreement and grasped Jill's hand.

"He seemed to be very efficient," Jill said. "One of the other tellers triggered the silent alarm as soon as she saw us heading for the safe. But he left the bank less than a minute before your squad cars arrived."

"Yes, that's true," Sue said. "He had a timer or something in his briefcase, and as soon as it went off he left. There was still lots of money in the vault, as you can see, but he just turned and left."

"Which way did he go as he left the bank?"

"I don't know. Jill and I stayed in the vault. I think we were probably in shock."

"This has been very stressful for you," Rob said, handing each of them his card. "If you happen to think of anything else in the next few days, please give me a call. You never know how significant the smallest thing can be."

"Well, that's just the thing," Sue said, taking the card.

"What's that?" Rob asked.

"I mean I've been robbed before, about three years ago, but this one was far less traumatic than my first."

"Why's that?"

Sue turned to Jill for support before she continued. "Well, it's just that he was so polite and reassuring. He even smiled at me. He did make veiled threats and that scared me a lot, but all in all he seemed to make a real effort to keep us calm. He never hurried or harassed us. He didn't even raise his voice."

"That's true," Jill said.

"You ladies conducted yourselves exactly right. You did nothing to antagonize the robber. Who knows, things might have turned out much differently if you had. Thank you for your time. Remember, if you do think of anything else, give me a call."

Sue and Jill nodded as Rob strode over to talk with the forensics investigators still busy with their work at the counter. The two had not been able to lift any usable prints. It seemed the thief had been pretty careful.

Rob returned to the office. He removed the card from the plastic bag and immediately began working at his computer. He opened up the police database and entered a search for the name on the card, Lance Knight. In seconds the computer brought up a photograph from the Department of Motor Vehicles. Rob studied the photograph carefully and printed a copy. Within minutes he had details on the suspect. Knight lived in Surrey. He was a surveyor and had a wife and three adult children. One by one, Rob inserted the bank videos into the player and watched them. It took several minutes before he found a clear view of the robber. As soon as he did, he stopped the tape. He studied the photograph he had printed and compared it to the image on his screen. He picked up the phone and dispatched one squad car to Knight's place of work and another to his home with orders to bring him in.

At this early stage of the investigation, Rob was not by any means ready to conclude that Knight was guilty. In fact, it seemed highly unlikely that he was. Knight had no criminal record, no financial irregularities. To Rob, he seemed like a model citizen. But right now this was the only lead in the case, and that photo sure looked a lot like the bank robber. *Maybe the captain was right about wrapping this up in a day,* Rob thought.

CHAPTER 2

L ance stared dumbfounded at the business card he held in
his hand. He was now five miles from the bank, parked in a
residential area of East Vancouver as he had planned. A real
estate agent had dropped off the card along with a flier at Lance's
house a few weeks earlier to announce that a neighboring house
had sold.

Lance had been busy transferring the bundles from the vault
and the loose bills from the tills into the briefcase. It was one of
those briefcases that expand accordion style when you undo the
straps, providing much more room inside. He had been delighted
that the wads of bills included hundred-dollar denominations.
Others were bundles of fifties, twenties, tens, and fives. He would
have the opportunity to count his take later. Now was not the time.
Lance had finished packing the briefcase and had then stuffed the
empty shopping bags into a plastic garbage bag. Then he had started
putting items from his pockets in the bag. The short-nosed pistol he
had picked up in the States had gone in, and then he had searched
for the robbery note. It was then he had discovered the card that
should not have been there.

How could this be? Lance wondered. Had he not used the back
of this card to scribble the robbery note? He retraced his steps,
remembering how he had stopped at the kiosk, written the note, and
attached it to the coffee card. *Could I have been that stupid?* Lance asked
himself. He vaguely recalled reaching into his pocket to pull out the
card he had stuffed in his shirt before leaving the house. Had he felt
a second card in his pocket as he reached in? He couldn't recall. Had
there been a second card, one that should not have been there? What

was that card? It couldn't have been the one he suspected it was. At the thought, his body shook involuntarily. Lance's elation at seeing all the cash quickly turned to dread. His mind struggled to reject the possibility. No way. If it was true, his life was ruined.

It had been his plan to recover the card with the robbery note before leaving. But the teller had placed it below the counter when she began emptying the till, and Lance had forgotten about it. That was his first mistake, but that was not what tormented him at the moment. It was the presence of the real estate card in his jacket pocket. That card should have been in the bank, stuck to the back of the coffee card. If this card wasn't stuck to the coffee card, what was?

Lance worked for a surveying company, and he carried business cards that he would occasionally hand to clients in the field. He often carried the cards in his jacket pocket but also had a few in his wallet, and now his worst nightmare might have come true.

Lance had been planning for months to rob the biggest bank in downtown Vancouver. He had planned the job meticulously, right down to replacing the plate on the car with a plate left at his place by a punk who had dated his daughter five years earlier. He was glad that his daughter had been smart enough to call it quits with that loser. The plate had sat in the basement along with other odd pieces of junk the guy had left. The province hadn't changed designs in decades, so Lance had simply shined up the plate a bit. He had put the current year's tag for his truck on the plate to complete the deception. Even if the plate had been spotted, there was little chance it would be traced to him. That ex-boyfriend was so stupid he would never remember what he had done with the plate.

Using cash, Lance had purchased the Impala from an older couple. But Lance had not registered the vehicle, and he had given a false name for the bill of sale, so it would be practically impossible for police to trace the car to him. He had kept the car a secret from his wife. She didn't need to know anything about it. He had attached the plates and had parked the car on a street a block away from his house. He had moved it often enough to avoid raising suspicion by the neighbors.

Lance had staked out the bank inside and outside. For months he had been entering the bank to make small transactions. Each time he had a goal in mind. On one visit he checked the location of surveillance cameras; on another he gauged the vault's accessibility.

On other occasions he studied the staff at the tills and in the offices. He parked outside the bank to determine its busiest times and also counted the number of armored cars leaving the site. Lance continued studying the bank until finally he had a sense of its rhythm. This enabled him to determine the date and time of day that would yield the biggest haul and that would be the safest for him.

He had rehearsed the heist as he drove to work in the morning, constantly reciting the words he intended to use and working on the tone. This had enabled him to appear calm during the robbery when in reality he was a ball of nerves.

When at last he committed to the job, Lance had to admit to himself that no matter how much planning he did or how well he knew the bank there were risks. A police cruiser could happen to be in the wrong spot at the wrong time. He might encounter a particularly aggressive bank employee or customer. He could always pull his pistol to intimidate such a person, but he was certain he could never bring himself to pull the trigger. The risks were real, but Lance's preparations were designed to mitigate the danger. He had never imagined that his stupidity might be his undoing.

Lance sat in his car staring at the card, a briefcase full of money on the passenger seat beside him. He could picture the police and bank officials chuckling when they saw his business card, which announced to all who could read, "Look here. It was me. I did it. Just drive to my house and pick me up."

His egregious error weighed heavily on him. How could he go home? Within an hour, the police would be at his house asking for a list of people to whom he had given his cards and demanding that he explain why his card had been used for a robbery note at the Citibank.

Lance realized he couldn't remain parked on a street in Vancouver within a few miles of the bank in a car that may have been identified by bystanders. He shut off the engine, leaving the key in the ignition. He walked with his stuffed briefcase and the garbage bag full of incriminating material to the next block where his 2001 Ford Taurus was parked. His plan had been to drive home as if nothing had happened and to continue with his life. Now he didn't know what to do, so after he tossed the garbage bag in a Dumpster, he drove aimlessly along the unfamiliar streets of Vancouver. Finally he came to an old motel just off Hastings in East Vancouver, one of the roughest areas of town. The glowing sign with a neon palm tree in relief said, "Blue Oasis." Lance parked and entered the lobby where he was met by a large, middle-aged East Indian man who hadn't shaved in days.

"Yes?" the man said, staring at Lance impatiently.

"I'd like a room, please," Lance said.

"You vant it by de hour or for de whole night?"

At first Lance wasn't sure what he meant but finally processed the question. "I'll be here two nights," he responded.

"Fifty-four-ninety with tax," snapped the clerk. "In advance." He held out his hand for payment.

Lance paid cash and within a minute he was seated on a lumpy bed in the tackiest room he could have imagined. A black felt picture of a stylized horse that hung over the bed seemed to date to the sixties or seventies. Lance hadn't seen one of those in years. The calcium buildup in the sink and the tub had long ago taken the shine from the porcelain. The blanket and the curtains were gray, faded by long years of exposure to the sun. The lampshade was tilted and sported a fringe at the bottom that was the style in the same decade as the picture. The dark, dingy aura and the foul odor that hung in the room hid the beauty of the sunny day.

Blue Oasis? Hah! Lance thought as he surveyed his surroundings. His plan had been to hide the briefcase behind boxes in the basement and to go on living his life the way he had always done. He had it all worked out. He would not tell his wife, Barb, what he had done, but he would say they had to start seriously budgeting if they were ever going to retire. He would slowly introduce the cash he had stolen so she wouldn't get suspicious. She would think their budgeting plan was succeeding as he gradually grew their bank account with the hidden loot. Later Lance would fake an inheritance when some old uncle or other family member kicked the bucket. He would draft documents complete with a lawyer's letter. She wouldn't suspect a thing.

At that point Lance would take Barb to some tropical spot to retire. Maybe South America! A Canadian dollar could buy a lot in some of those countries. He'd always been interested in seeing that continent. With the money from the heist and the sale of their house, they could tour South America, buy a nice beach house, and return just often enough to see the grandkids grow up. Lance would be able to provide much-needed assistance to his kids. They weren't doing badly, but a boost at this critical phase of their lives could make all the difference in the world.

But now, with his unbelievable stupidity, all those plans were in vain. If Lance went home, the cops would be waiting for him, and he would be dragged off in cuffs. He would lose his wife, his family, everything. He had no plan. He was paralyzed.

He picked up the phone on the bedside table. Should he call Barb at work? But what could he say? "Hi, honey. I just called to say that I've ruined the rest of our lives and that I'll probably never see you again. Bye. Love ya." Lance put down the phone and got up to turn on the old twenty-inch television sitting on the dresser.

Hours later, Lance shook himself and looked around. He was still on the bed, comatose, staring at the TV, but couldn't remember a thing he had seen. Where was he? *Oh yeah. I'm in the Blue Oasis, and that means the nightmare I just woke up from is true*, he thought.

He strode to the window, moved the curtains, and looked outside. It was late afternoon and growing dark. Then suddenly the television drew his attention.

"... robbery this morning at the Citibank. A lone perpetrator made away with an undisclosed amount. Police say there is an ongoing investigation and they are following up on all leads." The narrative continued over a video clip. It showed a uniformed female RCMP officer speaking into a microphone before a group of reporters. A short, younger-looking detective stood slightly behind her.

'An undisclosed amount,' they said. Lance hadn't bothered to count the money. He slowly opened the briefcase and peered inside. Most of the bills were still in their wrappers. He began to count. By the time he had finished an hour later, he had counted $737,280. This was beyond anything he had hoped for, but the money didn't hold the same importance anymore. No amount of money could buy back his life and the ones he loved. This was a big haul, but Lance couldn't enjoy it.

He looked at his watch. It was after six. By now Barb would be home and wondering what had happened to him. If the police had been there, the ugly truth would be sinking in. She would be shocked, grief-stricken, and probably in tears. "How could he have done this to me?" she would be asking through gritted teeth.

That thought tore at Lance's heart. He had met Barb at college and within a year had married her. She had quit college after the wedding, and they had immediately started a family. She was pregnant with Charlene Marie within the year, and the rest was history. Their lives had been pretty normal, though, like most families, they had struggled. They had encouraged their son, Jason, as he played hockey and other sports. Charlene, or Char as they called her, had wanted to go into dance, so they had gotten her lessons. In summers he and Barb had taken them and their youngest, Krista, camping or had gone on more distant vacations, usually to the States. California had been a favorite destination. Their trips to Disneyland and Yosemite had produced many photos and were a favorite topic of discussion when the family got together and remembered fun times. The kids had grown up beautifully and were holding down pretty good jobs, but Lance and Barb still struggled, never seeming to get ahead. *We were still relatively happy, I suppose,* Lance mused.

Lance's thoughts returned to the present and what was happening with Barb. He missed her more than he thought possible and reached for the phone to call her. But again, what would he say? How could he tell her how sorry he was for the pain he was causing? He had deserted her. If Barb knew, she no doubt had called Char and tearfully explained the situation. Lance hoped Char would drive the hour and a half to their house in Surrey to be with her mother and to provide what comfort she could. Jason would be no help, working long hours in the Alberta tar sands. Lance sank despondently back onto the bed and fell asleep.

· · · · ●●●◆●●●· · · · ·

It was seven o'clock at night by the time Rob stood alongside his partner, Doug Harris, on Lance's front porch. His time had been eaten up coordinating the work of the city police and of the other detectives he had at his disposal and by the ridiculous news conference he had to attend. Still, Rob was pleased with how the case had been progressing. The detectives had identified the getaway car as a 1996 Chevy Impala. Without a plate number, though, it had been impossible to identify the car's owner. It certainly wasn't registered to Lance Knight. Earlier, police squad cars had been to his home and workplace. No one had been at the house, but the surveying company had reported that Knight had phoned in sick that morning. This naturally raised red flags with the VPD. Before climbing the steps, Rob had conferred with officers in an unmarked car that had been parked just down the street all afternoon, but the stakeout team had reported nothing other than Mrs. Knight's arrival an hour and a half earlier.

The doorbell chimed inside the house, and the two detectives readied themselves as they heard movement toward the door. In a moment Barb opened the door.

"Yes?"

"Mrs. Knight?" Rob asked.

"Yes."

"We're detectives Passaglia and Harris of the Vancouver Police Department."

"Oh my God, Lance has been in an accident! Is he all right?"

"As far as we know, he hasn't been in an accident, ma'am. So you couldn't tell us your husband's whereabouts?"

"No, I expected him an hour ago," Barb said, "but he hasn't—" Suddenly her hands shot to her mouth as she gasped. "What's all this about?"

"We're just trying to locate him. We would like to ask him a few questions."

"What does this concern? Perhaps I could be of assistance."

"I'm sorry, Mrs. Knight, but one of your husband's business cards was used in a bank robbery this morning. We wanted to know if he could help us find out how that happened."

"What?" Barb gasped. "He couldn't possibly ..." Her voice trailed off.

"Would you mind taking a look at this photo? See if you recognize this person."

Rob held out a photo lifted from the bank video. It showed a side view of a man in a gray jacket leaning against the till with the lower part of his face visible.

She took the photo hesitantly and studied it. "I'm not sure who that is."

"Could that be your husband, ma'am?"

Her eyes shot up to meet the detective's. "What? No, of course not."

Slowly her wide eyes returned to the photograph. "I don't know,"

Barb said. "It's possible, I suppose." Suddenly she thrust the photo back at Rob. "I'm sorry, but I really can't be sure."

"All right. Thank you, Mrs. Knight," Rob said, taking the picture. "If your husband gets home, it's important that he call us immediately." The detective handed her his business card and the two men left.

"Well, that settles it. He's our man," Doug said as they descended the steps. "Do you think she's in on it?"

"Did you see the expression on her face when she handed the photo back to me? She doesn't know anything about this," Rob said as they strode back to their vehicle. "You could have knocked her over with a feather. I want teams to show photographs of Lance Knight to every hotel in the downtown area."

"Are you serious?" Doug asked in astonishment. "It could take days to get to every hotel in Vancouver."

"Start from the bank and work out from there. Don't worry. The way I see it, this guy will either turn himself in or hang himself within the next three days. Maybe we'll get lucky and find him first."

Doug laughed and shook his head. "Man, you're nothing if not thorough. No wonder they say you'll make captain by forty."

"Yeah, if this job doesn't kill me first. Oh, and when we get back to the office I want you to do the paperwork to arrange for a wiretap on the phone here."

Shortly before noon the next day, Rob had nearly wrapped up the case about twenty-four hours after starting his investigation. Lance Knight's driver's license photo had come in, and a positive match had been made with the picture from the bank video. He had not shown up for work the day of the heist, feigning illness, and had not come home the previous night. All this made his identity as the bank robber a certainty.

Based on these facts, Vancouver police had placed an APB on his Ford Taurus with an order for his immediate apprehension. Teams of officers were combing Vancouver's hotels and motels for Lance. Rob had spent most of the day researching his suspect. He was forty-three, somewhat older than he appeared, and was a successful salesman for a large surveying outfit. He had two daughters. Charlene, the oldest child, had gotten married last year and was living in Surrey with her husband, and Krista was attending the University of British Columbia in Vancouver. Jason, the middle child, was in Alberta, working at a high-paying job in an oil field. In addition to ordering the stakeout at Lance's residence, Rob had placed tails on the two daughters and was monitoring their phones.

Rob was especially troubled by the fact that Knight was not his usual suspect. Most of the thieves he dealt with were hardened criminals, people who had fallen into crime due to desperate circumstances. These men could not resist the lure of easy money and ended up pulling several heists, increasing the risk of capture. With this take, however, it was unlikely that Lance Knight would be pulling another heist anytime soon. Why would he need to?

Rob had little respect for bank robbers. They were typically egomaniacs who felt they were much too smart for the police. In the end, however, they all got caught and then they didn't feel quite so smart. Rob thought this case was a slam-dunk. A conviction would be a certainty. All he needed was an arrest, and Rob was working to ensure that happened soon. This guy obviously had realized his blunder by now and knew he was a wanted man. Where could he be now? He might have been able to make it across the border, but Rob's gut told him that wasn't so. A guy like this would have counted on returning to his wife and his family and fitting back into his old life. No, he was somewhere in the city, and it would take solid police work to find him. The teams Rob had working the streets were tightening the noose.

· · ● ●●◆●● ● · ·

When Lance awoke he could tell by the noise of the traffic outside that a new day had arrived. He looked at his watch and couldn't believe it was 11:15 a.m. He had slept more than fifteen hours, but it was a fitful sleep filled with uneasy images and a sense of foreboding and hopelessness. Lance looked at the television, which had been on all night long. It was still tuned to the channel that had reported the robbery. The news would be on in less than fifteen minutes. Maybe he would watch to see if there was an update.

Lance went down to the lobby. The same guy who had checked him in was behind the desk, reading what looked like a foreign-language newspaper. He hadn't even raised his head when Lance appeared. Lance slipped coins into a vending machine and retrieved two bags of nachos. He then went over to the pop machine, bought a Coke, and returned to the room.

Lance slowly munched on the snacks. Looking at the bag of nachos and the can of pop, he chuckled sarcastically. "Dining out at El Ristorante Blue Oasis—now this is living in style," he said.

The news started and sure enough he was the lead story. But this time his photo was front and center on the screen. "Police are searching for Lance Knight in connection with the robbery at Citibank yesterday. The man is at large and believed to be armed." A pretty news reporter appeared on the screen, standing outside his house. "CKOW sources report that the thief lives in the house behind me here in Surrey," she said. "In a humorous twist to this story, sources tell us that Knight wrote the robbery note on his own business card." As she said this, a flicker of a smile played across her lips.

"Ha ha! Very funny," Lance shouted at the TV screen. "Laugh it up. Do you know that what seems like an amusing joke to you has destroyed me?" Lance's anger gradually gave way to a deep depression. Yesterday was bad, but this was worse. His feelings wrapped around him like cords, holding him so he couldn't move and threatening to strangle him. Wave after wave of emotional pain washed over him and swallowed him up. But more than emotional, this pain was physical. It felt as if someone had slugged him in the gut. Lance slumped to the bed. He had been awake for just over an hour, and now he was escaping back into the neverland of sleep.

Much later Lance awoke from another fretful sleep. He looked at his watch. It was after six o'clock and almost dark. The reality of his situation hit him again, and he felt an unbearable depression. Lance removed his belt from his pants and wrapped it around his neck. A life with this kind of pain wasn't worth living. Lance searched for a place where he could hook the belt and end it all. He went into the bathroom and tugged on the shower curtain rod. Concluding that it would not support his weight, he returned to the main room. Maybe he could thread one of the belt holes through a nail in the wall. He searched the walls, but even in a dump like this management wasn't likely to leave nails in place. Lance stood on the bed and removed the ugly felt painting from the wall. Sure enough, he found a two-and-a-half-inch nail pounded about halfway in and bent up. Surely this was strong enough to hold his weight. Lance worked the belt hole past the head of the nail. This took him a couple of minutes, but finally the leather slid past the head.

Lance turned away from the wall, and with a heavy sigh he dropped his weight toward the bed and felt the belt tighten around his neck. He hung there, waiting for the makeshift noose to suck the life from his body. Suddenly panic struck him and he scratched at the leather wrapped around his neck and began kicking to gain his footing on the bed. But try as he might, he could not do it. Just before losing consciousness, Lance managed to lift himself a foot, but he lost his balance as the belt again tightened. Then all was darkness.

CHAPTER 3

Rob sat at his desk the following morning. He had gotten an early start and was pleased with the progress he had made with his files. He had two cases finished and ready for the prosecutor. He had followed up on leads in two other cases. In the first, he was pretty sure he had his man, and pending lab results he would probably be making an arrest. The other one now consumed his attention. He scribbled notes to decide his next move. He had not worked on the bank robbery since his visit to the Knight house the evening before. Nothing more had developed since then, but that did not bother Rob. The police search of hotels continued. Teams had visited all the major hotels in Vancouver and were checking on the smaller ones, but thus far the search had yielded no results. They still had quite a number of hotels to visit, but they would complete the sweep by the end of the day. Rob was confident that, one way or another, this case would be resolved within the next forty-eight hours. As he worked, Doug walked in, eating a thick, meaty sandwich.

"Passaglia," he mumbled between bites.

Rob looked up and groaned. "They wonder why I can never get any work done around here."

"Okay, fine. Then I won't tell you that they got the plate number on the '96 Impala," Doug said, turning and pretending to leave.

"What?"

"Yeah. You wanted that female witness on the street by the bank at the time of the robbery to undergo hypnosis. I thought you were crazy, but it turns out you're a genius. Under hypnosis, she remembered the plate number of the vehicle the perp used."

"And?"

"The plate belongs to a ..." Doug hesitated and took out a small notepad. "Richard Krejci. Registries got me an address and a phone number for him. He has no priors and no job. That's why I was able to phone him just a minute ago."

"Doug, you are an ace detective. What did he say?"

"Well, first of all he said those weren't his plates. When I told him the registries had him as the owner he was totally confused."

"Sounds like a space cadet."

"Yeah, pretty much, but it gets a little more interesting. I decided to do a history on him. He's been at about ten addresses over the past five years. He's living with his mother in Salmon Arm right now."

"Ever lived in Vancouver?"

Doug checked his notes again. "Once, three years ago, but he was here for only three months."

"You said it gets interesting. Right now you're boring the hell out of me, and I've got work to do."

"Ah yes. On a hunch I asked if he knew a person by the name of Lance Knight. He said that might have been the name of a former girlfriend's dad. He said he lived with the family for a couple of months several years ago."

"Great job, Doug."

"That's not all. I just got a call from the boys downstairs. They've found the vehicle. It was on a residential street about six blocks from the bank."

"Awesome. I want it towed to the lot, and get a forensics team over there to process it."

"Way ahead of you, Rob. Oh, by the way, did I mention that the sticker does not match the plate?"

"What? Did you run the tag?"

"Of course I ran the tags!" Doug hesitated for dramatic effect and Rob gestured impatiently. "The tags are for a 1988 F-150 pickup owned by a Mr. Lance Knight."

"Bingo," Rob said, slapping his hands together. "That means he's in his Ford Taurus." He got up and put on his jacket.

"Where are you going?"

"Why don't you and I go see Mrs. Knight and find out if she can tie up some loose ends for us?" Rob said as he left the office.

Doug stared after him and then hurried to catch up.

For the second time in as many days the two detectives stood on the door stoop of the small Knight bungalow in Surrey. A couple of news vans were still parked on the street. Rob pressed the bell and Barb opened the door.

"Good morning, Mrs. Knight. May we come in?" he asked, not wishing to attract the media's attention.

"Oh, it's you," Barb said. "Yes, come in. The reporters have been at the door three times already, and they keep doing video reports right in front of the house." As she moved aside to let them in, Rob noticed she was clutching a tissue.

As the detectives entered the living room, they encountered two other women, much younger but bearing an uncanny resemblance to Mrs. Knight.

"These are my daughters, Char and Krista," she said. "Have a seat, won't you?" She gestured toward the couch as she sat in a soft, oversized chair. Char sat on the arm of the chair close to her mother and put an arm around her, and Krista stood behind her. Barb unconsciously dabbed at her eye with the tissue.

"This must be terribly upsetting to you, Mrs. Knight," Rob said after settling onto the couch. "Tell me, have you heard from your husband yet?" He knew the answer to the question but did not wish to let her know that her phone was being tapped.

"Nobody's heard anything from him," Char answered. "We've been on the phone to everyone in the family, and nobody knows anything. There's got to be some mistake. My father wouldn't do something like this. He's never done anything like this in his life. He's held a steady job for over twenty years."

"Forgive me if I speak plainly," Rob said. "Officially, right now your dad is just a person of interest in this case, but there is no doubt that he robbed that bank yesterday morning."

With that, Barb gave several soft sobs, and her daughter hugged her tightly.

"I'm very sorry," Rob said, and he meant it.

"How can you be sure?" Char asked.

"I can't give you details. Let's just say that the evidence is overwhelming."

"How could he do this to me?" Barb sobbed. "We've been married for more than twenty years. We have a family, a home. Why would he throw all that away?"

Again Char squeezed her mother, but this time Rob could see a flash of anger in her eyes.

"Did you and your husband have any financial problems?" Doug asked.

"No, not really. Just the normal bills," Barb said, frowning.

"Do you know if your husband was involved in gambling?" Rob asked.

"No. He never gambled."

"Have you noticed any large amounts go missing from your accounts without explanation?"

"No!"

"Could you tell me what vehicle your husband is driving right now?"

"The F-150 is sitting in the garage, so he's driving the Taurus."

"What year is that?"

"Two thousand one!" Barb answered quickly.

"Do you know a Richard Krejci?"

Krista's eyes grew wide. "He and I used to go out," she said, "but that was years ago. What does he have to do with this?"

Rob ignored the question and asked, "Did Richard happen to leave any articles here?"

"He left a bunch of junk, but I think Lance threw it all out," Barb answered with a puzzled expression on her face.

"All right, ladies, I want to thank you for your cooperation. Once again, I want to express my sympathy for the hardship this has placed on you and your family. If he does contact you, please urge him to contact the police. Believe me, the sooner this is over with, the better off he will be." With that, Rob stood up and Doug followed suit.

The three women accompanied the detectives to the door. Char shook hands with Rob and asked, "Is there anything you can do about these reporters? I really wish they would respect my mother's privacy."

"I'm sorry, ma'am," Rob said. "There's not much we can do. If you want, you can post a 'No Trespassing' sign, but that's about it." The two detectives turned and left.

· · ·•••◆•••· · ·

For the third time in less than two days, Lance woke up not knowing where he was. But this time something was making him wheeze. Puzzled, he reached for the cause of the discomfort. He had a belt wrapped tightly around his neck. He removed it, threw it on the bed, and walked to the bathroom. Looking in the mirror, he saw that the belt had left a nasty red mark. Finally, Lance remembered that he had decided to end it all and that just before he had lost consciousness it seemed he would succeed. He returned to the bed and picked up the belt. He rotated it back to front so he could see the end. He examined the end of the belt and noticed that one of the holes had been slightly ripped. Lance glanced at the nail above him. It was still lodged in the wall but was now angled downward rather than upward. He guessed that his dead weight must have applied enough force to the nail to bend it downward, allowing the belt to rip past the head of the nail.

To his surprise Lance felt relief that he had escaped this close brush with death. "Okay, so I don't want to die. If that's true, I guess I had better get busy living," Lance said as he stared at himself in the mirror.

Lance drew a deep breath and braced himself. He could not think about his family; he couldn't allow the pain that had rendered him helpless to control him. He had to take control. This was the darkest hour of his life, but that didn't mean the situation was hopeless. He could make a new life for himself. Right now he was in danger. The police could burst through the door at any second. Unless he wanted to spend the next several years in jail he had to do some serious planning and quickly.

He opened the desk and pulled out an old phonebook. This half-star hotel wasn't going to provide stationery. Lance turned to the yellow pages, found a page with limited print, and carefully ripped it from the book. Then he picked up his jacket from the floor, rummaged through the pocket, and pulled out a pen. Lance hung up the coat, sat at the desk, and began making notes.

By the time he put down his pen and rose from the desk, an hour had passed and it was almost 6 a.m. Lance knew he had to leave this hotel. To avoid capture he had to keep moving. Lance was confident that the police would have identified his vehicle by now. He carefully folded up the yellow sheet that contained his escape plan. If he was disciplined and maybe a little bit lucky, it could save his life. Lance stuck the paper in his shirt pocket and quickly gathered his things. He took a look around the room to make sure he had not left anything behind. Then he slipped on his jacket and left.

If his plan was going to work, Lance first needed to find a commercial district. There were things he needed to buy. He got in his car and pulled out of the Blue Oasis lot. *I don't care if I ever see this dump again!* he thought. He swung west toward the downtown. Fifteen minutes later he was on a main thoroughfare caught up in the growing rush-hour traffic. His progress was slow, but Lance didn't mind. The best place to hide a vehicle was with thousands of other vehicles. He had plenty of time to kill. He needed another motel for a night or two, but he didn't want the undue attention that checking in first thing in the morning might draw. On his right about a block up was a Radisson hotel. Certainly that would be a major step up from the Blue Oasis and the hotel was close to three malls, but Lance's risk of being recognized would grow at a bigger, upper-class place.

Lance decided to keep driving. A few blocks ahead he spied the Crown to his left. It wasn't part of a big chain and housed a casino on the main floor. *This could be perfect*, Lance thought. He edged into the left lane as he passed the hotel. There were still quite a few vehicles in the lot since patrons no doubt had been gambling all night. At the next set of lights he doubled back.

To reach the entrance to the Crown, Lance had to turn down a short street since there was no entrance on the main drag. He swung onto the short street and almost jammed on his brakes. A large number of policemen stood near at least eight cop cars parked directly ahead of him.

Lance eased his foot off the brake pedal, his heart pumping a million beats a minute. He now realized this wasn't a roadblock or a stakeout; a bunch of cops were meeting at the doughnut shop across the street. The cliché was accurate. Officers leaned against their vehicles, sipping coffee from paper cups, or stood in small groups, shooting the breeze.

Resisting the urge to stare at them, Lance turned left into the hotel lot. He would have to watch himself. If he had screeched to a stop when he saw the cops like he almost did, it would have been game over. He checked his rearview mirror, and as far as he could tell he had attracted no attention. They were still at their cars, sipping coffee and joking. Lance parked near the casino entrance rather than the lobby entrance. He got out of the car, quickly walked through the casino directly to the lobby, and approached the reception desk.

"Hello, sir. May I help you?" the pretty receptionist asked.

"Hi there. Man what a night! I've been in the casino all night and I'm bagged," Lance said. "Can I get a room right away so I can get some sleep?"

The girl smiled and clicked away on the computer in front of her. "Certainly, sir," she said. "We can do that for you. I need a credit card to secure the room."

"No problem," Lance said, "but don't run it through. I'm gonna pay cash for the room. The poker gods were smiling on me last night." Lance pulled out his wallet, which he had stuffed with cash from his briefcase before leaving the car.

"All right, sir," the girl said. "That will be fine. We'll just run an imprint of your card in case there are extra charges. You understand."

"Yup, no problem. How much is the room?" Lance carelessly pulled out a wad of cash.

"That will be $149.65 including tax."

Lance counted out the cash from the bundle and handed it over.

The receptionist asked him for his information and typed it in as he gave it to her. She printed out a receipt and handed him his plastic key card.

"Very good, sir. You are in room 627 on the sixth floor. The elevator is just to the right. Please enjoy your stay."

"Oh, one more thing," Lance said. "Can you provide me with a shaver and some shaving cream? I'm sure I look like death warmed over."

"No problem, sir," the girl said with a chuckle. "I'll have the concierge send someone up with that right away."

Lance thanked her and headed for the elevator. He was taking a risk using his real name, but he had little choice since the hotel had an imprint of his credit card with his name on it. He would have to move quickly to do what he had to do and be out of the hotel as soon as possible.

Lance slid the card into the scanner and entered the room. He immediately pulled out a phone book from the desk by the window, found the listings for escort services, and dialed one of the numbers.

The phone rang five times, and finally a male voice answered,

"Desiree's Escorts." The man sounded as if he had been wakened from a sound sleep.

"Yeah, can I get a girl up to room 627 at the Crown, please?" Lance said.

"Yeah, I know it's seven-thirty in the morning. If you can't do it, I'll call someone else."

"Okay, that's good. Uh, I'd like a white or Hispanic girl, say in her early thirties, well-built, attractive. You know what I mean," Lance said, trying hard not to sound like he had never done this before.

"Fine. Oh, and can you tell her to dress discreetly? I don't want any trouble with hotel management. By the way, the elevator is keyed. Can she call up to the room when she gets here? I'll come down to let her up."

"Okay, about an hour. Tell her to hurry. Just a sec. I'll get you the address and phone number."

Lance provided the information and hung up. He pulled out the hotel stationery from the desk and began writing. He then set the paper and pen aside, went to the bathroom, and turned on the shower.

Lance was about to enter the shower when there was a knock at the door. He froze. He checked the view hole before opening the door. A man wearing the same style vest as those sported by the reception staff stood outside. Lance swung the door open.

"You requested a shaver, sir?" the bellhop asked. He held a small travel kit in his hand. Lance thanked him, gave him a small tip, and took the kit.

Half an hour later, Lance was in a hotel robe, freshly showered and shaved and toweling off his hair. He sat down on the bed, turned on the TV, and scrolled through the channels.

Ten minutes later he heard another knock at the door and froze again. *Oh no, it's not the cops, is it?* he wondered. Lance quietly crossed the room and checked the peephole. He exhaled softly. There at his door was the escort he had called for. *How did she get up here? She scared the wits out of me, that's for sure,* he thought. Lance quickly slid the briefcase full of money under the bed out of sight.

"You Lance?" the girl asked when he opened the door.

"Yes, Lance is my name."

"Yeah, sure," she said with a smirk.

The girl was about five foot four with dark, medium-length hair and a pale complexion. She was attractive enough, but the rough life was already starting to show with the lines on her face. She yawned widely.

"Come in," Lance said awkwardly. "Late night last night?"

"You know it," the girl said with a snicker as she entered the room and looked around.

"Look," Lance said hurriedly, "this isn't just a simple fuck. I've got something I want you to do first."

"Jesus, why is it always like this?" the girl said, throwing her hands up in the air. "As soon as they get you to the room the whole deal changes. Damn it."

"Relax," Lance said. "Hear me out, and then it's up to you. If you do what I ask, there's gonna be a lot of money in it for you. What's your name?"

The girl put her hands on her hips. "Name's Joan. Let's hear what you've got."

"Okay, that's better. I've got this costume party tonight, and I want to go as an East Indian. There's a twenty-four-hour London Drugs just down the block from here, and I'm sure they have a cosmetics section. What I want you to do is go down there and pick up everything I need." Lance handed her the list he had just written down. "You probably know more about this stuff than I do. If there's anything I've forgotten, pick that up too. Then I want you to make me up. What do you say? You name the price."

Joan shook her head disgustedly, and then her eyes shot upward as she began to think. She eyed him suspiciously. "Okay, sure, but it's gonna cost you $1,000."

"Deal," Lance said.

"In advance," the prostitute added.

"Here's two hundred dollars. That should be more than enough to get what I've asked for. Anything extra is yours, but don't skimp. As soon as you get back to the room, I'll give you the $1,000, okay?"

Joan shook her head in disgust one more time, snatched the money from his hand, and left the room.

Lance wasn't sure he would ever see her again. She could easily take the two hundred and never return. He hoped $1,000 was enough of a carrot to bring her back.

Lance tried to calm his nerves by watching an old movie on TV. He was too nervous, however, and began to pace across the room.

An hour later, Lance was still pacing. He angrily turned off the TV and started pacing again. *I knew she wouldn't come back,* he thought. *Now what am I going to do? I can't stay here all day.*

Lance returned to the desk, took out the phone book, and searched the Yellow Pages. Just then, he heard a knock. Lance ran to the door and looked through the peephole. To his relief, there stood the prostitute, smiling with a large shopping bag in her hand.

Lance swung open the door, and she entered. "You owe me a thousand bucks," she said, holding out one hand with the other on her hip.

Lance got his wallet and counted out the cash. The wallet felt much thinner than it had first thing in the morning. "Here you go," he said. "Let's get started."

He set the desk chair in front of the bathroom mirror. Joan pulled out the box of hair dye from the bag and began coloring Lance's hair. Soon his hair and eyebrows were black. Joan arranged the makeup on the sink counter. Then she reached into the plastic bag and pulled out an aerosol can.

"You're in luck," she said. "They had this." The can read "Instant Tan."

"What's that?" Lance asked.

"It's got methoxsalen in it. You just spray this stuff on. Any shade you want. With a little bit you look like you've got a tan; a little more and you're Mexican. I can turn you into a black guy if you want. For East Indian, somewhere in between, I think. Some of the girls use this stuff for specialty customers who want a certain kinda girl. Strip," she ordered.

Joan shook the can as Lance peeled off his pants. "This stuff's better than make-up," she said. "As long as you get a little sunlight it can last for days." Just don't get it wet right away." She had him close his eyes and began spraying his face. Every now and then she would stop to survey her progress. Lance peeked at the mirror whenever she paused. His face got darker as she worked.

Suddenly Joan stopped and stared at Lance. She sighed in exasperation and said, "Look, this is taking a lot longer than I thought. It's going to cost you another hundred."

Lance glared at her. "It hasn't even been an hour yet! Okay, let's make it $200 more, but if you bring up money again I want it all back. Now get to work."

"Fine! Fine!" she said, pocketing the bills. Joan returned to her task, and forty-five minutes later she stepped back and admired her work. She added a touch here and a touch there and smiled. Lance looked in the mirror, and sitting in front of him was an East Indian. Up close, his face might not have appeared quite authentic, but at a cursory glance he would pass for an East Indian even to most East Indians.

"Great job," Lance said. "Oh geez, don't forget my hands and arms. They're still white as ghosts."

In a half-hour his arms and legs were done. Lance admired himself in the mirror. "Now throw that can back in the bag just in case I have to make any touch-ups before the party tonight," he said.

"No problem," Joan said. "Just spray this on from about this far away until it looks good." She demonstrated. "When you want to take it off, soap and water will do the trick."

············◆·········

At that very second Rob stood in the parking lot of the Crown Hotel and Casino, peering through the passenger-side window of a tan 2001 Ford Taurus. A half-hour before he had been working at his desk when he got a call saying police had found the car on which he had put the APB. The quick discovery was extraordinarily lucky. Rob had immediately headed to the lot to see for himself. Doug and the two officers who had located the vehicle stood behind him.

"You see a bag of money in there, Rob?" Doug asked.

The two cops snickered. The car's interior appeared to be showroom clean; not a fry or a wrapper was visible.

"It could be in the trunk, I suppose," Rob said, straightening up. "Could someone get me into this vehicle?"

One of the officers walked over to his cruiser and came back with a long strip of metal designed for unlocking car doors. He worked expertly at the front driver's-side window and in less than a minute had the door unlocked. Rob donned plastic gloves and opened the door. He popped the trunk and moved to the back. The trunk was as pristine as the cab. Rob moved to the front of the interior. He looked under the seats and, seeing nothing, shifted to the back seat.

"I want this vehicle towed to the impound lot," he said. "Alert the forensics boys that the vehicle is coming in. I need a complete workover done."

He walked over to his vehicle, leaned in, and pulled out several posters. He handed the posters to the police officers. "This is the perp. Take a good look at this picture, and make sure that the other teams see it when they arrive." Turning to Doug, Rob said, "Why don't you and I stroll over to the lobby and see what they can tell us at the desk?"

The officers went to the car to call in backup as Doug and Rob strode toward the hotel.

The detectives approached the girl who had signed in Lance. She gave them a friendly smile and asked, "Can I help you gentlemen?"

Rob and Doug leaned in close, placing their elbows on the counter to ensure privacy, and showed her their badges. "Do you have a Lance Knight registered here?" Rob asked.

The girl's smile was replaced by a concerned look. "One second, please," she said. "Let me check." As she busied herself at her computer screen, Rob pulled out one of the posters and waited patiently.

"Yes, we do have a Lance Knight registered. He's in room 627. I signed him in just this morning."

Rob showed her the poster and asked, "Is this the man you signed in this morning, ma'am?"

"Why yes it is," she said. "What's he done?"

"I'm going to need a pass key," Rob said, ignoring the question. "If you have any staff on that floor, could you please have them leave the area immediately?"

"Of course," the girl said. She reached into a drawer, pulled out a card, and slid it to the two detectives. Rob snatched up the card, and the two hurried over to the bank of elevators. One of the elevators opened and an East Indian man emerged carrying a large, over-stuffed briefcase. They brushed past him and pushed the button for the sixth floor. Outside of the room the detectives drew their revolvers. Rob put his head against the door and listened. He shook his head at Doug, who nodded.

Doug carefully slid the card into the slot, and they heard the lock click. The two burst through the door, yelling, "Police! Don't move!" The room was empty. Rob motioned toward the bathroom. Doug quickly swung the door open, and Rob leapt forward. The bathroom was also empty. Rob held up a stained towel. "Hair dye," he said, "and it's wet, very wet. He's changed his appearance." Doug nodded.

"What's this?" Rob said, rubbing the white countertop and then inspecting his fingers closely. "Look at this, Doug. There's some sort of residue on this counter." He rubbed the substance between his fingers and noticed his skin darken as he did so. He stared at his fingers, thinking hard. Suddenly his eyes grew wide.

He bolted to the door and down the hall, leaving Doug in the room. When Doug recovered, he found Rob pushing the elevator buttons in irritation and ran to join him.

Rob held up his darkened fingertip. "This is that stuff people use," he said.

"What are you talking about?" Doug asked.

"Our man Lance is transforming himself. He's used this stuff to darken his skin. Look. This is some sort of tanning spray. And there was black hair dye on the towel. He's turning himself into an …" Doug and Rob stared at each other.

"East Indian?" Doug said, his voice rising. "Son of a bitch. We walked right by him."

Finally the elevator doors opened. Rob's eyes narrowed as they stepped inside and he pushed the button for the lobby. "Did you get a good look at the guy at the elevators?" he asked Doug. "I want you to get with a sketch artist ASAP. I'll have the boys fan out. He can't be more than a minute ahead of us."

"I didn't really pay much attention to him," Doug said.

The two men sprinted from the elevator and through the lobby as the astonished staff stared from the reception desk. They dashed outside and looked in all directions but saw no one of interest in the parking lot. Rob waved frantically at officers near the Taurus, and they came over on the double.

"We just missed him," Rob shouted. "He's on foot. I want you to stop and question any male on foot in this area." Two of the four officers took off. "Oh, and we have reason to believe he's darkened his skin," he yelled after them. "Take that picture you've got, but think three shades darker." He turned to the other officers. "You two go to bus stops in this area. You," he said, pointing at one of the officers. "Get in your car and head west. Flag down the first bus you see. Make sure Knight's not on that bus. Doug and I will cover the eastern routes. Let's go," he shouted, sprinting toward his vehicle with Doug following. The officers scattered to cover their assignments.

Suddenly Rob froze, staring at the busy street ahead of him. He turned as Doug and the two officers caught up to him. "You two get in your squad car and catch that bus," he said, pointing to a city bus heading off into the distance. "Come on, Doug," he shouted, sprinting back toward his car.

CHAPTER 4

Ten minutes earlier Joan had wrapped up her work. She had gathered her things in ten seconds and out the door in twelve, leaving without a word.

As soon as the hooker had left the room, Lance dressed, hurriedly threw the makeup and other items into the plastic bag, and with difficulty stuffed the bag into the briefcase. He forced the case shut and went down the hall toward the elevators. As he waited for one to arrive, he glanced at his watch. It was already ten thirty in the morning. Down in the lobby, the elevator doors sprang open, and Rob and Doug stood in front of him. To Lance they were simply two men in jeans and jackets. They stepped past him and entered the elevator and pushed the button. Lance entered the lobby and headed towards the exit.

He strode past the reception desk, left the lobby, and turned toward his car. As he stepped into the parking lot, he froze and his mouth fell open. Parked next to his Taurus was a police car. He could see the officer at the wheel speaking into a radio. With a gargantuan effort, Lance willed himself to move before the officers noticed a man frozen in place staring at the car. Still just outside the hotel entrance, he slowly turned away from the car.

Now he was without a vehicle, and within minutes the police would be in room 627 searching for evidence. It would be obvious that he had dyed his hair. How much more they could deduce, he had no idea.

Lance quickly strode away in the opposite direction from his car. He took the alley at the side of the hotel and was soon on the street backing the hotel. *I've gotta get as far away from here as possible,* Lance thought. *In a few minutes this place will be swarming with cops, and they'll be scrutinizing everybody*. He glanced back before approaching the intersection at which the hotel sat. Already another police car had turned into the hotel parking lot. Lance quickly crossed the street to a bus stop where an elderly man and two teenagers waited. He stood at the stop, his heart thumping heavily against his chest. To his relief, a bus pulled up in less than a minute. Lance didn't know where the bus was headed, and he didn't care. The important thing was to make a quick escape. As the bus passed by the Crown, Lance peered out the window at the scene in the parking lot. A third squad car had arrived, and a throng of policemen had gathered near the passenger side of his vehicle. Suddenly he saw one of the men point at the bus.

He got off the bus at the closest major intersection and walked briskly toward a stop on Cambie Street for buses heading north. He approached the stop, but as he did he heard a police siren coming from the route he had just taken. Lance slowly edged himself toward a storefront and turned to face the glass as if window shopping. The police cruiser sped through the intersection, and Lance listened as the wail of the siren faded.

Lance's sharp eyes noticed a second car pull up at the intersection. He could see the magnetized red light on the dash. The driver had his window unrolled and with his head stuck out the window was scanning the area intently. Lance took one step back and was hidden by the side of the covered bus stop. Lance could not see the intersection from where he stood, but the sound of accelerating engines told him the light had changed. He made a split-second decision and entered a flower store behind the bus stop. Lance strolled among the bouquets as he kept surveillance on the stop. Seconds later the northbound bus arrived. Lance was just about to leave the store to catch the bus when he noticed two men in jeans and jackets approaching the bus. They were the same pair he had passed at the hotel elevators. One of the officers' holsters was not completely hidden under his jacket.

Lance spun around toward the till and ordered the bushiest arrangement he saw in the store. As he waited impatiently for the florist to put the finishing touches on his purchase, he watched to make sure that the window display kept him hidden. The two men entered the bus. The florist finished the bouquet. Lance had the clerk write a love note on a card, dictating it with one eye fixed on the bus parked outside. Finally the bus pulled away, and the two officers walked back to their vehicle. One of the men stood by the car while the other entered the store opposite the car. Several seconds later the man came out of the store and entered the next. He was searching each store, and in a minute he would reach the florist's shop. Lance remained in the store, again circling through the displays. He didn't know what to do.

Five seconds later a second bus pulled up to the stop. Lance watched as a half-dozen people got on the bus. He carried the bouquet so that his face was partially hidden and stepped from the store as the last of the riders entered the bus. He hurried aboard just as the driver was about to close the door. In a second the bus pulled away as Lance stood in the aisle, studying the street behind him. There was no sign of the two men. He had not been spotted.

Fifteen minutes later he saw a large mall off to his left, so he rang the bell for the next stop, got up, and made his way to the rear exit. The bus pulled away, and Lance crossed the street to the mall. With his disguise he was fairly confident he could do what he had to do without raising suspicion. The only thing that bothered him was that he carried the briefcase, which held more than $700,000.

Lance entered the Canadian Tire store in the mall and moved quickly down the aisles. By the time he approached the till, he carried in his cart a ball cap, sunglasses, and a screwdriver with a variety of bits in the plastic handle. At the till he spied a rack of *Bargain Finder* magazines. He selected one with the title *Bargain Finder-Trucks*. If his plan was going to work, he would need another set of wheels right away. Lance knew just the kind of vehicle he was after.

Lance left the store and entered the main corridor of the mall. He spied a coffee nook and ordered a coffee, a sandwich, and a square. He noticed that his wallet was now almost empty. At some point he would have to slip into a bathroom and replenish his cash from the briefcase, but that could wait. Right now he had more important things to do. Lance spread out the magazine on the small table in front of him and began circling ads for vehicles that interested him. When he was finished, he moved to the mall lobby where there were a few pay phones. He tucked the folded magazine below a phone, spread several quarters in front of him, and began making calls. Lance had selected pickup trucks about fifteen years old. He crossed out any truck without four-wheel drive. He also had tried to select phone numbers with prefixes that indicated the truck owners might be a reasonable distance from the mall. He was on foot, and mobility would be a problem.

Thirty-five minutes and many quarters later, Lance was finished. It had been a frustrating ordeal. He often got no answer or an answering machine. Several trucks had been sold weeks earlier, and some owners confessed that their vehicles were in less-than-ideal condition. But finally he now had a small list of addresses in front of him.

Lance left the mall and entered a nearby parking garage. He climbed the cement staircase until he was alone on the fourth level where about half the stalls contained vehicles. Lance took a quick look around him and then moved behind a large SUV that would hide his presence. He took out the screwdriver from the shopping bag, knelt down, and removed the license plate from the SUV. With luck the owner would not notice the plate was missing for a day or so. Lance slid the plate and the screwdriver into the shopping bag and casually descended to ground level.

Lance crossed the street to the same bus stop where he had arrived two hours earlier. He waited fifteen minutes before the next bus arrived. During that time two police cars drove by on the busy street. Each time Lance had moved his hand to his face and had faked a large yawn. They weren't likely to notice him in his disguise, but he was not going to take any chances. Police were alert to body language, and boredom or fatigue would not attract attention while edginess might. In addition, Lance slid his briefcase under the bench at the bus stop so that it would draw as little attention as possible. Finally a bus arrived and Lance picked up the briefcase and the shopping bag and waited at the back of a short line to board. When he finally got on, he asked the driver how he could get to the first address on his list of potential pickups.

"Oh yeah, that's just off Kingsway," the bus driver replied. "I'll drop you at Boundary. Wait there for the nine, get off at Kingsway, and take the thirty-three to Marine. It'll be about a block from your stop."

Lance sat down and peered out the window. By the time he made it to his final stop, about an hour and a half had passed and he was getting a bit impatient.

He followed the directions the last bus driver had given him and was soon at the address he sought. Lance spied the truck he had come to see sitting in front of the house. It was a black, three-quarter-ton 1999 GMC 4x4 with a white canopy mounted over the box. He glanced at the interior through the passenger-side window. Nothing special: the seats were in fairly good condition, with gray, black, and blue plaid covers. The floor was made of a rubberized material and was covered with rubber mats. *No carpet,* Lance thought. *It's a work truck for sure.*

Lance knocked on the front door of the house. In a few moments a middle-aged lady appeared. She was dressed casually in slacks and a pullover. Her hair was beginning to gray, but Lance saw intelligence in her eyes. *No wrong moves,* he told himself. *Keep the story simple and straight.*

"I've come to see about the truck. I called earlier," Lance said.

"Oh yes. I'll get the keys," the woman said. "I'm afraid I won't be able to answer many questions, but my husband will be home in half an hour or so."

"That's fine, ma'am."

As the lady retreated into the house for the keys, Lance approached the vehicle. The last thing he needed was to be broken down on the side of the road. He intended to scrutinize this vehicle very closely before he purchased it. The truck was nondescript enough for his purposes. He had seen plenty of these still on the road even after fifteen years, so he assumed they were generally pretty reliable. Lance got down on his knees and was looking at the pavement underneath the vehicle when the lady returned with the keys. The truck had obviously been sitting in front of the house for some time, but there were no signs of oil, gas, or antifreeze leaks.

"Why are you selling it?" Lance asked as he got back to his feet.

The lady handed him the keys and said, "Neil bought it in 2009. It's been a good truck for him, but he just felt it was time for something newer."

"Have you had any problems with it lately?" Lance peered closely at her for any sign that she might be hiding something.

"Neil says it's starting to use a little oil. It's got almost two hundred thousand clicks on it, but other than that it runs great. Neil has always serviced his own vehicles. Changes the oil when it's time.

He did the brakes himself about six months ago. For the engine stuff, though, he takes it to his mechanic, so it runs pretty well."

Lance circled the vehicle, taking special note of the tires. They were a little worn but still had sufficient tread on them. They would be fine for his purposes. There was the odd scratch and dent but no rust. Generally the body was in pretty good shape.

After looking at the engine and taking the truck for a short test drive, Lance was fairly confident that the vehicle would meet his needs. He tried to keep his satisfaction off of his face. What a relief it would be to have a vehicle, albeit one that wouldn't be exactly legal with the stolen license plate. Obviously he wouldn't be able to register or insure it since the police would be alerted the moment his name came up on any government database.

"It said in the ad you were asking $5,000. Would you take $4,500 for it?" With his briefcase full of money, Lance didn't need to dicker, but the lady would be expecting him to offer less and might be suspicious if he didn't.

She hesitated for a few seconds and finally said, "Make it $4,600 and we've got a deal." Lance pulled out a wad of hundreds from his shirt pocket and began counting. The lady reached into the glove compartment for the registration. "Come inside and I'll fill out a bill of sale and the registration," she said. Lance gave her a false name and signed the bill of sale accordingly. He then returned to the vehicle and replaced the plate on the back with the one he had stolen at the mall. He hoped the owner had not yet discovered the missing plate.

Lance waved to the lady and shouted a thank-you as she stood at the door of the house. He got into the vehicle and pulled away in elation. He turned left at the first side street and left again at the next street heading toward Boundary Road.

A half-block later, however, he suddenly pulled over. One of the houses he had just passed was holding a garage sale. The garage door was open, and items were spread out on makeshift tables on the driveway.

Lance had noticed old tools and camping equipment stacked along the side of the garage. He got out and approached the house. A few people were milling around the tables, but he felt he could do what he needed to do without attracting suspicion. In the city he was in danger. He needed to hide in the wilderness until the heat died down. Then he would somehow have to get out of the country.

The old couple holding the sale smiled at him as he approached. "It's a retirement sale," the husband said. "Look around. It's all gotta go. If you don't like the prices, just let me know." By the time Lance was finished, fifty dollars had bought him several carpenter's tools, an ax, a camping stove and heater, a pair of worn coveralls, a hard hat, and a bright orange construction vest, the kind flagmen wear at highway construction sites.

Lance lugged his prizes to the back of the truck and threw them in the box. Buoyed by his success, he decided he would see what else he could find at the many garage sales in the area. Lance had found that the best sales were in older areas of the city like this one. One hour later he had bought a number of older but clean blankets and quilts and some clothes he thought would fit him, including a winter coat, a toque, and gloves. Lance knew that nights could get pretty cold up in the back country. He also lucked out by finding a place that had lumber. He had picked out a sturdy sheet of plywood and several two-by-fours, each about eight feet long.

It was now about 7 p.m. and just about dark. Lance swung onto the Trans Canada, the freeway out of Vancouver. The rush hour was almost done, but the Number 1 is never quiet, so there was still plenty of traffic. This suited Lance fine. If the police were monitoring the highway, his chances of slipping through were a lot better in a crowd than in sparse traffic.

Lance drove without incident toward Chilliwack, about an hour east of Vancouver. He took the exit for Chilliwack, but rather than turning left into town, he turned right toward the area's lakes and pressed on through the darkness and a soaking rain.

A half-hour later, the road began to circle a lake. Lance slowed down to watch for side roads going down to the shore. If he found the right one, he could not be seen from the main road, and there was little chance he would be disturbed during the night.

Up ahead was an unmarked trail leading toward the lake. Lance signaled as a vehicle came up behind him with high beams on and then quickly passed him. He turned onto the rough gravel path, which had grass growing in the middle and was obviously used infrequently. Lance squinted through the raindrops to follow the trail. It split and he chose the left fork. The path continued to drop toward the lake, and after another forty meters it ended on a gravelly spit of land right beside the large body of water.

Lance parked, turned off the engine, and yawned sleepily. It had been a long, stressful day, but after languishing in depression for so long, he found his accomplishments satisfying. Still, he was exhausted. He jumped out of the cab and sprinted to the back of the truck in the soaking rain. He opened the canopy and pulled out the blankets and the heavy coat he had bought. With the bundle in his arms, he dashed back to the cab. The raindrops pelted the windshield and the roof of the truck as Lance nestled under the blankets on the seat. He used the coat and one of the blankets to form a pillow against the driver's-side door.

For the first time that day, Lance thought about his wife and his family, and the emotional pain returned to the pit of his stomach. Lance shook himself. He missed his family terribly, but he could not let that eat at him. He needed rest because he would have to be alert in the morning. Lance tossed and turned for what seemed like hours, but eventually he fell into a deep sleep to the staccato of the raindrops.

Lance awoke to the sound of a vehicle coming down the trail. He opened his eyes and sat up. It was now daylight, and the rain had ceased. He crouched and peered through the window at his side mirror to see who was approaching, but the window was hopelessly fogged up. He unrolled it, and the first thing he saw was the red-and-blue lights mounted on the roof of the vehicle. It was the cops. Immediately his heart accelerated, and he was wide awake, weighing his options. Lance was trapped in this spot. He quickly rolled up the window and swallowed hard as panic swept over him.

Lance listened as the vehicle stopped behind him. He heard the car door slam and footsteps on the wet gravel. Lance pulled the blankets over him and feigned sleep, waiting for the rap on his window that he knew was coming.

To his amazement, the footsteps continued past his truck. As the uniformed officer passed, Lance caught a glimpse of him through the fogged window. He continued to walk toward the lake. But something was wrong. Lance wiped a small section at the bottom of the windshield and peered out toward the officer.

Lance's heartbeat slowed as he realized this wasn't a police officer but a fishing warden. He was approaching a man on the shore who held a fishing rod. Lance stared in disbelief. He had not heard the fisherman, who would have had to walk right by his truck to reach the shore. Lance realized how tenuous his situation was. At any moment he could be surprised, and his life would be over.

Lance watched as the officer spoke with the fisherman. The fisherman put down his rod and pulled out his wallet. He removed a card and handed it to the officer. The warden inspected the card and handed it back to the fisherman, who retrieved his rod and resumed fishing. After a few more moments of conversation, the warden waved and turned back toward his truck.

Lance scrunched down, pulling the blankets close. A few seconds later he heard a rap on his window and his panic returned. Lance sat up and unrolled the window.

"Sorry to disturb you, sir, but would you mind pulling your vehicle up a little bit so I can turn around?"

"Oh yeah. Sure. No problem."

Lance turned on the truck's engine and carefully pulled ahead. The strip of land was covered by loose gravel, but there was damp clay in some spots. He wanted to avoid those spots and to stay on the rock. He didn't know what he would do if he got stuck.

Lance watched in the rearview mirror as the warden turned around and then inched up the trail. When the warden had disappeared above the knoll, Lance climbed out of the vehicle. He ignored the fisherman but spied his vehicle parked on the side where the trail forked. Lance stretched and then went to the back of the truck. He pulled out one of the two-by-fours and a saw and began cutting. Two hours later he had constructed a platform just a bit higher than the wheel wells. He tossed his tools under the platform and spread the blankets on top of it. He now had a place where he could stretch out at night and a spot underneath where his tools and other supplies could be stored.

Lance climbed into the cab, carefully backed up the truck until he had space to turn around, and then drove up to the road above the lake. It was time to get away from civilization.

In a few minutes Lance was back on the Trans Canada and headed toward Vancouver. He would have to go back through the city to reach the north country. Lance was uneasy. By now the stolen license plate would have been reported, and police would have an APB out on it. However, this was a risk he would have to take.

Lance suddenly slowed because he could see police lights flashing up ahead on the side of the highway. He forced himself not to panic. *They probably pulled over some speeder,* he thought. But as he drew closer he could see that an accident had taken place. Lance slowed more to get a better look. On the highway stood a police officer signaling traffic to the left-hand lane and vigorously waving as he urged drivers to continue on without slowing down to gawk. Off to the side was a red Chevy Malibu with a badly crumpled hood and beyond that a blue pickup with slight damage to the rear bumper and the tailgate. *Man, he hit that pickup pretty hard,* Lance thought. *That Chev is definitely a write-off.*

Lance passed the accident site and resumed speed but suddenly hit the brakes and looked for the nearest exit. *This might be my lucky day,* he thought. He turned off at the next exit and doubled back on a business road that paralleled the highway. Lance could see the accident site directly across from him, so he pulled into the parking lot of a large greenhouse. A tow truck was now in front of the pickup.

He would have to wait for a while. Lance tilted the rearview mirror his way and inspected himself for the first time that morning. His face sported a thin stubble. It had been twenty-four hours since he had shaved. But of more immediate concern was the patchwork brown and white of his face. The spray was wearing off. Lance found the aerosol can in the shopping bag behind the seat and began spraying. By the time he was finished, he saw that the first tow truck had left with the pickup and a second had arrived for the Malibu.

Lance watched intently. When the Malibu was finally lifted onto the tow truck, he started his pickup. The tow truck pulled away, and Lance followed along the side road. He returned to the Number 1 and continued following the tow truck, which after about twenty-five kilometers took the first exit into the city of Abbotsford.

The tow truck passed through the business section of town and turned left at a set of lights at the top of a hill onto a road that twisted and turned next to a small river. They were soon in an industrial area with factories and warehouses. Lance was careful to follow at a safe distance. The tow truck continued past the large buildings and finally pulled into an auto wrecker's yard. As Lance passed, the driver got out of his vehicle and entered the front office in an old building that more than likely was once a home. It fronted an extensive lot surrounded by a high wire fence topped by barbed wire. On the lot were hundreds of automobiles in various stages of decomposition.

Lance drove ahead some distance and parked off the road opposite a meat processing plant. He saw the river below him through a narrow strip of trees. Lance entered the bush and quickly made his way back toward the auto yard, keeping out of sight as best he could. When he reached the lot, he spotted a man in oily coveralls holding the gate for the tow truck, which was backing into the lot. Lance moved among the trees, watching the tow truck through a tall chain link fence. The man in the coveralls directed the truck to an empty space toward the back of the lot. Once the vehicle was in the spot, the driver got out of the truck and the two men unhooked the vehicle. Lance waited until the truck had left the lot before he began walking among the trees back toward his pickup.

Now he would to have to wait. Lance reached the pickup and drove along the winding road, looking for a place where he could park his vehicle until dusk. Two miles farther along the road, he saw a sign that read: "Four-Mile Gulch Park." He turned in. The small park covered a small plain next to the river. A forest of huge trees shaded several small natural pools off to the left. The river was to the right. The park seemed nearly empty; Lance could see only one vehicle. He found a parking area and stopped. From his parking space, a path led through short shrubbery. With ten hours to kill, Lance meandered down the path. He hated the idleness. At times like this he could not stop thinking about Barb and the kids and the loneliness that haunted him, but there was little he could do.

Lance followed the path and soon came to a small footbridge spanning one of the pools at a narrow section between two larger bodies of water. Lance walked onto the bridge and leaned against the railing. He watched as a pair of white swans floated under the bridge. How free they seemed, with little to concern them except keeping their bellies full, which in this lush environment would be no problem at all. *Was all this worth it?* Lance wondered. *Maybe I should surrender to the police and let them cart me off to jail. I could serve my time and, when I'm finally released, resume my shattered life with my wife and my family. But would I still have a family after what I put them through?* In that hotel room after he woke up with a belt around his neck, Lance had decided to live. The plan he had scribbled on the yellow pages sheet had less than a 50 percent chance of success, but if he succeeded he could be back with his wife in just a few months—if she would have him.

After a long walk on the park trails, Lance decided to drive back into town. He found a camping store and bought a self-inflating air mattress, tarps, fishing gear, a cooler, and the best sleeping bag the store carried.

He went to a grocery store and bought a box of frozen burgers, buns, fruit, tomatoes, and vegetables. He also purchased frozen orange juice and as much frozen meat and fish as he had space for. It wouldn't keep for too long, but Lance hoped he would be able to eat the food as it thawed. At the back of his truck in the grocery store parking lot, Lance stored the food. He stuffed the frozen food as tightly as he could in the bottom of the cooler he had purchased and placed the fruit and the vegetables on top. By the time he was done, the cooler was full. In fact, he had to leave the bananas and oranges in the shopping bags with the buns.

As Lance made his way back down the winding river road, he spied an aluminum rowboat with a "For Sale" sign leaning against a garage. Lance decided to stop at the house.

A tall, gray-haired man, probably in his sixties, appeared at the door as he approached.

"Yes?" he said.

"Is that rowboat for sale?" Lance asked.

The man raised his eyebrows and thought. "Well, yes," he finally said. "I've had that sign on it for so long I had forgotten about it. Make me an offer and it's yours."

Lance had no idea what a small rowboat cost but imagined it must be $1,000 new.

"I'll give you a hundred for it," he offered.

"I'll tell you what," the man said. "You make it two hundred and it's yours."

"Sold," Lance said. "You don't happen to have some rope I could use to secure it, do you?"

Once again the man raised his eyebrows. "You don't have any rope?" he said with a snicker. "You didn't exactly come prepared, did you? Well, okay. I've got some in the garage."

The man helped Lance load the rowboat onto the canopy and secure it tightly with the rope and straps he provided. Lance was elated with his score. If he could augment his food supply with fresh fish, he might get by for several weeks in the wilderness. He was almost set to put his plan into action, but he faced one more hurdle.

Night had fallen and Lance was sitting in his pickup parked in the spot he had been in that morning, just a few hundred yards from the auto wreckers. Lance flashed back to the moment when he had passed the accident scene. He had remembered the time several years earlier when his wife had rolled their car. She had not been too badly hurt, just a large bruise on the back of her shoulder and shattered nerves. He had recalled the frustration of dealing with the insurance company after the accident. They had had to rent a car for two weeks before the company finally offered a settlement far below what they had expected. They had ended up buying another car when the settlement came through, but that was at least two weeks later. He had gone to the auto wreckers, hoping to get a few personal items from the car and to retrieve the license plate to put on the car they were buying. At that moment in his musings, Lance had hit the brakes. If the owner of the destroyed Malibu had anything close to the experience he had had, he would not be returning for his license plate for more than a week. That was more than enough time for Lance to carry out the first phase of his plan—to get through Vancouver and up to the rugged, largely deserted north country. The stolen license plate he had on the vehicle now was making him increasingly nervous. He would have to cross the Port Mann Bridge, which was a toll bridge that used license scanning technology, and he had heard that the police used it to identify stolen vehicles. He didn't want to take the chance.

The river road was pretty much deserted in the early evening, with just the odd transport truck going to one factory or another in the area. Lance got out of the pickup and retraced his path from that morning through the trees. When he got opposite the auto yard, he quickly crossed the road and followed the fence to the back of the lot. The eight-foot chain link fence had two strands of barbed wire running along the top. Lance was not going to let that stop him. He wrapped his fingers through the links and began climbing. The fence rattled loudly as he scaled it. Suddenly he heard a bark from the far side of the lot. Lance leapt back down from the fence as sixty pounds of snarling German shepherd charged at him. The dog stood on its back feet with its paws against the fence, growling.

This was something Lance had not bargained for. *It's never easy,* he thought, shaking his head and walking away. He realized the barking dog might attract someone's attention, so it was best to leave as soon as possible.

Lance returned to the truck and sat in the cab, contemplating his situation. He had a friend who was an animal control officer. It was his job to pick up strays and problem animals. He remembered a conversation he had had with Bill one day.

"I've been doing this job for ten years," Bill had bragged, "and I can't remember how many dogs have attacked me. But in all that time, I've been bitten only twice."

"Really. What size dogs?" Lance had asked, surprised by what Bill had said.

"Big ones, little ones. It really doesn't matter."

"I suppose you've got lassos and nets and such that you can stop them with."

"Nope. I use nothing but my bare hands," he had said, holding them up for Lance to study. "A dog has only one weapon, and that's its mouth. If you can neutralize that, the dog doesn't have a chance."

Lance got out of the cab, opened the tailgate of his pickup, and grabbed a hammer. The prize was too valuable for him to give up now. Hammer in hand, he returned to the lot. Lance studied the lot through the fence. The dog was nowhere in sight. Lance again followed the fence, this time as quietly as possible. He chose a different spot to climb, a point where a large, rusted white van was backed up against the fence. The dog would not be able to get at him if he entered here. Lance tried to climb the fence as quietly as possible, but it was impossible to prevent the fence from rattling as he neared the top. From the far side of the lot, he heard the dog yelp. The large German shepherd quickly approached and was barking angrily as Lance attempted to negotiate the top strands of wire without hooking himself.

Trying to ignore the snarling dog, Lance finally managed to cross the barbed wire and lowered himself onto the van's roof. The dog was beside itself with rage, leaping against the side of the van in a vain attempt to get at him. Lance jumped from the roof of the van onto the roof of a pickup on the opposite side from the dog. Lance leapt from roof to roof of the nearby vehicles. With one more leap he was on the hood of an old Cadillac, and with another bound he had reached the ground. Lance raised the hammer above his head and held out his other hand to block the charging German shepherd. He had less than a moment before the dog lunged, but he knew exactly what he was going to do. At the last possible moment Lance deftly stepped sideways. Momentum carried the dog forward. As it passed, Lance spun and brought the hammer down hard against the animal's skull. The dog yelped in pain and crashed to the ground in a daze. Lance charged the injured animal and again brought the hammer down on the surprised dog's head. The animal struggled with all its might to regain its balance, but it was too late. With one more well-aimed blow, Lance crushed the animal's skull and it lay dead at his feet.

Lance looked down at the animal with regret. He had always loved pets, and dogs were his favorites. Yet he needed that license plate, and he knew he would have to kill the dog to get it. He knew if he had any chance at freedom, he would have to sacrifice the life of this dog. Lance shook his head as he looked at the beast. Then he dragged it behind a vehicle and covered it as best he could with scrap metal.

Lance ran over to where he had seen the Malibu parked that morning and pulled out his screwdriver set. Within a minute he had the plate free, and he ran to the back of the lot. He flung the plate and his tools over the fence. Climbing onto an old two-ton truck, Lance was able to get back over the fence much more easily than when he had entered the lot.

Back at his vehicle, Lance quickly removed the plate and threw it into the bushes by the river. He then put on the plate he had taken from the Malibu and climbed in the cab.

Lance started the truck and retreated down the winding river road. Twenty minutes later he was back on the Number 1, heading for Vancouver. By the time he had passed through North Vancouver it was midnight. Lance didn't like traveling this late at night. It was too easy to raise the suspicions of patrolling police, but getting a hotel was just as risky, so Lance pressed on. He drove up the 99 toward Squamish. This night, fatigue was not a factor. As Lance drove, he couldn't get out of his mind the poor dog he had killed. He liked dogs and normally would never harm one. But desperate situations made for desperate actions.

By three in the morning Lance had passed Squamish and was about halfway to Whistler. Rain mixed with wet snow had fallen for hours. He stifled a deep yawn. Suddenly he spotted a sign that read: "Burnt Timber Campground, 64 km." A "Closed for the Season" sign hung below. *Perfect,* he thought. The gravel road went off to the left, which suited Lance. Since Squamish, the highway had been climbing steadily, and with the rise in elevation large snowflakes were dancing in front of his headlights. They hit his windshield and melted immediately. The road, however, was fast turning white and becoming slick. Lance believed the road to the left headed toward the coast, and the drop in elevation would mean he could escape the snow. He turned down the road, but twenty kilometers later he could go no farther. The pickup was straining against the intensifying snow, and his eyes were burning. Lance slowed until he found a place off the road to park. He pulled over and raced into the back under the canopy. He nestled in the blankets on the platform, spread the new sleeping bag over himself to guard against the cold, and immediately fell asleep.

In the morning Lance was wakened by the roar of a log truck as it sped down the narrow road. He lay in his blankets for ten more minutes, letting the rising sun gradually warm the inside of the canopy. He finally rose as yet another log truck tore past him. For such an isolated area, this was a busy road. Lance would have to be careful to avoid these mammoth trucks. He knew many of these drivers acted as if they owned the road, and with a full load of logs, they certainly wouldn't be able to stop for him. Lance pulled back onto the road and cautiously began the descent between evergreen and mixed forest. The road seemed to be headed west and gradually losing elevation. Lance slowed and pulled over each time a log truck sped by, but he still narrowly missed a collision as one behemoth came roaring around a tight corner. As the driver careened by with just inches to spare, Lance thought he glimpsed a smile on his face.

An hour later Lance watched for a sign for the campground. It had to be nearby. The icy snow had gradually vanished from the road, leaving rain-dampened gravel. Finally, almost having missed it, Lance spotted a small sign. He jammed on the brakes and made the turn. The road wound down to a small lake surrounded by a thick rain forest. Lance was surprised to see that although the campground was technically closed, a number of campsites were occupied by trailers of different sizes. This displeased him. The news shows still carried short reports about the heist three days earlier and about the close call at the Crown Hotel. The strange circumstances of the robbery had captivated the television audience, and reporters were covering the story from every angle. Lance still had his disguise but wanted to avoid contact wherever possible.

Lance picked a campsite as far from the occupied sites as possible and pitched his tent. He inflated the air mattress and brought in his sleeping bag, blankets, and heater. Most of the trailers seemed unoccupied, so Lance decided to take a walk down to the lake. The water was as smooth as glass and mirrored the snow-tipped mountains all around. Lance stood and admired the spectacular view for a few minutes. Then he collected firewood from a large pile in the center of the campground and lit a fire. He threw three burgers on the grill along with frozen buns. Once the buns were toasted, he applied ketchup and mustard and flipped the burgers.

"Hi there," a cheery voice called. "You're tenting it pretty late in the season."

Lance looked up and saw a woman, blond and about thirty, standing at the edge of his campsite with her daughter, who was about twelve. The woman was slim and attractive and smiled pleasantly. She wore a blue winter jacket open at the top. Her daughter had slightly darker blond hair. She was obviously the daughter because she closely resembled the woman beside her.

"Well, not really," Lance said with a smile. "I'm part of a survey team working in the area. The other guys are staying up where we're working, but I kind of like my privacy, so I decided to stay here instead."

"Oh, I'm sorry," the woman said with a frown. "I didn't mean to disturb you."

"Oh no, I didn't mean it like that. Sit down. I was just going to make some coffee, and I can put more burgers on the grill." The words were out of Lance's mouth before he was able to think. He needed to avoid people, but it had been three days since he'd had any real contact with another human being and he missed that. Besides, this human being happened to be beautiful. Lance mentally cursed himself for offering the invitation, but it was too late now.

"Oh no, that's fine," the woman said as she entered the campsite and sat on the opposite side of the picnic table. Her daughter wandered around the site, gathering pine cones in her jacket and singing softly to herself. "It's just that it gets pretty lonely here by myself all day with no one else to talk to but Micky. We don't even have phone service in this area with all the mountains. Geez, don't I sound like a needy loser?" She laughed.

"So what brings you to a deserted place like this?" Lance asked, hoping to relieve the woman's embarrassment.

"My husband talked me into coming to this godforsaken place. He's a tree faller. They're doing a lot of logging west of here. I'm sure you noticed the logging trucks coming in."

"Yeah, up close and personal," Lance said dourly.

The woman tossed back her head and laughed. "Yeah, I know what you mean," she said. "They scared the wits out of me coming down this road. Those drivers don't give a shit about anything except getting another load to the mill as fast as they can. My name's Jen." She extended her hand.

"Oh, pleased to meet you. I'm Rav," Lance lied, remembering his disguise.

"And it's good to meet you. We're going to go for a walk on one of these trails. There are supposed to be falls around here somewhere. I'm sure we'll be seeing each other. Enjoy your stay." She called her daughter and they strolled off.

Lance waved as they left and then sat staring at the fire. Jen had an infectious laugh and was beautiful and vigorous. He shook his head in disapproval of his weakness for the fairer sex.

The next morning Lance got up early, donned his coveralls and hard hat, and pulled out of the campgrounds. He had to stick to his story. Staying around would raise suspicion, and Lance wanted to avoid contact. He saw Jen was already up and sitting by a fire at her campsite with a coffee mug curled up in her hands. She smiled and waved to him as he went by. After hitting the sack, Lance had heard her husband pull in about eleven o'clock. His vehicle was already gone by the time Lance got up.

Lance drove out onto the gravel road and turned left, following the road deeper into the wilderness. He turned off onto another road after about five kilometers. This road soon got rougher and led up into higher elevations. Finally Lance spotted a cut line in the bush and pulled over as far as he could to the side of the road. For the rest of the morning he wandered down the cut line, which led up and down hills into deeper and deeper forest. Around noon he stopped on a high mountain outlook and pulled out the sandwiches he had prepared before leaving his campsite.

The spot was beautiful. From his vantage point Lance could see a silver ribbon of ocean gleaming between two peaks. Off to the left a large glacier curled below a towering gray mountain. He lay back in a bed of moss and stretched his aching muscles. He had probably followed the cut line for five or six miles, but the last stretch had been the worst. The trail rose precipitously, and Lance stopped several times on the way up to catch his breath.

Since starting his hike, Lance had been acutely aware of the danger of wildlife. His eyes constantly darted in all directions looking for any sign of movement. He knew black bears and cougars were in these woods, so he whistled and made as much noise as he could. He figured it was better to announce his presence than to surprise an animal. If an animal heard him, it was more likely to avoid him than to stalk him. Still the risk was there. Lance felt he had no choice. He was exploring these isolated woods because he wanted to find a location where he could live alone for a minimum of a month until the heat died down and he could made his escape. He was probably safe in the campground for the time being, but complacency could be his undoing. Lance continued climbing until he couldn't take another step. Sweat stinging his eyes and his muscles crying in protest, he dropped on the spot. Lance lay back on the moss and dozed. He dreamed of finding an idyllic ocean shore in a distant country far away from danger. His wife and his family were at his side, living in luxury with the thousands he had stolen.

Lance awoke and made his way back down the slope to his pickup. By the time he returned to the campground, it was after 5 p.m. Just before entering the campground, Lance surveyed himself in the mirror and gave his hands and his face a quick spray until he was satisfied with his disguise. He saw Jen sitting by her campfire as he pulled in. She seemed to have been frozen in that position from the moment he left that morning. He waved and parked at his campsite. As he did, he saw her get up and head toward him, carrying two cups. Lance prepared a fire in the grill as she entered his campsite.

"Hi," she said cheerily. "Can I offer you a cup of coffee?" Lance caught a whiff of the delicious aroma and reached for the cup.

"I can't think of anything I would rather have," he said, and took a sip. "Thanks. It's delicious!" She had mixed in some Kahlua, and Lance gave an involuntary sigh of satisfaction. After a full day of hiking, this definitely hit the spot.

"Where's your daughter?" Lance asked.

"Oh, Micky's in the trailer doing her lessons," Jen said as she sat down at the picnic table. "I've got her on homeschooling this year since we decided to come up here. It's like pulling teeth, though, to keep her working."

"Yeah, I can imagine," Lance said with a laugh.

Jen cocked her head to the side, gazing at him. "Rough day?" she queried.

"I am so stiff. We did a lot of walking today through some pretty tough country," he half lied.

"I bet you'll sleep like a baby tonight," she said.

"But it was a good day. Beautiful country."

"Oh, that's good," she said, smiling.

"So your husband left pretty early today. He must put in some long hours."

Jen shrugged. "Yeah. If I'd known it was going to be like this, I never would have agreed to come, but I'm stuck here now. I've been here almost two weeks, and this campground is deserted during the day. Most of the people here are working in the area just like you. There's Sharon over in site five, but I can take only so much of her."

Lance laughed. "Oh I see. What's wrong with Sharon?"

"Well, she's a lot older than I am, and all she talks about is her grandkids and the cutesy things they do. I'm sure that's really interesting to her, but it bores the hell out of me. I sometimes have to keep myself from rolling my eyes."

Lance guffawed. "I think I know exactly what you mean."

"So what are you guys surveying?"

Lance was thinking on his feet. "We're working for a mining company that wants to set up operations up here."

"Oh, that's interesting. So what kind of mining does the company do?"

"They don't tell me much." Lance wanted to avoid this line of questioning. He knew little about the area and even less about mining. "They don't tell us much, and I don't ask. I prefer to be like a mushroom, kept in the dark and fed you know what."

Jen's eyes sparkled as she laughed at his joke.

"So what do you do?" Lance asked, changing the subject.

"Well, I'm a safety program auditor, but I'm taking a month off before my next audit, and I thought I could use the rest and relaxation up here. When I'm on the job, we work pretty long hours."

They engaged in small talk as Lance got the fire going for a meal. "You guys might as well eat with me tonight," he said. "It's only going to be burgers, but I'm a master chef when it comes to those."

Jen laughed. "Deal," she said, "as long as you agree to eat with us tomorrow night."

Lance hesitated. This was not going the way he knew it should, but he was beginning to like Jen. Being with her helped pass the time and kept the demons from his mind.

"All right," Lance said. "If there are any fish in this lake I might be able to provide the main course."

"Fresh fish! That sounds great," Jen said. "Mike's got some rods in the trailer, and Micky might enjoy a little fishing. She's as bored as I am."

"It's a date," Lance said without thinking and then kicked himself for using the phrase. "I'm sorry," he said hurriedly. "I didn't mean it like that."

A tinge of color lit Jen's face as he said this. "No problem, mister. You better know I can take care of myself and won't be taken advantage of." She gave him a wink.

Lance held up his hands and laughed. "Okay, I've been put in my place. I'm going to start supper. You should get Micky and come back in about fifteen minutes."

Jen went back to her trailer, and a few minutes later she returned with Micky, who was lugging a watermelon. They sat and chatted as Lance finished grilling the burgers. They ate, talked, and laughed until darkness came and the stars peeked at them through the trees. Finally Jen thanked him for the meal, and she and Micky returned to their campsite for the night.

Lance cleaned up around the site and then went into the tent and lay in his bag. His legs thanked him kindly for the warm comfort his bag provided, and in no time he was sleeping.

The next morning Lance forced his tired body from the mattress and prepared himself as he had the previous morning. He waved at Jen, who was just coming out of the trailer, and drove on. He thought about the upcoming evening, fishing and eating with her and Micky, and the prospect brought a smile to his face. Once again, her husband's pickup was not there. In fact, Lance wasn't sure what the guy drove, because he had not yet seen the vehicle. He'd only heard it coming and going. He didn't recall it coming in that night, but with the fatigue he felt from all the walking he was probably sleeping too soundly to hear it.

Lance chose a different cut line in a different area and explored it. The weather had turned, and he put on his rain gear for the trek. He had found a couple of promising sites near the river, but neither completely satisfied him. He decided to continue exploring for a few more days to find the best one. The first cut line he chose this morning was much shorter, so he returned to his vehicle and drove a ways, choosing another cut line in the same area that looked like it might run close to the river as well. Lance needed a ready supply of water. He jumped from the cab and started down this cut line as the frigid rain pelted his raincoat.

He returned to the campground about the same time as the day before, thinking about the evening to come with Jen and her daughter. He liked this woman a lot but still missed his wife and his family terribly. The rain was subsiding, and Lance hoped they could get out in the rowboat.

Lance pulled into his campsite and stretched his tired muscles. A few minutes later Jen and Micky approached completely covered in yellow rain gear. The legs of Micky's outfit dragged in the mud as she walked. They had rods in their hands, and Jen carried a tackle box.

"Hey, are you ready to go?" Jen called out.

"Are you sure you want to do this?" Lance asked, gazing skyward. "It might be pretty wet out there."

"I'm game if you are," Jen said. "I've been thinking about fresh fried fish all day long."

"All right, let's do it," said Lance. He climbed in the pickup and backed up toward the lake.

Lance unloaded the rowboat into the water, and they got in. He rowed to a point of land that stretched into the lake and anchored. He selected a lure he thought might work, while Jen and Micky searched for their choices in their tackle box.

"These might help," Micky said as she pulled a plastic container from the bottom of the tackle box. She showed Lance a collection of earthworms, snails, and slugs. "I collected them today," she explained.

"Hey, good job," Lance cried. He selected an earthworm and affixed it to his hook. Jen got the first bite and squealed in excitement as she began reeling in the fish. Lance didn't have a net but managed to scoop the lake trout into the boat with his arms. It was among the bigger ones he had seen.

"Nice job," he said. "One more like this and supper is taken care of." He turned to Micky and said, "Okay, I'm not going to get skunked. Let's make a bet. If anyone gets skunked, they do the dishes tonight. Agreed?"

Micky and Jen laughed, and Micky said, "Okay, it's a bet, but I sure hope you like doing dishes."

They began casting in earnest. Ten minutes later Lance felt a wiggle on his rod, but when he jerked back he found nothing there. Immediately after, Micky cheered as her rod bent under the weight of a fish. A minute later Lance pulled the trout into the boat. It was just slightly smaller than the one her mother had caught. Lance drew in the anchor and headed back to shore. He dragged the front of the boat onto the gravel landing and helped Jen and Micky get out. The three of them headed for the trailer. Jen carried her rod and Micky's, while Micky proudly carried the fish.

The rain had stopped by the time they reached the campsite. Lance started the fire while Jen prepared the fish. Micky hopped in a circle, chattering all the while. She had obviously enjoyed the excursion a great deal.

Jen was a great cook. She seasoned and battered the fish to perfection and cut up potatoes into small chunks and threw them in the frying pan with the fish. She stewed some broccoli, and while everything cooked she mixed up a cheese sauce in a small pot that she placed to one side of the grill.

Lance couldn't believe it. The meal was delicious, and he ate until he was stuffed. He was used to much poorer fare on camping trips. Hamburgers and hot dogs were usually on the menu.

After supper Lance did the dishes as promised. He refused the help Jen offered, saying, "A bet's a bet." When he finished, Jen had a coffee and Kahlua ready for him. Lance put his coat on, threw a few more logs on the fire, and sat down on one of the lawn chairs circling the fire.

They chatted amiably as the night wore on. After they finished the coffee, Jen brought out some rye and they sipped on rye and Cokes as they talked. Micky sat with them, using a stick to play with the fire. She held the tip in the fire, bringing the stick out when it was lit. She whirled the stick around, and they watched the fiery orange streak the glowing tip made against the night sky.

At one point Lance said, "You know I slept really well last night. In fact, I didn't even hear your husband pull in."

He saw Jen's face tighten as she stared at the fire. "The bastard didn't come back last night," she said. "He's done this three or four times since we got here. After work he gets to drinking with the other guys and crashes in the camp they've set up. If he's been drinking, that suits me fine." Jen sniffed quietly.

Lance studied her face. The situation obviously bothered her, but she was doing her best to remain strong. "Oh, I'm sorry," he said. "Look, if you really want, I can take a day off work and drive you in to Squamish. I'll just tell the boss I was sick."

"No, don't worry about it. Mike has only one more week left on his shift anyway. And besides, it's been a lot better since you got here," Jen said, looking at Lance. "Thank you for today. It was fun, and Micky loved it too, didn't you?" She nudged her daughter with her elbow.

Micky stopped playing with the stick and looked up at her mother. Jen motioned with her head toward Lance.

Micky looked at him and said, "Thanks, Rav. It was fun."

"Yeah, it was," Lance said, "but next time I'm gonna be the one catching the fish."

The three of them laughed.

Finally as the night wore on and the rye had its effect, Lance stood and yawned. He thanked Jen for the meal and for the enjoyable evening and wished her good night. Micky had gone to bed an hour or two earlier.

Jen wished him good night through a yawn of her own, and Lance made his way in the dark to his tent. As he was climbing into the tent, Mike pulled in and parked next to the trailer. Lance quickly got into the tent. For some reason he felt a little guilty about the evening he had passed with Jen.

For the next few days Lance continued his routine of leaving the campground early in the morning and spending the day exploring the countryside for a place where he could survive for the next three or four weeks. He had found a number of spots but wasn't sure how well he would fare if the weather turned particularly ugly, as it was prone to do at this time of year. Lance was enjoying Jen and Micky's company in the evenings, and this may have delayed his decision on where to spend the next several weeks.

On the third day he chose a cut line that ran through a particularly hilly area. He was getting in better shape wandering the woods, but this area seemed to be taking a toll on him as he hiked. Each hill seemed to be higher than the one before. Lance noticed that he was taking more breathers as he scaled the hills. The unseasonably warm weather added to his exhaustion.

As was his custom, at around noon Lance pulled out sandwiches and a thermos of coffee at the top of the last hill he had climbed and enjoyed a picnic. The shade of the trees and the splendid panorama of distant snowy peaks refreshed him.

After a short nap he resolved to climb two more hills before calling it a day. So far nothing had caught his eye as a prospective campsite. If he did not find anything today he was pretty much resigned to a site he had found the day before next to a small lake. Lance got up, stretched, and continued on his way.

At the top of the next hill Lance stopped to regain his breath. The last stretch had been steeper than anything he had traversed that day. He was looking at the view the height provided when halfway down the hill he had just climbed he saw a black bear. The bear was an adult but not particularly large. The bear had obviously seen him first because it stood on its haunches studying him. Lance knew bears were generally as scared of humans as humans were of them, so although the bear made him nervous he was not about to panic. When the bear finally disappeared back into the trees, Lance turned and walked down the other side of the hill, hoping the bear would be long gone by the time he returned to the pickup.

He had begun scaling the next hill when he again paused. His breathing and his heart rate were slowly returning to normal when he spied the same bear. It had come out of the trees no more than sixty yards behind him and was walking in his direction. Now Lance was frightened. This was not normal bear behavior. If bears knew of a person's presence, they usually made themselves scarce, but this bear was clearly stalking him.

Just ahead there was a short drop-off before the hill again rose toward its summit. Lance turned and disappeared down the drop-off. He had to do something. The bear had cut the distance between them and would no doubt continue to do so until he was close enough to attack. Lance looked around and saw a stand of aspen trees nestled in the evergreen forest. He ran toward this stand, found a tree with branches conveniently spaced for climbing, and shinnied up the tree on the double. Lance got a foothold on a small branch, but when he put his weight on it, the branch snapped and he almost plummeted to the ground. He squeezed himself tightly against the trunk and shinnied higher until he was hidden among the leafy branches.

Not long after, from his perch in the tree, Lance saw the bear reach the crest and look around. It was obviously searching for its prey. He held his breath, watching the bear. The bear nosed around until it reached the spot where Lance had stood minutes earlier. The bear then began to nose its way slowly toward the bluff where he was hidden. The bear followed Lance's scent right to the bottom of the tree he had climbed, and then to Lance's chagrin it looked up.

When he realized that the bear had found him, Lance immediately climbed higher into the tree as the bear watched him. As Lance neared the uppermost branches, he saw the bear stand on its back legs and raise itself into the tree.

He was trapped! What could he do? The bear would slowly climb the tree until it reached Lance, and that would be the end of him.

Lance looked around him at the aspen grove. He had grown up in a small town in the interior of British Columbia. It was the kind of town where everybody knew everybody else. Children were allowed to roam with few restrictions since the town didn't have the safety issues that large cities did. Lance and his friends spent most of their time near his house in an aspen grove just like this one, building tree forts and playing in the trees. He and his buddies were a bunch of daredevils. One of the activities they enjoyed most was swinging from tree to tree. This gave Lance an idea.

Lance climbed as high as he dared and shifted his weight to get the treetop swinging in the direction of a nearby tree. Below him the bear was making a swift ascent. Finally the tree began to bend at a greater angle. As he pushed farther and farther outward,

Lance wasn't sure if the thinner trunk at this height would hold. The bear stopped about ten feet below him, perhaps disconcerted by the swaying of the tree. Lance hadn't done this since he was a kid, and he was much heavier now. But he had no choice, and with a final effort he stretched out and was able to grasp the nearby tree. He released his legs from the other tree and nearly lost his grip as the tree swung away from him.

Once the tree steadied, the bear continued to climb until it was at eye level with Lance. Some fifty feet above the ground and just ten feet apart, bear and human stared at each other. Lance was surprised at how the bear looked at him. It showed no anger or any other response with the possible exception of confusion. The two creatures eyed each other for the next fifteen minutes. Finally the bear, realizing it had no way to get at the nearby human, began to descend as Lance happily watched it go.

When the bear reached the ground, however, it immediately found the tree he was now in and quick began to ascend. This tree was taller and therefore thicker at the point where Lance clung. To swing this tree he would have to climb much higher.

When he reached a suitable height, Lance put all his effort into getting the tree swaying toward yet another tree nearby. He grasped the trunk of the other tree just as the bear got within reach. Lance swung himself into its branches in a moment of heart-stopping terror as the other tree snapped back to its original position. Once again he had escaped before the bear could reach him. Lance ignored the bear for a moment and immediately began plotting a new escape route.

This scenario played out three more times. The bear would climb the tree only to discover that Lance had switched to another. Once the bear scaled the tree at lightning speed, surprising Lance. The bear was inches from him with outstretched claws, and Lance desperately launched himself into the neighboring tree. After that, Lance had the tree swaying at all times, and as soon as the bear began to descend, he would swing into a new tree well before the bear could draw near. He also made sure he didn't choose a tree too far from another. Time and time again the bear charged up a tree only to find its prey had escaped.

Finally, late in the afternoon, the bear, having descended one more time, sniffed around on the forest floor, took one last look at its slippery prey up in the tree, and began to move away. Lance breathed a sigh of relief as he watched the bear disappear into the woods. He wasn't sure what he would have done if darkness had fallen while he was in this predicament. The bear might have been able to sneak up the tree and surprise him before he could react.

Lance stayed in the tree for another hour, watching for any sign of the bear. He feared the bear might be setting up an ambush. Finally Lance overcame his fears and climbed down the tree. Once he reached the ground he left the area as quickly as he could. Lance ran as much as his aching body would let him. He looked behind him in the fading light, imagining the bear was in pursuit. Sometimes his mind played tricks on him, and he thought he saw the bear in the shadow of the trees. It was dark by the time he reached his truck, panting raggedly.

Lance sat behind the steering wheel and expelled a deep breath. Several minutes later he managed to calm himself after his terrifying experience. He fired up the truck and pulled away.

"How was your day?" Jen asked when he finally arrived back at the campground.

"We had a few problems with a bear today," Lance said, smiling to himself.

"Really? Did you have to shoot it?" Jen asked, frowning.

"No, we managed to harass it enough that it finally got bored and left," Lance said.

Most evenings after his hikes, Lance spent time fishing with Jen and Micky. They had eaten together every night since they first went fishing and had become fast friends. Most nights Mike had pulled in late, and Lance hadn't laid eyes on him, but this night he was standing on the shore as they returned from their fishing trip.

With a wide smile, Micky held up three fish. When they made land, Jen said, "Hi, dear. You're home early. This is Rav, the guy I told you about. Rav, this is Mike."

Mike eyed Lance closely and then held out his hand. "Hi. Good to meet you," he said. "Thanks for taking care of my girls while I've been working." He put his arm around Jen and brought her close to him.

Lance helped carry the gear back to Jen's trailer and then dismissed himself, but Jen invited him to stay for supper and wouldn't take no for an answer.

"Okay, thanks a lot," Lance said, finally surrendering.

They ate supper and settled down by the fire with drinks.

"So what do you do?" Mike asked, turning to Lance.

"We're doing some surveying for a mining company," Lance replied.

"Oh? Where are you guys surveying?" Mike asked.

"We're up about twenty miles north of here."

"Oh really? We're working north of here as well. What road are you guys on?"

"To tell you the truth, I never paid any attention to the name of the road. When we first came, I just followed the rest of the crew and didn't pay any attention to road signs. It was pretty straightforward."

"What's the mining company?"

"Algoma," Lance replied, naming the first mining company that sprang to mind.

During the evening, Mike questioned him closely about what he was doing in the area. Lance lied as best he could, and his know-nothing approach finally seemed to satisfy Mike.

Lance made an excuse and returned to his campsite earlier than usual. He had spent little time at the site lately and busied himself there while Jen and Mike sat at their fire. Lance retired to his tent early and lay awake in his bag. His mind raced from one thing to another. He thought about the possible sites he had spied out and worried about how he would survive in these places. He pictured himself in the middle of a snowstorm in each of them, and the thought made him squirm. He also thought about Jen and the time they had spent together and the conversations they had had. He pictured her smile and the way she greeted him when he pulled into the campground in the late afternoons. It seemed to him that she had been looking forward to his arrival the last three days. Finally he thought of Barb and his kids, and the pain returned. Lance shook as he felt the agony he knew his family must be suffering as a result of what he had done. Finally, much later he fell asleep.

The next day as Lance was exploring a particularly rugged and overgrown cut line, he got lucky. About an hour into his hike, he suddenly came upon an old plywood cabin. The paint had peeled away, but the roof seemed to be in fairly good shape. The asphalt shingles looked a little curled, but he couldn't see any gaps. Lance tried the door, which swung open easily. Inside he spotted several traps hanging on the wall and an antique pot belly stove in the middle of the room. *How in the world did they lug that way up here?* he wondered. A galvanized chimney rose through the ceiling. In one corner of the cabin was a rustic bed made with two-by-fours. An old mattress lay on top of the planks. Lance's lip curled. There was no way he would sleep on that flea-bitten thing, but his air mattress would fit nicely on the planks. His heart beat fast as he gazed around the room. There was even a window in the back.

Lance look around outside. *This must be a trapper's cabin used during the winter,* he thought. Trees had grown up around the cabin and made it almost invisible. In fact, he had almost walked right by the cabin without noticing it. He blessed his luck. Lance wandered across the cut line and entered the trees on the other side. He scrambled down a hill on a well-worn path and found a fast-running stream. He spied a number of deep pools and then scrambled back up to the cut line.

This site is ideal, Lance thought. His search was over. This was better than he could ever have hoped for—a nearby water supply, a cabin with a heat source, and even a bed. Tomorrow he would make his excuses to Jen and leave the campground.

By the time Lance got back to his vehicle it was dark. Stars twinkled overhead from a patch of black sky. Lance paused for a few minutes, taking in the beauty of his surroundings. The last half-hour of his hike had been harrowing. He had stumbled several times over unseen logs and rocks on the cut line and he was scraped and bruised, but nothing could detract from the elation he felt over the discovery of the cabin. He would be able to live there in relative security for the next few weeks.

CHAPTER 5

After mustering all his resources around the area of the Crown Hotel, Rob finally faced the reality that Lance Knight had slipped through their fingers. The forensics unit descended on room 627 and confirmed Rob's suspicion that the mysterious substance was indeed a tanning spray.

But Rob did not wait for that report. The image of the dark man standing at the elevators burned in his mind. One of the first things he did when he finally got back to headquarters that afternoon was to summon a police artist. The artist worked his magic on the photo of Lance from the motor vehicle branch. He uploaded it into his computer and opened it into a software program. He pushed a few keys, and the face darkened on the screen in front of them. In just a few minutes the image of the man at the elevator doors appeared.

"Damn it," Rob said. "That's him. That's the man we walked right by at the Crown Hotel. Son of a ..." He arranged to have a new APB put out with Lance's darkened face side by side with the old photo. He contacted the television stations with the new information, and they agreed to run the story complete with the picture. Rob was somewhat disappointed, however, because despite his urgings the stations refused to do a follow-up. The public's attention to a story was short-lived, and in a metropolis like Vancouver there was always new fodder for the news agencies. This week, that new fodder happened to be the trial of a serial killer who had murdered more than forty women. Rob simply couldn't compete with that.

The incident at the Crown a week earlier gave Rob a new respect for his adversary. "I guess he's not as stupid as that mistake at the bank led us to believe," Rob said. "He's headed for deep cover. I know it." He got out of his chair and paced the room as Doug watched.

"I want a list of all stolen plates on my desk every morning from here on," Rob demanded.

"Stolen plates? Why?" Doug asked.

"Right now this guy's on foot, and he's not giving up. He's going to need wheels. To get them, he's going to need plates, and the only way he's going to get them is to steal them."

"Okay, Rob. Whatever you say." Doug left the office shaking his head.

The case had gone quiet. The wiretap on the Knight residence had yielded nothing. Rob had had a heated argument with the captain, who ordered an end to the wiretap, which was costing the department time and money. Rob extracted a promise from the Knight family to call him immediately if Lance made contact. He spent most of his time working on the rest of his caseload. Sooner or later police would get the break they needed. APBs were in place, stolen license plates would trigger an alert, and Lance's bank accounts and credit cards were frozen. The bank robber had little room to maneuver. The only thing that worried Rob was the incredible amount of cash Lance had. A person could open a lot of doors with $700,000.

Friday morning Rob sat with the telephone to his ear as Doug sat on the corner of the desk listening. "Okay. Listen, thanks a lot. You guys have been a big help," Rob said, hanging up the phone.

"That was the Abbotsford police," he said, turning to Doug. "I called them to follow up on some stolen plates. They had an interesting story to tell me. It seems that four days ago an auto wrecker in the area filed a complaint about a break-in one night. It never came to our attention because it was pretty much a local issue. Besides, as far as the staff at the lot knew, nothing was missing."

"Yeah, sure. I'm not really following you here, Rob," Doug said.

"Well, it didn't come to our attention until"—Rob checked his notes for the name—"Mr. Frank Abnell, whose vehicle was hauled to the lot a week ago, reported his plates missing."

"Uh-huh," Doug said.

"Well, it seems a day after the break-in, the auto wreckers found their guard dog dead."

"Dead?"

"That's right. It was bludgeoned to death with a blunt instrument, probably a hammer."

"Interesting," Doug said. "But what makes you so sure this case involves Lance Knight?"

"That's a lot of trouble to go through to get plates, wouldn't you say?" Rob sat up and leaned toward Doug. "I tell you what. Next staff party, just for entertainment we're going to give you a hammer and have you go up against an angry eighty-pound German shepherd. I gotta tell you, my money's on the dog."

"Not me. I'm scared of dogs," Doug said, shaking his hands and laughing.

"I've got a hunch this guy's gone deep and he's used these plates to do it. I want you to contact the Wells Gray, Hope, and Squamish detachments. See if you can talk them into sending squad cars to the provincial parks and campgrounds in their areas to look for a vehicle with this plate number on it." He slid a piece of paper with the number across the desk to Doug.

"Okay, will do," Doug said, scooping up the paper. He left the office to make the calls. The three departments guaranteed their cooperation and promised to send squad cars to all campgrounds in their vicinity to check for a vehicle with the tag BRC 2891.

· · ● ● ● ◆ ● ● ● · ·

Lance drove back down the deserted road toward the campground. The closer he got, the more his elation at discovering the cabin was replaced by a pang of regret deep in his gut. He thought about Jen and the evenings he had spent laughing and joking with her. He would miss those times. Lance had to admit he was falling for this girl.

Just before reaching the campground, he pulled over, took out the tanning spray, and darkened his face. Lance had done this every evening. During the day the makeup became streaked with sweat as he climbed up and down the cut lines.

When he was finally satisfied with his appearance, Lance pulled into the campground. There had been so little traffic in and out of the place that he no longer worried about being discovered. As he climbed from the cab of his truck, he spied Jen approaching him.

"You're late," she said.

"Yeah, it was quite a day. Boss said we had to get the line we were on done today. I don't know what the hurry was, but I'm beat."

"Well, you're in luck. Supper's ready. Micky and I borrowed your boat today and we got lucky. I hope you don't mind."

"Oh no," Lance said. "Use it whenever you want."

Jen grabbed his hand and said, "Come on. Supper will be getting cold." Lance was taken aback by the unexpected gesture. He struggled to gather himself as she led him back to her campsite and sat him at the picnic table where a Coke bottle stood beside a bottle of rye.

"Help yourself," she said, "and if you wouldn't mind, pour me one too. I'll bring out the food."

"Micky, supper's ready," Jen called out as she turned toward the trailer. Micky appeared out of the darkness on a path from the lake just as Jen emerged from the trailer bearing plates and a frying pan.

Lance took the plates and set three places on the picnic table while Jen retreated into the trailer for the rest of the food. The frying pan was loaded with sizzling fish. Jen had prepared what seemed a feast to Lance. She also served beautiful young carrots, a salad, and potatoes whipped in a cheese sauce.

They ate until they were satisfied. Then they sat by the fire talking until late in the evening. Finally Jen and Lance put the leftovers in the fridge and heated water to do the dishes. Jen washed as Lance dried. Lance could not stop thinking about how much he would miss her when he moved to the cabin.

"I'm going into Squamish tomorrow," he said, making a sudden decision. "Do you and Micky want to come with me?"

Jen looked up at him. "You don't have to work tomorrow?"

"Nope. It's the weekend and the crew has gone back to Vancouver. I want to pick up some groceries and enjoy a bit of civilization. What do you say?"

"Well yes, that sounds wonderful," she said. "I can't wait. Thank you."

"Okay, tomorrow morning we're going."

It was after one in the morning when Lance rose from the campfire and said good night to Jen. Yet again Mike would obviously not be returning to the campground.

"Are you sure you don't want to sleep in the trailer?" Jen asked.

"That tent can't be the most comfortable place to spend the night. We've got plenty of room."

For a moment Lance was tempted to say yes, but he thought better of it.

"No, no. I'm quite comfortable with my mattress and my heater. Besides, I'm not sure what I might do. I sleepwalk, you know," he said with a laugh.

"That wouldn't be so bad," Jen said, staring at him.

"Thanks, Jen, for everything. Good night!" he said, ignoring the look in her eyes.

"No, thank you. I think I would have gone crazy by now if it wasn't for you."

Lance gave her a quick hug and left for his tent.

The next morning Lance got up early and did a little cleaning up inside the tent and around his campsite. He dumped the water from the melting ice in his cooler and went through the food. Some of the meat looked suspect, so he tossed it in the garbage. He would have to stock up for his sojourn in the cabin for the next few weeks.

Lance soon noticed movement at Jen's site, and about fifteen minutes later Jen and Micky came over.

"Are you ready to go?" he asked.

Micky climbed into the middle, and Jen followed as Lance fired up the engine. He noticed the truck needed fuel.

On the way into town, Lance counted three squad cars heading into the campground region. The trip to Squamish took more than an hour. When they arrived, Lance said he had to pick up some things for work, so he dropped off Jen and Micky at the Safeway grocery store and agreed to meet them for lunch. Lance then drove around until he found the local library. It was a squat brick building just off the town's main street.

Lance parked and walked in. The library was housed in one room. The spare stacks surrounded three long tables in the middle. Lance headed over to one of the two computers under a colorful sign that said "Internet." It was time to put the next phase of his plan into effect. He sat down at the computer. Lance wasn't sure how to find what he was looking for, so he decided to take the direct approach. He opened the search engine and typed in "fake ID."

Lance's eyes grew wide. The search engine immediately found thirty or forty sites advertising passports, social security cards, and driver's licenses from any US state and even some provinces in Canada. Lance searched through the sites, nervously hoping no one would notice what he was doing. Finally he found one that promised complete discretion. All a person had to do was send a number of passport-size photographs, fill out a form indicating which state or province the ID was for, and give a credit card number. The company would do the rest. Ten days after receiving the photos, it would send the fake identification. The company wouldn't charge the card until the person received the order and was satisfied. Satisfaction was guaranteed! If a person didn't like the job the company did, he could send the documents back free of charge.

Lance decided to go with a US passport and a driver's license from California. Safety in numbers, he reasoned. California was America's most populous state. He had a better chance using ID from a state like that than, say, from Rhode Island. Besides, he was somewhat familiar with California, having worked there for a year before he was married. Lance felt he would go unnoticed by the enormous bureaucracy of such a large state.

He highlighted the website and returned to the search engine. This time he entered "obituaries California." Immediately several pages of obituaries popped up, and Lance scrolled through them. Most showed men and women in their twilight years. These he dismissed out of hand. Many were scant on details. He was looking for an identity he could easily assume. Eventually, he found a few men who had passed away in the last couple of years and whose obituaries seemed to offer a fair amount of information about them. He reviewed these and finally settled on a Mark Fenwood of Red Valley, California, who had died about six months earlier. Quite a few sites contained this name.

Lance waded through them. Most were for Mark Fenwoods from other areas of the country, but then his eyes settled on a Facebook account that looked promising. He clicked on the link and suddenly he was looking at his target's photograph along with dozens of postings on the home page. The family had not bothered to cancel the account. Lance scrolled through the posts, jotting down anything of note that he felt could help him fill out the identity. He was amazed at how much information he could glean about this person online. He even obtained a passport number and an expiration date from a scanned copy of the document the man had in his files.

Lance returned to the first site, placed the information on the form, and entered his credit card number. The ad said he wouldn't be charged unless he was satisfied. He hoped that even if his card was frozen, as he imagined it was, he would get the documents before the company ran it. A shady business like this wasn't likely to do a whole lot of verifying. He instructed the company to mail the documents to Lance Knight, General Delivery, Squamish. He had to ask the librarian for the Squamish postal code. After hitting the "send" button, Lance sat back. He was astonished at the ease with which he was able to get information from the web. In fact, he found this sobering him. If he had gotten this much information in little over half an hour, how much did the police know about him with the vast resources they had? If he was going to make his escape, he would have to totally reinvent himself, breaking all connections with his past.

Just to be sure, Lance repeated the application process on a number of promising sites. One asked for payment in cash along with the application. Lance was pretty sure that sending cash through the mail was illegal, but he shrugged, printed out the application, borrowed an envelope from the library, and stuffed it with the money and the form. He added a few extra sheets in hopes that this might prevent the post office from detecting the cash.

Lance finished the applications, scribbled down the names of the websites, and then searched the library's sparse collection. Eventually he found a small paperback titled *Survival Techniques in BC's Wilds*. Lance glanced around, tucked the book into his jacket pocket, and left. *Who knows*, he thought, *there might be some valuable information in here that will help me extend my stay at the cabin.*

He had a lot to do before meeting Jen and Micky for lunch. Lance found a photography studio and had several passport-size pictures taken. Then he crossed to a drugstore and bought a box of envelopes. Fifteen minutes later he had the envelopes with his photos ready to be mailed.

Lance drove back to the grocery store where he found Jen and Micky standing with bags of groceries in their hands.

"Been waiting long?" Lance asked.

"No. We just got out five minutes ago," Jen said. "Let's go eat. It's on me. We're famished. We didn't have breakfast this morning."

"Me neither," Lance replied. They drove down the town's main street and soon found a small, elegant restaurant. They went in and ordered a three-course meal. Lance noticed that Jen was more animated than usual, laughing and conversing happily. Her mood seemed to have improved with the opportunity to get away from the campground, if only for the day.

"We're going clothes shopping," Jen declared after the meal. "Do you want to come, Rav?"

"Oh no, I'm not falling into that trap," Lance said with a laugh. "You two go have a good time. Besides, I still have a lot to do."

Once Jen and Micky disappeared down the street, Lance climbed back into the truck and drove to a service station. While an attendant filled his vehicle, Lance went into the bathroom, locking the door. He scrubbed with soap and water until his white skin appeared from under the tanning spray. Lance peered at himself. This was the face he had owned for forty years but hadn't seen for more than two weeks. Lance paid for the gas and left. He was amazed that no one took even a second look at the transformation that had occurred. He found a second photography studio and again had passport pictures taken. He now had two sets—one of himself as an East Indian, another of himself as a white man. He slipped the new photographs into envelopes along with the extra applications he had printed, scribbled the website addresses on the envelopes, and inserted cash, hoping the companies would be honest enough to provide the service even though they already had the money in their hands. Then he mailed the letters at the post office.

Lance drove away and parked in a secluded spot. A few minutes later, using the rearview mirror, he was again the East Indian whom Jen and Micky knew. He went to the store and bought as many groceries, mostly frozen, as he felt he could lug over the long cut line to the cabin.

By the time he was done, Lance had about forty-five minutes until he was to meet up with the girls and head back to the campground. He hesitated, debating with himself. Lance yearned to call his wife, but he knew that a phone call to Barb could lead to his capture. There was a chance the police had a wiretap on the house phone. But there were many things he wanted to say to her, and his decision to cut all contact with his past meant he would not have another opportunity for a long time. Lance decided to make the call. Even if there was a wiretap and police could trace his call, by tomorrow he would be off in the wilderness and would have disappeared from the face of the earth for all practical purposes.

Lance went to a pay phone near the center of town and picked up the receiver. As he dialed, his heart fluttered. He wasn't nervous or excited or even fearful. He felt as if he were standing on the other side of a veil about to peer into a life that once existed but now seemed strangely ethereal. Barb picked up the phone on the second ring.

"Hello!"

Lance could hear the tension and sadness in her voice, and it almost tore his heart out.

"Hi, Barb. It's me."

There was a long pause on the other end of the line, but finally she said hello. There was no tenderness in her voice. It was void of emotion.

"Listen, Barb, I just want to say how sorry I am for putting you through everything I've put you through."

There was no response.

"Barb, I love you so much, and I hate what I've done to you."

"Don't! Don't you say that to me! How could you do it?" she said, her voice shaking. "You can't begin to know what I've gone through. There have been police and reporters camped outside our house asking questions. And I don't have any answers."

"I'm sorry, Barb."

"Why didn't you tell me what you were going to do?"

"If I had, you would have tried to talk me out of it."

"That's exactly what I would have done. How could you do something so stupid?"

"Look, I've been working at the same stupid job for almost twenty years, and what do I have to show for it? I'm still in debt up to my neck. We struggle every month just to buy food and to pay for our house. I was sick of it."

"You had a wife and a wonderful family, and you've ruined everything." Barb began to sob bitterly.

"Listen, Barb, I'm going to leave the country. I've got a lot of money, and I want to be with you. Once I get settled, will you join me? We can live the rest of our lives together with no cares in the world."

Barb continued to sob. Finally she said, "I can't live off of stolen money. I won't do it. Lance, you've got to give yourself up. What you are doing is wrong and dangerous."

"I'd be behind bars for ten or fifteen years. We're talking armed robbery here. Please, Barb. I want to be with you. Let me ask you this. If I gave myself up, would you be there for me when I got out? I need to know that."

Again there was a long pause. "Ten years is a long time, Lance. I can't tell you that. Who knows what will happen in ten years? I'll be over fifty. The way these last two weeks have gone, I'll probably be dead in ten years."

"Listen, Barb, I've got to go. Think about what I've asked you. I'll call you in a few weeks. I want you to think seriously. Will you forgive me and come away with me? I promise you, Barb, it will be wonderful."

"You've made lots of promises to me," she said angrily, "and right now none of them means spit." The final word came out as a hiss, and with a loud click she was gone.

"Barb, Barb. Hello. Hello."

When Lance hung up the phone he was stricken. He stood by the booth for a minute or so and then slowly headed for his truck.

CHAPTER 6

ob was in downtown Vancouver, seated in his favorite Vietnamese restaurant with Doug, less than a block from headquarters. The place was neat and clean with simple plastic chairs at small tables. Several huge, intricately stitched oriental tapestries were the only extravagance. Rob liked the simplicity of the place and found he could get a decent meal for less than any of the many fast-food dives in the area charged. He was bent over his bowl of pho, about to scoop a spoonful of noodles into his mouth, when his phone rang.

"Passaglia," he said, wiping his mouth with a napkin.

"Lance Knight has surfaced, sir," the voice said. "He just placed a phone call to his wife. We traced it to a pay phone in Squamish."

"How long ago?"

"Five minutes ago, sir."

"Okay," Rob said. "I want a transcript on my desk ASAP." With that, he disconnected.

He looked at Doug and said, "Get me the head guy at the Squamish detachment stat."

Rob headed to the till and paid for his half-eaten meal. As they left the restaurant, Doug handed him the phone.

"Hello. This is Inspector Lamy."

"Hello, Inspector. This is Detective Passaglia of the VPD. We've just received information from a wiretap indicating that Lance Knight is in Squamish as we speak."

By the time the pair returned to headquarters, Rob had given the inspector all the information he had, and the inspector had promised to put as many units on the street as he could spare. Rob had also convinced him to put out an APB on the plate that had been stolen from the auto yard in the Fraser Valley. Rob wished he could give the inspector a vehicle description, but he had nothing.

Rob sat at his desk and Doug sat down across from him. "So what's he doing in Squamish?" Rob wondered. "Have we identified any friends or family in the area?"

"No," Doug responded. "We've interviewed Knight's family extensively, and nothing about Squamish ever came up."

"That means he's probably alone up there. But why Squamish? His first move should have been to try to cross the border."

"There are plenty of places to hide up there," Doug said. "You're right in the middle of the coastal rain forest."

"Of course!" Rob said. "He's decided to lie low until things cool off a little."

"So I suppose we're off to Squamish," Doug said.

"Why?" Rob asked. "If he's lying low like we think, we'll know within the hour if the Squamish PD has had any luck. If they don't get him by then, he'll scurry back to his nest."

Doug got up. "I've got some work to do," he said. "I'll check back in an hour or so."

Rob was deep in thought as Doug left. He turned to his computer and accessed the maps database. He printed out a large map of the Squamish area and circled spots on the map. Finally he picked up his phone and dialed. Inspector Lamy answered on the first ring.

"It's Detective Passaglia. Do you have any news for me?"

"Nothing so far, but I'll contact you right away if we nab him."

"Actually, I have another favor to ask," Rob said. "Would you mind having your men drive through all the campgrounds in the area? I count eight places in your area. It shouldn't take more than a day to cover them all."

"Campgrounds? Why campgrounds? Most of them are closed for the season."

"With all the media coverage this case has had, Knight's face is still one of the most recognizable around. He has to go deep. Camping out is one of the ways he can do that."

"Makes sense. Okay, if we don't come up with anything today, I'll have a sweep of the campgrounds done tomorrow."

◆

Lance drove to the prearranged meeting place and waited. Soon Jen and Micky approached the truck with more shopping bags in their arms. They were both in excellent spirits. "Rav, this has been wonderful. I can hardly wait to show you the clothes I've bought," Jen said.

Lance smiled weakly. His somber mood put a damper on the girls' happiness.

"Rav, what happened?" Jen asked. "What's wrong with you?" She and Micky looked at him curiously.

Unwilling to tell her the truth, Lance said, "I'm sorry, Jen. I didn't want to tell you this until later, but I've been transferred. I'm leaving the campground soon. We've got a big job in the interior."

"Oh no," Jen said.

"I am really, really going to miss you two," he said, smiling.

"I'm going to miss you too," Jen said. "If not for you, I would have gone crazy by now."

"Well, I guess we better get going."

He pulled away from the curb. About a mile out of town a police car came up behind the pickup. Lance spotted it and immediately became tense. Jen glanced over at him as he watched his rearview mirror. The police officer pulled out to pass and studied the occupants of the truck as he went by. He then sped off into the distance. Jen continued to study Lance but said nothing.

The return trip to the campground was a quiet one. Lance's mood continued to put a damper on Jen and Micky, and Jen's observation of him during the encounter with the police car had made her pensive. When they reached the campground, Lance dropped off Jen and Micky at their site and then followed the circle to his own site and parked.

Lance did not feel like visiting, so he picked a trail he had not hiked before and went for a long walk.

He thought about what Barb had said to him. She was angry, and he didn't blame her for that. However, the uncertainty of his future with her weighed heavily on his mind. The depression he felt the first few days after the robbery swept over him again. Lance walked slowly and let his thoughts carry him. *I made a decision that I was going to live. I was going to get out of this situation. Everything I have done over the last week has been based on that decision. I can't let the possibility of losing Barb dissuade me. She has to live her life, and I have to live mine.*

She asked me to give myself up but couldn't promise she would be there for me, so that is no option at all. I've got a plan to beat this, and I'm going to carry it out. I'll call Barb in a couple of weeks and see what she says. In the meantime, I've got things to do. I can't lose my focus. Tomorrow I move to the cabin for a couple of weeks, and then I'm out of here.

Lance's mind wandered to Jen. He regretted having brought her down with his bad mood after the phone call. His mood lightened a bit as he thought of the times he had spent with her. Once or twice a smile flickered across his face as he thought of the jokes they had shared and of some of the things they had done. He also remembered things she had said that meant a great deal to him. In particular, Lance recalled how she had taken him by the hand the night before and had led him to her campsite for that wonderful supper she had prepared for him. As his mood lightened, his pace quickened. Lance noticed that night was falling, and he retraced his steps. On the way back he was amazed at how far he had walked. It was nearly dark by the time he returned to his campsite.

For the first time since he had met Jen they passed the evening apart. Lance cooked some burgers and ate slowly. Occasionally he glanced over at the girls as they moved around their campsite. He went to bed early and tried to sleep. He tossed and turned for half an hour, going over in his mind all that had happened—the happy start to the day with Jen and Micky, the horrible phone call with Barb, and then the uncomfortable trip back to the campground. Finally, exasperated, he threw back the covers and left the tent.

Lance saw Jen sitting at the picnic table, staring at the fire, and decided to join her.

"Hi, Jen," he said, sitting down beside her.

She jumped, startled by his unexpected approach. "Phew! Hi there," she said, recovering. "You couldn't sleep?"

"No. Not at all."

"Me neither."

"Look, I want to apologize for the mood I was in on the way back."

"Oh, that's all right," she said. "In a way I guess I should be flattered that you're so strongly affected by having to leave."

"I am honestly going to miss you. But what I would really like right now is to see all those clothes you bought today," Lance said, brightening.

"Well, okay then," Jen said with a smile. "Sit here and I'll be right back."

A few minutes later, she returned carrying her shopping bags and wearing a new dress. It was a short red number that complemented her curves nicely.

"Wow," Lance said.

Laughing at his reaction, she twirled in front of him and asked, "Do you like it?"

"Like it," Lance said. "You better tie me to a tree or I might not be able to control myself."

Jen laughed and posed seductively. She sat next to him and one by one pulled out the outfits she had bought.

Lance complimented her on her choices, and then they sat quietly enjoying the fire.

"Well, I guess I should go back and try to sleep. It's already midnight," Lance said.

"Oh, don't go," Jen said. "I'm not tired at all. Are you?"

"Actually, no," he said.

"Why don't you come to the trailer? We can play cards or something. Obviously, Mike won't be coming back tonight. Micky sleeps like a rock. We won't disturb her."

Lance immediately agreed. They went inside and played cards, talking quietly while Micky slept in the back of the trailer.

After a number of hands Jen placed the deck on the table. "I'm disappointed you're leaving," she said, looking at Lance. "I thought you had another week here."

"Jen, I want you to know that I think you're something special. I'm going to miss you guys," Lance said.

Jen brushed the hair out of her eyes and stared at him. "I'm going to miss you too. Here," she said, opening a drawer and producing a pen and paper. "Will you call me some time?" She wrote her name on the paper and underneath scribbled her cell phone number.

"Thanks, Jen. Yes, I'll call you," Lance promised, stuffing the paper in his pocket.

Jen came over and stood beside him. Her expression was inscrutable. "I'm going to miss you, Lance," she said. "Thanks for everything, friend." She bent down to kiss him, but just as her lips were going to touch his cheek, Lance impulsively turned his head and their lips met. Jen straightened up in surprise and brought her hand to her lips.

Lance was immediately embarrassed at what he had done, and the warmth of a blush reddened his face. But then Jen bent again, and now they were kissing passionately. As they kissed, Lance felt her pull him to his feet. Her tongue searched his mouth. Fumbling with the zipper, Lance let her dress fall to the floor. Still locked in a heated embrace, Jen stepped out of the dress, kissing his face and neck and pulling him toward the bedroom. Lance followed, eagerly caressing her breasts and kissing her deeply, seeking her tongue. Soon they were naked and on the bed, and they made desperate love. They lay on the bed, Jen cuddled in his arms, and then they made love again, this time slowly. When they finished, they fell asleep in each other's arms.

Lance woke up at about five the next morning and quietly rose and dressed. He looked down at Jen still asleep in the bed and yearned to cover her face with kisses, but instead he turned and left the trailer.

It was still dark outside as Lance walked back to his campsite. He quietly loaded his sleeping bag, his mattress, and his ax onto the truck and then brought down his tent and loaded it as well. He worked quickly, and by the time he had finished, the sky was brightening in the east.

He had to leave. Lance didn't know if his phone call to Barb had betrayed his location to the police. He'd seen plenty of TV shows in which the cops traced people just by using phone signals. Lance inspected the site, got in the truck, and drove toward the exit. Suddenly, he stopped and swung back into the campground. He had decided that he didn't need his boat anymore and had left it down by the lake. He had just thought of another use for the boat, so he drove to the lake, wrestled the boat onto the canopy of the truck, secured it tightly with ropes, and left the campground.

Lance drove quickly to the cut line that led to the cabin. He parked on the side of the road and got out to survey the ditch that separated the cut line from the road. He knew he would have to hide the truck because it could reveal his whereabouts. Lance walked the entire width of the cut line, looking for a place where he could navigate the ditch onto the cut line. Finally, at the far end where the cut line met the forest, he spied a dip in the land. The bank was not as steep there. Lance felt certain he could make it up onto the cut line at that spot. He got back into the truck, eased the vehicle into the ditch, and then gunned the motor. The truck bounced and lurched up onto the cut line. There was no path for the vehicle to follow, but the cut line was fairly level, so Lance could navigate the cut line. He drove slowly until he found a spot big enough for his vehicle about half a mile from the road.

Lance got out of the truck and dropped the boat from the canopy. He loaded his bags, his mattress, all his clothes, and all the tools he had purchased into the boat. To bring all that he would need for the next two weeks to the cabin, Lance estimated he would have to make three or four trips back and forth. But if he could drag the boat, he could have everything there in just one trip.

A Cat had bulldozed a small gap into the forest, and Lance decided this was the perfect place to park his truck. The gap was not easily visible from the middle of the cut line. A person could walk right by it without noticing his truck. The spot was obscured by saplings that had sprung up on the cut line. In a few years a crew would probably clear the cut line of these trees, but that was of no concern to Lance. What did concern him, however, was how he could get the truck past them.

Lance took his ax from the boat and cleared a path just large enough to get his truck through. He removed only the trees thick enough to block his path. The smaller ones he felt he could drive right over, and they would help to hide his truck once they straightened up again. For an hour Lance hacked out a path, and by the time he was done the sun shone down on him. He got in the truck and gunned the motor. Small trees fell in every direction and branches scraped the windshield, but in a few seconds the vehicle was nestled in the spot he wanted. It was perfect. Some of the saplings behind him had already straightened, just a little worse for wear, while tall fir trees loomed in front and to the sides. Lance dragged the larger trees he had cut down and stood them against the truck. For good measure, he wandered into the deep forest, cut down several more young trees, and stood them against the truck as well.

Finally Lance returned to the spot where the rowboat sat full of his stuff. He looked back at his work and was satisfied. From where he stood the truck was invisible. There was an obvious path leading to the spot, but he believed all traces of that would soon fade. Lance tried to straighten some of the trees his vehicle had bent over. Some of them might continue to grow, but others were badly broken. He had done the best he could and hoped that would be good enough.

Lance fashioned a harness out of rope to pull the rowboat. He tucked his winter coat between the rough rope and his skin and started off. The boat slid easily behind him as he walked down the center of the cutline. About fifteen minutes later Lance reached the first of the inclines he would need to scale. He looked back along the way he had come and his heart skipped a beat. A vehicle passed on the road in the distance. That didn't worry Lance much. The vehicle at that distance was the size of a toy car, and there was little chance the driver had noticed him or the boat. What did worry him was the wide path of flattened grass his boat had made. Lance shrugged. He guessed that in a day or so the grass would straighten up, hiding his trail.

Lance looked up toward the summit of the hill he was about to scale dragging the boat behind him. He paused momentarily and then started up.

Three-quarters of the way up the hill, Lance was doubting the wisdom of his decision to drag the boat. His face was beaded with sweat and he was breathing hard. He had already stopped four times to regain his breath and to wipe his brow. Lance looked up. The mountain seemed to climb forever, but after dragging his load this far there was no way he was going to abandon it now. He braced himself and started again.

It was another fifteen minutes before Lance reached the summit. Gasping for air, he collapsed into the boat onto the clothes and bags lying at the bottom. Shielding his eyes from the sun, he rested until his breathing slowed. His muscles throbbed. How many more hills like this one lay ahead before he reached the cabin? Three, maybe four; Lance couldn't remember. He got up and started down the other side.

Suddenly he had an idea. He dragged the boat to where the hill began a steep descent. He gave the boat a mighty push and jumped in. Lance immediately regretted his decision. The boat careened down the steep slope at breakneck speed, whirring past trees. He was terrified. At any moment the boat could hit some hidden boulder or log and toss him out, possibly leaving him with a broken neck. He pictured himself slowly dying as his wrecked body lay in the cut line. But soon the boat slowed and came to rest on the upward slope of the next hill.

With shaky legs Lance climbed out of the boat and looked back up the hill. It had taken him forty-five minutes to climb the hill and less than twenty seconds to descend. Lance repeated this descent three times but with his foot dragging behind the boat to slow it and guide it a bit. Finally he reached the cabin with the sun still high in the afternoon sky. It had been a grueling trip, but he figured his decision to bring the boat had saved him many hours of trudging back and forth on the cut line. Lance threw his gear into the cabin and left.

He crossed the cut line and went down to the stream he had found on his last visit. He took off his boots and soaked his feet in the icy water. Lance snoozed beside the creek for a while and woke up to the sound of snuffling some distance away.

About twenty meters away a black bear was edging its way into the stream from the opposite bank. The bear had not seen him yet. Lance slowly got to his feet. The bear noticed the movement and lifted its head. Lance backed away toward the path up the bank. At this distance, if the bear charged he was dead. Fortunately the bear seemed more interested in the salmon in the stream and watched as Lance scurried away. By the time he disappeared over the lip of the gully, the bear had lost interest in him and was fishing.

For the rest of the day, Lance cut down dead trees from the forest, sawing several logs to size for the old stove in the cabin and stacking them neatly behind the door.

Lance packed the stove with kindling and logs and lit a fire. He lay in his new bed stiff and sore but pleased with all he had accomplished this day and with the relative security he now felt. He soon fell asleep to the crackle of the logs burning in the stove.

During the night, the weather turned and he heard the pitter patter of rain on the roof. In the morning, Lance awoke and walked in his underwear to look out the cabin window. The rain had turned to snow, and about five inches lay on the ground. He smiled and blessed his luck. The snow would cover the tire marks and the flattened grass. Lance dressed, threw on his winter coat, and went outside. Off in the distance he heard a helicopter engine. It could be a police helicopter. Lance hurried to the rowboat and dragged it into the thick woods. Leaving it out had been careless. The shiny sides of an aluminum boat would be easily spotted from the air if the sun hit it just right. A rowboat sitting near the top of a mountain would be curious indeed to anyone who spied it.

Next Lance went inside to inspect the fire. The evening's blaze had been reduced to warm embers. These would produce very little smoke, so he left them alone. He decided that as a precaution he would not burn a fire during the day when a trail of smoke could be detected from the air. He would wait until dark before starting a fire. This meant the cabin would be a little chilly at the beginning of the evening, but by the time he drifted off to sleep he expected it would be warm and cozy, as it had been the previous night. Lance picked up his saw and went into the woods where he had left the trees he had felled the day before. He worked on the logs all day until he had a large pile of firewood stacked unseen in the trees. He brought an armful into the cabin and went back out to saw more logs. He remembered talking to a wise guide who had taken him hunting in northern British Columbia. "If you're ever out camping and you need a fire for the night, cut logs until you think you have enough to last you the night, and then cut three times that much," the guide had told him. Lance knew this was true because he had gotten up at least three times during the night to add firewood and had used the whole stack he had brought in the day before.

For the next few days, Lance spent his time fishing the stream or walking the edge of the cut line in search of grouse. The rest of the time he busied himself felling trees and hacking them into logs for the fire. The days were cool and snow fell a few more times, making walking the cut line somewhat difficult. Even with all that, Lance had plenty of leisure time, which he spent reading the survival manual he had stolen from the library. He would study the book and then trudge the woods looking for the plants the book said were edible. He rarely found any of them, but when he did he happily picked them and brought them back to the cabin.

Lance took to hiking in the direction of the sea, which was visible far off in the distance. To do so, he had to cross the stream at the bottom of the gully on the opposite side of the cut line. From there he descended quickly into mixed forest. This had two advantages. For one thing Lance was pretty sure that at this elevation, frost had not hit the area. This meant he had much more luck foraging for fruits, berries, and vegetables. Second, the area seemed extremely remote.

Lance saw no roads or power lines or any other sign of civilization. One day while hiking in this area he came across a clearing. The ground was soggy, and his socks became sodden. Up ahead, he spied tall plants with dry purple flowers. Lance thought he recognized them. He quickly found the page he was seeking in the survival manual, which he always brought with him. He nodded. "Camas," he declared. He grabbed a stick and began digging. After gathering a half-dozen bulbs from the plants, he tucked them into his backpack and headed back to the cabin. The next day he boiled the bulbs, and when it seemed they were soft, he mashed them into a smooth paste. He fried a couple of hamburger paddies. His heart skipped a beat. He swore the paste he had prepared tasted just like sweet potatoes. Lance vowed to return to the spot the next day to gather more bulbs.

Another day, closer to the cabin, he found some low-lying cranberries and picked them. He decided to fry up some of the frozen chicken he had brought. The cranberries would go nicely with the chicken. At the cabin, Lance boiled and then simmered the cranberries, reducing them to a red sauce that he spooned onto a plate next to two pieces of chicken. The fruit and vegetables he found added nicely to his food supply, which was mostly frozen meat.

He noticed, however, that the cooler was already less than half full. The meat was keeping frozen quite nicely, though, since most nights the temperature dipped below freezing. Fortunately, Lance had had the foresight to store the cooler up in a tree in the shade of the forest. When it snowed, he repacked the cooler tightly with as much snow as he could fit in. He needed his food supply to last as long as possible because once the food ran out he would have no option but to return to civilization.

Lance had thought he would be living a life of leisure up in the cabin. He soon discovered he was mistaken. With firewood duties, cooking, and his daily food gathering hikes, Lance was exerting a lot of effort. He prepared large meals to keep up his strength. Lance didn't mind all the activity since it kept him from thinking about his deeper problems—the loss of his family, his confusing feelings for Jen, and how he would avoid capture once he returned to the city.

One day, in a grove of pine trees he found mushrooms growing in plentitude. Lance picked a bunch and dreamed of the steak and mushrooms he would enjoy. Back at the cabin, however, he turned to the page in the manual describing what he thought were ponderosa mushrooms. The entry contained a bold-faced warning that these mushrooms could be easily confused with a similar mushroom that was poisonous. Lance studied the pictures of the two types of mushrooms and carefully read the descriptions. He thought his mushrooms were the good kind, but he had some doubts. In the end, Lance threw the mushrooms into the forest. The last thing he needed was to become violently sick up here all alone.

Lance's disappointment was short-lived. The next day he found a crab apple tree near the meadow where he had discovered the bulbs. He filled his backpack with ripe apples, and for the next few days, he munched on them as he hiked. He even baked a small apple pie one evening, using the flour, salt, and sugar he had brought with him.

By the end of two weeks the place began to seem like home, and he felt almost carefree. Lance found it very strange that here he had few worries while out in the real world he faced chaos and danger. Still, one small mistake could spell his doom, and he could not afford to relax for even a second.

Lance worked hard cutting wood, keeping the cabin clean, and most important making sure the site appeared uninhabited. He also had plenty of time to think. He thought about Jen and about their last night together when they had made love. Thinking of that filled him with happiness, but he also felt slightly guilty when his thoughts turned to Barb. This brought back the hurt and anger he felt during their phone conversation. When he returned, he would call her again. Lance hoped that by that time she would have reconsidered joining him. Something deep down, however, told him she would never change her mind.

Lance felt no need for his disguise, so he stowed the spray in a corner, and gradually his face and hands changed back to white. Lance noticed he was getting into much better shape. Though he had never been fat, his life had gradually become more sedentary. But over the past few weeks with all his hiking in the hills, culminating in the grueling trip to the cabin, his muscles were responding. He could saw firewood for hours straight without breaking a sweat. His new conditioning felt good, and Lance was proud of the extra bulge in his muscles.

He also explored his surroundings. He kept more to the deep woods, however, to avoid creating trails that would be visible from the air. Each day Lance went deeper into the woods than the day before, taking care not to lose his orientation so he could easily make his way back to the cabin. The first day, about fifty yards from the cabin, he found a large tree that had toppled, roots and all. This had left a hole in the ground almost six feet deep. Lance immediately returned to the cabin, wrapped up the briefcase containing the money in plastic bags, and buried it in the hole, covering it with a good two feet of soil and gravel.

One morning Lance was seated against a log close to the edge of the tree line. He often chose this log as a resting place because it fit the contours of his body. He had stuffed a blanket behind him to cushion his head. Lance stretched out, allowing the sun to warm him. Later he would cut more wood and do a little more exploring. But there was plenty of time for that. Right now he was going to take a little nap.

"What the hell are you doing here?"

Lance almost jumped out of his skin at the sound of the voice. He opened his eyes and sat up. A short, thin man with a week's growth of whiskers stood glaring at him.

"I asked you what you're doing in my cabin."

Lance stammered as he slowly recovered from the shock of having someone appear out of nowhere.

"I ... I ... I've been staying here for the last couple of weeks."

"What the hell for?"

"Just to get away for a little while. I was up here working, surveying, when I found this place. Got my sister to drop me off when my days off came up."

"Well you can clear out right now," the man barked. "This is my cabin. I built it with my own damn hands, and now I want to use it." The man dropped a load of chains he had been carrying from his shoulders and turned and entered the cabin."

Lance gaped at the chains lying in front of him. They were, in fact, traps.

The man came out of the cabin. "Looks like you've been doing some cleaning up around here," he said. His eyes wandered to the firewood stacked in the trees, and he looked appreciatively at Lance. "That's gonna come in handy," he said.

The man looked to be about fifteen years older than Lance. Gray hair fell carelessly from the even grayer toque on his head. His face wore what looked like a permanent scowl.

"Look," Lance said, "I've got no way out of here for about three days until my sister comes and picks me up." He thought to himself that by that time his fake ID should be waiting for him at the post office in Squamish and that he could get on with the next phase of his plan. "If I can stay till then, I promise I'll stay out of your hair."

The old-timer stared at Lance for several seconds and finally shrugged. "We'll see. In the meantime, you can make yourself useful. Follow me and be quick about it."

He started off down the cut line to the north, the opposite direction from where Lance had his truck hidden. Lance sat in confusion for a second and then sprang to his feet and followed.

The stranger led him without speaking a word for at least twenty minutes. Once or twice Lance tried to engage him in conversation, but he got little more than a grunt in response. Social graces were clearly not this man's strength, and he made it obvious that he was not happy to find Lance at his cabin.

Lance had not explored the cut line as far as the two of them were now walking. He had tried to keep out of sight, so he had confined most of his explorations to the woods. Finally they came to a place where the cut line was broken by an escarpment that dropped a good twenty feet to a gravel road below. Lance stared down from the cliff as the man turned into the trees to the right. An animal trail led along the escarpment and suddenly turned directly down into the escarpment. The stranger disappeared down the trail and Lance followed. The trail followed a break in the cliff just a few feet wide. The trail dropped precipitously and then wound down until Lance found they were at the base of the cliff. At this point his guide turned back to his left, and suddenly they were at the edge of a gravel road next to a gray pickup with a red quad behind it.

Lance stared in disbelief. He had no idea a road ran so close to the cabin. In all the time he had been there, he hadn't once heard the sound of traffic. His mind went back to the arduous trip he had made to get to the cabin and he cursed silently.

"Here, grab these," the man barked, pointing at traps lying in a wooden box on the back of the pickup. He gathered up bedding and several grungy backpacks filled with who knew what.

Lance draped the traps over his shoulder as he had seen the stranger do earlier and then reached for a couple of long canvas bags.

"Leave those goddamned things where I had them," the old-timer snarled. "Grab those." He pointed to a bundle of wooden stakes. "Hurry up. I don't have all damn day." As Lance picked up the bundle, the man eyed him for a second and then was gone back up the trail.

Lance puffed and scrambled his way up the sharp incline with his heavy load, and when he reached the top he caught sight of the stranger, who was already forty feet ahead of him, striding back up the cut line.

A half-hour later, Lance arrived back at the cabin, sweaty and sore from his efforts. He dropped the chains and the bundle with the traps the man had brought earlier. Lance heard banging inside the cabin, and a moment later the stranger came out. "Let's go," he said, glancing at Lance before heading back down the cut line.

Lance shook his head as he stared after the old guy heading back down the cut line. He was older than he was and didn't look particularly strong, but he was wiry and showed no signs of tiring. Despite his improved conditioning, Lance realized this guy was in much better shape. He was having a lot easier time of the work than he was, that was for sure.

Lance scrambled after him. An hour later they arrived back at the cabin, each carrying a load of supplies on one shoulder and a huge cooler between them.

"In here," the man ordered as he headed to the door. Inside he let go of his side of the cooler without waiting for Lance, who, off-balance, awkwardly dropped his side of the cooler.

"Well, don't just stand there," the man said. "Put those things over there." He pointed to the bags Lance held on his shoulders.

"Yes, master," Lance said, frowning as he dropped his load. He felt like a slave.

The man added firewood to the stove. "That saved me a few trips," he said more to himself than to Lance.

"You're welcome," Lance said more than a little sarcastically. "I'll take that as a thank-you."

"I'll let you stay," the man declared, "as long as you don't get on my nerves and you don't keep me awake with your snoring. You can damn well sleep outside if you do. Oh and that reminds me. The bed's mine. I built it, and it's mine. You're welcome to the floor. Open up that cooler and start cooking."

Seeing Lance stare, he asked, "You can cook, can't you?"

Lance again shook his head at the stranger's gruff manner and rummaged in the cooler for food. Getting along with this guy would be a challenge, but Lance had no choice. *Thank God I won't be here much longer,* he thought.

Lance grilled trout fillets he had caught in the stream below the cut line before the trapper's arrival. He cut up potatoes into thin slices. Then he fried them in butter and added frozen carrots and peas. The men ate in silence. By that time it was dark. The trapper went outside to smoke, leaving Lance to do the dishes. Finally the man returned, made up his bed, and lay down. Lance curled up in his sleeping bag on the air mattress close to the stove.

The next thing Lance heard was the trapper stirring from his bed and moving around the small cabin. Lance opened his eyes and glanced out the window. Morning was beginning to show in the sky through the trees. Lance rose and quickly rolled up his bag, stowing it and the deflated mattress against the back wall.

"We have a long day ahead of us," the trapper said. "You might as well give me a hand with my trap lines. We'll call it your payment for room and board."

"Agreed," Lance said. "By the way, what's your name? If we're going to be working together, I suppose we should get to know each other."

The man gave Lance a hard stare and then said, "Folks just call me Cojer. I suppose that will do. I've got eggs and bacon in my cooler. Throw them on the pan and let's get going. We'll need to get an early start if we're going to set my lines."

Lance nodded and before long the cabin was filled with the aroma of eggs and bacon cooking atop the stove. "My name's Lance," he said as he flipped the eggs and maneuvered the bacon. He had decided to use his real name, assuming that the risk was minimal.

Lance set a plate of eggs, bacon, and home fries in front of Cojer. He grunted, which Lance assumed was his version of thank you.

"You're welcome," Lance said, and Cojer glared up at him.

"Don't be a sarcastic ass," he hissed.

The men wolfed down breakfast, and Lance gathered the plates and the cutlery and dumped them in the pot of water he had just put on the stove. The water was barely warm, but sensing Cojer's impatience to get moving, Lance washed the dishes in the tepid water while the trapper went outside to get ready for the day.

When Lance came outside Cojer was waiting with a load of traps draped over one shoulder and his rifle in hand. He pointed to a pile of traps and a heavy mallet and abruptly turned and started down the cut line. Lance quickly gathered up the traps and the hammer and hurried after him.

After about fifty yards Cojer turned down a cut line only a few meters wide. However, it ran straight as an arrow, so when they came to the crest of a hill Lance could see that the trail cut a snowy line through the trees for at least two miles ahead. Cojer stopped a number of times to set traps, especially in areas where he found animal tracks. After an hour he decided to show Lance how to set a trap. His explanation was specific and detailed. Until then, Lance had thought the old guy was incapable of stringing two sentences together, but Cojer made his expertise clear. Lance listened carefully and followed instructions while Cojer watched. When he was satisfied with the job Lance had done, he turned abruptly and moved on down the trail.

Lance hurried after him. As they progressed down the trail, they found the tracks of what Lance surmised to be a big cat. Cojer took note of the tracks and followed them. He stopped periodically in places where he wanted a trap set. While Lance worked, Cojer pulled out an old tin can and a brush and painted the trees nearby with liquid from the can. "Cunt spray," he said with a grunt. "If that don't bring that cougar in, nothin' will." Each time Lance finished, Cojer wordlessly inspected his job. Occasionally he would shoulder Lance out of the way and make adjustments, and then he would turn and continue down the trail.

When they reached the long descent, Cojer turned right into the trees. They arrived at a slough after a five-minute walk into the forest. In the middle of the slough was a large beaver lodge. Cojer circled the slough and found a number of slides the beavers had worn. On each of these Cojer placed a couple of traps. Then he slowly made his way across the thin ice out to the lodge where he placed more traps. Looking on from the shore, Lance saw that Cojer knew his trap line well and did his work expertly.

As they plodded through the snow, Lance began to tire and to work more slowly, which irritated Cojer. He was still setting traps when Cojer finished his work and moved on. Whenever he had to wait at a place where he wanted a trap set, he swore bitterly at Lance. "Hurry the fuck up," he said. "We don't have all day."

Two or three miles down the trail and several traps later, Lance looked up and to his surprise Cojer had disappeared. Lance hurried ahead to find him. Cojer stepped back onto the trail about twenty yards ahead of him, waving for him to follow, and then vanished again into the trees to the left. Lance reached the spot where the trapper had been and found another trail winding through the trees to the left of the trail they had been on. Cojer was quickly disappearing around a grove of tall Douglas firs, and Lance hurried after him. When he rounded the corner, Cojer was waiting up ahead. He snatched the mallet impatiently from Lance and deftly set a trap close to some tracks.

The men wound their way along the trail, setting traps every quarter-mile or so. Lance was exhausted but was determined to keep up with the old man. He took comfort from the fact that they were quickly running out of traps. He knew the work would soon be over. After about an hour of weaving through the trees, Lance was astounded when they suddenly emerged from the bush onto the gravel road right in front of where they had left the pickup the night before.

Cojer dug into one of the boxes mounted on the back of the quad and tossed Lance a sandwich wrapped in plastic before opening one of his own. The two men chewed hungrily on the sandwiches and drank water from bottles Cojer pulled out of his pack. After eating, they lounged for about ten minutes. Then Cojer unloaded the quad, using the hydraulic lift on which the quad was mounted. Once on the ground, the old man hopped on the quad and pushed the start button. The quad immediately came to life.

The rest of the day went much more easily as they were now on a far wider cut line on the opposite side of the gravel road and were using the quad most of the time. In addition, Cojer set most of the traps himself, probably because he could do it more quickly. Lance was relegated to pulling traps out of the back and handing him tools and materials. As the day progressed, Lance became fairly adept at anticipating what was needed next. This was fortunate because Cojer was not in the habit of asking politely when what he needed wasn't immediately at hand. They proceeded down the cut line for about five miles and then turned left onto another that intersected it.

When they finished this cut line, Cojer turned back onto the first one. They crossed another gravel road before turning to the right down a new trail. The day continued much as it had until they came across the tracks of what was obviously a huge grizzly. Cojer threw a large trap down, pointed to where he wanted Lance to set it, and then rummaged in the seemingly bottomless boxes mounted on the back of the quad. As Lance drove the stake, Cojer circled the area with a small can, administering liquid to the bases of all the nearby trees.

Lance struggled to set the trap and lost his grip. The trap sprung shut, narrowly missing his fingers. Cojer whirled and shouted, "Jesus Christ! Be careful. You want to lose some fingers?" Cojer knelt, pushed Lance aside, and in seconds had the trap set.

As twilight arrived, they finally returned to the escarpment where the pickup was parked. They dismounted, loaded the quad onto the deck, and headed back up the winding trail, which brought them to the top of the escarpment and onto the cut line where the cabin sat. They followed the now-familiar trail and arrived back at the cabin just as darkness drove the last rays of light from the sky. Lance again had cooking and dish washing duty while Cojer lounged against a tree outside the cabin and smoked. After his chores were done, Lance pulled his bedding from the corner and settled into his bag early. He fell asleep from exhaustion almost immediately and didn't awaken until he heard Cojer stirring in the morning.

The next day the men retraced their steps, checking the traps they had set. They progressed quickly as most traps remained empty; however, when they arrived at the beaver's dam, Cojer reached into the cold water and pulled up a trap that held a plump beaver. Cojer held the animal at eye level, examining it carefully. Its fur glistened in the sunlight. "Not bad," he said, and promptly started back down the trail to the narrow cut line. Lance concluded that the pelt must have been the best Cojer had ever harvested since this comment was the closest thing to a positive statement he had made in the two days Lance had known him. The men spent the day walking the cut lines and checking traps and then headed down a new, shorter trail. To reach this trail, they again unloaded the quad and took the gravel road for about a mile, with Cojer driving and Lance seated behind him. Suddenly Cojer veered off the road and onto a hidden trail, startling Lance. Cojer must have noticed the fright his sudden move had caused, because he chuckled quietly. They again arrived back at the cabin at twilight, and the evening routine mirrored that of the night before. Lance cooked while Cojer smoked outside and prepared the pelts he had harvested.

As they sat down to supper, Lance expected Cojer to remain sullen and silent, but to his surprise, the old man suddenly became curious. He asked Lance when his sister was coming to pick him up. Then he wanted to know where Lance lived and what he did for a living and all manner of details about his life. Lance grew uncomfortable as the questions continued. He much preferred the disinterest of the night before. Lance lied as best he could and tried to deflect the questions by asking about Cojer's life. However, Cojer gave curt answers and returned to the offensive. It seemed to Lance that this had turned into more of a grilling than a conversation, and he couldn't help but think that the old man's questions were motivated by suspicion. To Lance's relief, the conversation finally ended. He got up to do the dishes and once again retired early and fell fast asleep.

The next morning Lance awoke suddenly to a kick in the side. His eyes sprang open, and he saw Cojer standing above him with a rifle pointed at his head.

"I know who you are," Cojer said. "I knew there was something fishy about your story, and last night it hit me. You think I don't watch TV? You're that bank robber. Now you're gonna get up very slowly and we're going outside. Be careful and do exactly what I say. You make one wrong move and it will be your last."

Lance pushed back the covers and slowly rose from the floor as Cojer backed up, keeping the rifle trained on him.

"You wouldn't really shoot me, would you?" Lance asked.

"Why not?" Cojer said with a shrug. "I don't give a shit about you, and it would be no less than you deserve. I'd be doing society a favor. Outside!" He gestured with his rifle.

Lance walked out of the cabin with Cojer close behind.

"Now get your ass over to that tree and sit down." Cojer motioned to the tree where Lance usually rested. As Lance complied, the trapper tossed the backpack he carried to the ground. He rifled through the bag with one hand while aiming the rifle with the other as Lance sat by the tree. Cojer pulled out long strips of leather from the bag and moved behind Lance.

"Now give me your hands," he ordered. When Cojer trained the rifle on him, Lance finally stretched his arms out behind him around the tree. Cojer immediately grasped them and quickly wrapped the cords around his wrists, tying them tightly. Cojer moved back to the pile of gear he had set by the wall of the cabin and returned to Lance with a long, thin rope. He used it to bind Lance's ankles and then wrapped the other end of the rope around a tree. He gave a strong pull on the rope, dragging Lance forward. Lance winced at the sudden strain this position put on his shoulders. He feared that they might be dislocated.

"Now you just wait here while I take a look around. I bet you've got the loot stashed around here somewhere," Cojer said. He picked up the rifle and set off into the woods. To Lance's chagrin, the trapper was heading toward the spot where he had hidden the briefcase. Lance waited helplessly, shivering in the sweats he had worn to bed. The sky was overcast and foul weather was on the way. A stiff breeze chilled him to the bone. From time to time Lance caught the sound of breaking twigs as the old man moved through the woods. A half-hour later Lance's nightmare became a reality. He heard a loud whoop from deep in the trees. His treasure had been found, and now all was lost.

A minute later Cojer emerged from the trees, carrying the briefcase. "You stupid, fucking idiot," he said with a grin, holding up the case for Lance to see. "I knew it was there as soon as I saw the uprooted tree. You couldn't find a better place than that? And now all your work and risk have been for nothing." With that, Cojer entered the cabin.

A few minutes later he came out, toting his bedding. He tied this to his backpack and stuffed the rest of his equipment inside. Finally he straightened up and sidled over to where Lance sat bound. He looked up at the threatening sky and said, "Well, this is the last you'll see of me. I'm going to pick up my traps and whatever's in them and clear out. I usually spend at least another week here, but I think I'm gonna pack it in. My take this year has been damn good," he sneered holding up the briefcase.

"If you're lucky you might eventually work your way free, or you may just freeze to death if it starts snowing, and it looks like it might. If you do, don't worry. Some animal will come along and clean up your bones. Whatever happens, I don't really give a damn." With that, Cojer rounded the corner of the cabin and disappeared down the cut line.

Lance glared after him. He was despondent. After all he had been through and had sacrificed, he had nothing. He would be left penniless and without a family or would go to jail. Worse, he might die on this mountainside. Lance shivered as the cold wind increased to a howl. He struggled against the leather thongs around his wrists, but they didn't give at all. The old fart had done his job all too well. Lance wondered how he would ever escape.

Fifteen minutes later the nasty weather arrived with Lance lying semi-prone, both arms jacked up behind him and around the tree. A mixture of rain and sleet came in sideways, driven hard by the wind. In seconds Lance was soaked and freezing. The temperature dropped, and the rain was soon replaced by wet snow. The snowflakes struck him and melted. Water dripped from his face and hair and ran in freezing rivulets down to his neck and then inside his sweater and down his back.

Lance jerked and struggled desperately against his bonds. He noticed a slight change. The leather thongs, now soaking wet from the rain and snow, had turned slick, and he was able to stretch the leather just a bit. This gave him a glimmer of hope, and he renewed his efforts. Finally Lance was able to rotate his wrists ever so slightly. With the fingers of the opposite hands, he strained to reach the leather binding his wrists, but he could not quite do it. He tried to rotate his wrists so they were at ninety-degree angles to each other. With all his might he fought against the bonds and stretched his fingers once more. He could not reach the cords. Lance roared in frustration. He again tried to maneuver his wrists to gain the infinitesimally small length he needed to reach the cords. Finally Lance had enough leverage to sink his fingernail into one of the thongs.

Now he worked feverishly, oblivious to the snowstorm raging around him. He scratched at the thong, and it began to slide over the other cords. One by one he moved the cords so they no longer overlapped. This made the cords less tight by degrees, so now he had more movement in his wrists. Lance began to pull his left hand through the cords, but they tightened again as they moved from his narrow wrist to his hand and his knuckles. He worked his thumb against the cords to stretch them past his knuckles. Ever so slowly the cords slipped closer to the knuckles of his left hand. In a few minutes he was able to stretch the first cord past the knuckles. But three more cords bound him. He strained against these cords and thought he had been able to stretch them just a little more, but now he shivered badly as the snow and the ferocious wind cooled him to the core. He had to get free now. If the storm ceased and the leather dried, it would shrink and tighten once more. Lance carefully felt the cords with his thumb. He could not allow them to become tangled with each other. Finally he chose a cord that seemed to overlap the other two and tugged at it. It slowly began to slide along his wrist and past the other cords. Again he scraped and strained, and finally another slippery wet cord was past his knuckles. Two more to go.

Lance strained to spread his wrists to gain more slack. Just two cords were now binding his wrists, and so he was able to stretch them slightly more. He repeatedly attempted to hook his thumb around one of the cords. His frustration mounted as he failed. Finally, just as he was about to give up, he caught one of the cords. He pulled and the cord moved slightly. Now he was able to gain a better hold on it. Slowly, agonizingly, he slid the cord along his wrist. As he moved it up his hand, it tightened against the wider obstacle.

Lance was now shivering uncontrollably as the snow continued driving against his side. It was starting to freeze in his hair and on his sweats. Finally the third cord was over his knuckles. The last cord gave way easily and his wrists were free. He sat up and quickly untied the rope that bound his legs.

Struggling to his feet, Lance sprinted to the cabin. Cojer had put out the fire in the stove, but the cabin was still warm. Lance tore off his soaked sweatshirt and pants and threw them aside. He got a towel and dried himself and then quickly pulled on pants and a warm shirt. He grabbed his coat and bolted from the cabin.

Lance had no idea how long he had taken to free himself, but he hoped he still had a chance to catch that fucker Cojer. The old man had said he was going to pick up his traps. Surely by now he was on the quad retrieving the last of them, but there was no way Lance was going to give up now.

He raced down the cut line toward where he had seen Cojer's pickup. Fifteen minutes later Lance approached the gravel road.

He was breathing hard and his sides ached. His heart raced as he sprinted down the narrow path below the escarpment. He could not yet see if the truck was still there, but in just a few seconds he would know.

As Lance moved past the last trees blocking his view, his desperation turned to elation. The truck still sat on the opposite side of the road in the ditch. Lance stood by the cut line, regaining his breath, but now he could hear the distant hum of a motor.

Lance thought quickly. The snow had continued to fall and now covered the road. If he crossed the road, Cojer would see his tracks. He quickly moved into the thick brush and searched for something he might use as a weapon.

He found a fallen branch that looked solid enough. This club would have to do, for now the sound of the approaching quad grew louder. Lance quickly hid behind a cluster of trees about twenty feet from the side of the road.

Seconds later he saw the quad. Cojer drove onto the road and made a wide circle, pulling up behind the pickup. He got off the quad and surveyed his surroundings in all directions. Lance made himself as small as possible when Cojer stared in his direction. Cojer held his rifle in his hands. Finally satisfied, he leaned his gun against the side of the pickup and began tossing traps and pelts into the back of the truck. Lance crouched, waiting for his opportunity.

Cojer finished loading the traps, returned to the quad, and grabbed the briefcase from the seat. He took one more look around. He seemed to look straight at Lance for a moment, and Lance instinctively crouched lower. But then Cojer walked at a leisurely pace to the cab of the truck, picking up the rifle on the way. He dropped the briefcase and stood by the door, appearing to search his pockets for his keys.

Lance moved from the bushes into the ditch. Cojer's back was to him. This might be Lance's only chance. As he quietly moved across the ditch, Cojer unlocked the door and swung it open. As he tossed the case and the rifle into the cab of the truck, Lance pounced.

The snow quieted his approach until the final moment. Cojer whirled as Lance appeared. Lance raised his club to swing, but Cojer extended his arms to block the blow and ducked low. At the last instant, however, Lance changed trajectory and swung lower, catching Cojer's arms with a glancing blow. Cojer came up hard and gave Lance a mighty shove, leaving him sprawled on his back in the middle of the road in the gravel and the wet snow. Lance looked up to see Cojer reaching into the cab for the rifle. Lance scrambled to his feet and charged, striking Cojer in the stomach with his head just as Cojer brought the rifle to bear. The force of Lance's charge knocked Cojer back onto the seat. A shot rang out. Lance was dazed from the explosion right by his ear, and Cojer brought his legs up sharply, striking Lance in the ribs and taking his breath away. The old man got to his feet and pushed Lance from the truck, and Lance was on his back once again. As Lance climbed to his feet, Cojer shut the door to the cab and fired up the engine.

Lance despaired. The briefcase was in the cab with Cojer, and in a second he would be down the road. As the tires spun on the gravel and gained traction, the pickup lurched ahead. Lance grabbed onto the truck and rolled over the side into the box. He rattled in the box among the traps and pelts as Cojer swayed this way and that, but finally he was able to stand up. Lance picked up the heavy mallet from the floor of the box and broke the back window. He would have struck Cojer in the back of the head had he not lost his balance from the motion of the vehicle. Lance was thrown against the back of the cab as Cojer jammed on the brakes. When the vehicle stopped, Cojer climbed out with the rifle, a string of obscenities flowing from his mouth. But Lance was ready and leaped on him as he left the cab. The two men plunged to the gravel, and the rifle skittered away from them. Lance rolled on top of Cojer and brought his fist down hard. He felt Cojer's nose turn to mush. Cojer's head rolled from side to side, and Lance struck him again and again. Cojer groaned in pain. Lance thought he may have broken his nose and jaw.

"Now who's the fucking idiot, you bastard?" Lance shouted at him in a rage. "You could have gone straight to your truck and driven away with $700,000. But no, you had to pick up your precious traps. Stupid! Stupid!"

Cojer lay grimacing, holding his nose. Suddenly he lunged for the rifle, which lay five feet away, but Lance stepped over and put his foot on the rifle before he could reach it. Cojer lay face down on the gravel road. Lance picked up the rifle.

Lance noticed that a large logging truck had rounded a corner in the distance. He quickly grabbed Cojer by the ankles and dragged him behind the pickup. He hoped the rig was too far away for the driver to see what he was doing. He dragged Cojer from behind the pickup and laid him in the ditch out of sight behind the quad. He returned to the road and busied himself next to the open door of the cab as the big truck approached. Lance gave a wave as the truck passed and then watched it recede into the distance.

When it had gone, he returned to where Cojer lay moaning. "I'm going to give you more of a chance than you gave me," Lance said. "The quad is still sitting back there about a mile away. You can get out of here with it. You don't mind if I borrow your truck, do you?" He snickered. Lance returned to the cab, hopped in, and turned the key that still hung from the ignition. He fired up the engine, made a U-turn, and drove off. *Well, it looks like I've added car theft to my rap sheet,* Lance thought.

He turned right at the first gravel road that intersected the road he was on. Lance followed this road for about five miles until he came to another gravel road and again took a right. He soon recognized this as the road that led to his cut line. In fifteen minutes Lance found his way back to where his pickup was hidden. He parked Cojer's pickup in the ditch, grabbed the briefcase, and walked onto the cut line for the final time. He arrived at his pickup, retrieved the key from under the bumper, and climbed in. The motor turned over. He feared he might get stuck in the heavy snow, but in a minute he was back on the gravel road. Ten minutes later he swung onto the main road and headed toward Squamish. Lance knew it would be some time before Cojer would recover to the point where he could drive the quad, but he could not stop himself from glancing at the rearview mirror. He willed himself to maintain a safe speed on the treacherous road.

Ten minutes later he was at the entrance to the campsite where he knew Jen would be sipping a cup of coffee, but with a knot in his stomach he drove on. Before Cojer could raise the alarm, Lance needed to get to Squamish to pick up the package that he hoped had arrived by now.

CHAPTER 7

L ance walked into the post office. A small woman in her fifties with short brunette hair stood behind the desk, talking to an elderly woman with packages in her hand. Lance approached the desk, and the two ladies turned toward him.

"Can I help you, sir?" asked the woman behind the counter.

"Uh yeah. Is there a general delivery package here for Lance Knight?"

"Just one moment. I'll check," the woman said. Letters of all description were neatly sorted on a back shelf. She reached for a handful of packages and papers from one of the compartments. Near the bottom she found what she was looking for and pulled out a small manila envelope.

"Here it is. I'll just need some identification, please," she said.

Lance took out his driver's license and handed it to the woman. She studied it and was about to hand him the envelope, but then Lance saw a flash of recognition in her eyes. The lady glanced up at his face and said, "Yes, sir. Just one more second, and I'll give you your package." With that she headed into the back with the envelope and his driver's license.

Lance knew that his luck had run out and that he had to act now. He placed both hands on the counter and vaulted over it, running after the woman. He saw she had moved into an office and was picking up a phone while clasping his driver's license.

She screamed as Lance burst through the door. "I'm sorry, lady, but I'm going to need these," he said. He snatched his license and the package from her. Leaning in a corner was a bar with a hook on one end, and Lance seized it. The woman screamed again and recoiled from him as he raised the bar over his head.

Lance brought the bar down hard on the phone, shattering it into a heap of plastic and electronics. He spun around as a male postal worker standing in the doorway shouted, "Hey, what the hell do you think you're doing?"

Lance glowered at the man and raised the bar again. "You better back away if you know what's good for you," he said, shaking the bar menacingly. The last thing he needed was a scuffle with this burly dude, and he knew if push came to shove he would never be able to strike him with that bar. He had to intimidate him.

The man looked at Lance and then up at the bar and slowly backed out of the office. Lance ran past him into the back room where the mail was sorted. Mailbags seemed to be stacked everywhere, and on the other side of the room a female postal worker stood frozen with a heap of mail in her hand. Lance ran to the back door and out into the alley behind the post office. He raced down the alley and turned left through a narrow space between the post office and the neighboring building. In seconds he was back on the main street, dashing toward his truck. He ran across the street, jumped into the truck, and squealed off as the elderly lady who had been in the post office moments earlier stared wide-eyed after him from the sidewalk.

Now what was he going to do? Within seconds the police would be notified, and every officer in town would be in pursuit. Lance raced toward the outskirts of town, heading for the road he had come in on. Suddenly he turned into a residential area. He knew he would have no chance of outrunning the police if he stayed on the main roads. He wound his way through the back streets of town, heading as best he could toward the outskirts. Finally he came to the last road he could take in this direction. He could see the forest through the backyards of the houses he passed. He spotted a large sign that read: "Deer Run Golf Course." Lance turned into the parking area and saw the darkened clubhouse up ahead. He hesitated for an instant before shoving his truck into four-wheel drive and heading out onto the snow-covered golf course. His truck plowed through the snow from one green to another until he came to a final green that backed onto the forest. Lance got out of the vehicle and walked to the edge of the green. He saw that the forest dropped down into a steep gully.

He quickly surveyed the trees and ran back to his vehicle. He put the truck in gear and edged it toward the trees.

The front wheels bounced over the edge, and the truck entered the gully. Lance frantically worked the brakes and the steering wheel, skidding the truck down the gully while avoiding the many stands of trees that blocked his path. About halfway down he jerked forward as the truck slammed into a tall Douglas fir. Lance left the vehicle, dragging his thick green coat with him. He quickly stuffed the manila envelope into the briefcase and pulled the case out of the cab. He stumbled and slid to the bottom of the gully where a small stream flowed. Lance knew the police would eventually realize he was no longer on the road and would investigate. The tracks in the snow would lead them to his abandoned vehicle. He had perhaps half an hour of lead time before this happened, maybe even two hours if the police were particularly incompetent. But he had to make the best of the time he had.

- - ••••◆••••• - -

Rob walked out of the interview room and was met by smiles from detectives who had been watching the interview from the observation room. A couple of them approached him, and they exchanged high fives.

"Beautiful job in there, Rob," someone said.

A man had murdered his wife, and the team had been working on the case for the past week. The detectives had not been able to secure enough evidence to prove he had committed the crime. They needed a confession to wrap up the case.

During the interview Rob quickly built a rapport with the husband and then took the direct approach, accusing him of the crime. He led the man to believe police had more evidence than they actually had. The guy soon cracked and made a full confession.

While they were celebrating, Captain Harding entered the room. "Your man has just showed up, Rob," he said.

"Who?" Rob asked.

"Lance Knight. Seems he terrorized the staff at the post office in Squamish and fled."

"Jesus," Rob said, racing from the room.

Minutes later Rob phoned the RCMP detachments in Whistler

and North Vancouver, asking them to set up roadblocks north and south of Squamish. He had also talked to Gary Roberts, the police chief in Squamish, who recounted the incident at the post office as reported by the staff. Knight had no more than a five-minute head start, and police had a description of his vehicle as well as a relative direction of travel. Squad cars had been sent at high speed north and south on the highway and on a secondary gravel road he could have accessed.

Rob thanked the chief for his efforts and told him about the roadblocks he had ordered. "If you've got the manpower, can you run a search of the town?" Rob asked.

"You don't think he'd stick around here, do you?" Gary asked incredulously.

"This guy has proved to be very resourceful," Rob said. "He's smart and he doesn't want to be caught. With him, you have to expect the unexpected."

Rob wrapped up the call, grabbed his jacket, and left the office. "Let's go, Doug," he said.

Looking up at Rob's retreating form, Doug sprang from his desk, got his jacket, and hurried after him. "Now where are we going?" he asked.

"Squamish!"

Three hours later Rob and Doug stood above the gorge on the edge of the golf course with a team of policemen. They had taken Rob's advice and had sent patrols throughout the town. Just minutes before, the tire tracks in the snow had led them to the gorge and to the vehicle. Doug and Rob had just climbed back up from the ravine. The vehicle was empty and the engine cold. The fugitive had at least a two-hour head start.

"I want a search mounted immediately," Rob told Gary.

"Right," the police chief responded. "We'll radio in the order right away."

"He'll be on foot. This is our best opportunity to catch him. Where do you suppose he'll go from there?"

Gary whistled and said, "If he's smart he'll just circle around and come back into town somewhere, or he could try to get to the highway and hitch a ride."

"Can you get the local TV and radio stations to alert the community that we've got a fugitive situation here? Get his photo from the files and put it on the air. If he's coming back into town, I want to eliminate his options."

"Sure, no problem."

"What if he decides to head out that way?" Rob pointed toward the thick forest.

The chief shook his head. "You mean out into the bush? I don't like his chances if he does. This is some of the roughest terrain in Canada. He would have to travel a hundred kilometers minimum in any direction he goes. The mountains west of here are glacier-covered. He's got to cross at least three fast, ice-cold rivers. To the west is the Pacific Ocean, and that's no walk on the beach either. I would have to say it would be impossible. If he tries it, though, we'll never find his body."

"That's why we need a search team out here to find him," Rob said. "I'm sure the bank would appreciate its money back."

"Don't worry. In less than an hour we'll have trackers, dog teams, and maybe even FLIR after this guy," Gary assured him.

"FLIR?" Doug asked. "What's that?"

"Forward Looking Infrared helicopter," Gary said.

"Oh!" Doug said, a little embarrassed.

An hour later Rob met with Gary and with Bill Higgins, the search coordinator, at the detachment headquarters. Topographical maps of the area around Squamish were spread out on a table as Bill reviewed the search strategy.

"We have a team of trackers with dogs starting from the vehicle," he said. "They will report back once they've established a direction of travel. Once we know that, we can reduce our containment area. This guy made a smart move dumping the truck in the ravine. That's given him a pretty good head start. For now, though, we figure he might come out on this trail or possibly this one." He pointed to the trails as Rob and Gary studied the map closely.

"What are these?" Rob asked.

"Recreational hiking trails used by the locals," Bill said.

"We have units patrolling this old logging road here," Gary said, pointing to the map. "It's only ten miles from the golf course. We also have foot patrols monitoring the southwest perimeter of the town just in case he tries to come back into town. Within the hour we'll have teams on the two trails Bill mentioned."

Bill turned to Rob. "You said he's charged with armed robbery.

If he's armed you should call in the emergency response team for support."

"So far the only indication we've had of a weapon is the note. I have team members on standby, though, just in case we need them," Rob said.

"With units here, here, here, and here, we've established a pretty good perimeter," Bill said, touching the map in several places.

Rob was not convinced. "What happens if he just goes cross country through here?" He traced a straight line across the map.

Bill looked up at him in surprise. "Have you ever tried to travel cross country in our rain forest?" Bill asked. "These woods are thick with underbrush. It's a real rat's nest in there. If he tries it he'll get bogged down. Our trackers will have him in a couple of hours."

"It's still a huge perimeter. That's got to be thirty square miles of dense forest," Rob said.

"Well, that's the best we can do for now," Bill said. "With a three- or four-hour head start, there's no telling what direction he could have taken."

Rob shook his head.

"Don't worry, Rob. Like I said, once the trackers start reporting in, we can start to squeeze him in. We'll catch him," Bill said.

"What's the situation with the helicopter?" Rob asked.

"We can have it in the air tomorrow morning if we need it."

Rob straightened up. "Okay, I guess that covers it," he said. "There's not much more I can do but wait. In the meantime I should join my partner. He's interviewing the post office staff. If you get any news give me a call."

Rob arrived at the post office to find Doug had finished questioning the woman who had waited on Lance that morning. Doug closed his notebook and strode over to meet Rob.

"She's made a positive ID that it was Lance Knight," Doug said. "He was picking up mail when she recognized him. I talked to the other two employees as well. They can't tell me much other than the fact that he scared the shit out of them."

"Picking up mail?" Rob asked.

"Yup, he had a manila envelope waiting for him. General Delivery. She brought it into the back office when she was going to call the police. That's when he got aggressive. He entered the office, grabbed the envelope from her, and took off."

"Hm. Sounds like whatever was in that envelope was pretty important to him. Did she say where it came from?"

"No luck there, Rob. The post office is checking the routing on it. They might be able to come up with something in a day or so, but right now we've got nothing."

"What could it possibly be?" Rob wondered.

Doug scratched his head. "It might be tickets for a flight, I suppose."

"Maybe, but how would he have paid for them? We've got a hold on his credit cards."

Rob's phone rang. It was Gary. Rob hoped he had good news regarding the search. In fact, there had been another sighting of Lance Knight. An older woodsman had admitted himself into the Squamish hospital with a broken nose, claiming the fugitive had attacked him.

Rob and Doug immediately drove to the hospital to question the victim, Cojer. He said Knight had attacked him at a campground north of Squamish. The two detectives soon decided that something about the old timer's story did not add up. The details he provided were sketchy and at times inconsistent. When they probed deeper into his story, Cojer erupted with a stream of profanity. He complained about police incompetence and hurled insults at the two detectives. The ruckus brought nurses to the room, and they sedated him. Rob and Doug left the hospital shaking their heads and headed back to Vancouver.

Lance's advantage was that the police had no idea where he was headed, but with no compass he had little idea himself. He had planned to drive south and to attempt to cross the border. Now, after the disaster at the post office, he would have to travel southeast through the mountains on foot, hoping to come out somewhere in the populated Fraser River valley and to head for the States. But first he had to trek sixty to eighty kilometers through this damned forest. The mountains were home to glaciers, grizzlies, and cougars, and he would need to get past all of this while avoiding the team that would surely be pursuing him. He had heard stories of men who had gotten lost in this wilderness and who were never seen again. With no compass to guide him, this could easily be his fate. Lance took a bearing and decided that the stream at the bottom of the ravine seemed to run more or less east to west. He needed to head south, and to do that he had to cross the stream and to scale the steep bank.

Lance hopped from rock to rock to avoid getting wet and was soon on the other side of the small stream. He immediately began to scramble up the steep slope on the far side of the ravine, fighting his way through the thick underbrush that blocked his path. At the top of the slope, he finally burst through onto a narrow animal trail. Although this path did not head in exactly the right direction, Lance followed it, putting distance between himself and his truck in the ravine. The well-worn trail wound ever upward. Finally he came to a clearing high up on the mountainside. Lance stopped and surveyed the panorama in front of him. He looked toward what he believed was the south and in the far distance saw a snow-covered peak that rose above closer mountains. He would use this mountain as a landmark to keep traveling in what he hoped was the right direction. Lance took a hard look at the peak, memorizing its features, and moved on.

He continued quickly through the clearing and back into the deep forest. The animal trail continued to wind upward until the forest gradually thinned. Soon he might be above the tree line. But the path became less distinct and forked several times. Each time Lance chose the path that seemed to be the most used, enabling him to travel more or less in the direction of what he now considered his mountain—the mountain that would keep him moving south. Lance ducked under spruce branches and struggled over fallen trees to follow the path, and finally it disappeared. He backtracked until he found the path again and chose another fork. He walked ten minutes and passed several forks in the trail before this path vanished. Again he backtracked and followed another path. This one also soon petered out. Undecided about what to do, Lance stopped. He had basically been running around in circles. Ahead the forest closed in on him, but he was done taking paths that led nowhere, so he headed straight into the woods.

Lance made little headway over the next half-hour as he fought against the underbrush and the fallen trees, moving deeper and deeper into nothingness. Eventually he confronted long vines with sharp barbs. Scratched and cut, Lance tried to make it through, but the undergrowth became so thick that finally he couldn't take one step more. Dejected, he retraced his steps back to where he had lost the trail. This took the better part of an hour, but finally he found a trail. Whether it was the same one or a different one he had no way of knowing. He followed this trail until he came to a fork and took the path to the right. Lance had wasted a lot of time, but he was again moving quickly. At one point he even spotted his mountain and was satisfied that he was still angling in the right direction. But soon after that this trail also petered out.

Lance raised the briefcase above his head and plunged into the dense underbrush. He fought his way forward through clinging bushes and over dead trees down the side of the mountain. With the noise he was making, any pursuers would learn his exact location. The struggle was sapping his strength, and several times he had to pause to control his ragged breathing. Lance was completely engulfed in an infuriating tangle of vines and long, sharp thorns. He could see only a few meters in front of him and could only hope he was headed in the right direction, but he continued downhill.

Finally when he thought he could go no farther the forest opened onto another well-worn trail. Lance eagerly followed it. This new path hugged the side of the mountain. As the path dropped into a steep valley to his left, Lance could hear the sound of rushing water below him. He began to run.

A half-hour later he arrived at a place where the trail leveled off into a small clearing at the side of a rushing river. Lance prostrated himself at the edge and drank the cold, clear water. When he had taken his fill he rolled over and closed his eyes. He lay still for about ten minutes before finally sitting up and looking around.

The trail he had been on ended at the river's edge, and the river seemed to run east to west. If Lance wanted to continue south, he would have to cross the river. The other side was just ten yards from where he stood, but he knew he could never reach it in the roiling current. He looked east and west and finally decided to head east. There was no path by the river. Lance climbed over boulders and fallen trees and eventually came to a place where the river cascaded over a precipice twenty feet above him. Lance raised himself onto a huge boulder rounded smooth by eons of pounding water and from there wedged himself up onto another like it. Tossing the briefcase ahead of him from boulder to boulder, he made his way to the top of the falls. Then, standing by the cascading water, he surveyed the river upstream.

Here the river widened and deepened, dammed by the boulders at the top of the falls. But farther upstream he could see the tops of boulders with white water splashing around them, indicating shallower water. Lance skirted the side of the river, slowly making his way upstream. Finally he came to where the water appeared to be shallower. The river was even wider here, perhaps twenty yards to the far side. This was probably his best chance, and he had to keep moving.

Lance took a step into the icy water and then a second and a third. The water suddenly rose to waist level, and Lance gasped as the cold water hit his groin. Holding the briefcase above his head, he pressed on. Now the water was at chest level, and Lance felt a tug toward the waterfall. His feet slipped on the slick river bottom as he advanced. Now the water was just below his chin, and he stretched his neck, fearing he would soon be submerged. The current was steadily forcing him downstream, but now he could feel the river bottom rising. He gained his footing and soon found himself in the middle of the river in waist-deep water. Lance slipped and slid his way back upstream in the shallower water and then turned toward a gravelly beach on the opposite bank. He splashed his way toward the shore, but the river bottom suddenly dropped and he was totally submerged.

Flailing with one hand and hanging on to the briefcase with the other, Lance struggled to reach the other bank just six feet away as the current carried him downstream. Kicking his way to the surface, Lance reached with his free hand and grasped the edge of a boulder. He was slowly losing his grip on the slippery rock, and he feared he would have to let go of the briefcase to keep from being swept over the falls. *No damn way,* he thought. *After all this has cost me I'll go over before I let go of this.* With a mighty struggle, Lance raised himself chest high in the water and threw the briefcase discus style. The case landed beyond the water by a few feet. Now, with both hands gripping the rock, Lance felt more secure. He half pulled himself arm over arm back upstream toward the beach. The icy river was numbing his limbs. Finally as he struggled past a large boulder, he could see the beach. The river bottom grew shallow as he approached. He gained his footing and scrambled onto the opposite shore, shaking uncontrollably.

Lance quickly stripped off his drenched clothing and wrung it out as best he could. He spread the clothing on the warm gravel in a narrow strip of sunlight and huddled in the same sunny area, trying to control his shivers.

Finally Lance rose, crossed the beach to where he had flung his briefcase, and opened it. The water poured out and with it a number of bills. The money was completely soaked. Lance drained the water from the briefcase, carefully replaced the money and his documents, and closed it. He returned to his clothing and dressed. The clothing was still wet and felt cold against his skin, but he had no time to waste. He knew that if the weather turned cold he could suffer hypothermia. Lance picked up the briefcase and walked along the river to the edge of the rocky beach. He discovered a small path leading into the shadowy forest and headed upward into the gloom of the forest.

Lance climbed for the next fifteen minutes. He was cold and sore, and his wet clothing chafed against his skin, leaving it red and raw. Eventually he found a gravel logging road. For the first time in hours Lance could see his mountain, and even better the road rose directly toward it. But if he took this road he would be out in the open and could easily be spotted by a patrol. Lance had had enough bushwhacking for one day, however, and he strode down the middle of the road in the direction of his mountain. He hoped he would hear any traffic long before police could spot him. As he advanced he constantly surveyed the edge of the road for places where he could seek cover if need be. The road was in ill repair and seemed deserted. Lance walked and jogged along it for a good hour.

The road rose steadily, and soon the cliff to his right and the deep forest to his left gave way to a more gently sloped clear-cut zone. The space was wide open with nothing but grass and old stumps. This area made Lance nervous. If a police helicopter flew over, he had no cover. He hoped to escape this area as soon as possible. He regretted his decision to leave the cover of the forest, but he could see his mountain looming directly in front of him.

Lance hurried on, running when he had the strength, walking quickly when he did not, and he was relieved when the road plunged into virgin forest on both sides. Lance suddenly froze. He had heard something. He waited and listened intently. There it was again, ever so faintly. He dashed into the forest and crouched behind the tall trees. Seconds later a police cruiser appeared. The driver surveyed the woods on the side where he hid, and the other officer scanned the opposite side. In the back was a German shepherd. Luck had been with him. If they had come a minute earlier when he was in the clear-cut zone, they would surely have spotted him. Now Lance knew for sure he was being hunted. Had they been able to find his trail and to deduce his direction of travel? His heart pounding, Lance crept to the side of the road. The car had moved out of sight, but Lance could see another section of the road in the distance. He waited until he saw the car round this section and vanish.

Lance bounded from the trees and sprinted in the opposite direction, looking back every few seconds as he ran. Out of breath, he doubled over. He had panicked, and panic was the one thing that would get him caught. Surely the tracks he left along the road would be clearly visible if the police returned. What should he do? Should he head back into the forest? The forest rose from the side of the road like a barrier. He recalled the bushwhacking of that morning, and he had no desire to repeat that torture. He turned and continued down the road ever watchful for escape routes and oncoming vehicles.

He came to a section where the road had been cut through the mountainside. Jagged rock rose on both sides for the next quarter-mile. This was a death trap. If anyone came along, Lance could flee in neither direction. He began to run as fast as his tired legs would carry him, his briefcase flapping at his side. He must traverse this area as quickly as possible. He stayed in the center of the road where traffic had hard-packed the gravel. Here his footprints would be the most difficult to spot.

Finally he reached the end of the cliffs and ducked into the trees and down the steep bank. He dove under a large tree and lay panting rapidly and sweating profusely. Lance remained there for several minutes before sitting up and looking around. He saw a worn path running below the road in more or less the same direction. He scrambled down the slope and onto the path. Now he could continue under the cover of trees in the direction he needed to go. Finally, however, the trail veered sharply downhill, so Lance climbed back to the gravel road above him.

He followed the road nervously for the next forty-five minutes. It wound ever upward through deep forest. He came to a section of the road where the area on the left had been logged out. Lance hugged the heavily forested right side as he proceeded. This section was particularly twisty, with hairpin turns first to the left and then to the right. Lance had traversed several of these sharp corners and was navigating yet another right bend when he froze. On the road about fifty yards ahead were two police cruisers. Four officers leaned against the hood of one of the cars.

Lance edged his way back around the curve, but before he could disappear he saw one of the officers point in his direction. They all scrambled to their vehicles. Lance dove into the trees and crashed down a slope through heavy bush as the wailing of sirens grew closer. In seconds he descended onto a well-worn trail. He turned down it and raced away from the officers. This was no good. In seconds they would be on this path, and he would be spotted. He darted back up the hill into the thick cover and stopped.

He could hear the thrashing of his pursuers several yards back as they descended through the underbrush. They would be expecting him to flee from this area as quickly as he could. Lance was well hidden in the thick underbrush, so he waited. He heard the heavy footfall of one of the men as he ran past Lance along the path below.

Lance slowly edged his way back up toward the road under cover of the underbrush. With each step, he took care to make absolutely no noise. He knew that reinforcements had been called and that soon the area would be swarming with police. Finally he reached the edge of the road and poked his head out. Twenty-five yards down the road were the two cruisers, and two officers stood looking into the woods, their backs turned to him. They had their eyes on the spot where minutes earlier he had plunged into the thicket. Below him Lance heard more crashing as at least one of the men had returned and was now searching the underbrush.

Lance was desperate. He had to get away from this area before a team with dogs arrived. If this happened it would be only a matter of time before he was captured. He took a breath and crawled onto the road. Inch by inch he crept across the road, not wanting any sudden movement to attract the attention of the men yards away from him. Every now and then one officer turned his head to say something to the other and Lance froze, but so far they had not noticed his prone body on the road. Now he was more than halfway across and edging toward the ditch, quietly dragging his briefcase.

As he gained the ditch Lance heard a third cruiser approach. He lay flat in the grass of the narrow ditch. It was the cruiser that had passed him earlier, the one with the dog. The cruiser quickly pulled up to the other vehicles, and the two officers descended with the dog into the bush. Lance climbed into the clear-cut zone on the far side. Fortunately the officers remained focused on the bush where the others were searching.

Lance gained the cover of a thin row of trees on the mountainside. He rose from his knees and passed through this narrow band of trees onto a rough path that loggers must have used. He was now out of sight from the road. He moved onto the path and began to run. Every so often Lance could see the cruisers far below him through the band of trees.

To his chagrin, the path descended and soon merged with the gravel road where the squad cars were parked. Lance could hear another siren in the distance. He saw a small cliff on his left. The rock was jagged, cracked, and weathered. There was no time to lose. He quickly yanked his belt from his pants, looped it through the handle of the briefcase, and began to climb, letting the case dangle at his feet. He ascended easily from one handhold to the next, but the sound below told him the vehicle would soon be in sight. He scrambled more quickly upward and was now forty feet above the road.

Lance pressed himself against the rock as the cruiser came into view. He was in plain sight. If anyone glanced up, Lance would be spotted, but the officers were racing to the site of the search, and he clung to the rock face unnoticed as they passed below.

Lance continued his ascent with great care. If he lost his grip, he would plummet to his death. There was no turning back. He had to continue higher and higher up the cliff. He planned his moves several steps ahead and rose inexorably toward the grass and the willows that rimmed the top of the rock face. Finally Lance reached a spot about ten feet from the top, but there was a slight overhang and it seemed there was no way to reach the vegetation above. Then he saw a small root protruding from the rock above him. Lance reached for it, wrapped it around his hand, and pulled. There was a loud snap as the root gave way.

Fortunately, Lance didn't fall far. His right foot hit an outcropping of rock just inches below, and his right hand still gripped a small crack. He dropped the root from his left hand and scrabbled for something to latch on to while his left foot swung crazily outward.

Lance held on desperately with one hand and willed his body back toward the rock face. His left hand regained its previous hold, and then his left foot found purchase. His heart pounding at the fright he had just experienced, Lance clung to the rock. His legs and arms shook from the strain of the effort he had made to prevent himself from plummeting to his death.

But Lance could not hold on much longer. He looked right and left for a way up and noticed a crevice twenty feet over that angled upward and created a gap in the vegetation at the top. If he could reach it, he could gain the safety of the bluff. But to do that he would have to descend about fifteen feet, for he could find no holds without descending. This he hated to do because it felt like surrendering what he had worked so hard to gain.

Descending was even more difficult than climbing, because his body blocked his vision of what was below. Lance had to feel blindly for footholds while clinging to the rock, but finally he found a place where he could begin moving left, and he soon reached the crevice. The ledge was wider here, and he did not have to use his hands, which by now were in intense pain. He sat on the ledge and rested for several minutes.

Lance carefully sidestepped his way upward along the crevice. Finally he reached for some small willows and pulled himself up. Pushing with his weary legs, he clambered onto the level ground of the bluff.

Although exhausted from the climb, Lance felt he had no time to waste. The dogs were no doubt following his scent and would soon be at the base of the cliff. He headed for yet another clear-cut zone on the side of a rounded hill. At this elevation his mountain was now clearly in sight and Lance walked toward it.

It was now late afternoon. Lance quickly descended the hill in the cover of the forest and soon came to the gravel road. He saw what looked like a path on the other side of the road, so he backtracked toward it and descended onto the trail. It seemed more like a hiking trail than an animal path, so Lance made good time along it for the next two hours even though he had to climb over fallen trees that lay across the path and leap over several small streams. He was happy that he had distanced himself from the place where he had been spotted. Lance felt a little safer. Yet this was a hiking trail and now that police knew he was in the area, they were bound to search it. If the police found tracks, they would match his pace. But Lance didn't think they would be able to use quads. The trail was just a bit narrow for that.

Late afternoon was turning to early evening, and Lance wondered what he would do when night fell. He pictured himself shivering in the dark huddled under a tree as wild animals prowled. Even now the shadows were growing and the features of the forest were becoming obscured. Lance continued to walk, looking to make as much headway as possible.

As he pondered these things, Lance heard the trickle of yet another rivulet he would have to cross. He came to it, jumped it easily, and walked on. But then something made him stop. He retraced his steps back to the stream. His nose had caught a faint whiff of sulfur as he had passed. He knelt down and felt the water. It was hot. An idea formed in his head. There were a number of hot springs in the British Columbia mountains, and he had just found one. He left the path and followed the stream uphill. But the stream trickled through underbrush over large rocks and he could advance no farther, so he returned to the trail and instead followed the stream downhill. Finally he splashed into hot water. He squinted in the dim light and saw that the lay of the land had formed a shallow, sandy pool about ten feet in diameter. The warm water trickled over rocks at the far end of the pool and down into a ravine.

Lance placed his briefcase on a large rock by the side of the pool and quickly stripped off his clothing, placing it on top of the case. He dropped to his knees in the center of the hot spring. He dug into the bottom of the pool and found he could push his hands into the sand past his wrist. Lance spotted a chunk of decaying bark and wood that looked like it might serve as a rudimentary shovel. He retrieved it and scrambled back into the warm water. The evening air already felt cool on his naked skin. Lance quickly pushed the sand toward where the water gurgled through the spaces between the rocks at the edge of the pool. He jumped from the pool, gathered twigs and leaves, and packed them into the dam he was building. After an hour of dredging and damming, the pool was about fourteen inches deep. In the darkness Lance felt for larger rocks and dislodged those he could, continuing to build up the sides of the pool. This night at least, he was not going to be cold. He felt his way to where he had set the briefcase and bundled up his jeans, fashioning a pillow. He waded once more into the hot pool, placed his jeans on a flat rock he had set beside it, and lay down. Lance struggled to get comfortable and then tried to sleep.

Such a lonely place this was in the dark, silent forest. Lance tried to calm himself, but he could not shake the thought of bears and cougars stumbling upon him in the dark and making a meal of him. His mind wandered to his wife and to the anger she felt and then to Jen, who had become so special to him while he stayed in the campground. He thought again of establishing a new life in some foreign country. His thoughts became confused as one moment he was living an idyllic life with his wife and the next with Jen. In this state of mental turmoil he at last drifted off to sleep. He knew he was sleeping, because a few times during the night he suddenly awoke sputtering and spitting when his head slipped off the rock into the water. He continued to drift in and out of sleep throughout the night.

CHAPTER 8

Back in Squamish Rob and Doug sat in a meeting with their counterparts from the town's police department. It was 9 p.m. and the group had gathered around a large topographical map of the area outside of Squamish mounted on a cork bulletin board. They had received the report that Lance had been sighted on the logging road. The location of the sighting was identified by a pin with a tiny red ball poked into the map. The field units had later reported that the dogs had picked up Lance's scent and had led them to the base of the cliff Lance had scaled. They had discovered Lance's footprints along the gravel road and had found the curious scrapes he had made crawling across the road in embarrassingly close proximity to where the cruisers and the officers must have stood at the time. The team had driven as close to the top of the precipice as possible and had again put the dogs to work. At the edge of the cliff the dogs had picked up Lance's scent and had followed it to the entrance of the hiking path. By this time, however, it was nearing dark and the search had been called off, to be resumed in the morning.

"Where are you, Lance?" Rob said, peering at the map.

The entrance to the hiking path had been identified with a yellow-headed pin. "We need a team here tonight," Rob said, pointing to the pin. "We don't want him doubling back and slipping our containment again. How soon can we get a team there?"

"I've already contacted A group, and they are being dispatched to that location as we speak," Gary said.

"Good!" Rob said, still studying the map. "Now taking into account approximately three hours of lag time before we found this path, he has to be somewhere about here." Rob drew a haphazard circle on the map some distance from the pin to the southeast. "What's the terrain like in this area?"

Gary drew alongside him, studying the map. "Considering what he's traveled through today, he's going to find it a lot easier to make progress. The terrain is still up and down with some fairly steep climbs, but the path is well maintained and he can make good time."

"He may consider walking through the night," Doug said. "Lord knows that's what I would do. It's going to be near freezing up there, and I'd rather be walking than sitting huddled under some tree freezing my ass off."

"Good point," Rob said. "Okay, if he travels all night the best he could possibly do is about here." Rob placed a red pin on the map. "We should have another team about here." He poked a second yellow pin on the map about ten kilometers forward from the red pin. "Can we have another team here before morning?"

Gary squinted at the map. "First light this time of year is about 7 a.m., and the only way along that trail is walking or maybe bicycles. The best I can do would be to have a team there by noon."

"No good!" Rob removed the pin and placed it another fifteen kilometers along the path. "I need a team here by one in the afternoon. We need someone who is familiar with this area. Do we have anybody?"

"I've done a fair bit of hiking on that path, sir," an officer said.

Rob spun and looked at him. He was at most thirty years old, thin and fit. Rob imagined he enjoyed hiking and the great outdoors. "All right," Rob said. "Now think. We're concentrating right now only on this path, but we have to consider all possibilities. Are there any other paths or routes he could take?"

The officer furrowed his brow. "Well, he could try breaking trail, but that would be slow going and would take its toll on him. When all is said and done, though, with the gorge on this side and Mount George here, he's got pretty much only two options." The officer pointed to squiggly topographical lines indicating a rapid incline in elevation. "He'll be forced down to the path here." He pointed some distance beyond the pin. "Or he's got to summit here and come down the other side of the mountain and join this path." He ran his finger along another faded gray line similar to the path the pins outlined. "This one goes pretty much northeast and comes out at Lake Esther."

Rob removed another pin and placed it on the spot the officer had indicated. Then he reached for two more pins and placed them along the path to the north. "Let's get these points set up tomorrow. You better get tents down there too, but out of sight. I want lookouts posted day and night. This guy's slipped through my fingers for the last time. And let's get bicycle teams on both of these paths. They might get lucky."

"Yes, sir," Gary replied and picked up the phone to carry out the orders. With that, the meeting broke up.

· · · · ● ● ● ◆ ● ● ● · · ·

Lance slowly realized that the night was losing its grip, so he rose from his watery bed. The frosty air immediately made him shiver, so he hurriedly threw his clothes on. His pants, which he had used for a pillow, were damp from having slipped into the water along with his head during the night.

It had been twenty-four hours since he had eaten. Yesterday he had been so focused on escaping his pursuers that he had not given a thought to food, but now he was famished. He would need to eat soon because he could feel his energy level had dropped. Suddenly Lance had an idea. He would put the hot water to one final use before moving on. While at the cabin, he had read in the survival manual that pine needle tea was a good source of nutrients. Just by the pool stood a bluff of pine trees. He stripped needles from a tree and placed them on a large rock near the pool. He then ground the needles to mush with another rock. With his hands he brought water up from the pool and filled a small indentation in the larger rock. As best he could, he mixed the mush into the hot water. Finally he bent down and sipped the water. It had a distinctly piney taste with a hint of sulfur. Lance grimaced at the foul-tasting concoction. Despite the taste, he refilled the small indentation several times, mixing in more pine needles and sipping until the edge of hunger lifted.

Lance had no idea what time it was, but he wanted to get moving before the manhunt resumed. He picked up his briefcase and climbed up to the trail.

For the next hour Lance hurried along the path, but with each step, he felt the forest closing in on him. The twilight of dawn had changed to the full light of morning, and the possibility of encountering a search party grew. Finally Lance could stand the tension no more and climbed off the path, scrambling as quietly as possible through the dense underbrush. His progress would now be slowed, but at least in the cover of the brush he no longer felt the danger that seemed to loom on the pathway. Yet he knew if he was discovered now all would be lost. Tracking dogs would easily pinpoint where he had left the path and would follow him. He had to keep going.

Finally after an hour, Lance made his way to a rocky clearing, and to his dismay he discovered that despite the hour of climbing he could still see a section of the path no more than a hundred meters below him. He suddenly caught a flash of yellow on the path. Lance instinctively ducked behind a rock and then peaked at the trail. A second flash of yellow passed through another opening on the path. This time he could clearly see two policemen on bicycles. Lance shuddered. If he had stuck to the trail, the silent riders would probably have been upon him before he had a chance to react. Once again his instincts had saved him.

Lance decided to keep as far above the trail as possible. He climbed slowly through the rock and underbrush until finally the forest gave way to the alpine terrain of the mountain heights. At last, with a final easy climb he gained the ridge. He was more open to detection from the air, but there were still enough trees so that he could hide if he heard the thrum of a helicopter engine. Besides, with the thinning of the underbrush he could make better time along this ridge. A second advantage Lance found was that from time to time he encountered an open vista where he could see the mountain he was using as his guide. He was reassured to know that although he was moving at an angle to the mountain, he was basically headed in the right direction. At some point he would need to descend to get back on course, but that could wait for now.

Lance continued on in the high country and was surprised at how much the pine tea he had concocted that morning had sustained his energy. Still, the terrain was uneven and difficult. Each step was an effort, and at this elevation, his rests grew more frequent as he gasped for breath in the thin mountain air.

About midday, when Lance came upon yet another point where a panorama of the countryside was open to him, he noticed that his mountain landmark had disappeared behind a closer mountain. He decided to descend, and so for the rest of the day he dropped into one valley after the next, clambering up one side and then down the opposite side until finally he reached a crest where he saw his guiding mountain looming before him. If he climbed down from this crest, Lance would be at the base of the mountain he was using for his landmark. To be sure, however, he would have to scale the mountain to a point where he could reorient himself.

Lance lifted his gaze and took a step toward the rock wall he would be climbing for the next several hours. Then he stopped. His mind was willing, but his spirit and body were screaming in protest. He turned back and despondently began to descend into that one last valley. *The sky is already turning a dark blue,* he rationalized. *It would be dark before I could get high enough to conduct a proper survey anyway.* Lance knew such laziness could result in his capture, but still he descended.

Lance stumbled across a small path and decided to follow it. The path was too narrow and too obstructed by rock and rubble for cyclists to navigate, so he continued on it for a few hours. Lance suspected this trail would eventually intersect the main trail he had left early in the morning, and sure enough, just as darkness fell it did. Rather than risk the main trail, Lance chose to continue following the much smaller one. He leapt from the edge of his path to grass on the edge of the opposite side of the main trail to avoid leaving any tracks for searchers. He scanned the ground, and when he was satisfied that it was free of tracks, he gingerly turned and made his way along this path away from the main trail.

The path continued to descend gradually, and Lance continued to follow it as the light faded. He still berated himself for not ascending when he knew he should, because the farther he descended the less he would be able to navigate. The winding trail followed no clear direction, and now the features of the forest were disappearing as Lance's second night in the bush loomed. With no real idea of where he was or where he was heading, Lance pressed on. The deeper the trail led, the darker it became until finally he found he was extending his arms to avoid crashing into trees he could not make out right in front of his face.

Lance stopped and opened the briefcase. He remembered he had placed his cell phone in the case. He hoped it still worked after having been soaked. He had turned it off and had taken out the battery because he had heard the police could locate a person by tracing a cell phone signal. He would chance that now. He inserted the battery, pressed the "on" button, and waited for the phone to power up. Soon the cell came on and flashed the message "No service in this area. Shutting down." The phone chimed as it shut down. Frustrated, Lance turned the cell back on, and when it came to life he quickly pushed the menu button and selected "utilities." He chose "scheduler" next and then held the cell phone up and shone the light in a circle around him. It wasn't much light, but it would do. Lance was resolved to walk all night. He pressed on with his briefcase in one hand and his cell phone in the other illuminating the way.

Lance continued on the trail through the night. The path rose and fell but for the most part went downhill. From time to time Lance stopped and looked at his phone. During his trek the power bar had dropped from two bars, indicating half charge, to just a sliver of red, and now there were nothing. Soon after, the cell beeped the message that it was low on power and would be shutting down. Lance cursed as darkness fell. He gained a few more minutes of light by turning the cell on again, but each time the phone soon beeped its message and the cell automatically shut down. On the third try the cell refused to come back on.

Stubbornly pressing on in the darkness, Lance edged his way forward like a blind man, using his arms to guide him. He continued on in this fashion for a half-hour. He almost lost the path a number of times, wandering off headlong into the underbrush.

The path turned sharply downhill, and Lance continued to feel his way along for the next five minutes before stopping suddenly. What the hell was he doing crashing and banging in the darkness? The sounds could alert wild animals, which would have no trouble stalking him. What's more, he had an ominous feeling. Something made him turn around. He listened for the sound of an animal creeping up on him. Several times he imagined he heard something, and each time his heart jumped. He searched for a large tree he had banged into just before he stopped. Finally he found it. Lance placed the briefcase on the uphill side of the tree and sat on the case, using the tree as a backrest. He crossed his arms around his knees in an effort to keep warm. Lance longed for the warmth of the hot spring and realized how incredibly lucky he had been to find it the previous night. Tonight he would have to keep himself warm as best he could. He thought sleep would be impossible.

As Lance huddled at the base of the large Douglas fir tree, Rob sat at his desk in a trailer that had been quickly set up as the command post on the west shore of Harrison Lake. The post was set up in a small gravel parking lot for a popular hiking trail The command post consisted of three work camp style trailers. One served as Rob's office and the other two as bunks for the teams he commanded. The command post was placed here because it seemed Lance was headed in that direction. Rob commanded a dozen teams in the manhunt, but so far the fugitive seemed to have vanished into thin air. Rob studied the terrain maps in front of him while the faint sound of a generator thrummed outside his door. The generator powered the trailers and portable light stands had been set up to illuminate the command post. He had teams posted on all the trails in the vicinity of Lance's last known location. He had his man trapped between the river, which was impassable because of the deep gorge, and the snow-capped mountains to the north. Just to be on the safe side, the Squamish detachment had teams posted along the paths on its end in case Lance decided to double back. It was only a matter of time before he would be captured. Rob also had two teams of bicycle police patrolling the two main paths and had deployed a helicopter that had been searching the higher ground.

This had been a particularly frustrating day for Rob, but true to his dogged nature he persevered. He was now studying the maps for probably the twentieth time that day. He had rented a scooter and had surveyed all the trails he could navigate, and now he was methodically tracing each path to ensure he had every escape route covered. Finally his gaze returned to the river. He searched the contour markings and was finally satisfied with the reports the locals had given him that the gorge was too steep and that it would be impossible for anyone to cross that river and live. There was a knock at the door.

"Come in!" Rob called, glancing at his watch. It was already after one in the morning. Sergeant Palmer entered.

"I saw your light on and thought you would like the report sooner rather than later."

"What is it, Sergeant?"

"One of the bicycle crews finally reported in an hour ago. It seems they discovered some signs of Knight."

"What? Where? Why the hell did it take them so long report?"

"You know how bad radio service is among these peaks. I didn't get the report until midnight. I was sleeping when they called it in. I figured you'd be sleeping, but when I came outside to take a piss I saw your light on."

"Well next time I want to know immediately. I'm unhappy that I'm getting a report that's already an hour old. Is that clear?"

"Yes, sir."

"Okay, show me where they found the sign," Rob said, turning toward the map.

"Right about here, sir," Palmer said, pointing to the map. "It looks like Knight made himself a little hot spring pool and spent last night there."

"Holy shit! Really? I can't imagine that could have been too comfortable." Rob traced a line from where the trail left the Squamish area to where the sergeant had indicated. "He's traveling in our direction. He's had a whole day's travel on us, but he couldn't have done any better than, say, here. Let's tighten the web. I want teams situated here, here, here, and here. We should be able to move the two Squamish teams up to here and here. We should make contact with him at some point tomorrow, assuming he hasn't frozen to death. It's getting damn chilly out there."

"Yes, sir. I'll have the posts set up first light tomorrow morning."

Rob hesitated, frowning at the map. "And I want a team patrolling the paths on the south side of the river."

"South side of the river!" Palmer exclaimed. "There's no way he can get to the south side of the river, sir. It's impossible. You've got a team covering the drawbridge, and that's the only way to cross."

"I know, damn it, but I want a team over there anyway."

"Yes, sir. Good night, sir," Palmer said. He stopped briefly on the trailer steps and shook his head. *This guy might just have a screw or two loose*, he thought.

Rob studied the map for a few more minutes and finally doused the light. He immediately fell into a relaxed sleep. This whole episode would soon be over.

CHAPTER 9

Lance was mistaken about his ability to sleep. Without realizing it he drifted off. A few times Lance woke up chilled and rubbed himself, jumping up and down to get his circulation moving, but mostly he slept. Exhaustion caught up with him, his body shut down, and he descended into unconsciousness despite the discomfort he felt. Sooner than he could have guessed, the sky lightened.

Lance rose, again rubbing himself and bouncing to get warm. He would press on now in the dawn. Lance picked up the briefcase, took a few steps, and froze on the spot. His eyes swelled into giant orbs as he stared in front of him. He was in exactly the spot where he had stood the night before when that uneasy feeling had gripped him, preventing him from going on. Just two steps in front of him the trail led to a precipice and then jackknifed back into the bush. Lance edged himself to the rim of the precipice and peered over. There was a sheer drop of at least one hundred feet. Had he continued on in the night he surely would have plunged over the cliff to his death. What had made him stop? Was some angel watching over him, protecting him from danger, or had his senses subconsciously detected the emptiness in front of him and sent a danger signal to his mental command center?

Lance pondered these things as he stared at the chasm below him. His heart beat a little faster, and even in the cool morning air a bead of sweat covered his forehead. He shook his head, grateful that his stupidity last night had not cost him his life. With renewed resolve that he would survive no matter what, he turned away from the cliff and followed the path into the bush. The trail skirted away from the cliff, and Lance hoped that at some point it might drop into the deep valley. Every so often the trail would suddenly bend to the right, providing another view of the deep chasm. Lance followed this path until suddenly he emerged from the trees into bright sunlight and onto a trail much like the one he had abandoned early yesterday morning. The trail was obviously designed for humans. Lance blinked against the sunshine allowing the sun's rays to warm his frozen limbs. He followed this new trail downhill, aware of how exposed he was on such a well-worn path. He came to a brown sign that said, "Drawbridge 1 km." Lance quickened his pace.

He walked for another five minutes and then stopped. *This is too easy,* he thought. *They have to have a trail like this covered.* He turned off the trail and soon found the path that skirted the ravine. Within ten minutes he came out onto yet another promontory overlooking the chasm. But this time when Lance looked back, he could see the drawbridge that stretched across to the south side. He was wondering whether he should return and cross when suddenly he spied movement. Lance instinctively crouched and studied the place where he had detected the activity. He stared for two minutes and was beginning to doubt he had seen anything when suddenly a man stepped to the edge of the ravine, stretched widely, relieved himself, and turned back into the bush. Sure enough, police were watching the bridge, and if he had continued along that path he would have stepped right into their grasp.

Lance turned away from the drawbridge and for a half-hour continued along the little path skirting the ravine. At times the path seemed to wither away to nothing and Lance wondered whether he had lost the trail, but each time he picked it up again and slowly made his way, pushing aside branches and stepping over rotting tree trunks. Finally he came to a slightly more established trail and took it toward the ravine. In less than twenty paces Lance came to an old log platform constructed over the edge of the gorge he had been skirting. He could see the drawbridge only as a faint line against the horizon. Just below the platform he spied a guy wire stretched across the deep valley and disappearing on the other side. Lance could not make out just where the guy wire was attached in the far distance.

He scratched his head. Should he rappel across the valley? He would be open to view from the drawbridge, and while he crossed the police could easily make their way to the other end of the line with their cuffs ready. On the other hand, Lance had been wandering aimlessly for the last several hours, and the search party might close in on him at any time. It could have been his imagination, but he thought he had heard voices a number of times recently. Perhaps the main trail was not that far away. Lance thought for a few seconds and then scrambled down from the platform to the metal cable. He undid his belt and looped it through the handle of his briefcase. He then looped the belt around himself and the cable, using the last hole to make the belt as long as possible. When he put the weight of his torso onto the belt, he had two inches of slack, but the briefcase handle pressed painfully against the small of his back.

Lance edged himself out over the lip of the steep valley, hanging upside down on the cable. Supported by the belt in the middle, he began to slide along the cable, using his hands and legs. He made fairly good time as the belt glided easily over the cable. He tried his best to reduce the friction of the belt on the cable. If the belt snapped, not only was he probably a goner, but the briefcase along with the cash would fall into the gorge far below. Gravity helped his efforts as the line sloped downward. Before long he was dangling above a large, fast river in the middle of the gorge.

He felt more exposed than ever, but he needed to rest. Slowly he allowed the belt to take more of his weight and relaxed his arms and legs. Away from the trees Lance surveyed his surroundings. Behind him he could make out the peak of the second mountain he had used as a landmark. He turned in the opposite direction and looked along the gorge. He could see two mountains ahead, but they were obviously not as high as his two landmark mountains since they had no snow on the peaks and were treed right to the summit. Lance had crossed the highest part of the range, and once across the gorge he could continue to descend. Where he would come out, he was not sure, but it would not be difficult to follow the gorge and the river far below him.

Somewhat rested, Lance again made his way hand over hand across the wire, moving as fast as he could, careful not to allow the belt to slide across the metal cable with too much friction. Finally he was most of the way across the gorge, and as far as he knew he had not been spotted by the lookout on the drawbridge. But now a new problem arose. Lance had progressed as far as he could on the downward slope of the cable and could easily make out the platform about fifty feet ahead, but the guy wire from this point angled sharply upward. Lance was not at all sure he could scale this section without slipping helplessly backward. Lance strained as he placed one hand over the other while pushing with his legs, his feet entwined around the cable.

Slowly Lance struggled closer and closer to the platform. His arms and legs ached from the exertion. He hesitated and again allowed the belt to take his weight, but as soon as he relaxed he felt himself slipping backward. He grasped the cable with all his might, stopping his descent. There would be no more rest now, and the last twenty feet were the steepest yet. Lance was so close to the other side, and yet the distance seemed impossible. His muscles screamed at him that they could go no farther. He looked below him. If he released himself from the cable here, he would face at least a forty-foot drop as the mountainside sloped sharply downward. Lance yearned to release his grip and to allow himself to slide back down the cable, but he could not give up so close to his goal. With all his might he pulled himself upward and forward. He wanted to rest, but the effort to hold himself where he was would soon drain his strength. He gave another mighty pull that brought him yet closer. Sweat fell from his brow in huge droplets and his breath grated against his chest as he pulled again and then again. Suddenly the belt snapped and Lance plunged into the ravine.

◆

Despite getting just a few hours of sleep, Rob had stirred at first light. He had orchestrated the placement of the posts at exactly the spots where he wanted them. He had made a call to the K-9 division, and a team would be on the ground within an hour. Working methodically, he had drawn the web around the fugitive ever tighter until at last there would be nowhere for him to run. That is if he could still run. The guy would be enduring temperatures that dipped toward the freezing point and terrain fraught with pitfalls, including the wildlife that roamed these woods. What's more, he hadn't had food for more than sixty hours and had probably gotten little sleep. Rob gave him a fifty-fifty chance of surviving. If he was killed, chances were they would never find his remains. Rob thought idly that if that were the way things turned out, he might dedicate a few vacation days to seeing if he could find the money.

He pondered all of this as he sipped his third cup of coffee and chewed on a sandwich. He had been on lots of stakeouts and knew there was little more he could do but wait. Still, he insisted on hourly reports from all his teams, including the one at the drawbridge. But so far he had heard nothing out of the ordinary.

Rob made a number of phone calls to his detachment, reporting to his superiors and ensuring that all loose ends had been covered on this case and on several others he was leading. He had just finished one such report when his phone rang. His heart quickened. This could be the news he had been waiting for.

"Passaglia," he answered crisply.

"Captain Passaglia," came the voice on the other end, "it's Matt Ross."

Rob rolled his eyes. Ross, a crime reporter for the *Vancouver Sun*, was an ever-present thorn in his side.

"Sorry, Matt. No time to talk now."

"Where are you?" Matt asked, ignoring the brush-off. "I've been looking all over for you. Any news on the Knight thing?"

"Nope. Sorry, nothing new."

"I heard there was something happening up in Squamish. The local hubbub is that Knight was sighted there. Is that true?"

"Come on, Matt. You know I can't confirm or deny that!" The last thing Rob wanted was for the press to get wind of the manhunt and to descend en masse on his turf, messing up his operation. He had been lucky so far. His command post had been set up far enough into the wilderness that few, if any, people living around the lake knew of its existence.

"So you're saying he's not in the Squamish area? From what I've learned, this Knight is a total amateur. What I've got so far is that he's never been in trouble with the law before, decides to rob a bank one day, takes off into the woods, and seems to have disappeared without a trace, and you guys haven't made any headway since this went down. Is that pretty much it?"

"All except for the part about us not making headway."

"All right. Now we're talking! What do you have?"

"What I have is no further comment, Matt. I'm hanging up now."

He quickly pressed disconnect and left his trailer for Sergeant Palmer's.

He glanced at his watch as he entered Palmer's trailer. It was already approaching 11 a.m., just about time for the hourly reports.

"Did all units report in last hour?" Rob asked.

"Yes, sir, except for the one on the south bank," Palmer said. "Still nothing to report, Captain. Should I call the south bank team and get a status report?"

Rob thought for a moment. "No. Let's maintain radio silence as much as possible. We don't want to inadvertently alert Knight to our presence, and we certainly don't want the press getting wind of what we're doing here."

"True enough, sir." Suddenly there was a crackle on the radio. "That should be the south bank team now."

⋯ ⋅ ∘ ∘ ●●◆●●● ∘ ∘ ⋅ ⋯

Lance awoke, his back aching severely. He looked up and spotted the cable about fifteen feet above his head. Things had happened so quickly that Lance wasn't sure how he had ended up lying tangled in a shrub. He gingerly sat up. His back pained him and his arms ached. He stung from cuts and scrapes on his face and limbs. He peered around. He had obviously fallen from the cable to the shrub perched on a small ledge. Two feet to his left was a bottomless ravine.

Oh no, the money! Lance thought as he leaned over the ravine. He quickly turned, looking for any sign of the briefcase. He leaned further out over the cliff and there it was. Just about five feet below him sat the briefcase no worse for wear, dangling from the belt still around the handle and tangled in some brush clinging to the side of the ravine.

Lance scrambled out of the bush and clambered over to the ledge where the briefcase sat. Clinging to the rock, he slowly lowered himself over the ledge. With one small foothold and one hand holding the rock above, he carefully reached down. If he dislodged the briefcase it would fall into the ravine. He had no idea how he could climb down if it fell, and besides money would be scattered all over creation. Finally he grasped the handle and pulled himself and the briefcase back onto the ledge. Lance breathed a sigh of relief.

He got to his feet and climbed up to more level ground. He began to walk down the trail that clung to the edge of the gorge. The terrain was much more rugged than on the opposite side, so Lance was forced to risk staying on the trail. He made good time as the trail descended to the rapidly flowing river at the bottom of the gorge. The path skirted the river where the terrain allowed but ascended from the valley for long stretches too. At times Lance wondered if he had lost the river completely.

Suddenly he heard the muffled sound of conversation. He quickly ducked beneath a spruce tree whose low branches concealed him from the path. The voices grew louder and then two police officers appeared after coming around a bend in the path. One of them held a radio in his hand. He was long and lean and was moving along the trail with long strides.

"We've been following this path all morning, sir, and there are no tracks at all," he said into the radio.

The officer listened to the squawk on the radio for a few seconds and replied, "Okay, will do, sir. Over!"

"What did he say?" asked the other officer, who was middle aged and slightly more rotund than police regulations normally allowed.

"He wants us to go all the way up to the drawbridge and then head back."

Lance's mind raced to the trail he had been on. He hadn't been especially careful to hide his tracks, and he knew they would surely find signs of his presence and alert their commander to what they had found.

"How far's that?" the older man asked.

"It's about three miles, mostly uphill."

"No fucking way. I've been climbing this godforsaken mountain for hours. It's obvious he's not on this trail. Reports say he was sighted on the opposite side of the gorge. Why are we even here? How the hell could he get over here? I don't mind coming up here and helping out you canucks with your problems once in a while, but I've busted my ass enough."

"That detective who's come down here from Vancouver wants this thing done right," his partner replied. "He's nothing if not thorough. Even though the trackers have this guy's trail on the other side of the river, he wants this side searched too. If we turn around now he'll know we didn't go all the way up."

"Like hell he will. I'm going to go back to the spot at the top of the waterfall and have a little nap. If you want to go on, go ahead. I'll wait for you there."

"You know I haven't been trained in tracking."

"It's up to you either way," the other officer said with a shrug. "I've climbed my last step today." With that, he spun around and headed down. The other officer hesitated for a moment and then followed him back down the trail.

Lance sighed in relief. Now all he had to do was track the trackers and they would lead him out of the wilderness. He waited for ten minutes and then slowly followed the officers down the trail. Lance was confident he was going the right way, encouraged by the odd scuff mark or footprint. Now the trail descended steeply, and the sound of rushing water grew steadily louder.

This must be the waterfall they talked about, Lance thought. He remembered that the officers planned to rest there for a while, and not wanting to stumble upon them, he left the path and found a place thick in the bush where he was well concealed. Lance waited patiently but eventually drifted off to sleep.

When he awoke, the sun was shining in his eyes, and his arm and leg muscles were still feeling stiff from the fall and the gargantuan efforts he had made on the zip line that morning. He rose slowly, wondering if he could take another step. Lance gazed at the sky, and its color told him that it was late afternoon. He must have slept for several hours. Lance started back down the trail, confident that the policemen were long gone from their resting place at the top of the falls. Still, as the sound of the falls increased, his caution grew and his pace slowed. Finally the trail reached a flat, rocky bluff, and just beyond that he spied the water churning over a precipice. From the edge of the clearing Lance searched for any signs of the officers.

Finally satisfied, he came out into the open and looked for signs of the trackers having been there. Near the edge of the river he saw the tread marks from the officers' boots. It looked as if they had splashed water, possibly getting a drink from the stream, and then stepped on the wet rock. The water had long since dried, leaving just the image of the boot prints behind. Lance surmised that it had been at least an hour since these tracks were left. He smiled to himself. He was tracking the trackers, and if he did it right they would guide him to his escape.

Lance followed the path, which led steeply downhill toward the sound of cascading water off to his left. That the officers had reached the point they had on foot meant Lance was only hours away from leaving the wilderness. He quickened his pace as he sensed that his third night in the woods—or was it his fourth?—was coming quickly. Darkness had fallen by the time he emerged from the narrow trail and reached a clearing where a small parking area was located. The area was circular and surrounded by tall trees with a gravel exit road at the far end. The lot was empty.

Lance crossed the parking area and continued along the deserted road in the darkness. He kept his ear tuned for the sound of a vehicle, but for the next two hours he strode along the gravel road undisturbed, his briefcase swinging at his side. His heart quickened and his pace slowed. When he caught a glimpse of lamp posts shining far in the distance, it was his first sight of civilization since he had plunged into the ravine at the golf course in Squamish three days before.

He approached the area carefully, staying in the shadows as much as possible. As he got closer he could see a much larger parking lot on the far side of a paved road. In the lot were three trailers with lights glowing in most of them. Near them, were a number of police vehicles. Lance had stumbled onto the makeshift staging area for the search that was underway for him. Beyond the parking lot Lance thought he could make out the dark waters of a rather large lake. He skirted the encampment and came out on a road leading down to the lake. About a mile from the police encampment he came upon a few rows of cabins nestled between the lake and the paved road heading north and south.

Lance crossed the road and ducked into the trees, giving the cabins a wide berth. He scurried along a gravel road hugging the shore of the lake for another quarter-mile and passed quietly between two darkened cabins. He found a stand of bushes close to the lake, squatted low in their cover, and waited. One by one lights from the cabins were doused until finally except for the distant street lamps all was in darkness. Lance moved out from the bushes down to the beach. He passed several piers until he came to one where an aluminum rowboat with a small motor on the back was tied up. He glanced around furtively, and summoning his courage, he crept onto the pier toward the boat. He bent low and squinted into it. He loosened the rope from the post and scrambled into the boat. He opened the gas can lid and shook the can. Lance smiled with satisfaction. It sounded like plenty of fuel remained. He picked up the oars and rowed far out into the lake before tugging on the cord to start the motor. He pulled once and the motor sputtered. He pulled a second and a third time with no better results. To his relief the motor whined to life after the fourth tug.

Lance idled far out into the water before he opened the throttle and turned southward toward a faint glimmer of light reflecting off the water far off in the distance.

Once again Lance was gambling—gambling that he could reach the distant lights before the rowboat owner raised the alarm, gambling that the gas in the tank would not run out and leave him stranded in the middle of this huge lake, and gambling that he would somehow weave his way through all the pitfalls before him to a new life.

CHAPTER 10

Rob sat at a desk in one of the trailers in the staging area twenty-five miles north of the small community of Harrison. The trailer housed his bedroom and his office, which was next to a meeting room with a large map of the area. The light stands illuminated the area, which stood in stark contrast with the dark forest that surrounded it. Rob had made a quick trip to Vancouver to deal with several pressing issues and had driven back to the encampment in the dark. He had kept in close contact with the search teams pursuing Lance Knight.

Tracking the fugitive had been difficult. He had led police on a chase through extremely wild country, some of it too rough for the dogs to follow the scent. The teams often had to retrace their steps to make sure they did not lose the trail. The rocky landscape had yielded precious few signs. Hopes had risen with the sighting of the fugitive on the logging road. However, he had disappeared once again despite the establishment of a containment zone around the area. The following morning the trackers had stumbled upon the hot pool about two hours after he had left.

Despite the difficulties and setbacks, the search team had established that Lance's direction of travel would eventually lead him directly to the long, glacier-fed Harrison Lake. As a result, Rob decided to relocate the team's base of operations to the spot on the west side of the lake.

With the coming of the weekend, the search had been expanded, and despite his objections the search force had called in US tracking experts to help. About thirty officers were now prowling the woods in an effort to arrest the fugitive. Rob was still in charge of a number of these teams, but now a second task force had been established. Coordinating their efforts was a headache. Teams had fanned out in the sectors to the west of Harrison Lake and reported in to the command center every hour. They operated from first light until dark. Despite all that effort, there were no positive signs. Rob knew tomorrow would be crucial. They would have to nab this guy by then. If they didn't, it meant he had probably not survived or had somehow managed to escape the containment zone.

Rob was organizing the next day of the search. All trails and roads on the map were highlighted, and he used pins and sticky notes to plan the activities of each team in his charge. Once again he had been impressed by Lance's ability to adapt and to innovate. Rob's mouth was agape when he heard about the hot pool Lance had constructed. If he was going to capture this guy, he would have to be more thorough than ever before.

He checked his plans one last time and gave a loud yawn. It was late and tomorrow would be yet another long day. Rob doused the light and climbed into bed unaware that the man he sought was in an aluminum rowboat less than two kilometers away.

The next morning the alarm rang at four-thirty, an hour and a half before first light. Rob shaved and had a light breakfast before heading to the rallying point. He spent the next half-hour debriefing the teams on their areas of search. Finally he dispatched the teams so they would be at their designated starting points by first light. Rob would now be receiving and reacting to the reports the teams called in.

At 10:30 a.m. Rob was at his desk sipping a cup of coffee when an RCMP officer entered the trailer.

"Sir," he said, "we just received a complaint from one of the cabin owners down the road that his rowboat has gone missing."

Rob stared at the officer. "Shit!" he finally shouted. "That's got to be him. How did he get by our posts? He must have traveled half the night." He rose from the desk and began pacing. "All right," he said, turning to the officer. "Call all the search teams back. Before we break up the search I want the teams reassigned to canvas all hotels in the area."

"Excuse me, sir! Did you say call all the search teams back? How can you be sure he was the one who stole that boat? It might have been some local hooligan. You're going to call off the search based on one missing boat?"

"It was him. I'm getting to know this guy all too well, and I promise you I'm gonna nail his ass. Make the call. Task force B can continue the search on the trail," Rob said over his shoulder as he turned to leave.

"Where are you going?" the officer asked, following him from the trailer.

"Harrison," Rob responded as he climbed into his vehicle. "Call the teams back in. I'll be back in two hours, and I want my team assembled here by then."

Rob sped into town armed with a picture of the fugitive and began asking around. It did not take him long to find a number of people who had seen what they described as a hobo who had shown up in town early that morning. When shown the photo, however, they could not say for sure it was Lance. After cruising the community without any sight of the fugitive, Rob headed back to the command center.

By the time he returned, most of the teams had reassembled, curious about the morning's developments. Others were expected within the next hour or so. Sergeant Palmer looked up as Rob entered the command post.

"Sir, the team on the south side of the river just called in. They picked up Knight's tracks and followed them to a rappel line about a kilometer this side of the drawbridge," he said.

"Rappel line?" Rob fumed. "When the hell was someone going to tell me about a rappel line?"

Palmer flushed. "It seems the locals didn't bother mentioning it since they figured it was impossible to use without the proper equipment."

Rob bit his tongue. He posted a large map on the bulletin board and called the officers to attention. "Okay, men," he said. "You no doubt have heard we have evidence that the fugitive slipped by us during the night. I just got back from Harrison and confirmed the sighting of a stranger in town. We can't confirm it was Knight, but we will proceed on the theory that it was. He can't be far ahead of us, so we're going to do a sweep of the nearby communities. This guy has been in the woods for three days without food or shelter. He looks like shit from what they said in town, and I'm sure he feels like shit. I want every hotel, motel, and restaurant searched. Sergeant Palmer, you will talk to everyone operating a taxi, a bus, or any other mode of transportation you can think of to ask them if they picked up anyone matching his description. We'll concentrate the search here."

He turned and pointed to Abbotsford on the map. Abbotsford was the largest community in the area with a population of almost 150,000.

"It's a ten-minute drive to the border, and he's likely to attempt to cross," Rob said as he turned back to face his men.

"Excuse me," one of them said. "That's not what I was called up here to do."

Rob glared at the man, who spoke with a slight American accent. "You were assigned to this search team, and until you are reassigned you will do as you're asked," Rob said in an acid tone. Turning to the rest of the group, he issued his instructions. "Team one, you take Agassiz; two, you're going to take Hope; three, Chilliwack ..." Rob sent the bulk of the force to Abbotsford. Squad cars began pulling out of the parking lot onto the paved road, and within minutes the command center was deserted. Rob picked up the phone and made arrangements for Doug to meet him in Abbotsford. He was sure Lance would be heading there.

· · • •••◆••••· ·

The motor whirred steadily throughout the night. Occasionally Lance shook the tank to satisfy himself that he still had enough fuel to reach the distant shore. He kept his eyes peeled, for he knew that logs floating on the surface of these mountain lakes could sink or tip a craft of this size. Lance could not see such obstructions in the dark, but if he was to make the small town at the end of this lake by first light he could not slacken his pace.

Finally after several hours, the blackness changed to a deep purple. Lance shook the tank, listened to the slosh of the fuel, and swung the bow toward the shore. Just a little fuel remained, and he would not fare well trying to swim in the cold lake. Lance once more headed toward the lights that began to rise from the surface of the water as he drew closer to shore. At any moment he expected the motor to sputter and die, but it droned on as the sky continued to lighten.

The motor sputtered and died just as Lance thought he might reach the small town that was now clearly visible beneath the pale blue sky. He immediately picked up the oar and headed for a treed area between the cabins, which were showing signs of life. He was keenly aware that the missing rowboat might already have been reported. The best he could hope for was another hour before the authorities realized he might have slipped by them during the night.

Lance quickly beached the boat, dragging it as far into the trees as he could. He uncoupled the gas tank and headed for the road with the tank in one hand and his briefcase in the other. He didn't plan to return for the boat, but he thought his chances of getting a ride would improve if he appeared to be a boater who had run out of gas. Once on the road, Lance placed the briefcase in the grass close to the trees and held the red gas tank as conspicuously as possible. He stuck out his thumb when the first vehicle came along, and sure enough, the driver of the two-tone blue pickup pulled over for him. Lance darted back and picked up his briefcase, swinging the gas tank into the box before climbing into the cab.

"You were out pretty early this morning," the older gentleman said with a smile. "How did you make out?"

"This is the best part of the day," Lance said. "I thought I would get in a couple hours of fishing before I headed in to work. I got skunked this morning, though, and worst of all I ran out of gas. Why didn't I check the tank before I headed out? I'm always doing stuff like this."

The man laughed. "Best-laid plans, eh? Here's hoping the rest of your day goes better."

"Thanks. Just drop me off at that first gas station," he said as they pulled into town.

"No problem. Look, I can take you back to the boat if you want. I've got some time on my hands." the man said as he signaled to turn into the gas station.

"No, no. I'll just call my wife. She'll be up now," Lance lied. "She can pick up the tank here. Besides, I have to head in to work." He held up the briefcase. "Hey, thanks for the lift." Lance hurried out of the cab, reached in the box for the gas tank, and turned toward the pumps before the Good Samaritan could protest.

The gentleman sat with a puzzled expression on his face. *There was definitely something off about that story,* he thought. *Who goes to work dressed the way he is? Unshaven! Unkempt! Not to mention dirty and with a definite scent of BO.* Finally he shrugged and pulled back onto the road.

Lance walked slowly toward the entrance to the gas station, feigning a call on his dead cell phone while listening for the vehicle to pull away. Once the man had left, Lance quickly turned away as the attendant was about to come out to assist him.

Lance took the first side road he saw. Even at this time of the morning there were people in the commercial section of town, mostly store owners preparing to open for the day. He needed to head for a quieter part of town; the fewer people seeing him, the better. He turned right on the next street he found. As Lance passed a still-unopened jewelry store, he caught his reflection on a large mirror inside. He stopped and stared. There facing him stood the most abject derelict he could imagine. His clothes were dirty and ripped from three straight days of bushwhacking. Long, graying stubble grew from his face and neck, and what made all of this stand out in weirdness was the briefcase that dangled at his side and the gas tank in his other hand. No wonder the guy who picked him up looked at him so strangely. His appearance told Lance he needed to get away from here as soon as possible. Just the sight of him would raise suspicion. No one who saw him would forget him, and the police could be on their way this minute. Lance hurried away from the store.

He walked two blocks and entered a residential area. Lance quickly dropped the gas tank next to two garbage cans and continued on without looking back. He turned left at an intersection and hurried toward what he assumed might be the town's main thoroughfare two blocks ahead. The traffic on that street was already growing.

When he arrived at the street Lance spied a phone booth outside of a small restaurant that appeared to be doing a brisk breakfast business. He could call a taxi, but how was he going to do that? Even though he carried hundreds of thousands of dollars, he had no change and no credit card that he dared use.

Lance walked over to the booth and picked up the phone book. He flipped through the Yellow Pages and found the taxi section. As he feared, there was no taxi service in the small town of Harrison. The closest taxi company was in Agassiz, which Lance guessed was about ten minutes away. He was so close to having eluded the police, and now here he was stuck at the door to freedom. He needed to get out of here and to get out immediately.

Lance looked at the restaurant. He could go in there and get change, but he imagined all eyes turning toward him as he entered. Then he had an idea.

He quickly crossed the road and headed for the restaurant, but rather than enter it, he placed his briefcase on the sidewalk by the entrance and sat on it. As the first group left the restaurant, he asked, "Could you spare a bit of change?" A man threw him a dollar coin. This was perfect. Lance did not want to be noticed because he would immediately arouse suspicion. But people naturally avoided eye contact with street beggars, and that's exactly what he seemed to be. Lance waited another minute or so and held out his hand each time someone left or entered the restaurant. Most people ignored him, but in just a few minutes he had plenty of change for a phone call.

He hurried to the phone booth, quickly found the number of the Agassiz taxi company, and dialed.

"Chizzum Taxi," a woman responded after a few rings.

"Look," Lance said, "I'm in Harrison and I desperately need to get to Chilliwack."

"I'm sorry, sir. We don't serve that area."

"Please, ma'am, ask one of your drivers. You can tell him that whatever the fare would be, I'll double it."

There was a long pause. "Please hold," the lady said with a sigh.

Lance waited, praying that the change he had fed into the phone would be enough to get this settled.

"I have a driver who says he'll come, sir, but it will be a hundred dollars."

Lance expelled a breath of air in relief. "That's fine," he said. "Tell him there's an extra fifty in it if he can be here in ten minutes."

"All right. I'll tell him. Address?"

"It's 975 Harrison Highway," Lance lied. "It's kind of hard to spot, so just tell him to stop in front of the 'Entering Harrison' sign on the outskirts of town and I'll watch for him." Lance hoped there actually was an "Entering Harrison" sign.

"I'll tell him. Thank you, sir."

Lance hung up and hurriedly crossed the street, eager to escape any curious eyes that might be watching him from the restaurant. He soon was one block off the busy main road. Lance looked around and could see no one, so he turned south and walked down a residential street that paralleled the highway. This street ended after a few blocks, and Lance again found himself on the highway. On his side of the road were cornfields now reduced to stubble. On the other side were residences that abutted a small, tree-covered mountain. Lance walked in a ditch next to the cornfields, keeping himself out of sight as much as possible. Within five minutes he found what he was after. On the side of the road was a large wooden sign with a wooden sculpture of a Sasquatch. The sign read simply: "Welcome to Harrison." This was perfect. He would wait for the taxi here.

Lance looked around. He stood at the edge of a cornfield. There was a farmhouse maybe a quarter-mile to the south. To the north he could see rows of houses on the outskirts of the hamlet. On the opposite side of the road were a number of houses with expansive yards. Lance soon grew impatient. He quickly crossed the road and ducked between two treed yards without fences. He made his way up the mountain in back until he found a spot above the houses where he had a clear view of the road below him but still would be practically invisible. Lance sat on a large boulder and waited, his eyes constantly scanning the road from which his taxi would be coming.

It seemed like an eternity before he finally saw the taxi speeding down the road in the distance. Twice before he had started down from his perch before realizing that an approaching vehicle was not the taxi. But now he was certain, and he scrambled down the side of the rock as quickly as he could go without breaking his neck.

By the time he reached the highway, though, the taxi had passed by, heading into town. Lance was exasperated, but within a minute he spied the cab. The driver had made a U-turn and was headed toward him. Lance waved his hand and the turn signal came on. The taxi stopped and Lance climbed in the back.

A large, dark-complected man frowned at him from the front. "That's $150," the taxi driver said, doubting the man in the back seat had two coins to rub together.

"Here's a hundred," Lance said. "The fifty was for ten minutes. You took twelve."

Without another word the man took the money, turned, put the car in gear, and sped off. Within five minutes Lance was sleeping soundly in the back seat. Half an hour later as the taxi approached Chilliwack, he was awakened by the driver's voice. "Where would you like to go?" the man asked.

Lance stirred and when his head finally cleared, he said, "Take me to a hotel. Not too expensive."

Ten minutes later the taxi pulled in front of a small hotel near the center of town. Lance grabbed his briefcase and got out. He stood watching as the taxi sped away, and when it had disappeared he walked away from the hotel. He needed to make following him as difficult as possible. Lance was still groggy, but he had to cover as much ground as he could before the police spread their dragnet and caught him in it.

He guessed it was nine or ten in the morning. At some point during his long trek his watch had stopped working. Lance wandered toward a park with a pond at its center. On a bench sat a couple of old-timers watching ducks swim on the pond.

Lance approached the two men. "Excuse me," he said. "Would either of you know where the bus station is in town?"

The two men looked up and then glanced at each other. "Sure," one of them finally said. "Just take that road behind you. Head up the hill about four blocks, turn left on Veddar Street, and it's on the very next block."

"You're in luck," the man behind the counter at the station said. "The Abbotsford bus is leaving in five minutes. If you hurry you can catch it."

The deeper into the urban sprawl Lance moved, the safer he felt. He had gone from the hamlet of Harrison to the small city of Chilliwack and now was headed to Abbotsford, a city of more than one hundred thousand. An even greater advantage to Abbotsford was that it sat just miles from the US border. Lance paid for his ticket and climbed on the bus.

Lance again drifted into a deep sleep almost the minute the bus left the station. It was no wonder, for he had spent most of the previous night on Harrison Lake in the rowboat, and the night before he was in the depths of the forest, shivering next to a tree. He awoke a half-hour after departure to find the bus was making its way along a busy street in Abbotsford. Lance sat up and surveyed his surroundings. The street had many stores on either side. Up ahead a large sign advertised what seemed like a high-end hotel. Lance immediately scooped up the briefcase and headed toward the front of the bus.

He waited there, studying the hotel as the bus sped past it. Two blocks later the bus stopped at a red light and Lance approached the driver.

"I live quite close to here," Lance said. "Could I get off now? It would save me some time."

The driver turned and scowled. "We're not supposed to do this," he said, shaking his head, but he reached for the lever and the bus door opened. Lance scrambled off the bus onto the sidewalk and immediately headed back toward the hotel.

Several minutes later Lance was soaking in the now-muddied waters of the bathtub in his hotel suite. Dried needles, grass, and a leaf or two floated on the water. He had run the bath as soon as he had gotten to his room. Lance wanted the water as hot as he could stand it, especially after the ordeal of the last week. He wasn't sure he would feel warm ever again. Once the tub was filled, he eased himself into it and lay there nearly comatose from exhaustion. He spent the next hour in that position, allowing the dirt and the grime to soak off of him. Finally he stirred and showered and shaved, using the razor from the courtesy kit he had gotten at the front desk.

There was a knock at the door. Lance immediately tensed. Finally he summoned the courage to approach the door. He looked through the sight glass. It was a hotel busboy. Lance frowned and opened the door.

"Your burger, sir, and the T-shirt you asked for from the gift shop."

"Oh, right," Lance said, taking the items. His heart stopped pounding. He had completely forgotten about the order he had placed when he checked in.

Over the next few hours, Lance shopped at retail businesses on the street where the hotel was located. He began by buying shirts, blue jeans, a jacket, underwear, and socks. He changed into one of the outfits at the store, leaving the wide-eyed clerk with a handful of worn and torn pants, a shirt, and a coat in her arms. He then found a sports store where he bought a bicycle and a fluorescent orange-and-red riding outfit complete with racing helmet and riding shoes.

He also purchased a small backpack and had the bike outfitted with a rear rack that included storage pouches. Just a few minutes later, Lance abandoned the briefcase in a back alley, and as he rode along the street on his new bike, the backpack bulged with the money he had crammed into it.

He also found a stylist's shop that could get him in within a half-hour. When the girl had finished with her last customer, she told Lance, "I'm ready for you now, sir. This way, please."

When he was seated, she asked, "So what can I do for you today?"

This did not look like a standard barbershop, and Lance hesitated to ask for a simple haircut. "Go nuts," he heard himself say. "I'd like something different."

The girl appraised him thoughtfully. "I think I know just the thing," she said. She explained what she had in mind, and an hour later Lance walked out of the shop as a blond with darker highlights and a moderate spike on top.

He planned to make a few more purchases, but they could wait. Right now Lance's stomach was aching. He needed a more substantial meal than the burger he had eaten that morning, and just ahead on the left he saw what looked like a nice restaurant.

Lance ordered a porterhouse steak with all the fixings. After eating, Lance cycled back to the hotel. The meal had been excellent and he felt a little groggy. Perhaps he would have another nap before completing his preparations.

Lance pedaled to the hotel entrance and chained his bike to a signpost with the lock he had purchased at the bike store. He strode into the lobby and made for the bank of elevators past the reception area.

"He registered this morning at 9:35," the clerk was saying to two men dressed casually in plaid shirts and blue jeans.

"Can you describe him, ma'am?" Rob asked.

"Well, he seemed quite disheveled to me. To be honest, at first I thought he was ... well, a bum, but then he paid cash." Lance heard the reply as he angled away from the desk and the elevators toward the restaurant to the left.

"For one, sir?" an attractive girl asked him.

"Uh, yes please," Lance said, glancing back to the desk. "Uh, could I have this table?" He pointed to a small table close to the entrance of the restaurant that was partially concealed by a plant mounted on an ornate post.

"Certainly, sir. Have a seat."

"Just bring me an orange juice, please. That's all I'll need," Lance said, trying without success to keep the urgency from his voice.

Lance's heart was racing. He could see a porter approach the two men, and the three of them walked toward the elevator out of his view. How was it possible that they could be so close on his trail? Was it just dumb luck or was someone in his head guessing his moves before he made them?

Now what was he going to do? Lance looked toward the entrance and saw two men dressed casually, much like the two who had been at the desk. They stood away from the entrance in a designated smoking area, each with a cigarette. They were doing their best to look laid-back, but their alertness said otherwise. Lance had barely noticed them when he rode up, but now he eyed them suspiciously. Hadn't he seen one of them before? He thought hard and then it hit him. This was one of the two men he had overheard talking along the trail that led to the zip line—the plump officer who had refused to hike the trail. Lance's biking gear had obviously thrown off the police. He wanted to get up, walk to his bike, and ride off, but the two men out front had him frozen in fear.

Lance saw a vehicle pull up outside. The two men strode to the passenger-side window and conferred with a man inside. As they did this, Lance made his move. He threw some change on the table and strode quickly toward the exit, leaving his glass of orange juice half finished. The man in the passenger seat motioned to the driver and the car sped off. Once he reached the exit, Lance put on his sunglasses and glanced in the direction the car had taken. The car was parked next to the hotel about twenty-five yards past the entrance, and the two occupants were now striding toward him and the two who had been near the entrance. Lance's heart leapt in his chest, and he quickly turned away from the men toward his bike chained to the signpost. Lance squatted as low as he could, keeping his back to the men as he struggled to unlock the chain. Finally it came loose, and Lance quickly wound the chain around the frame and mounted the bike.

"Stop," he heard one of the men command from just behind him. Lance's heart pounded as he slowly turned to face the man.

"Your key," the man said, pointing. "You don't want to lose that."

"Oh, thank you," Lance mumbled. He collected the key and rode off.

Lance pedaled as fast as he could away from the hotel, his heart pounding. Before he left the hotel driveway, a police cruiser passed by on the street, and he encountered yet another shortly after he turned left onto the street. As this one passed, the officer in the passenger seat seemed to study him hard. Lance feigned a relaxed expression and turned his head away from the cruiser. He made a right into a street-side mall, and as he did he noticed that the cruiser he had just passed had moved into the left lane and was about to make a U-turn. As soon as Lance was out of sight of the cruiser, he pedaled as hard as he could through the parking lot. He took a narrow lane between stores that came out onto a graveled alley that ran in back of the stores. He sped along the alley, and when he saw a deep ditch with thick underbrush under a few tall trees on the opposite side of the alley, he careened into the brush without diminishing his speed. His momentum carried him deep into the shrubs before he toppled to the ground. Breathing heavily, Lance pulled the bike toward him until he was sure it could not be spotted. He soon heard the rumble of tires moving in the alley above, but Lance kept his head low, resisting the urge to take a peak to verify if it was the police cruiser.

As his panting slowed, Lance thought. This city seemed to be swarming with police. They must have discovered the missing boat on Harrison Lake and anticipated his move here. They were searching hotels, and by now hotels had been advised to report any suspicious persons seeking rooms. With this kind of pressure he would not last long on the loose. He had to find someplace to lay low until the search grew less intense.

Then he remembered. Wasn't Abbotsford where Jen had said she lived? She had scribbled her phone number and address on a piece of paper and had handed it to him while they were at the campsite. He had glanced at it and had slipped it in his pocket but had not noted it.

Lance edged his way up toward the alley and poked his head out of the grass growing at the side. He looked both ways and seeing nothing he ran down the alley and into the lane toward the street-side mall. He made it into the mall and headed toward the biggest store in the complex, a grocery store. No doubt the police would still be in the area, trying to catch sight of him. Lance reached the store and took stock of his surroundings. Close to the entrance he spotted a bank of phones. He strolled over and opened up the phone book tethered to a booth. He turned to the R section and found several entries for Robinson. One entry read: "Robinson M: 384 Andersol Avenue." That was it. There was no sense calling Jen. At this hour she would be at work and Micky would be at school. He turned into the store and moved up and down the aisles. Lance thanked his lucky stars when he found a city map in the stationery department. He picked up a bottle of water and a small bag of apples and headed for the beauty department. To his relief the store carried the same tanning spray he had used while at the campsite when he met Jen. He picked up a can and headed for the till.

He made his purchase and headed for the front of the store. Lance watched a corner bus stop through the store windows. He waited near the entrance, occasionally checking a nonexistent watch and peering back and forth as if waiting for a ride. He waited twenty minutes before he saw a bus approach the stop. During that time he had seen at least a half-dozen cruisers go by. Lance left the store and headed at a trot to the bus stop.

Once on the bus, he paused beside the driver. He was an older man and his face wore a permanent scowl.

"I need to get to Andersol Avenue," Lance said.

"Which block?" the driver asked without turning to face him.

"Three hundred block," Lance answered.

The driver thought for a few seconds and said, "I'll tell you when it's your stop. You'll need to transfer to bus eleven. Just give the driver your address. He passes within a block of there."

"Thanks," Lance said. He sat beside an older lady near the front of the bus.

About fifteen minutes later the driver pulled over and turned toward him. "This is your stop," he said. "Just wait at the stop across this street. The bus should be coming by in about five minutes."

Lance thanked him and disembarked. He quickly crossed the street to the bus stop and waited. This was a residential area with houses dating from the late nineties. They all had siding in pastel shades as had been the style about twenty years ago.

It was more like ten minutes before the bus arrived, but to Lance it seemed like two hours. He had never felt more exposed. He prayed that no police cruiser would come by while he waited. To his great relief, he spied the bus approaching and scrambled aboard when it stopped in front of him.

"Andersol, three hundred block," Lance said as he mounted the two steps toward the driver.

The driver smiled and nodded. "Have a seat. I'll let you know." Lance wasn't at all sure how long it took to get to his stop. He drifted off once more. Finally the driver roused him. "This is your stop," he said. "Andersol is the next block over." He pointed.

Lance stepped down from the bus and headed toward a gas station near the bus stop. In the bathroom he took out the spray can and got to work. After ten minutes, Lance studied his appearance. He thought he looked slightly ridiculous with his new blond spiked hair and his darkened skin, but there was nothing he could do about that now. He pulled the pants and shirt he had purchased earlier out of the backpack and changed out of the bike gear then he left the bathroom and headed for Andersol.

The houses on Andersol were much newer than those near the bus stop. They were larger too. Each one had an attached two-car garage in front. Lance strolled down the street until he spotted number 384. It was a beige house with white trim. The lawn and shrubbery were neatly appointed. Lance did not stop at the house. It was still too early for anyone to be at home. Instead he turned into a small park. There were a few trees in the park, and Lance sat down, leaning against one of them. Once again he was out like a light.

When at last he awoke, the sky was darkening. Lance got up and brushed off and straightened his clothing. He turned nervously toward the house. It had been more than a few weeks since he had seen Jen. He was showing up unannounced and had no idea how she would react. But he was desperate and so he strode across the street.

He rang the bell and waited, almost hoping no one would be home. But he heard the sound of steps approaching the door. It swung open and there was Jen. Her expression was blank for an instant and then she laughed.

"Rav," she said, "is that you?"

"Yeah, it's me," Lance said. "I thought I'd go for a new look. What do you think?" he asked, running his fingers through his hair.

She looked at him for a second and shrugged. "I didn't expect to see you again, but this is wonderful," she said. "Come in!"

Lance followed her into the living room. "Micky," Jen called, "you'll never guess who's come to see us." She turned back to Lance and studied him. "My God, what happened to you?" she asked. "You look awful." Instantly she realized what she had said and her face reddened.

Micky rounded the corner from the hallway, her head tilted curiously. When she saw Lance she beamed. "Hey, Rav!"

"Hi, Micky. It's good to see you again. I missed you guys."

"Actually you're just in time for supper," Jen said, guiding him to the dining room. She pulled a plate from the cupboard and quickly set another place. The aroma of chili con carne filled the room. Jen cut slices of garlic bread and spread the meaty sauce over the bread on each of their plates. It was all Lance could do not to wolf down the food. The meal was delicious.

When they had finished, Jen pulled a box of ice cream from the freezer. She filled three bowls and covered the ice cream with sliced strawberries. This time Lance lost control. His bowl was empty before Jen and Micky had eaten a few spoonfuls. Jen raised her eyebrows, but she gave him a refill.

"What happened to you, Rav? You look like you've been run over or something," Micky said.

"Micky!" Jen said, shocked.

"No, it's okay," Lance said. "It's a long story, but the crux of it is, I got lost in the forest while doing a surveying job and I just found my way out. I hope the same thing never happens to you. It was terrifying!"

"That's awful! Jen said.

"No way!" Micky said. "How long were you lost?"

"Two days, I think. I hope I'm not being too forward by asking if I can stay over for a couple of days."

"Of course you can stay," Jen said. "I'm working for the next couple of days, but you can relax here while I'm away. It looks like you could use the rest."

"You're sure it will be all right with Mike."

Immediately the mood in the room darkened. Micky stared at her plate.

"There is no Mike," Jen said. "I'll explain tomorrow. But right now you're going to bed. I'll show you your room. You get some rest and we can talk tomorrow night." As Lance followed her down the hallway, he felt a wave of fatigue overtake him.

"Look at you," Jen said as she swung open the door to the spare bedroom. "You can barely keep your eyes open. Good night, Rav."

Lance undressed and climbed into bed. When at last he stirred, the alarm clock flashed 1:17 p.m. Had he really slept for fifteen hours? Lance showered and shaved and then went to the kitchen. He spied a note on the counter that read: "Food in fridge."

Lance opened the fridge and pulled out a plate covered with plastic wrap. On it were an omelet and fried potatoes. Lance stuck it in the microwave and ate. The omelet was filled with creamy parmesan cheese. Lance savored it to the last morsel. He filled the sink and washed his plate and utensils.

When this was done he moved to the living room and turned on the TV. He found a station that carried the local news. To his relief, there was no mention of a fugitive at large. He switched the channel and found a *Friends* episode. To his surprise he still felt tired, so he clicked off the television and returned to the bedroom. The covers were still ruffled. Lance climbed in and pulled them to his neck.

When he awoke his senses were aroused by the smell of chicken frying in a pan. He got out of bed and darted into the bathroom in the hallway. He did a quick survey of his face. A few touch-ups and he'd be fine. But first he wanted to clean up. Lance swung open the mirror to search the cabinet and then moved to the drawers. He found shaving cream and a shaver. He lathered up and shaved quickly. He dried his face and then applied a bit of tanning spray until he was satisfied.

Lance returned to the bedroom and noticed a change of clothes had been laid out on the dresser. They fit pretty well. After one more quick look at himself, he walked out to the kitchen.

"Hello, sleepy head," Jen said. "Now this looks more like the Rav I met at the campground." She nodded approvingly. "How are you feeling?"

"Thanks to you, I feel much better," Lance said, smiling.

"Micky's in the living room watching TV. Why don't you join her? Dinner will be ready in five minutes."

After supper the three of them sat on the sofa in front of the TV, and Jen put in a movie she had picked up. One of Micky's friends called and she disappeared into her bedroom, leaving the two of them alone.

"So how did you get lost?" Jen asked.

Lance thought quickly. "The boss asked me to do some staking before I headed home while he drove the others to the city. I don't know how it happened, but I became disoriented. I spent two nights in the trees. I couldn't find my truck. It's still up there somewhere. I wandered this trail and that but couldn't find my way. I didn't manage to find a road and catch a ride until the third day. I doubt the company I work for even knew I was missing."

"That must have been awful."

"It was."

Lance turned his attention back to the movie. Jen sat quietly for a minute and then said, "Mike came home last weekend. It was obvious he had been drinking, and he was in a foul mood. We had a big fight, which ended in him slapping me in the face, so I returned the favor. It wasn't the first time that kind of thing had happened. Micky was upset and crying. The next morning I resolved that I wasn't going to put her through that anymore, and I asked him to leave. He cursed and yelled but finally left."

"Do you think the two of you have a chance to fix things?"

"I'm done with all this. I'm not happy, but at least I feel more tranquil. All the stress is gone. You showed me how a gentleman treats a woman, and I won't settle for anything less now."

They talked for the next hour, paying little attention to the movie. At ten o'clock Jen called out, "Bedtime, Micky. Don't forget you have school tomorrow."

Micky came out of her bedroom, kissed Jen on the cheek, and wished Lance good night before heading back to her room. Jen restarted the movie, and this time they gave it their full attention. Lance felt a tension being this close to Jen. He tried his best to repress his feelings and focused on the movie. It ended sometime after eleven. Lance realized he had no idea what it had been about.

"Well, I guess I'll go to bed, he said, rising from the couch. Good night, Jen."

"Good night, Rav," she said.

Lance had stripped down to his shorts when the bedroom door swung open. Jen stood in the doorway, looking at him. Lance raced to her and kissed her deeply. The first time he had made love to her had been wonderful. But he had felt a strangeness after having slept with only one woman for so many years. Tonight, however, Lance was able to relax with Jen, and they made long, luxurious love. Sometime in the wee hours of the morning she left the room for her own bedroom as he slept.

Lance stayed the next night as well, repeating the routine of the day before. Jen and Micky were gone by the time he awoke. He spent the day in the house, and in the evening Jen cooked another wonderful meal. After Micky had retired for the evening, Jen sat close to Lance on the sofa and they chatted. But the conversation this evening was lighter. Jen laughed at Lance's jokes and told some of her own humorous stories. They made love again that night, and Jen returned to her own bed when they were finished.

The next evening changed everything for Lance. It was a couple of hours after supper when the doorbell rang. Lance immediately tensed as Jen moved to the door. He sat on the sofa and listened to the sound of a tense, hushed conversation that went on for five minutes. But Lance bolted for the door when he heard a loud smack and Jen's scream.

When he rounded the corner he saw Jen holding her face and heard the loud cursing of a man on the other side of the open door. Lance pushed past Jen and swung the door wide. There on the step stood Mike. Lance moved onto the step and closed the door behind him. The smell of booze assaulted his senses.

"Rav!" Mike said in surprise and then recovered. "Well, things are starting to add up. How long have you been sneaking around behind my back, you dirty son of a bitch?" he said, poking Lance hard in the chest with his index finger.

"Go away, Mike. You're not solving anything this way."

"Don't tell me to go away! This is my house," he shouted. With that, he swung wildly. Lance ducked under the punch and Mike stumbled badly. He steadied himself and took another mighty swing.

A month ago this fight might have been close, but while on the run in the backwoods Lance had acquired a wiry strength and agility he had not known since his youth. He blocked the punch easily and delivered a mighty blow to Mike's midsection that doubled him over. He pushed Mike's shoulders, sending him reeling backward. Recovering, he charged at Lance with his head down.

Surprised, Lance tried to evade him but too late. Mike bulldozed him hard against the door while Jen stood with her hands over her mouth in horror. Lance thrust his arms up and under Mike's arms, forcing him off, and then struck him hard on the chin. Mike sprawled onto the lawn. When he pulled himself up, a trickle of blood ran from the corner of his mouth. Lance moved toward him.

"Rav, don't!" Jen cried. She had moved onto the step and stood wringing her hands. Lance swung again, landing a blow to the gut, once more doubling Mike over.

Still bent over, Mike charged again. The two of them fell to the ground together and wrestled, rolling over and over on the lawn. Finally Lance gained the upper hand, climbing on top of Mike and forcing both of his hands to the ground. Mike struggled with all his might but could not escape. At this point Lance heard the sirens.

He tried to separate himself from Mike, but the harder he struggled the more Mike clung on. He was still clutching Lance's legs when the police arrived.

Fifteen minutes later, Lance sat by himself in a jail cell at police headquarters. He had no choice but to present the fake ID he had obtained in Squamish, even though he knew it had probably been compromised. The police would run the ID and would soon put two and two together and arrest him for the bank robbery along with a myriad of other offenses he had committed in the past weeks. He'd be transported to a penitentiary, and that was the last he would see of the outside for the next ten to fifteen years.

CHAPTER 11

I t was four in the morning and Lance sat on a bench in the cell. Three men shared the cell with him. One had been brought in about one in the morning reeking of alcohol, obviously intoxicated. The drunk had immediately lain on one of the cots in the cell and had fallen into a fitful sleep. He was now snoring loudly. The two others were on another cot. One was lying on the cot with his head propped up on his elbow, while the other sat next to him on the edge of the cot. They were talking quietly. They had been in the same spot since the police had deposited him in the cell late the previous last night. Lance had no interest in what they were discussing or in how they had ended up in this cell with him.

Lance was preoccupied with his own situation. The euphoria of the last few nights with Jen had slowly faded as he contemplated his predicament. He had been the object of a massive manhunt, and now he sat helpless in a jail cell, awaiting his fate. He knew that in the morning he would be confronted by the short, dark-haired detective he had spied on two occasions and would be taken back to Vancouver to stand trial for the botched bank robbery. Lance thought of the media frenzy his arrest would cause and of the disgrace his wife and his children would feel as the television cameras showed him hauled into the courthouse in cuffs. He pictured Jen and Micky sitting in front of the television with their mouths agape, feeling betrayed. They had let him into their home, unaware he was a fugitive from justice. Jen would cringe to think she had shared her bed with him.

Lance could not get these images out of his mind. When he arrived in the cell he had paced back and forth for the first two hours, haunted by them. Finally the man sitting at the edge of the cot had angrily demanded that he sit down. Lance sat on the bench and had remained there since that time. The depression that had gripped him the first few nights after the bank robbery had returned. But now it was even more intense than before if that were possible.

How could he have suffered so much for nothing? He had been tied to a tree by a crazed mountain man and left to freeze to death. He had wandered through the British Columbia rain forest lost, exhausted, and hunted by the police for four days. He'd almost fallen into a deep ravine. At any moment he could have collapsed from exhaustion. And for what?

Lance thought of the American border just kilometers from where he sat. He should have snuck across the border when he had the chance. He seemed to have been so charmed, managing to escape all his pursuers. He had walked right by them on more than one occasion. The plan he had formed on that sheet of paper had recently seemed so possible, but now it was ripped to shreds. How stupid he had been. What did he have to live for? He would be an old man by the time he had finally paid for his crime. He had destroyed his marriage and disgraced his family.

What would prison be like? He had heard so many stories. Rape! Violence! No escape except by taking the drugs that were so rampant. Rehabilitation was no option for him. His life was over. He wished he were dead.

Lance's mind was slowly clouding, and he was sinking into oblivion. A fitful sleep finally returned. Two hours later he was jolted from his sleep by shouting. He bolted upright. The two men who had been conversing so amicably were now in the middle of the cell shoving each other. The drunk had also stirred and was watching the ruckus. Two police officers came quickly, and keys rattled as they hurriedly unlocked the cell. They raced in between the two men, pushing them to separate corners of the cell. Soon the two were handcuffed. One of the combatants was ushered out of the cell and down the hall as the other hurled obscenities at him.

"You shut up now, or you'll be going into the isolation cell," one of the policeman shouted. This seemed to have an immediate calming effect. The man had obviously had some experience with this and had no desire to repeat it. He moved back to the cot and glowered.

Satisfied that everything was under control, the officer moved to the cell door. Lance wondered why he hadn't taken the opportunity to escape during all the confusion. "Go back to sleep," the officer said, turning to him. "It's five-thirty in the morning." As the officer left, Lance looked over at the drunk. His eyes were already closed and his mouth open. Asleep.

Lance was ushered into an interview room several hours later. A policeman carrying a portfolio entered and sat across from him.

"I guess you know what this is all about," he said, staring hard at Lance.

Lance gulped but could find no words. He stared back at the police officer and then hung his head.

"You have the right to an attorney," the policeman said. "If you waive that right we'll proceed."

"Go ahead," Lance replied dejectedly.

"You're being charged with assault," the officer said, opening up the portfolio. "You'll need to sign here, acknowledging that you understand the charge and verifying that you will appear before a magistrate on the date indicated."

Lance was unable to process what he had just heard and stared dumbfounded.

"Do you understand the charge?" the officer repeated with a bit of frustration in his voice.

The wheels in Lance's brain turned slowly, but finally he said yes.

"We'll hold you here for the next week until your records come back," the officer said.

Again Lance sank into despair.

"Unless," the officer said emphatically, pointing at Lance, "unless you can promise that this is the end of this incident. You will not engage in any further violence against Mr. Robinson. Is that clear?"

"Yes, of course," Lance blurted. "I have no desire to see him ever again. You have my word on that, officer."

"Very well." The officer smiled briefly before his expression turned grave. "But you understand that if we have any further dealings you'll be back in that cell. We can hold you until your court date if we so choose."

"No problem, sir. You won't see me again, I promise. Uh, until my court date, of course," Lance added quickly.

"Very well," the officer said, standing. "You'll be remanded to your own custody based on that assurance. You can go."

A half-hour later after his miraculous release, Lance was still in panic mode. He had retrieved his bike from the ditch and his backpack from the house and had immediately left Abbotsford and was pedaling toward the border with no idea how he planned to make good his escape from Canada.

* * * * * * ◆ * * * * * *

"You just cut the old plant off right at the soil like this." The young man took the clippers and deftly snapped the brittle twig right at ground level. "Then take one of these clips and attach the new one to the wire."

The man was no more than twenty-five but showed obvious skill as he demonstrated the tasks the new field worker was to do.

"Take your time and do it right," he advised. "As you get used to it, you'll get faster. Now you try it."

Lance took the clippers and snapped the next twig. He took a clip from his instructor and clipped the branch to the wire. The young man bent down, inspecting and adjusting Lance's work. "That's good," he finally said. "Just remember to clip it below this branch. These things won't be growing anymore at this time of year, but come spring they grow fast, and the clip can strip the branch right off if you do it above."

Lance nodded.

Yesterday he had been pedaling toward the border as fast as he could go when he had seen the sign saying, "Laborers wanted." In the distance he could see the buildings at the border crossing. He feared the officers had been alerted that he might attempt a crossing, so on an impulse he had swung into the yard at the farm where the sign was posted. Lance had been hired immediately and told to start the next morning. He left the yard and pedaled back in the direction he had come. When he was a sufficient distance from the yard, he got off his bike, crossed a neighbor's field, and circled around. He approached the farm, carefully keeping the out buildings between himself and the house. He stole back and forth among the buildings, most of which were unlocked, until he found a shed holding large sacks of fertilizer. Lance quietly brought his bike into the shed, arranged the sacks into a bed, and spent the night there in relative comfort.

In the morning he rose early, got back onto the road by means of the neighbor's field, and then rode the bike into the yard as if he had just arrived. Immediately after he made his entrance, a white van with Hope Valley Farms stickers on the doors arrived. About a dozen workers stepped out of the van, stretching as they exited. All of the workers appeared to be Asian. Lance worked on his row for a full day alongside them. At first they were much quicker than he was, but as the day wore on Lance was able to quicken his pace, almost matching theirs. His work in the field had brought him closer and closer to the border, and it was all he could do to keep himself from dropping the shears and sprinting those last several yards to climb the light barbed wire fence that marked the line.

In the evening the young man who had trained Lance started the van. Stiff and sore, Lance climbed in with the others, leaving his bike propped against a shed. They were driven into Abbotsford to the light-rail transit station. Lance climbed out with the rest. A few of the workers were met by family and drove away, but a few others waited for the arrival of the next westward train. Lance followed them. The train arrived and Lance rode for the next half-hour, listening as his fellow workers jabbered on in Chinese or some other foreign language. They rode to the next major center, which Lance learned was Langley. The rest of the workers exited the train there, and so Lance did as well. Against his better judgment, he sought out a hotel room and collapsed on the bed. The comfort was a welcome relief, and Lance slept until early the following morning.

For the next two days, Lance worked at the farm during the day, eyeing the border yearningly, and then returned to his hotel room at night.

As Lance labored in the fields, he studied the border. There were two gravel roads along the fence line—one on the US side, the other on the Canadian. From time to time border patrols had passed along those roads, raising a cloud of dust us they drove. He had seen both Canadian and American patrols, but the American patrols seemed far more frequent. Lance had also noticed a gravel road leading away from the border at the far corner of a raspberry field about half a kilometer from where he was working. An American patrol had parked on the side of that road earlier in the day almost out of sight. Lance could tell the patrol vehicle was still there by the gleam of the late afternoon sun off the windshield.

He decided that if he was going to attempt to cross the border he would need to know the level of surveillance the patrols maintained at night. That evening he went to a high-end hunting and camping supply store and purchased the highest-quality night vision binoculars the store had. The following day he put them in his backpack along with his lunch and went to work.

At the end of the day rather than board the van with the others, Lance strode toward his bike. He waved the young farmhand away, motioning toward the bike. The man smiled in understanding and drove the van carrying the rest of the crew out of the yard. With the departure of the workers, the yard immediately grew quiet and Lance gazed toward the border.

Lance had discovered that Hope Valley Farms kept none of its sheds on the property locked except for a few that housed machinery, so he headed toward one with a window that faced the border. He was not worried that the owners would spy him moving among the out buildings. The farmhouse stood off from the rest of the farm operation and was separated from the buildings by a tall hedge. In the three days he had been on the farm, he had seen only the daughter, and she had walked straight from the house to her sleek sports car and had roared off.

Lance then moved to the fertilizer shed where he had spent the first night. He was still stiff and sore from the day's work, so he lay down in his makeshift bed and soon fell asleep. When he awoke it was pitch dark. He glanced at his watch. It was eleven. Lance stole over to the building with the window facing the border, and for the next four hours he trained his binoculars there. He found the evening patrols usually did their rounds with their headlights off. He mentally patted himself on the back for his decision to purchase the binoculars, for he was able to spot the patrols easily from the window. The patrols maintained a schedule more or less consistent with the daytime hours. Still, there were large gaps of time between patrols. These ranged from about forty-five minutes to as much as two hours.

Satisfied with the knowledge he had gained, Lance returned to the fertilizer shed. Tomorrow night he would cross the border. Lance flopped exhausted onto the fertilizer bags and immediately went to sleep. At 6 a.m. his cell alarm went off. Lance pulled his bike into the main yard and waited. The rest of the crew would soon arrive.

Lance was able to spy on the border until near dark. He noticed that in the late afternoon a patrol had parked in the same spot as the day before and had stayed there for a couple of hours. The patrol finally made a U-turn on the gravel road and disappeared from the border. When the rest of the crew left, Lance again pretended he was going to leave on his bike.

Around 6 p.m. a heavy rain began. Lance waited another hour, leaning against the rain-spotted window as pitch darkness fell. When the rain slowed, Lance crept out of the shed, collected his bike, and stealthily carried it across the field toward the gravel road. By the time he reached the border, mud had caked his riding shoes and he was sopping wet from the cold drizzle. Standing at the barbed wire fence, Lance looked around, using his binoculars. All was darkness in both directions save for a soft light in the sky to the west from what he surmised must be the border crossing less than a mile away. With all his might he flung his bike over the fence. It rattled noisily as it landed on the gravel on the other side. Lance hoped the rough treatment had not damaged the bike. He then quickly grasped a fence post and climbed, landing softly on US soil.

An irrational sense of relief filled his heart and mind as he did, but Lance knew he was far from safety. He picked up his bike, mounted it, and sped down the gravel road leading south into the dark, rainy night.

Lance continued to ride south. The road wasn't exactly suited to the tires on his bike, but he had found a well-worn tire path and was making good time. About half a mile ahead, an intersection was illuminated by the approach of headlights from the west.

This is an odd time for someone to be driving around here, Lance thought. *Did I trigger some sort of alarm when I crossed the border?* He steered his bike down into the ditch and was in the cover of dark trees by the time the headlights came into view at the intersection far ahead. As soon as the vehicle rounded the corner a powerful search lamp made the gravel road appear as day. Lance immediately grabbed his bike and dove for deeper cover.

As the pickup slowly passed, the searchlights illuminated the trees above him. Lance pressed himself against the ground, cursing the fluorescent colors of his outfit. The pickup drove on, however, and Lance sat up, watching it go with search beams probing both sides of the road.

Lance took off his helmet, tied it over the rear reflector of his bike, and made for the road. Though the patrol truck had passed, he knew he had to flee. He brought his bike onto the gravel road and pedaled as hard as he could in the opposite direction.

Lance continued for another half-hour along the gravel road. He estimated he had penetrated ten miles into the States. His breathing was becoming labored from his exertion when he saw a sign that read: "Mount Baker Hiking Trail," with an arrow pointing to his right. In the darkness Lance made out the entrance to a parking area on the right. He turned in and soon found a well-groomed path leading into the trees. Without hesitation Lance took the trail. In the rain it wasn't too difficult to spot the sides of the trail as everything shimmered with the dampness, so he made good time. He was a little more relaxed in the cover of the trees and had slowed his pace somewhat. But then Lance heard the distant pounding of a helicopter engine. It was getting louder and seemed to be heading straight for him. Lance mustered all the speed he could without careening off the winding trail. The helicopter passed very close overhead but then flew off rapidly to his right. Lance breathed a sigh of relief. He knew that the helicopter might be equipped with heat signature cameras and that he might have been spotted.

For the next ten minutes Lance raced along the path, slowing down only when he skidded wildly from the path after a sharp turn. He careened into a willow bush, his helmet clipping the trunk of a nearby lodgepole pine. Fortunately the bike seemed none the worse for wear, and chastened, Lance continued on his way at a more reasonable pace until the path crossed a paved road. He turned onto the road and proceeded cautiously, eventually finding the main highway leading south. By early morning's light, a signpost announced he was arriving in Everly, Washington.

Just some twenty miles from Canada, Everly was obviously a border town. Most of the windows of businesses in town sported large signs announcing that the Canadian dollar was accepted at par. Milk, cheese, and chicken prices were advertised in window paint. Money exchange booths lined the main street, all boasting attractive rates. Lance pulled in at a gas station, rolled his bike to the back, and then entered the station restroom with his backpack and the other bag from his rack. He dumped the expensive binoculars into the trash. A few minutes later he emerged from the restroom dressed in a new shirt, new pants, and a jacket carrying just his backpack.

Lance wasted no time. He immediately went to the closest money exchange booth. He moved from that one to the next one just down the street. Each time he exchanged small amounts of Canadian cash to avoid suspicion. Five hundred dollars was the maximum he would cash. Within half an hour, he had visited nine exchange places and now carried more than $3,000 in American money.

Lance then walked to the bus station and bought a ticket to Seattle. He was somewhat uneasy about the fact that the bus would not reach the city for another two hours. Lance nervously checked his backpack into the luggage claim at the depot. It was the first time he had left his money unattended since the trapper had made off with it almost two weeks before, and Lance didn't like the idea of doing it now. But toting a backpack pointed him out as a stranger and possibly as a foreigner. With all the activity at the border, authorities were obviously aware of an illegal crossing, and Everly would be a logical place for them to search.

He crossed over to a restaurant and ordered a full breakfast— eggs, bacon, hash browns, and pancakes. Lance ate slowly, and when he was finally finished he spent time in a couple of curio shops that displayed art, lamps, and knickknacks.

Fifteen minutes before the bus was to arrive, Lance returned to the depot and retrieved his backpack. Eventually the bus pulled in and he boarded it, tucking his backpack into the rack above his seat. Lance waited for the bus to take off. Then to his horror a border patrol officer stepped aboard. Lance was seated about halfway back and watched anxiously as the officer moved from row to row asking to see identification from each passenger.

Lance's heart raced as he handed the officer his fake ID. This was the first time he had used it in the States, and he had no idea if it would pass inspection.

"California, huh?" the officer said, studying the passport. Lance was thanking his stars he had the foresight to order the fake ID. He had no way to judge its quality, but it seemed to be working.

"So what brings you up here?" the officer asked, turning his attention from the passport.

"We had a family wedding in Vancouver, and then I went with a couple of long-lost cousins to Mount Baker for a few days of skiing. They dropped me off here and headed back up to Canada."

"Where do you live in California?"

"Redwood," Lance said, remembering the forms he had filled out.

"Have a good trip," the officer said. He handed Lance his passport and turned to a couple across the aisle.

Lance made an effort to relax as the officer inspected the next couple's documents. A few minutes later the officer had finally completed his check and stepped off the bus. Lance thought the hiss of air as the door shut was the sweetest sound in the world. At last the bus moved away from the curb, and they were on their way to Seattle.

It took Lance a while to relax, but he finally did. He gazed out the window, watching the scenery fly by. When he got to Seattle, Lance did what he had done in Abbotsford. He still had forebodings of arriving at a bus depot only to be met by four or five police officers who would haul him off to jail. So Lance again watched for a hotel, and when he found one he asked the driver to drop him off at the first red light. This time he had to hike back up a long hill almost a mile before reaching the place he had seen. Set on a long, narrow strip parallel to the street, it was a typical roadside hotel with two floors. He could choose a room facing the street or facing the back of the hill, the clerk told him. Lance selected one facing the street, but it was still early afternoon, so he had to wait for room service to finish cleaning the room.

Once he got to the room, he reached for the phone and ordered a pizza. He felt it was time to reevaluate his situation. The last week had been a grueling affair, and he needed to take stock and to regain his strength for the next phase. Lance felt that he was fairly safe from capture for the time being but that he would have to keep moving. His most significant problem was the Canadian cash he carried in his backpack. The fact that it was Canadian and that it was such a large amount would immediately raise suspicion. He had started to work on that problem at the border by converting some of the money into US dollars. More than $3,000 in American funds would give him a helpful cushion, but he still had hundreds of thousands of Canadian dollars. Lance didn't know what to do. Should he try to start an account? Should he exchange all the money? No matter what he did, it was bound to raise suspicion.

His second problem was that being in the States was still somewhat risky. The American press had picked up the story of the man who had used his own business card for a holdup note. This was considered a novelty news item, and the coverage had not been as intense as it had been in Canada, but there was still a danger he would be recognized. If he was captured, extradition would be inevitable. Lance had decided he could achieve safety only by escaping to Central or South America. This created yet a third problem—passing security at border crossings. His fake identification had worked well enough at the money exchange booths and on the bus when it was inspected by hand. But at a customs station, inspectors would check all documents electronically. Since Mark Fenwood would no doubt show up as deceased, it was a virtual certainty that Lance's IDs would be flagged as false.

For the rest of the day, Lance did not leave the hotel. He ate pizza, watched TV and dozed off two or three times while doing so. He rose early the next morning feeling refreshed and booked passage on an afternoon bus to Los Angeles.

Lance arrived in L.A. at about three-thirty in the morning. With hundreds of thousands of dollars in his backpack, he found it a scary prospect indeed to walk through all the vagabonds and strange people milling around the bus station even at that hour. Lance put his head down and strode toward one of the taxis parked outside. "Take me to the nearest hotel," he told the driver, trying not to betray his nervousness.

The driver nodded and swung away from the curb. Within minutes they were on a four-lane freeway and with the scant traffic at that hour were traveling at high speed. They continued on the freeway for fifteen minutes. The longer the cabby drove, the more nervous Lance became. They had now traveled about fifteen miles on the freeway. It was becoming obvious that the cabby was either taking a tourist on a joy ride to boost his fare or, worse, was headed for some seedy area where his passenger would be robbed.

Finally Lance exploded. "I said the closest hotel," he shouted. "Your meter is already at twenty-five dollars. If I'm not parked in front of a nice hotel by the time that thing reads thirty I'm not paying."

"No, no," the cabby protested. "There are no hotels in this area. I'm taking you to the closest ones."

"Yeah, right," Lance retorted, "and Uncle Sam's my mother. You heard what I said."

"There are hotels this way," the cabby said as he took the next exit.

Five minutes later they were sitting outside a Best Western. Lance got out of the cab with his bags and handed the cabby thirty dollars.

The cabby pointed at his meter. "It's forty-two," he said.

"Well, thirty is all you're going to get from me," Lance said. He was fuming.

The driver swung open the door and climbed out of the cab to confront Lance. "You owe me forty-two dollars," he said emphatically, standing nose to nose with him.

But Lance did not back down. "You deliberately went out of your way to increase your fare. There's no way this is the closest hotel," he said.

"This *is* the closest hotel," the cabby insisted.

Lance turned toward the lobby. "Come on," he said. "Let's ask the clerk if he thinks this is the closest hotel to the bus depot."

The cabby hesitated. "I tell you what," he said, trying to placate Lance. "You give me thirty-five and we'll call it even."

Lance hesitated. What was he doing? He was arguing with a taxi driver who was ready to beat him senseless over ten bucks while he carried hundreds of thousands in his pack. Wordlessly he handed the cabby the extra five dollars and stomped into the hotel to get a room.

After rising late the following morning, Lance went down to the lobby and asked the clerk what buses would take him to a more commercial area of the city. There was no way he was going to trust his fate to a taxi driver again. The clerk was very helpful, providing him with a small map and detailed written instructions. Lance caught a city bus outside the hotel and bought a transfer. He was on the bus for a good half-hour. *That driver last night sure took me out to the boondocks*, he thought. Finally, an hour later after exiting the first bus and transferring to another, Lance arrived at the district the clerk had described. Lance immediately found a post office and asked if he could get a post office box. The clerk nodded and brought out paperwork for him to fill out. Lance used the information from his fake driver's license, and soon he was issued the key to the box.

"Oh, and strictly no junk mail or fliers, please," he said. "I'll be picking up mail only every two weeks when I've completed my shift."

Lance left the post office. He now had a local address. Next he headed for a Continental Bank across the street.

"I would like to open an account here," Lance told a teller. "The problem is I have only Canadian money. You see, most of my clients are Canadian, and I'm usually paid in Canadian funds."

"That will be no problem, sir," the teller said. "It just means you won't be able to access those funds for five business days. How much do you wish to deposit into the account today?"

"Uh, only $1,000 Canadian today," Lance said with a smile. "I will be depositing about $10,000 more in about a week once I've completed some pending transactions."

"And that will all be in Canadian?" the teller queried.

"Yes," Lance said.

"All right," she said. "I'll place a note on your account saying the deposit is expected. Could I please see some ID?"

Lance showed her his California driver's license and his passport, which she accepted without question. He counted out the Canadian bills, and the teller handed him his bank book and a banking card. "Now remember, sir," she said, "please don't use this until Wednesday. As I said, we will be putting a five-day hold on the balance until the exchange has been cleared."

Lance thanked her and left the bank. Over the next three hours Lance visited six other banks. At each bank he followed the same procedure, depositing $1,000 and saying a larger deposit could be expected. Each bank accepted the cash and his identification with no questions. Two did not even require a holding period.

Over the next three days Lance repeated the process over and over again until his story became more like a script. He perfected and expanded it with each telling. By the end he had accounts at twenty branches throughout L.A. He made sure to have no more than two accounts with any national banking institution.

One evening after dining at a nice restaurant connected to the luxurious Hilton Hotel in downtown L.A., Lance strolled over to a pay phone in the lobby and placed a call to his wife.

"Hi, Barb. It's me," he said when she answered the phone.

There was a long pause, but finally she said, "Hello."

"How are you doing?" he asked, his voice a mix of concern and just a little awkwardness.

"Um. Some days are better than others."

"Are the kids with you?"

"No. Char went back home yesterday. She had to get back to work. She was a great help while she was here, though."

"Yeah, she's a nice girl. Listen, Barb. I know the bills must be piling up." Lance had managed the family finances, and after two weeks he could imagine the stack of unpaid bills.

"It seems like that's all we ever get in the mailbox," she said.

"I'm going to send you some money so you can pay the bills." There was silence on the other end of the line.

"You want to send me money you robbed from the bank?" Barb said at last.

"Listen Barb. I've gotten out of the country. Don't you see? I've almost made it." He hesitated. "Barb, I want you to join me. I miss you and I want you with me."

Again there was silence. Finally Barb said, "I can't do that, Lance. I wouldn't be able to live with myself living off stolen money. I'll sell the house before I do that."

Now Lance was angry. "You would rather I go to jail for the rest of my life?"

"I don't wish you ill, Lance."

"Just tell me how we can be together, Barb."

"I think I want a divorce," she said suddenly.

Lance's heart instantly became a lump of clay.

"I do. I do want a divorce," she repeated, this time with more certainty in her voice.

"You can have your divorce," he said despondently, "but I won't be back anytime soon to sign the papers." With that, he hung up the phone and left the lobby.

Rather than take the bus, Lance started walking. The hotel was on a busy thoroughfare, so as soon as possible he turned off that street and found himself in a fairly affluent residential area. Lance walked and walked. He knew he had jeopardized his marriage, but it was not until he heard Barb say with such certainty that she wanted a divorce that he realized it was all over. As he walked,

Lance assimilated that new reality. For two hours he walked, hardly paying attention to where he was.

In the end, Lance completed a catharsis. He knew he loved his wife and his kids and always would. When the time was right, he would attempt to bridge the gulf he had created with them. But somehow he had gained a new focus in the last two hours. It was forward-looking. He would build a new life for himself. He had his health. He had mental acuity. He knew he had potentials. What those potentials were or would be he could not say, but he was going to move toward them. He would find stability on some distant shore and then begin to live a full life. Pain remained just below the surface, but Lance felt more than anything a calm reassurance. He found a bus stop and made his way back to his hotel.

CHAPTER 12

"He's in Los Angeles!" Doug said as soon as he sat down in Rob's office.

"Damn it! I knew it. I figured he must have managed to get across the border. How do you know he's in Los Angeles?"

"The boys on the wiretap of Knight's home just sent us a transcript. Knight called his wife last night. Apparently everything is not sunshine and roses in the Knight household. She told him she wanted a divorce."

"Hmm! That's interesting. I guess we won't be able to lure him into a rendezvous with her. Did you get an address?"

"He phoned from one of the downtown hotels in L.A. Used a pay phone."

"He's being pretty careful," Rob said. "Still, I guess you better give the hotel a call and see if they have anyone registered under the name of Lance Knight or Mark Fenwood."

"Mark Fenwood?"

Rob opened his desk drawer and pulled out several manila envelopes. "These came in this morning," he said.

"What are they?" Doug asked.

"Our boy's been busy," Rob said. "These are fake passports, all in the name of Mark Fenwood. Look at the photos. He's got some with him made up and others normal. I guess he hoped he would cover all the bases. They've come in from four fake ID places."

"That must be why he was at the Squamish post office," Doug said. "He was picking up his fake ID."

"Yup," Rob said. "At any rate, I'll contact the Americans to be on the alert at all the California airports and border crossings. If he uses his real ID or the fake ID, we've got him."

* * * * * ◆ * * * * *

Lance spent the next three days relaxing. He did a lot of window shopping in the mornings but bought very little. In the afternoons, once the day had warmed up, he went for a stroll along one or another of the many beaches in the L.A. area. In the evenings he took in a picture show.

Once those three days were up, Lance put the next phase of his plan into action. He revisited the banks, and as promised he made larger deposits of Canadian cash. The deposits varied depending on how comfortable Lance felt about each branch. They were between $5,000 and $10,000 in Canadian dollars and always in odd amounts. In the end Lance had accounts totaling $138,000 in US money. He stored each bank card along with the rest of his cash in the backpack. He still had more than $500,000 in stolen Canadian money, and it felt like an albatross around his neck.

Lance had now been in L.A. for nine days. It was time to prepare to cross the border. He took a bus from L.A. to San Diego and got a room at a hotel on the south side of that city just minutes from the border in Tijuana. Lance used the same story at several bank branches in San Diego, and after a week he now had laundered close to $250,000. He had more than thirty bank cards in his backpack, each carefully labeled with the name and address of the branch.

One day at a major department store, Lance chose a large suitcase and went to the notions department and bought a sewing kit. In the evening he carefully cut away the fabric from the base of the suitcase. The next day he purchased a hot glue gun and a sheet of thin plastic and constructed a false bottom. Then he carefully placed the rest of the money—some $250,000, all in hundreds—in short stacks along the bottom with most of his bank cards. He pushed the plastic down on top of the cash and hot glued it in place. Finally he resewed the lining fabric over the new base. The work took him three evenings. The sewing took the most time since it had to look perfect. Lance did several sections over and over again until he was satisfied. He packed the suitcase with the clothes he had purchased, got on the light-transit train across the street from his hotel, and headed for the border.

At the border checkpoint he stood in a line of Americans and Mexicans waiting to cross. The facility was low tech compared with any customs station he had encountered in Canada or the States. There were no computers in sight. This reassured Lance. The line advanced steadily toward the examination area where he was required to fill out a tourist card saying where he was going and how long he intended to stay. He filled it out and rejoined the line, card in hand.

Each person passed through a metal detector and then pushed a button. If the light came up green, the person was waved on through. If it came up red, however, the person was ushered to a table and was required to open all luggage in front of a border guard, who inspected it closely. Lance could see an older man dressed in a white straw campesino hat at the table protesting loudly in Spanish. He had the misfortune of triggering the red light. He had three cardboard boxes bound with twine and copious amounts of wrapping tape. As he removed all this packing, the guard stood totally unconcerned with the man's protests.

Finally it was Lance's turn. He stepped through the detector, hoping it would not alarm. The guard pointed to the button. Lance anxiously pushed it, hoping it would come up green. Unfortunately, however, it came up red. He was directed to the table next to the one where the guard was searching the cardboard boxes. Dozens of belts, vests, and other leather goods lay strewn on the table, and the guard continued to empty the boxes. Lance concluded that the man must be a merchant selling goods at one of the open marketplaces that abounded around San Diego.

A second guard approached Lance and asked him to open his suitcase. Lance took his key and unlocked the case. He waited nervously as she went through his belongings. He was acutely aware of the small imperfections he had left when he had sewn the lining. He hoped she would not notice them. The longer the search continued, the more glaring they seemed.

Finally she closed the suitcase and took the tourist card he had filled out along with his passport. Her eyebrows lifted slightly as she examined the documents. "Please come this way," she said in a heavy accent. She indicated a spot behind where two guards stood examining the papers of the people who were not required to have their bags searched. She said something in Spanish to one of the guards and left. The man nodded and continued processing the travelers entering the country. Lance watched as person after person passed by. Why was he being detained? He looked at the entrance to the station and for an instant considered bolting for the door.

Finally all of the passengers from the train had been processed. The guard turned and faced Lance. "Where are you from?" he asked. His English was much better than the woman guard's.

"I'm from Redwood, California," Lance said.

"And you are an American citizen?"

"Yes!"

"Have you been to Canada?" the guard asked, keeping his voice casual.

Immediately Lance's heart began thumping loudly in his chest. How had he known? What would happen now? His mind spun, looking for an appropriate response.

"Uh, yes, actually. I lived in Canada for a few years."

"But you don't live there now?" the guard asked.

"No, of course not," Lance answered.

"Well, you filled out the tourist card with a Canadian address and presented us with an American passport," the guard said, holding up the card Lance had filled out.

Lance stared horrified. Sure enough, in his nervousness he had put his British Columbia address on the card. "Oh, I'm sorry," he said. "That's my address from three years ago. I can't believe I used it."

"Very well. Please fill out a new one. You know it's your responsibility to have these papers filled out correctly. If you don't, you are liable to imprisonment, and I'm sure you don't want to spend even a few nights in a Mexican jail."

Lance mentally kicked himself. He had been so preoccupied with the search of his luggage that he had filled in his correct Canadian address. Stupid mistakes like this one could ruin everything.

He redid the paperwork and handed it to the guard. The guard took his time studying the new card but finally said, "Thank you. You are free to go. Bienvenidos a Mexico."

Lance took a taxi to downtown Tijuana and immediately caught a bus headed for Mexico City. The trip was an arduous affair, lasting some thirty hours with just two breaks in which he had time only to go to the bathroom and to buy snacks. He dozed, watched the countryside go by, and finally arrived in the capital city's main bus terminal in the early evening.

The terminal was a round structure with many brightly lit booths for bus lines on its circumference. Numerous walkways led from this main area to exits. Vendors at the booths were all shouting at the same time, touting discount fares to this or that region. Several beckoned to Lance and to other travelers. Lance wanted to escape the racket and immediately sought an exit. He took one of the wide lanes with a sign that read: "Taxis." He emerged from the noisy terminal onto the street and headed toward a line of taxis. Drivers immediately beseeched him to use their taxi. Lance made a beeline for the closest taxi and directed the driver to take him to the airport. He arrived in no more than ten minutes.

Lance walked the entire length of the airport and was disappointed to find that it differed very little from other North American terminals he had been in. All the major international airlines had offices here as did the national airlines of Mexico. He would face the same problems getting through security here that he would have faced in the States. Almost certainly he would be required to present his passport, which would then be entered in the system. Within seconds, no doubt, the passport would be identified as false. Lance left the airport not knowing what to do. He did not want to continue using buses. His back and his legs were stiff and achy after the marathon trip from the border.

He found another taxi and pointed to a hotel sign atop a tall building in the distance. The driver looked in that direction and nodded in understanding. Fifteen minutes later Lance was registered in an extravagant hotel in downtown Mexico City.

The next morning he approached one of the receptionists, a pretty miss with long, ebony hair, in the lobby and asked her about airports in the area. She mentioned the airport he had visited the night before but knew of no others in the city. Lance thanked her, left the hotel, and strolled past the rows of nearby stores. He found a bookstore and purchased a map of the city. Then he had breakfast in a restaurant bustling with patrons. The place seemed to be hundreds of years old and was obviously very popular. After dining he returned to his room.

Lance spread out the map on his bed and studied it closely.

He noticed immediately the airport he had visited and continued studying the map. Finally, on the top corner he found what he was looking for—the long lines of an airport's runways on the outskirts of the city and a faint blue label identifying it as the Aeropuerto Atizapan. Gathering the map, Lance quickly went to the front of the hotel where a couple of sleek sedans marked as taxis were parked. He approached one of the cars and motioned to the driver. Then he moved to the hood and spread out the map. The driver climbed out and studied the map with him. Lance pointed at the airport he had found, and the driver nodded.

"You wait," Lance said, holding out his arms and shaking his hands in exaggerated gestures to communicate with the driver.

The man smiled at his awkward attempt and said, "Yes, sir. I'll be happy to wait for you at the airport."

Embarrassed, Lance climbed into the cab, and the driver headed off with a chuckle. The ride to the airport took an hour. They finally turned onto a narrow paved road that led up into the hills surrounding the city proper. At the end of this road they came upon several hangers and a number of small private airplanes. The taxi passed a dilapidated warehouse with windows just under the overhang of the roof. Many of the windows were broken. Beyond the warehouse they saw a small terminal sitting beside the main runway.

Lance got out of the cab and entered the building. The inside was dark, and Lance thought at first that the building was deserted. When his eyes adjusted, however, he saw three booths on the far side. One of the booths was unoccupied, but employees were on duty at the other two. An old blackboard at each counter listed several destinations along with departure times. Lance read the first blackboard's listings. He didn't recognize any of the destinations. He moved to the next booth and studied the board there. Most of the destinations were similar, and he still failed to recognize any of the names. Then near the bottom of the list he saw the listing "San Jose de Macoris, Republica Dominicana."

Dominican Republic, he thought. He got the attention of the girl at the desk and pointed to the listing. The girl looked and nodded. She began to explain in a long stream of Spanish, none of which Lance could understand.

Lance held out his arms and waved his hands. "English," he said.

The girl shrugged her shoulders helplessly and shook her head.

"Momento," Lance said, and ran from the terminal. He brought his driver in with him and explained what he wanted. The driver and the girl spoke briefly, and the driver turned to Lance. "Transporte Energia has a flight from here Thursday morning," he said. "It is a flight operated by a large mining company mainly to transport workers from here, but they do take other passengers when space allows."

"Ask her if there is room on the flight this Thursday and how much it is," Lance said. The driver asked and listened carefully to the girl's responses.

"There are three available spaces on the flight this Thursday," he said. "It leaves at 7 a.m. sharp and the cost is two thousand pesos." Lance did a quick mental calculation and came up with a fare of just over $200.

"Tell her to book me on the flight," he said.

The driver did so and then turned to Lance. "You will have to pay in advance, please."

Lance withdrew the equivalent in American money and handed it to the girl.

The girl studied the bills in consternation and looked questioningly at the driver.

"I'm afraid she can accept only pesos, sir," the driver said.

Lance had only US dollars, but unwilling to give up this opportunity for a quick exit from the country, he pulled out several more bills for the girl.

"No, no, sir. This is not necessary," the driver said. "I have pesos. Give me the $200 and I will pay her." Lance thanked him effusively, and moments later the transaction was completed.

"Your name, sir?" the driver asked.

"Mark Fenwood," Lance answered. The girl repeated the name but murdered the pronunciation. For the next minute Lance and the driver repeated the name over and over again to no success. Finally the frustrated girl handed Lance a clipboard and indicated the space where he should write his name. He left the building with receipt in hand, and the driver took him back to the hotel.

The following day was a leisurely one for Lance. He slept late and strolled the streets around the hotel for a few hours. Finally he checked out of the hotel and caught a taxi to the Atizapan area of the city. He booked a room in a hotel a relatively short distance from the airport. Having time on his hands, he called Jen and they talked animatedly for three quarters of an hour. He went to bed early, making sure the alarm was set and asked the lobby for a wakeup call.

The next day he got to the small airport early. One by one the other passengers arrived. Lance was a great curiosity to the other men. Only members of the work crew usually took the flight. They obviously knew each other. To have a white, non-Spanish-speaking passenger on the flight was odd to say the least. Finally they boarded a four-prop twenty-four-seater. No one spoke to Lance and there were no stewardesses. After a bumpy, four-hour ride, they landed in an airport not unlike the one they had left—dilapidated and abandoned for all intents and purposes.

The rest of the men boarded an old bus that whisked them away in a cloud of black smoke. Lance caught a taxi into the small city of some fifty thousand inhabitants. Located right on the Caribbean coast, it was on the opposite side of the island from most of the tourist spots. That pleased Lance and he decided to stay. He found a small place to rent about a block from the beach. It was older and showed signs of deterioration from the salt air breeze, but it was clean and had obviously been maintained by the owner. The place had some simple furniture and a comfortable bed. Lance rented it for the month.

Lance lived a relatively simple existence, confident that he had escaped the arm of the law and could now enjoy freedom and security. He usually went to the market in the morning and bought the food and supplies he would need for the day. This was becoming less of an ordeal, for bit by bit he was gaining a rudimentary knowledge of Spanish, so communicating by hand signal was no longer necessary. He walked just about everywhere he needed to go. *What's the hurry?* he told himself. However, he was a little lonely since it seemed no one in this city had even a basic knowledge of English. The island was fairly small, though, so he did see the odd tourist who had wandered over to the restaurants and beaches on his side. From time to time he struck up conversations with some of these people to pass time.

Lance was considering extending his lease on the place for a second month when something happened to change his mind and to make him feel trapped on the island. He had struck up a conversation with a tourist couple who had wandered into a restaurant where he was enjoying a coffee. He discovered they were from British Columbia, so he announced that he was also Canadian. They enjoyed a pleasant conversation, talking about home and places of interest on the island. Then suddenly the man blurted out that Lance looked a lot like the guy who had used his own business card in robbing a bank. Lance laughed it off but soon found an excuse to leave.

The next morning Lance was enjoying a breakfast of sliced local fruit in his room. The encounter with the Canadian family had rattled him, and he had vowed that he would do his best to stay away from any places frequented by tourists. He was downing the last few slices of fruit from the platter when he heard a rap at the door. Lance frowned as he approached the door. When he swung it open, there stood the Canadian tourist he had encountered the day before. The man was holding a pistol trained on him.

"Hi," the man said with a grin. "The name's Frank Wells. This is certainly out of the way. May I?" He motioned inside. Not waiting for permission, he brushed past Lance, entered the room, and sat down on the corner of the bed.

Astonished, Lance followed him inside. "How did you find me?" Lance asked.

"When I said you looked like Lance Knight—and that is who you are, is it not?" Lance didn't answer. "At any rate I thought it was merely a resemblance until you left so quickly afterward. That made me suspicious. When you left, I sent my wife back to our hotel in a taxi, and I followed you in another taxi here to your place. When I got back to the hotel, I did a little bit of internet searching and came up with this." He held up a full-page photograph of Lance from the *Vancouver Sun*. Frank took a satisfied look at the photo and nodded. "Yup, it's you all right."

"What do you want?" Lance asked, chagrined.

"It's obvious, isn't it?" Frank said. "I can take you and this newspaper clipping to the local police and have your ass arrested. I don't know what the extradition laws are here, but I'm sure they will be interested to learn they have a wanted bank robber in their midst. I *can* do this, but I think maybe we can make an alternate arrangement, just the two of us. I think $50,000 should be enough to make this problem go away."

"Let's just say I agree to this," Lance said. "How do I know I can trust you?"

"From where I sit, I don't think you have a choice," Frank said, again pointing the pistol at Lance.

Lance drew back from the pistol and winced at the shot he thought was about to come. "Don't shoot!" Lance yelled. "All right. I'll pay."

"That's better," Frank said with a smile. "Let's have it!"

"I'm afraid all I have is a few hundred dollars," Lance said, holding up his wallet.

Frank stood up and crossed quickly to where Lance stood. "I'll take that," he said, grabbing the wallet and pulling the bills from it. "Now where's the rest?"

"I've put the rest in a bank account."

"Is that true? Then I suppose you will have no objections if I have a look around."

Lance shrugged. For the next fifteen minutes he sat on the bed as Frank rifled through his drawers and turned the room upside down. Lance's heart raced as the man tore open the suitcase with the money hidden in the lining. He searched every pocket and emptied the contents onto the floor. Once again, however, Lance avoided detection despite a rather amateurish job of stitching.

Finally Frank straightened up. "Okay, let's go," he said, motioning with the gun.

"Where are we going?" Lance asked, raising his hands.

"Why, we are going to find a bank where you are going to withdraw whatever money you can, of course."

Lance's mind raced as he sought a solution to his predicament. He moved to the door followed closely by the extortionist.

As they slid into a taxi, Frank said, "You just cooperate and we won't have a problem. We're going to go to the bank, and you're going to take out the maximum you can. If that doesn't work, our next stop is the police station. Do you understand?"

"As you say, I don't have a choice," Lance replied weakly.

"Damn right you don't, and don't forget it."

As instructed, the driver took them to a nearby bank. When they arrived, the bank was not yet open, but a dozen people were lined up at the doors. Frank told Lance to exit the cab and led him to the line. The stranger was obviously nervous at this unexpected turn of events. "Don't even think about trying anything," he said through gritted teeth.

For the next fifteen minutes they waited, both men sweating in the morning sun beating off the stone streets and buildings. When the doors finally opened, the two filed in with the rest of the customers, now numbering well over fifty. This was a bank out of the Wild West. The building was supported by heavy stone columns and dark-gray stone walls. There were few adornments other than old wooden benches on either side of the entrance. The tellers stood behind heavy black bars, dealing with the first customers.

Lance noticed that those ahead of them were taking tickets from a dispenser to the left. Frank crooked his head, motioning for Lance to do the same. Lance approached the machine. He was jostled as others pushed past him to get tickets as quickly as possible. Lance realized these tickets determined the order in which patrons would be served. He hesitated. Exasperated, Frank pushed past him and snatched a ticket. They moved to benches on the right side of the bank and waited with the others. Frank kept his right hand in his jacket pocket, careful not to expose the pistol hidden there. As the tellers finished with a customer, they would call out the next number, and the person holding that ticket would approach. Five tellers were dealing with customers while a sixth sat behind another cage, tackling a stack of paperwork.

Frank nudged Lance and showed him the ticket, which had the inscription A34 in bold red lettering. Lance nodded. Finally one of the tellers called, "A treinta-y-cuatro." Lance recognized the number but did not react. Obviously his blackmailer understood even less Spanish than he did, for he hadn't reacted either. The teller called the number three more times.

"That must be us," Frank said, elbowing Lance in the side. "Come on!"

As the two men approached, the teller held up a finger. "Una persona solamente," she said.

Lance understood immediately that she meant only one person at a time. His companion had also understood. "No problem. We are friends," he said, motioning between Lance and himself. "It's okay!

Amigos! You don't mind if I'm here, do you?" Frank said ominously as he shouldered Lance.

"Uh, no, no. Of course not," Lance said.

"Una persona," repeated the teller.

"It's okay. It's okay," Frank said. The two of them now stood in front of the teller's cage.

"Una persona," replied the frowning teller, this time much more forcefully. Seeing the disturbance, an armed guard approached.

"All right! All right!" Frank said, backing away from the guard. "Don't try anything stupid," he snarled at Lance in a lowered voice. "I'll be listening." Frank squeezed himself into a small space on the bench nearest the teller's cage, forcing the person on each side to slide away to give him room. They glared at him and muttered under their breath. Frank paid them no mind, however, and stared intently at Lance's back.

"Ingles!" Lance said, knowing Frank could hear him. "Ingles," he repeated. The teller stared at him confused and finally nodded. "Un momento," she said and turned away. "En privado," Lance said suddenly in a much lower voice. The teller hesitated and looked back at him. Lance nodded and intoned the phrase again quietly. "En privado." The teller nodded and waved him back to the benches behind him. "Sientese, señor," she said.

The front row of benches where Frank sat was full, so Lance went to the back row and sat down. Frank immediately rose and joined him.

"What the hell was that about?" he asked. "What did you say to her?"

"I simply asked if I could speak to someone in English. Don't worry," Lance said.

"Oh, I'm not worried, because you know what, if I don't leave this bank with some money, you and I are going to the police station. That's the deal and there will be no compromise, so I strongly suggest you get this business done before I lose patience. Why did she send you back to the benches anyway?"

"I'm not sure," Lance said honestly. "I only assume she went to get someone who could speak English."

By this time the teller had returned to her cage and had resumed dealing with customers. About ten minutes later a younger bank officer dressed neatly in a sharp-looking dark suit and a tie approached her and said something to her. The teller scanned the benches and when she spotted Lance, waved to him to come up. Lance approached with Frank following him closely.

"This way please, sir," the bank officer said, motioning toward a closed door. Lance headed for it, but when the young man noticed that Frank intended to follow, he held up his hand. "I'm sorry, sir. Could you please wait on the benches? We should not be too long."

"Finally someone who can speak English," Frank said, smiling. "Listen, this business concerns both of us. We can explain it all momentarily. Please!" He smiled again at the banker.

The man hesitated, and as he did Lance desperately sought to make eye contact with the teller. She noticed and spoke rapidly to the banker. Lance had no idea what she had said.

"I'm very sorry, sir," the banker told Frank. "These are bank regulations. I'm sure you understand." With a glance and a motion of his head, he signaled to the nearby guard, who guided Frank back to the benches. Frank glared at Lance for a second and then gritted his teeth and retreated.

The banker ushered Lance into the office. He offered him a seat in one of the two wooden chairs in front of the desk and moved around the desk and sat in his own large leather seat.

"I'm Sr. Luis Consuelo. How may I be of service?" he asked, extending his hand to Lance.

Lance hesitated and then decided to take his chances with the man smiling kindly in front of him. "Look," he said, "the reason we came is so that I can withdraw $50,000 from my account. Unless I miss my guess, that type of withdrawal will be practically impossible. Am I right?"

"I'm afraid you are correct, sir. We do not have that kind of currency in our little bank. Such a transaction would take several days, possibly over a week."

"That's what I thought. The truth is, I suspect the man outside is nothing but a con artist. Do you understand what I mean by a con artist?" The banker nodded and motioned for him to continue. "Well, he has offered to sell me a piece of property, but the fact that he insists on a cash sale makes me rather suspicious."

"Yes, we have problems with such people in the Dominican, I am afraid. However, I'm not sure how I can be of assistance in this matter."

"Well, the fact is I would like to be rid of him. If there is an exit I could leave from unseen, I'd like to get away from him and go. I don't want to deal with him anymore."

The banker sat considering the matter for a several seconds. Finally he rose.

"I'm sure you realize, sir, that this is highly unusual and is really no concern of the bank."

"Yes I do, but I'm desperate. Please help me."

The banker hesitated but finally strode to the back of the office and opened a door that Lance had not noticed until now; it blended well with the woodwork. "Follow me, please," the banker said. He led Lance down a hallway past several other offices to a heavy door at the end of the hall. He punched some numbers into the panel, swung the door open, and suddenly Lance was staring out into a back alley.

"Thank you," Lance said. "I wish I could repay you in some way for your kindness. Unfortunately, I have no cash right now to offer you."

"That is not necessary. Simply promise me that you will not return to this bank. You will have ten minutes, at which time the bank guards will usher your friend out of the bank. I suggest you use those ten minutes to get as far away from this bank as possible."

Lance grasped the man's hand and pumped it vigorously. "I will. I promise," he said.

Lance ran down the alley toward the busy street. He stepped into the street and waved his hand over his head. All the taxis he saw had passengers and sped by, but finally after what seemed like an interminable time a taxi swerved toward him. Lance gave the address and entreated the driver to hurry. The taxi pulled away.

When the taxi arrived, he asked the driver to wait and sprinted to his room. He burst through the door, grabbed his suitcase, scooped up items left strewn on the floor, zipped his bag closed, and dashed out, leaving most of his clothes and grooming equipment behind. He tossed his suitcase in the back seat with him and said, "Drive!"

As the car approached the corner, another taxi turned onto the lane. Frank sat red-faced in the back. Lance dove down behind the front seat as the taxi passed. A few seconds later Lance peeked out the back and spied Frank running toward his room. Lance spoke to the driver and thirty minutes later was deposited in a ramshackle part of town. He took a room with cement walls, a cold shower, and plenty of cockroaches for companionship. He arranged with the lady of the establishment to have his meals provided in his room. He rarely ventured outside.

Lance stayed there for the next few days and then traveled to the main city, Santo Domingo. He visited a travel agency and asked about flights. The agent checked schedules on the computer and announced that all flights for the next twenty-four hours were full with the exception of a flight to Lima, Peru, which left later that afternoon.

"I'll take it," Lance said.

"Very well," the lady said with a smile. "Could I please have your passport?"

This was the part that made Lance nervous. Would he find that he was trapped on this island? He took out his passport and handed it to her. She copied the passport number along with the other information Lance gave her. His nervousness increased when he saw her frown in confusion at the screen.

"This is odd," she said. "It's not accepting your passport number."

"Great," Lance said. "This has happened to me more than once."

"Don't worry. I'll try it again," she said.

Lance sat impatiently. He knew the number would never be accepted. He was about to make an excuse and leave the office when the lady said, "I can't seem to get it to work. I'm sure this will work, however; it hasn't failed yet." She again entered data into the computer.

In a few seconds she said, "There we go. Sir, you are booked on the flight to Lima, Peru, leaving at four-fifteen this afternoon. Please be at the airport one hour before flight time."

Lance gaped. Finally he said, "Great! That's wonderful!" He paid for the fare in cash, and she printed the flight information along with his boarding passes.

He thanked her for her help and got up to leave the office. "By the way, what did you do to make my passport work?" he asked, his curiosity getting the better of him.

The lady smiled. "Oh, I simply used my own passport number. Don't worry. This has happened before. They won't be cross-checking your information at the airport here in the Dominican Republic. You're all set."

Lance traveled back to San Jose de Macoris. He packed his bags and cleaned out the room. Then he walked down the block to where his landlord lived and told her he was giving up the suite because an emergency had arisen. He then caught the bus back to the airport.

Lance was amazed that he was able to board the plane without once having to produce identification. It seemed his ticket was enough. He arrived in Lima that evening and waited in a long line to clear customs. Evidently several flights had arrived at just about the same time, creating a terrible backlog. Finally, however, he reached a customs officer, who stamped his passport after a cursory glance. Lance exited the airport and sought a taxi. He was pleased to find an organized taxi system, and a cabby agreed to take him to the nearest hotel for ten American dollars. Ten minutes later the taxi pulled up in front of a small but elegant place called the Hotel Hatun.

Lance spent the next few days orienting himself to the city of Lima and to the country of Peru. Up until the point when the travel agent in the Dominican Republic had announced that a flight was available, he hadn't given Peru a second thought and knew next to nothing about it. He spotted a place with internet service and spent a couple of afternoons reading everything he could find about Peru. He had heard of Machu Picchu and the Nazca Lines and was surprised to find that both were located in Peru. But Lance didn't intend to be a tourist. In fact, he would make it a point to avoid tourists, especially after what had happened in the Dominican.

He soon discovered that tourists rarely visited northern Peru, so the next morning he had a taxi drive him to a bus depot and he boarded a northbound bus. Lance looked out the window as the bus journeyed through a desert landscape. It appeared so desolate that he imagined himself at the end of the world. About six hours after leaving the capital, the bus crested a high hill and a panorama spread out far below him. The blue Pacific stretched to the horizon. Row after row of white breakers waited their turn to pound the golden sand of a long beach. Beyond the sand lay an agricultural landscape. The lush fields made a profound impression on Lance since this was the first significant greenery he had seen since leaving the city. A small town was nestled among these fields. Lance pressed his nose to the window and studied the view as the bus wound its way to the village far below.

When the bus arrived, the door opened and several people

climbed aboard and squeezed their way down the narrow aisle, looking for seats. On impulse Lance jumped from his seat and pushed his way toward the door against the flow of passengers. He stepped from the bus into the bright sunshine. The only place to stay in town was an old hotel on the main street. A clerk led him up a long flight of stairs and showed him a number of rooms. Lance chose one with a small balcony that offered a clear view of the Pacific. He dropped off his bags and returned to the street to investigate. The spot was perfect. He strolled the streets and then walked along the beach. He did not once see another white face or come across anything that could be remotely construed as touristy. Yet the place seemed idyllic. Lance discovered that the town was named San Sebastian.

He stayed there for the next three weeks. After the first week he moved from the hotel into a clean room at the back of a small family home. He even considered buying a little house just above the beach on the outskirts of town.

Lance used $50,000 in Canadian money to open an account in the local bank. This raised a few eyebrows, but the bank accepted the deposit with no fuss other than a hold on the funds for two weeks to allow the main bank in Lima to exchange the dollars into sols. This did not bother Lance at all since he had gotten as much of the local currency as possible from street vendors while in Lima.

Lance continued these transactions at regular intervals and traveled to Lima where he chanced starting a large account with the rest of the cash in his suitcase. This amounted to nearly $250,000 in Canadian money, but again the bank agreed to open the account with little fuss. Lance felt at peace now that all the loot was in safekeeping and he had found the beautiful little village. He smiled contentedly as he left the bus. But one missing piece kept him from knowing true contentment. Lance took long walks and did a lot of thinking. Finally, he did something he had done a few times since leaving Canada; he phoned Jen. This time, however, Lance had something specific he wished to discuss with her.

"Oh, hi," Jen said, brightening as she always did when she recognized his voice.

"Hi, Jen. How are my girls doing?"

She laughed at the question and assured him they were fine.

"Listen, Jen. I've got something I want to ask you."

"Oh? What is it?"

"I want you and Micky to come visit me."

"What? In Peru?"

"Sure! Why not?"

"Well, for one thing I've just started an audit, and it's going to take me a couple of weeks to finish. And there are other clients who want me to do work for them."

"Jen, I'm not asking for you to come tomorrow, but you should come when you can. You deserve a real holiday, not like the last time when you got stuck in that campground and were pestered by a certain surveyor every time you turned around."

She laughed. "You were my salvation. I would have gone crazy otherwise."

"Seriously, Jen, I want you to come. It's beautiful here. You just tell me when you can come, and I'll pay for the tickets."

Jen did not know what to say.

"I have some things I want to discuss with you, Jen."

"That sounds interesting," she said. "Now you've got me curious."

"Say yes, Jen. Say you'll come."

Jen sighed. "Let me think about it, Rav," she said. "Call me back in a couple of nights, and we'll talk about it."

Lance agreed and changed the subject. They chatted about their daily lives for a while and eventually said good night.

Two evenings later Lance did as Jen had asked and called her back. During their conversation she finally agreed to come but said she would come alone. She would arrange to have Micky to stay with her sister for a week. They discussed details and finally decided she would come after Christmas once she had completed her final audit of the year. Lance said he would make the arrangements and wrote down all the information he needed from her to book the flights. Once they made the decision they were excited about seeing each other again. They chatted animatedly for several more minutes before hanging up.

CHAPTER 13

R ob exited the plane in Lima, Peru, and patiently waited as the long line of passengers coiled its way through customs. Finally he reached the booth, and after a few perfunctory questions he was through and headed toward the exit. He had a room booked for the night. In the morning he would meet the outfitters for the four-day hike he had planned. In the afternoon he would fly to Cusco, and the day after he would be on the trail.

He could hardly believe he was here. Three weeks before Peru had been as far from his mind as possible. That suddenly changed when Captain Harding approached his desk one morning and sat down uninvited across from the detective.

"Rob, I'm freeing up your caseload," the captain said.

Rob looked up from the paperwork he was busy filling out.

"What the hell for?" he protested.

"Because you're going on a vacation."

"To where?"

"I don't know where, and frankly I don't care. All I know is that you're taking a vacation, and it's starting as soon as possible."

"Why?"

"Because you've been working for three years and you haven't taken a single day off in that time. Hell, you've accumulated almost two months of holiday time. The department is on my back about it. I don't want you taking all that time off at once. If we can do without you for two months, we can do without you period, so take a couple of weeks every few months until you use up your vacation time."

"Maybe I should," Rob said.

"Maybe I didn't make myself clear. That wasn't a request. You're taking two weeks off. Enjoy your vacation," the captain said, looking pointedly at Rob.

Since the captain was adamant that Rob take time off, he grudgingly agreed. That evening at home he read an article about the Inca Trail in *National Geographic* and was intrigued. The next day he went to see a travel agent he knew and made arrangements for a trip to Peru.

At this moment, however, Rob was anxious. The tension and the heat had gotten to him. He had done little traveling, and the unfamiliar customs procedures made him uneasy.

He hoisted his backpack to his shoulder and followed the other passengers to the exit. As he left the customs area, Rob was met by several taxi drivers who immediately began hustling him. He ignored them and wove his way through the terminal.

Rob was entering a country, in fact a continent, he had never visited. He spied the many taxis lined up outside and headed for them. He hoped they would know the location of his hotel; otherwise he had no idea how he would get there.

Up ahead was an East Indian man with a wide smile on his face. A woman with mousy blond hair darted past Rob, nudging him slightly, and leapt into the man's arms.

Rob glanced at the couple hugging each other as he went by and smiled at the tenderness of the scene. He took five more steps toward the entrance and then froze. He twisted around and studied the man closely. He was still in the woman's embrace. Rob would know that face anywhere. It was the man by the elevators at the Crown Hotel. It was the man on the poster whose photo the technician had altered according to Rob's instructions. Rob knew with 100 percent certainty that he was looking at Lance Knight.

Rob looked around the terminal and spotted a policeman stationed at the exit.

"Do you speak English?" he asked urgently.

"Yes, sir. May I be of service?"

Rob pulled out his badge and showed it to the officer.

"I am a Canadian police officer," he said, "and that man is a fugitive from Canadian justice." Rob turned and pointed to Lance. The man and the woman, arms around each other, were heading directly toward them.

"Are you sure?" the officer asked, studying the couple skeptically.

"There is no doubt in my mind," Rob said. "He robbed a bank in Canada. I worked on the case."

"Very well," the officer said. "Please wait here." He headed toward the couple.

Lance and Jen were walking toward the exit when the officer suddenly appeared in front of them. He put his hand on Lance's shoulder and said, "Please step over here, sir." With his head he indicated an area free of traffic against the terminal wall.

Lance headed there with the officer following him, his hand still on Lance's shoulder. Jen followed the pair helplessly, trailing her suitcase behind her. When they reached the wall the officer waved, and Rob approached them from near the exit.

"Are you sure this is the man?" the officer asked Rob.

Rob looked hard into Lance's eyes and said, "I've never been surer of anything in my life."

Lance thought there was something oddly familiar about this man. He could not place where he had seen him, but he knew he had.

"Lance Knight, I'm Detective Rob Passaglia of the Vancouver Police Department, and you are under arrest."

"Turn around and put your hands behind your back," the Peruvian officer said, reaching for the cuffs in his belt as bystanders began to notice the drama unfolding near them.

Lance twisted around suddenly before the two men could react. He reached in his pocket and tossed a key to Jen. "Go to the hotel, Jen," he said as Rob and the officer seized him. In an instant his hands were behind his back and the cuffs were applied.

"Wait at the hotel, Jen. I'll be there tomorrow. This is all a mistake," Lance shouted as the officer pushed him toward a door marked "Policia." Rob followed. Just before he disappeared behind the door, Lance took one last look at Jen, who was standing dumbfounded all alone in the airport.

Inside the small room assigned to the police, Lance was ushered to a chair at a table.

Rob sat down across from Lance while the officer who had arrested him conversed in Spanish with another policeman. It was obvious that neither was sure of the protocol in this situation. The second officer picked up a phone and spoke to someone while the other officer listened.

"You came so close to getting away with this," Rob said to Lance.

"So what happens now?" Lance asked.

Rob shrugged. "To be honest, I don't know. I imagine you'll be held in custody here until extradition is worked out, and then you'll be flown back to Canada to face the charges."

Suddenly Rob thought about the woman involved in the happy reunion. He quickly returned to the terminal and looked up and down the huge hall, but there was no sign of her. Rob raced to the exit. Ignoring the taxi drivers swarming around him, he scanned the area. A long row of taxis were parked in the lane bordering the terminal. His sharp eyes searched the passengers along the lane and inside the taxis, but he still could not find the woman.

"A blond woman just came out. Did you see her?" Rob asked the taxi drivers around him.

The drivers looked at each other and shrugged their shoulders.

Rob doubted they had understood a word he said. He went back into the terminal and crossed into the airport police station.

He immediately confronted Lance. "Who is she?" Rob demanded.

"Leave her out of this," Lance said dejectedly.

"We'll find her," Rob replied. "It's only a matter of time, and when we do she's going to have some explaining to do."

"I said leave her out of this," Lance told him angrily.

Rob decided to change tack.

"You sure led us on a chase," he said. "We almost had you several times. Do you know I walked right by you at the hotel?"

"It was wonderful for me too," Lance replied sarcastically. "I thought I was going to die in those woods."

"Why did you do it?" Rob asked.

"I felt I deserved it."

"You *deserved* it!" Rob repeated in astonishment.

"Yeah, I've worked all my life, and what do I have to show for it? When a person puts in all that time he should have something to show for it. I had nothing. Any time I needed new clothes or wanted to take my wife out for a simple meal, I had to ask myself if I could afford it. We had so much debt that we would never be free of it."

Rob leaned forward, locking eyes with Lance. "I'll tell you what you deserve," he barked. "You deserve to go to jail for eight to fourteen years, and I'm going to see that that's what happens." With that, he got up and conferred with the policemen.

Finally, well after midnight a paddy wagon arrived at the airport and Lance was whisked away. Rob wanted to accompany him in the wagon but was denied entrance. The police gave him the address of the jail where Lance would be held and said Rob could see him in the morning. Rob supposed he would not be going on the hike. He would need to find the Canadian embassy to apprise the government of the situation. That would have to wait until tomorrow, though. He yawned widely. Right now he needed to get some sleep. Rob left the airport and took a taxi to his hotel.

· · ·●●●◆●●●● · ·

In a daze, Jen looked out the window of the taxi as it passed through the city. Lima seemed otherworldly with the occasional modern-looking building sitting between tiny, worn-down shops of every description. A feeling of abandonment shot through her. Why in the world had she agreed to come here?

This was stupid. She would to have to compose herself. Rav had told her he would see her tomorrow once everything had been worked out, but what had happened? Why had he been arrested? Right from the start, Jen had felt there was something mysterious about him.

After a long ride the taxi pulled up to the Hotel Hatun. Jen walked in and talked to the lady at the desk, who was friendly and spoke good English. It was obvious that the staff had been expecting her. A porter escorted Jen to her room. The room was shiny and clean. Lance's suitcase sat open in a corner. She ignored everything, climbed into bed, and slept fitfully.

Jen spent the next day at the hotel, hoping Rav would show up and the nightmare would be ended. But he did not show up that day, or the next, or the third. Eventually she began to stray from the hotel for short periods. She had no idea what to do. Her return ticket was not for another week. Would she have to wait until then? By this time Jen doubted Rav would ever show up. She wondered what was happening to him. On the second day she had gone to a police station, but the police wouldn't or couldn't tell her anything.

Tomorrow she would see if she could return home. She missed Micky intensely. A day after arriving, Jen had phoned her but had struggled to keep from sobbing. Micky had immediately sensed something was wrong. Jen had assured her that she was fine and had ended the call quickly, not wanting to add to the worry her daughter felt.

CHAPTER 14

L ance was taken downtown and placed in a cell in the main police station several blocks from the center of Lima. He slept very little if at all. He was extremely worried about Jen and about his situation. Rob visited him that afternoon and said he had gone to the embassy that morning. The embassy would petition the Peruvian government, and Lance would soon be on his way back to Canada. Copious amounts of red tape had to be cleared since Canada and Peru did not have an extradition treaty, but in a short time he would stand before a judge in Vancouver.

The detective asked Lance what he had done with the money, but he would say nothing. Once he was in Canada he might be able to use what he knew to plea bargain. Realizing he would get nowhere, Rob rose to go.

"There's nothing more I can do now," Rob said, "so I'm going to hike the Inca Trail like I planned. I'm leaving for Cusco tomorrow." Lance nodded disinterestedly and Rob was gone.

Over the next few days Lance sat in isolation save for when guards brought him food. The depression Lance had felt at the Blue Oasis motel in Vancouver came back redoubled. He did little but stare into space as the hours dragged by.

On the afternoon of the fourth day of his incarceration, Lance heard the jingle of keys and the cell door opened. Sunk in depression, he did not look up for several seconds. When he did, he saw Barb standing by the door.

Lance blinked twice and then his eyes grew wide. He jumped to his feet.

"Barb, how in the world did you find me here?" he asked.

Barb gave a quick smile and said, "Your capture made the front page of the *Vancouver Sun*. When I read about it, I booked a flight and here I am. The kids couldn't understand why I came, and I'm not even sure I can explain it myself."

"So how are the kids?"

"They're holding up reasonably well. They still don't understand how you could do what you did. They love you, but you'll never understand how betrayed they feel."

"Believe me, if I could rewind what I've done, I'd do it in a heartbeat. You know I would never intentionally hurt them or you."

Barb just shrugged.

"I'm surprised they let you in to see me," Lance said. "I haven't had a visitor since they locked me up."

"Well, that was actually quite an ordeal," Barb said. "I've been here for a day and a half. I knocked on every door I could think of. I think they finally decided I wasn't going to take no for an answer, so it was easier to let me see you. But they've made it pretty clear that this visit is a one-time-only deal."

"So why did you come, Barb?" Lance asked, letting out a deep breath. "The last time we spoke you said you were moving on."

Barb sat down on a chair at a small desk. "I need an explanation, Lance," she said. "I want to know why you were so willing to throw our lives away. I need it face to face and eye to eye. Why did you do it, Lance?"

Lance thought deeply for a few seconds. "As I said, it was never my intention to throw our lives away. I wanted to give you the life you deserved, one where we didn't have to worry and could always be happy."

"We were happy!" Barb said. "At least I thought we were."

"Come on, Barb. Happiness isn't eking out an existence, wondering how we are going to get by every month. And what about retirement? What happens once the paychecks stop? Sure, we have a few thousand in the government tax free retirement savings plan for that day, but how long do you think that will last? Staying in a rut all your life means that's the way you'll end your life. That wasn't for me. I did something about it. I admit I never anticipated the consequences, but at least I tried to do something about our lives."

"We had a house, a family. That's all I ever needed, Lance."

Lance hung his head, at a loss for words.

"Do you know how I feel? It's like you took a knife and stabbed me in the heart," Barb said, gently patting her chest. "Ever since the day you robbed the bank, I've sat and wondered how you could do this to me, to us. It's a betrayal, Lance, pure and simple. You've betrayed me! You've betrayed your family! The kids don't know what to think. They're crushed, Lance. So am I!"

"I'm sorry, Barb. I don't know what to say. If I had known what would happen, I never would have done it."

Tears trickled down Barb's cheek and she sobbed quietly.

"I suppose I'll be sent back to Canada soon, and I'll be sent away for a long, long time. I asked you before and you couldn't give me an answer. Now I'm asking you again, Barb. Do you think we can rebuild our marriage? Will you wait for me and give me a chance to make up for this, to make it up to our family?"

"I don't think you can fix this one, Lance. How can you do what you've done to me and to our family and fix it? Tell me that!" Barb said, glaring into his eyes.

Lance's expression turned gray. He had never felt lower than he did at this moment. "Well, that's it then," Lance said. "My life is over. I wish I was dead." He slouched in his chair.

Barb stared at him. Finally she stood up, tears streaming down her cheeks.

"There's one thing I can say for sure,'" she told Lance. "To me you are dead. I flew down here to get the answers I deserved, and I guess I got them, inadequate as they are. I think I'll go now. Goodbye, Lance!" She turned and left the room.

Lance sat in his chair, staring after her. The visit had brought home the pain he had caused, and it hurt to think what he had done to those he loved. The gloom he had felt over the past several days intensified. His head pounded and he was barely conscious as his surroundings whirled around him.

The following morning Lance was led into an interrogation room. Two men entered, both wearing ill-fitting suits. The older man was thin with an impossibly black mustache. His hair was flecked with gray. He sat on the table in front of Lance while the other detective, a shorter, stockier man with native Indian features, leaned against the door. The detective at the table spoke.

"My name is Detective Lopez, and this is Detective Ramirez," he said, nodding toward the man at the door. "How have you been? I assume you have been treated well."

Lance shrugged.

"Tell me what you did with the money. It's $1 million, I heard. You must have it here in Peru with you, yes?"

Again Lance said nothing.

"Within the next day, you will be moved to the Jose Larco Penitentiary. I assure you, my friend, you do not want to go there. I can, how do you say it, pull on the strings and make sure you stay here. All you have to do is tell us what you did with the money."

Lance remained silent.

With that, Ramirez lunged at him, grabbed him roughly, and spun him in his chair. He pulled his pistol and held it to Lance's temple, shaking with rage.

"Where is it?" he screamed in his face.

"I don't know," Lance said, frightened.

"I'll shoot you right here, you fucking pig's tit," the man yelled in Spanish as he pressed the muzzle harder against Lance's head.

"I hid it," Lance said desperately. "It's in Mexico."

In the next instant he saw stars and felt warm blood trickle into his eyes. Ramirez had struck him on the head with the butt of his pistol.

"You're lying," Ramirez raged. "Tell me another lie and I'll bust your teeth." He held the pistol in front of Lance's nose so he could see it. His blood was on the barrel.

"Listen, friend," Lopez said. "You do not want to make this man angry. Why don't you tell us where the money is? We know you are lying. You don't want to go through this, do you?"

Ramirez slapped Lance hard across the face and screamed at him again.

For the next hour the men shouted at him, cajoled him, and beat him. A significant mouse had already developed on his forehead, his lip was split and bleeding, and there were contusions on his cheek and his chin. Still, Lance refused to tell them what they wanted to know. The two were obviously hoping that they might strike it rich if he revealed where the money was.

Finally, barely conscious, Lance heard the door to the room open as a third man entered. Through eyes that were nearly swollen shut, Lance saw that this man was much more neatly dressed and that he was upset. He sputtered a stream of abuse at the men, who cowered in the face of the vehemence. The Spanish was rapid, but Lance had now been exposed to the language for more than two months. He did not understand everything that was said, but he heard the word *Canadian* several times and the phrase *Canadian ambassador* and finally the word *hospital*.

He deciphered that the man was outraged at the abuse Lance had suffered and that he feared the actions of the two men would cause an international incident if the embassy learned of them. His final command was that Lance be taken to a hospital immediately.

An ambulance soon arrived, and he was put on a gurney and loaded in. Under guard by a uniformed officer who carried a submachine gun, the ambulance whisked him to a hospital. At the hospital he was immediately sedated. Lance awoke the next morning feeling nauseous. He had been placed in a hospital gown, and his wounds had been treated. He touched the bandages on his head gingerly. He attempted to roll away from the guard, who sat in a chair in a corner of the room, but realized his right hand was cuffed to the bed frame.

Later a doctor came in and told him he was being kept in the hospital for a day for observation. Lance had suffered a concussion and severe lacerations to his forehead. "Take these," the doctor said, handing him two pills. "They will help you sleep."

Lance popped the pills into his mouth with his left hand and drank the glass of water proffered by a nurse. When the doctor left, however, he turned his head away from the guard and quietly spit the pills out onto the bedsheet. He wriggled his body until he felt the damp pills slide under him.

Lance surveyed his surroundings. He was in a private room—at least as private as a room could be with an armed guard seated in the corner watching his every move suspiciously. A door opened to a cubicle where a toilet and a sink were located. Beyond this the room was quite simple. There was no sophisticated equipment. Above the bed was a window with a heavy metal lattice covering. Lance was cuffed to the wrought iron headboard on the old bed. The room gave him a feel for what North American hospitals might have been like in the thirties or forties. In fact, Lance had a bed much like this one thirty years earlier when he was a kid. His mind drifted back to his childhood days and to a much simpler existence. Then the idea hit him.

He rolled over as best he could away from the guard and lay still. After a few minutes Lance began to snore. He hoped the guard found the noise convincing.

Finally, a couple of hours later, he heard the guard get up, walk over to the cubicle, and close the door behind him. The sound told him the guard was urinating in the bathroom. Eventually the guard came out and exited the room. Immediately Lance sat upright in the bed and pushed against the headboard. As he suspected, the wrought iron frame slid upward easily. A few hours before when he was reminiscing about his childhood, he remembered that the headboard telescoped into a bottom piece. He recalled that as a teenager he had hidden his girlie magazines in the tubes of his headboard. That was what had given him the idea, and now he had to move quickly.

One more push and the headboard separated from the rest of the frame. He hoped the guard had not heard the screech of metal against metal. Lance threaded the cuff past the tube, and now he was free. He went to the bathroom and cursed under his breath. He had hoped his clothes would be there, but they were not. He went to the door and peered up and down the hallway; there was no sign of the guard. Lance quietly left the room, the cuff dangling from his wrist. Everything depended on what he did in the next few seconds.

He sprinted down the deserted hallway and walked past a nursing station next to a bank of elevators. He pushed the button to the elevators and stood listening to the whirring of the mechanism behind the metal door. He glanced anxiously in the direction of his room. Finally he lost patience and bolted for a heavy door next to the elevators. This was the entrance to the stairway. Lance descended as quickly as he could with vertigo threatening his balance and his head pulsing with pain. He had no idea what floor he was on. He had dropped four flights of stairs when he heard the door high above him burst open. The guard had discovered his absence and was in pursuit. At the bottom of the stairs, Lance swung left through heavy doors out into a hospital ward as footsteps pounded above.

Lance tucked the cuffs into the sleeve of his gown and hurried down the hallway, heedless of the curious looks from staff and patients. He rounded a corner and sprinted down another long corridor. He turned left and then right again and came to another set of stairs, which he quickly descended. Lance could tell he was now on the main floor, because he could see an extensive lobby with exit doors to the outside off to the left. He turned to the right. The guard would head straight to this lobby to prevent him from escaping the hospital. Lance bent over and feigned a limp as he moved slowly down the hall. It was all he could do to keep from running, but finally he reached a set of glass doors. He pushed his way through.

Lance entered a smoking area at the back of the hospital. He was on a patio where patients and staff members stood puffing away. Lance ignored them and moved to the far end of the patio. He crossed onto the lawn bordering the hospital and came to a brick fence at the boundary of the hospital property. He leapfrogged the waist-high fence and sprinted from the hospital grounds toward stores on the far side of a busy street.

Dodging traffic, Lance crossed the street and burst into a store where customers sat in cubicles in front of computers. Just inside the entrance two young men sat behind a counter, and behind them were phone booths.

Lance turned to the youths and pointed at the booths. "Emergencia! Emergencia!" he cried frantically.

"Un sol," one of them said.

Lance displayed his hospital gown and held out his empty hands to show he had no money. He again pointed at the telephones, yelling, "Emergencia." Finally one of the youths shrugged and waved him toward a booth. Lance dashed into it and called information for the Hotel Hatun. Once he had the number, he pushed the buttons quickly. A receptionist answered the phone, and he gave her the number of Jen's room. The phone rang once. No answer. It rang a second time and then a third. Finally on the fourth ring, Jen picked up.

"Hello," she answered uncertainly.

"Jen, it's me."

"Oh my God," she said. "Where are you?"

"Jen, listen. Do you know where the PagoPoco store is? It's near the hotel."

"Yes. I've seen it."

"Meet me there in an hour. Bring me a change of clothes."

"Why? What's happening?"

"One hour, Jen. I don't have time to explain right now." With that, he hung up and left the establishment.

Shortly after, a collectivo pulled up. This one sported the names of locales in Lima painted in bright letters on the sides and the front of the van. Lance recognized none of the names. He had seen many of these vans during his time in the city. They were one of the main forms of transportation. The door swung open, and Lance darted in and took one of the few remaining seats.

The other passengers stared at the strange white man wearing a hospital smock. A young lady near him slid over as far away as possible. The van sped on, stopping at most of the intersections. Lance watched the others in the van. A boy operated the door. At each intersection, the boy would swing the door open, jump out, and shout out the stops on the route, ushering waiting passengers into the van. Before long, the van was packed. Once it was underway, the boy would collect coins from the newest passengers. Lance had no change. All he had was a hospital smock and a set of handcuffs attached to his wrist, which he concealed as best he could under the sleeve of the smock. He feigned sleep to avoid making eye contact with the boy. This seemed to work as the collectivo pulled out into traffic once again.

The van continued on. Lance estimated it had gone about twelve blocks, but it was difficult for him to say since he kept his eyes closed. Finally he felt a tap on his shoulder. He opened his eyes. The boy had his hand out, gesturing impatiently for payment. Lance pretended he did not understand. The boy said something to the driver, and the driver immediately pulled to the side of the road and stopped. The boy swung the door open and sternly signaled for Lance to get out.

Lance climbed out of the van. Behind him he heard a gasp from the young woman who had sat near him, and not a few snickers. He had forgotten that the smock was open in the back, and he whipped his hand back and gathered the material together. This action caused the cuffs to swing into full view. Lance quickly pulled the cuffs back into his sleeves. Everyone in the collectivo seemed to be staring at him as it pulled away. Lance watched as the van disappeared down the busy street.

This was ridiculous. If a cop spotted him dressed as he was, he would end up back in jail.

Soon another collectivo stopped at the intersection. To all appearances, this one was full, but Lance squeezed aboard anyway. He had to stay out of view as much as possible. He must look strange with his bloodied face and the hospital gown. He climbed in next to a short, middle-aged woman. The strange man in a hospital smock made her extremely uneasy. She immediately got up and left the van.

Before long Lance was asked to leave this van as well when it was discovered he didn't have the fare. He caught van after van. Sometimes he rode just a few blocks; other times he stayed on for twenty or more before being kicked off. Some vans refused him entry dressed as he was.

Lance didn't recognize any of the places where he was deposited. This latest forced stop was obviously a main connecting area. There were benches installed along the sidewalk. Many collectivos and a few ragtag buses were haphazardly parked along the street. The buses picked up passengers and roared off in clouds of black smoke while several boys from the collectivos ran among the crowd advertising their destinations. There was a great deal of hustle and bustle. Suddenly Lance spied a policeman. He was staring at Lance and began to approach. Lance sprinted off in the opposite direction as he heard the piercing sound of a whistle behind him.

After a couple of blocks he looked back. The policeman was nowhere to be seen. Lance bent over, panting heavily. How was he going to meet Jen? He had no idea where he was, and he stuck out like a sore thumb.

Lance surveyed his surroundings, hoping against hope he would recognize something. He stared down the block at the businesses on the opposite side of the street.

Desperate situations call for desperate actions, Lance thought. He walked down the block and quickly crossed the street, ignoring the stares of those he passed. He approached a large bank. Lance realized that this bank bore the same name as the branch where he had opened the large account on an earlier trip to the city. That was great, but he had no identification.

Looking as he did, it was difficult if not impossible for him to be unobtrusive. Nevertheless, Lance stood off to the side and studied the entrance. Customers entered and exited the bank through large glass doors. A security guard stood at the entrance, and another held post just inside the doors. Lance waited for his opportunity.

Finally Lance saw several customers coming and going from the bank. As a result, the doors were wide open. *Here goes nothing,* he thought. Lance threw the smock at his feet and charged toward the entrance completely naked.

The guard outside was so startled that Lance was able to rush right by him. Now he was inside the bank and headed toward the tellers. Suddenly rough arms were around him, and he was thrown to the floor by security guards.

"Socorro! Socorro! Me robaron! Socorro!" Lance yelled at the top of his lungs. "Help! Help! I've been robbed," he repeated in English.

At this the guards paused in confusion. They looked to the interior of the bank. A scowling man in a neat suit was hurrying toward the commotion. "Lo boten!" he shouted at the guards. Lance didn't understand but knew he would be tossed back in the street since the guards hauled him to his feet and were pulling him toward the entrance.

"Please! Please wait! I've been robbed! I have money!" Lance shouted at the bank manager. The manager blinked and then held up his hand to the guards. He spoke rapidly to them and signaled with a jerk of his head.

In the next instant, Lance was being ushered to an office and was pushed into a chair in front of a large desk. The bank manager followed and closed the door behind him. He sat in his large chair and studied Lance.

In a moment the most beautiful Hispanic woman Lance had ever seen entered the office. She was tall and slender with long dark hair flowing over her shoulders. Lance was happy that due to the stressfulness of the situation there was no response in his nether region. The manager spoke to her in Spanish. She nodded and left the office. The manager continued to stare at Lance.

Soon the woman returned, this time with a towel that she red-facedly proffered to Lance. The manager again spoke to her in rapid staccato Spanish.

The woman turned to Lance and in clear English said, "Excuse me, sir, but Señor Guanilo would like to know the reason for the disturbance you have caused in his bank." She smiled at Lance. He could tell she had relayed the message with much more politeness than the manager had delivered it.

"Thank you," Lance said. "I was cuffed, beaten, and robbed

no more than a block from here. They took my clothes, my wallet, everything."

The woman translated for the manager and Lance continued.

"My name is Mark Fenwood," he said, "and I have a rather large account with this institution. Please ask him to check this for me. I have an account with $250,000 in it. I opened this account a month and a half ago at the Larco Avenue branch. As you can see, I am in a desperate situation." He turned toward the manager. "All I am asking is to withdraw a small amount from my account. I realize there may be a substantial fee for this, which of course I'll be happy to pay." He smiled at the woman. "Please be sure to tell him everything I just said." Lance hoped the mention of the large fee might whet the manager's appetite and keep him from tossing him from the bank.

The woman spoke at length with the manager, who posed a few questions. The woman was able to answer these without speaking to Lance.

With a furrowed brow, the manager folded his hands in front of himself for a good minute and then spoke once again to his lovely assistant.

The woman turned to Lance. "This is a very dangerous part of the city, señor," she said. "We are very happy that nothing even more terrible happened to you. It is most unusual that your robbers saw fit to remove your clothing. I suppose they thought it might delay you from alerting the authorities. Still, it is very unusual. However, the manager has said we will look into what you have told us about your account. Unfortunately, this might take a long time. If you don't mind, we will ask you to wait here."

"Under the circumstances," Lance said, "I don't mind at all."

At that, the manager smiled at him and left the office with his assistant. While he waited, Lance scooped up a paperclip sitting on the desk and fiddled with the lock on the cuffs. In just a few minutes the cuffs popped open, and Lance threw them into a waste can. He made sure the cuffs were covered by papers in the can. He didn't want any questions about them, realizing they were a weak part of the story he had spun.

It was almost an hour before the manager and the assistant returned. This time the manager was all smiles. He shook Lance's hand and spoke to him in rapid Spanish, none of which Lance understood. He handed Lance a blanket, which he immediately wrapped around himself. The manager gestured at the assistant. He shook Lance's hand again and left. She was carrying a number of papers and hurriedly moved behind the desk.

"I apologize, Mr. Fenwood, for the wait. It was necessary to verify the information you provided us. We have checked your branch and have found what you have told us to be true. Please sign at the bottom of this sheet."

Lance took the sheet, signed it, and passed it back. The woman took the sheet and compared the signature with the signature on another document in her stack of papers. This was obviously a document he had signed when he opened the account. Next, she pulled out a photocopy of his passport picture and compared it with Lance's facial features.

"Everything appears to be in order," she said. "The manager has agreed to allow you to withdraw a maximum of three hundred soles. Is that satisfactory at this time?"

"That's great," Lance said.

"Very well," she said, pulling out another paper. "Here is a check in that amount. All you need to do is sign it."

Lance looked at the check. All the details had already been filled in with the exception of the signature. He quickly signed.

"Unfortunately, Mr. Fenwood, a service fee of 150 soles will be withdrawn from your account. As part of this service, however, we would be happy to send someone to a store on the next block to get you some clothing." As she said this, her face reddened perceptibly. "This store sells very inexpensive clothing that should suffice until you can gain access to your own clothing. We can have you on your way in no more than fifteen minutes."

"Awesome," Lance said, beaming. "You guys are awesome."

The woman smiled and had him sign documents authorizing the service fee and confirming his identity. Lance signed the papers without bothering to read them. The woman scooped up the documents and left.

She was soon back, this time with a bag of clothing in her arms and a wad of cash. Lance took the bag. Inside were a simple white T-shirt, blue jeans, socks, and a pair of nondescript running shoes. The woman went over the purchase amounts that had been deducted from his account. Finally, she wished him luck and left him to change.

Once out of the bank, Lance hurried back to where the collectivo had dropped him off. Lance soon found a taxi at the terminus. He gave the driver the address of the hotel, settled on a fare, and climbed in.

After traveling for forty-five minutes, he jumped from the taxi and entered the PagoPoco store. He hoped Jen was still there. It had taken him well over two hours to arrive.

He raced from aisle to aisle, searching for Jen. Finally he saw her walking aimlessly in the men's clothing section, carrying a bundle. Lance ran to her.

"Jen," he cried as he wrapped his arms around her.

Jen's wide eyes wandered over his face for several seconds.

"My God, Rav," she gasped. "I hardly recognized you. What happened to your face?"

"I ran into the butt end of a pistol," Lance said as he took the clothes from her. He stopped in front of a mirror and stared at his face. He hadn't had the opportunity to see it. He was surprised at how horrible he looked. Both eyes were blackened. On his forehead were two gashes. There was also bruising and swelling around his mouth. No wonder Jen had stared at him so. "Fortunately, though, this whole confusing misunderstanding has been resolved. I'm so sorry to have put you through this, Jen."

The two of them left the store and returned to the hotel.

CHAPTER 15

"**Y**ou did what?" Rob cried angrily.

His eyes were wide. He blinked slowly, and his newly tanned face was turning red as he stared at the official seated in front of him in the central administrative office of the police service in downtown Lima.

Head Detective Raiz Raiz adjusted his collar uncomfortably under the glare of the incensed detective. Rob had just returned from his hike on the Inca Trail, which accounted for the tan he had acquired in the past week. He had taken a late afternoon flight from Cusco, and when he discovered that his connection back to Canada was delayed, he decided to check on Lance before catching a flight later that night.

"Yes, I'm afraid it's true," Raiz said. "It seems two of our detectives became overzealous, shall we say, in their interrogation of the prisoner. He had to be hospitalized, and even though he was under twenty-four-hour surveillance, he managed to escape."

"How the hell did he do that?" Rob asked.

"Apparently he managed to disassemble the bed he was in while the guard went for coffee. Please rest assured that those involved in these, uh, mistakes have been properly disciplined."

"Wow, that's a relief," Rob snarled, his face still red.

"The Peruvian government apologizes for this unfortunate incident. We have a number of the prisoner's belongings, which I will be sending over to the Canadian embassy."

"Belongings?"

"Well, yes. You see, in the hospital he was in a gown, so we have all his clothing and, of course, his wallet, which was confiscated the day he was arrested."

"Do you mind if I have a look at these things?"

"I'm sorry, but that would be highly irregular. We must go through the proper channels in these matters. I'm sure you understand."

"I understand that there's been nothing proper at all in the way your police department has handled this matter. You know as well as I do that your detectives were trying to shake down this guy in hopes of pocketing the money. Maybe I'll just go pay my embassy a visit and explain exactly what has happened."

"Ah señor, there is no need to do anything so rash."

"How about a look at those belongings? I'm sure your staff members with their busy schedules haven't had time to examine them."

Raiz hesitated. "Very well, señor. My secretary will show you to a room you can use to conduct your examination. I'll have a porter bring the items to you."

Ten minutes later the box arrived from downstairs. Rob opened it and spread the contents across a table. There was not much to examine: one bloodstained blue short-sleeved shirt, one pair of tan khaki pants, one set of white briefs, a pair of blue socks, a pair of dark brown leather shoes, and one black leather wallet. Rob picked up the shirt and checked the pocket. Empty. He then picked up the trousers and checked all of the pockets front and back. Also empty. This was a little surprising, but any change in those pockets might easily have found its way to other pockets. Finally he picked up the wallet and opened it. There were no bills in the main sleeve. Rob chuckled. It would be highly unusual to have no money at the airport. A person would certainly need taxi fare to exit. Someone in the police department had obviously lifted the dough. There was one bank card and one credit card, both from Transcontinental Bank, an American company. Rob scribbled down the numbers on each of the cards. He would check these out once he got back to work in Vancouver. They might be able to freeze the funds in the account.

Next he pulled out several papers from another compartment of the wallet. One by one he examined these. He found three business cards. One was from the Hatun Hotel. Rob doubted this was much of a lead. The likelihood of Lance still being there after a full day was minimal. Still, it would be worthwhile to see if the hotel's records held a phone number, an address, or anything else of interest. The second card was from an engineer in Lima. *Why would he have that card?* Rob wondered. The last card was from a travel agent, also located in the capital. Could he be planning to leave Peru? This was another lead that ought to be checked out. Rob unfolded what looked like receipts. The first two were from restaurants in the city, and another was from a store, also with a Lima address. At the bottom of the last receipt was the name Musica de Rosario, San Sebastian, Ancash. Rob copied this information in his pad. Checking all the other compartments and finding nothing, he began to stuff the contents back into the box. He left the room and returned to Raiz's office.

"Ah yes, Detective Passaglia. You have finished your examination of the belongings, no? Have you found anything interesting?"

"Possibly," Rob said as he sat down in a hard wooden chair in front of the his desk and opened up his notepad. "He had a couple of bank cards—American, I believe. He was using the alias Mark Fenwood. I will run a check on those cards once I get back to Canada. He also had a business card for the Hatun Hotel. You might have someone check it out. The hotel may be able to provide some information."

"Hmm. Yes. Perhaps that would be useful."

He picked up the phone and made two calls. First, he called the hotel and asked if anyone was registered under the name of Mark Fenwood. The hotel said this person was registered and was in fact at the hotel at the moment. Next he ordered a police squad to descend on the Hotel Hatun. When he hung up, he turned to Rob.

"Good news, señor!" he said. "Your man is still at the hotel. I've dispatched a squad, and they will have him back in custody within the hour."

"Let's go!" Rob said, standing up and hurriedly putting on his jacket.

"No! No! No!" Raiz said. "I'm afraid I cannot allow this. You are not in your jurisdiction. What could I tell your embassy if you were shot or killed during the arrest? The team I have dispatched is the most capable unit in Peru. They know their business and will soon have Señor Knight in chains."

Rob could see from the expression on the man's face that he

would not compromise on this question, so he sat back down, sighing in annoyance.

"It was very good work that you found that card, señor. I compliment you. You are an excellent police officer."

"Thanks for the compliment," Rob responded, "but I'll feel a lot better once I know Knight is back behind bars."

"Please do not worry, señor. Tell me, what else did you find in your inspection of the belongings?"

"He also had a business card from a MagicPeru Travel Agency here in Lima," Rob said, checking his ever-present notebook. "This may indicate he intends to leave Peru shortly. You might want to give them a call and see if they have sold any trips to a Mark Fenwood."

"I see," Raiz said as he scribbled down the details. "All will be done as you have asked."

"And then there's this." Rob withdrew from his pocket the receipt he had examined earlier and passed it to him.

Raiz studied it. "San Sebastian," he read. "I know this place. It is only an hour from my home city."

"Really? Where is it?"

"It is about six hours straight north of Lima. It is a very small village right on the coast."

"What would Lance Knight be doing with a receipt from San Sebastian? Is it a bus stop where passengers have time to shop for CDs?"

"Oh no, that is ridiculous! San Sebastian is a very small town, señor. The buses pick up and drop off riders, but that is all."

"It's possible, then, that he may be living there. I tell you what. I'll phone my chief in Canada and see if he'll give me a couple of days. If Knight isn't caught tonight, I'll go up to San Sebastian to see if he's there and bring him in."

"I'm afraid, señor, that is impossible. As I've already said, you have no jurisdiction here."

"Send a couple of your men with me. I'll just be along in the role of a consultant. They can make the arrest."

"That also we cannot do."

"Why not? If he's there, it will be an easy arrest. I imagine he sticks out like a sore thumb."

"Sticks out like a sore thumb," Raiz repeated. "What is this?"

"I mean he should be very easy to spot."

"Ah, yes," he said with a laugh. "I believe you are right."

"Level with me here, Raiz," Rob said, leaning forward. "Are you going to make any effort at all to place this man under arrest?"

"We are making every effort to cooperate, as you can see. But you have to understand this is not a matter for Peru. He is a Canadian. He is a fugitive from Canadian justice. Really this is Canada's problem, not ours."

Rob felt deflated. He thought of the many hours he had spent on this case and of how he had believed a week earlier that his work had been rewarded with the capture at Lima's airport. Now he wondered if Lance Knight was going to disappear once more.

"With respect, Raiz, I don't think you appreciate the gravity of this situation. Peru has let a Canadian bank robber escape in a hospital gown. You have been presented with evidence of his whereabouts, and I hope you will be able to bring him. But I've learned that Lance Knight is a very slippery individual. If this turns out badly, this will not be helpful to international relations. What happens if he decides to start robbing Peruvian banks?"

Raiz laughed. "I'm sure, señor, you will find that Peruvian banks are much more difficult to rob than their Canadian counterparts."

Rob decided to make one last try. "Very well," he said. "You understand, of course, that I must report this lack of cooperation to the embassy."

Raiz stared at Rob and then became pensive. "I have the perfect man for the job," he said. "This man is like a boa constrictor. Once he has his target in his folds, he does not let go. I will have him lead a task force to San Sebastian if it is necessary. If the fugitive is there, he will be captured."

"Excellent!" Rob rose from his seat, satisfied he had done as much as he could do. "I'll call you once I get back to Canada to find out what happened," Rob said. "We can exchange information. In the meantime, I have a flight to catch."

"It has been a pleasure, señor," Raiz said, extending his hand. "Have a good flight home." When Rob had left the office, Raiz picked up the phone.

CHAPTER 16

Lance and Jen left the hotel and found a small park where they strolled and chatted. Lance noticed that Jen had become somewhat reserved. She helped him as much as she could, but the openness in the relationship that had begun at the lake was gone. After all that had happened since Jen had gotten to Peru, Lance could hardly blame her. Still it hurt.

The room at the hotel was simple but clean and homey. Lance had booked a room with two beds, hoping that would be satisfactory. As it turned out, they had not spent a single night in the room together. When they returned they sat on separate beds and faced each other, ready for the conversation they both knew needed to happen.

"Okay, here goes," Lance said, sighing deeply. "At the airport when I said everything was a big mistake, I was not being exactly honest."

Now it was Jen who let out a loud sigh.

"Jen, I robbed a bank in Vancouver."

Tears began to flow down her cheeks.

"When I met you at the campground, I was hiding out. My real name is not Rav. It's Lance Knight. I'm not East Indian. I am a surveyor, but I wasn't working as one when we met. Everything about me was a lie. The only thing about me that was true was the relationship that developed between us, Jen. I really got to know you, and that last night together, well ..."

"Are you married?"

"Yes!"

"Oh God." She put her head in her hands.

"I lost my family as a result of what I did. That part of my life is over. My wife has made that clear. My wife wants nothing to do with me. If I could, I would take it all back, but I can't do that, so I want to start rebuilding my life. Jen, I want that new life to include you."

Jen raised her head from her hands to look at Lance.

"Look, Jen," he said as he crossed the room and pulled out a small canvas bag from his suitcase. "I have more than $700,000." He opened the case and showed her several bank cards and bank books he had accumulated. "That's enough money to live comfortably for several years. We can begin to build the life of our dreams."

"Why did you do it?" Jen asked.

Lance's brow furrowed as he considered the question. Then he asked, "Have you ever felt that after all your efforts you deserved more than what you were getting at the end of the day?"

"Yes, of course."

"That's how I was feeling, but I guess the way I was feeling was more intense than usual. I think I was the ideal employee. I worked day in and day out, always giving my best effort. I hadn't taken a sick day in years. Yet when the end of the month came around, I had nothing left. I paid my bills, bought the groceries, no exorbitant spending, no luxury purchases, yet still the bank account was always zero or worse by the next pay day."

"I know that feeling very well," Jen said, a cynical expression on her face.

"That got to me more and more. I saw others in the community with more money than they knew what to do with, and yet they didn't work nearly as hard as I did. So I guess you could say I held my own mini-revolution."

Jen chuckled at that.

"I'm not saying what I did was right, but I'm not sorry for what I did. My only regrets are what it has cost me. If things had gone the way I had planned, I would have walked away from the rat race and drifted off happily into the sunset."

Jen looked into Lance's eyes. "I understand exactly what you're saying," she said. "I'm sure lots of people have thought about doing what you did, including me. The only difference is you acted on it. Most of us, thank God, never will. Somehow you overcame your conscience. But imagine the chaos if we all acted on the ideas that popped into our heads like you did."

"True," Lance said. "Jen, my plan when you agreed to come

was to take you to my home in San Sebastian and then tell you everything I just told you. It was just an amazing coincidence that the detective who headed the case against me was on the same flight as you. But we can still do that, Jen. There are dozens of bus lines in Lima, and each one has its own terminal. The chances that the police will watch all of those terminals are minimal. I still want you to see San Sebastian, Jen. Will you come with me and see this place? It's like heaven on earth."

"I need to think about all this, Lance. I can't tell you right now."

"I understand," he replied. "Let's go out for supper, and after that I'll take in a movie or something. Leave you alone. Give you time to think."

"All right," she said. "Thank you."

"Okay," Lance said, rising to his feet. "By the way, is this room arrangement okay? Do you mind being roommates? If you want, I can get you your own room."

"No, it's fine. I think I need you with me right now. The week all alone was horrible, not to mention terrifying."

"I'm sorry about that," Lance said. When Jen made no reply, he got to his feet and said, "Great. Let's go eat. I'm starved."

The two left the hotel and walked slowly to a small café named Cerise. They were given a table on the patio. It wasn't the most ideal location, with the constant roar of traffic on the busy street, but the food came quickly and they savored it. After the meal they engaged in light conversation, forgetting for the moment all that had happened over the last week.

Finally Lance paid the bill and they returned to the hotel. At the entrance he paused.

"I'm going to get out of your hair for a while now," he told Jen. "Give you some privacy to think about everything."

"That would be very nice," she said seriously.

"Okay. I'll be back in about three hours," he said, squeezing her hand. Lance walked off and Jen turned toward the hotel gate.

As promised Lance took in a movie. It was an American action flick with Spanish subtitles. The sound was turned down, but he could follow the English dialogue with no problem except when those around him conversed. They had no problem following the plot line, because they were reading the subtitles. Lance depended on the audio, however, so these little conversations irritated him—more so, probably, because of his anxiety over what Jen would decide about going with him to San Sebastian. If she said no, he could hardly blame her after all he had put her through. Still, he knew that would hurt. As Lance strolled back to the hotel, he realized he wasn't sure how the movie had ended, so distracted had he been worrying about Jen's response. At times, he almost wanted to sprint back to the hotel, but the next instant he wasn't sure he ever wanted to arrive. When he got back, he found the lights to the room were all on, but Jen was sleeping soundly in her bed. Lance shook her gently.

"Good morning, sleepy head," she said with a smile, rubbing her eyes.

Lance smiled back. "Good morning," he said ironically. "You know, of course, it's ten o'clock at night."

Her look and tone immediately became more serious. "I've been thinking a lot about what you asked me," she said.

Lance could see by her countenance that the answer was going to be no. He swallowed and braced himself for the bad news. "Yes?" he said.

"I was shocked when you told me you robbed a bank," Jen said. "I don't condone what you did. I'm not sure why I always end up with guys like you. No offense. I'm not sure we can have a future, Lance. I have to think about Micky. The truth is, though, you are right. I did feel we made a connection, and I have grown fond of you. I wouldn't have come to Peru if that wasn't true. I'm such an idiot! I've decided I'll come with you to San Sebastian. I'm probably crazy to do it, but what the hell."

Lance leapt from the bed and gave her a mighty hug, forcing the air from her lungs. "That's great," he said. "We'll leave tonight. As I said, you're going to love it."

Jen laughed at his reaction. "Well, I guess I better pack then. I'm not making any promises, though," she said, again becoming serious.

Embarrassed, Lance released her and grabbed his suitcase. They busied themselves packing for the next several minutes, and then they were off. As they exited the hotel, Lance looked at the street and froze.

He and Jen stood on the steps of the hotel with their mouths open. They could not believe what they were seeing. A religious procession was taking place on the street in front of them. Priests in colorful vestments led the way. Six men followed, carrying a large glass case on a platform supported by poles on their shoulders. Inside the case was a statue of Mother Mary. Her cloak was white with gold patterns. Behind these men walked forty or fifty people dressed in their Sunday best. It took the procession about five minutes to pass the hotel.

Once it disappeared Lance and Jen stepped onto the sidewalk with their suitcases. A taxi driver saw them and immediately pulled up. Jen climbed into the back seat, and Lance negotiated with the driver as he loaded their bags into the trunk. At that moment, Lance heard the wail of sirens. He looked in the direction of the sound and saw a huge police van careening toward them. Lance quickly joined Jen in the back seat. As the taxi pulled away from the curb, the van pulled up to the hotel and a dozen or more men burst from the rear, carrying machine guns. Lance looked in the rearview mirror. The squad was rushing into the hotel. Lance glanced over at Jen. She was oblivious to the action taking place behind them. They sat in silence as the taxi entered the main drag.

After the scare at the hotel, Lance was on high alert. He avoided the terminal he usually used to travel to San Sebastian and took a taxi to a location on the northern outskirts of Lima where he had noticed the bus stopped on previous trips he had made. When they arrived, a half-dozen travelers were already waiting on the curb for the bus to arrive. Lance paid the fare at the makeshift terminal on the side of the road, and they hurried to join the line. Ten minutes later the bus arrived and they climbed aboard. They had to stand in the aisle for the first hour because all the seats were taken, but seats became available when passengers disembarked at the first major town. However, these were single seats, so Lance ended up sitting a few rows behind Jen. Being separated made Jen uncomfortable, and she glanced back at him frequently. They were not able to find seats together until five in the morning, the final hour of the trip.

Lance did not want Jen to miss the vista that had so captivated him on his first trip. "Look at this," he said as the bus rounded the corner high above the little town. She leaned across him and stared out the window. The small village sat gleaming in the valley far below just as the sun peaked over the mountains to the east. The sight was spectacular.

"That's San Sebastian?" Jen finally said, her mouth agape as she surveyed the beautiful view.

The next day Lance showed her around the town. They took a long walk on the beach. He arranged for them to see the interior of the vacant beach house he had been thinking of buying. The owner agreed to allow them to have a meal there that evening. Lance arranged for one of the local fishermen to anchor offshore near the house. At the end of the day's fishing, his son came ashore in a rowboat, bringing a large fish. He started the fire pit and cooked the fish for them, wrapping it in banana leaves. The boy served the steaming fish on plates with sweet potatoes and corn. Lance and Jen dined at a table in the backyard and watched the sun change from gold to crimson and then dive below the horizon. After the meal they strolled back to his apartment in town.

Lance slept on a borrowed cot, leaving the large double bed for Jen. That evening she pulled him into the bed with her, and they made love slowly and tenderly before falling asleep in each other's arms.

Almost as if no time had passed, Jen awoke the next morning to the sound of rattling pots and pans as Lance was already preparing breakfast.

"Hi, sleepyhead," he said when he saw her stir.

Jen laughed, remembering she had said exactly the same thing to him a couple of days before. They ate lightly. Lance had cooked up a bowl of porridge for each of them.

Jen was due to fly out late that evening. They were both quieter than normal, realizing their time was short. They had a simple lunch—fried chicken, rice, and a vegetable. They washed dishes together and then sat down at the kitchen table.

"I want you to consider moving down here permanently to live with me," Lance said. "I'm falling head over heels in love with you, Jen."

"If I had a dime for every time a bank robber has said that to me," Jen replied. She laughed but quickly turned serious when she saw him cringe. "Rav—Lance, I mean—I've grown very close to you. I truly have." She took his hands in hers. "I know you're not a criminal at heart. You're that sweet man I met at the campsite. But I can't even consider moving down here until Micky is done with school. I can't put her at risk like that. You understand that, don't you? I'm afraid my answer has to be no." Tears welled in her eyes.

"I understand, Jen. Really I do. But why don't you let her see this place before you decide? Bring her down at Easter break. I fell in love with this place as soon as I saw it, and I think you did too."

"San Sebastian's great," Jen said. "It's like a paradise, but I don't know. I have to be the adult here."

"You had Micky in correspondence classes at the campground, didn't you? Bring her at Easter. I'll pay your fares and you can decide then."

"Maybe I'll talk to her about it. I'll think about it. That's all I can promise you. You don't know how traumatic it is for a kid her age to be pulled away from all her friends."

"Yeah, I think I do and you've got a good point," Lance said. "Okay! Talk to her and see what she says. At the very least you can have a vacation at Easter. I can show you gals some of the sights."

"We'll see," Jen said with a laugh.

Before either of them wanted, it was time to return to Lima for Jen's flight. They walked hand in hand to the town plaza and caught the bus. This time they had seats together, much to Jen's relief, and they sat quietly, watching the passing scenery. Finally they arrived in Lima, disembarking where they had boarded. This time they chose the stop not to avoid police but simply because this one was closest to the airport.

Lima was much windier than San Sebastian had been, and swirls of dust struck their faces as they stepped down from the bus. They hurried to a line of taxis, shielding their faces from the sandy attack.

In twenty minutes a taxi had them at the airport. The driver pointed to a long line of taxis outside the terminal and spoke in Spanish. Lance saw the problem immediately. Because of the heavy traffic, the taxi would take forever to cover the last hundred yards, so they agreed to walk to the airport from the street. Jen checked in at the counter and was back at Lance's side in five minutes, one of the bonuses of flying first class. He squeezed her close and they exchanged a long kiss, lost briefly in the magic of the moment. Finally Jen pushed away from him. One final kiss and she was walking away, trailing her suitcase behind her. At the doors to the gates she looked back at him, gave him a little wave, and was gone.

Lance turned and walked out of the airport, shoulders sagging and head down.

The next day Lance walked from his apartment in San Sebastian toward the market a block away to buy the groceries he would need that day. He had arrived on the bus late the previous night and had slept in that morning. Ahead on the next block on the opposite side of the street, he saw a man dressed in jeans and a short-sleeved checkered shirt. Following him were two soldiers with machine guns slung over their shoulders. In front of these three marched a local policeman, whom Lance recognized. As soon as he entered the street, their heads cocked slightly in his direction. Then, as if avoiding looking directly at him, almost as one they faced directly ahead but quickened their pace up the street toward him.

Lance did not like the look of this at all. He put on his own performance. He stopped and quickly searched his pockets. With a shake of his head, he did an about-face, walked rapidly back to the corner, and turned back toward his place. As he rounded the corner, Lance glanced back toward the advancing group. All charades were obviously over, for they began to charge toward him and the two soldiers unslung their weapons.

He sprinted past the long staircase leading up to his apartment and toward the end of the street. If he could round that corner before his pursuers reached the street, they might stop to make sure he hadn't gone up to his apartment. This would gain him some time but precious little. Lance got to the end of the narrow street and rounded the corner as fast as he could, turning left. He again glanced back. There was no sign of the men yet.

Lance continued down the block, breezing by a middle-aged couple approaching him. They stopped and stared after him. Lance had run about a block and a half down the dirt street when he spotted his four pursuers coming around the corner after him. The two soldiers now had their machine guns in hand but lagged behind the other two.

Lance reached the end of the block and kept running. The buildings on the opposite side of the street gave way to a sugarcane field. He swung across the street and plunged into the cane, which was at least twelve feet tall and very thick. Lance immediately disappeared from sight. He desperately pushed the stalks aside, making his way deeper into the crop.

His pursuers reached the cane field just thirty seconds after Lance had entered it. One of the soldiers sprayed the sugarcane with machine-gun fire. The man in the checkered shirt jumped at the sound and turned angrily on the soldier, shouting at him to stop. "Pare idiota," the man demanded. He approached the cane field and signaled the others to spread out and follow him in.

Lance heard the whir of bullets, some uncomfortably close, and he covered his head with his hands. He was sorely tempted to put them in the air and surrender. Instead he turned and pressed deeper and deeper into the stalks. Lance wished they didn't make so much noise as he brushed by them. He stopped and could clearly hear the men moving in the cane behind him. It was difficult to tell exactly where they were, but he feared they might stumble upon him at any second.

Suddenly, he heard a loud cry of pain off to his right in the cane field and the sound of men moving toward the scream. "Serpiente! Serpiente!" someone was screaming. "Me pico!" Lance had enough Spanish to understand that the man had been bitten by a snake. Lance remembered seeing a cane field burning just after he had arrived in San Sebastian. When he had sounded the alarm, however, one of the locals had smiled and had explained that farmers set the fires because the fields were filled with all sorts of nasty vermin, including poisonous snakes.

Lance slowly moved away from the sound of the screaming, hoping not to make too much noise.

Ten minutes later he came to the opposite edge of the cane field and out onto a beach. He again heard the crack of cane in the field behind him as the men resumed their hunt. Lance looked toward the ocean. Tall waves crashed on the shore forty yards from where he stood. Should he seek refuge in the sea? Lance made his decision. Instead he turned left and sprinted along the edge of the cane field parallel to the shore, hoping his pursuers would not emerge from the stalks.

A thirty-second sprint brought him to the end of the field, and he turned away from the ocean and out of view from the shore. To his right lay another field of cane. Sweating profusely and breathing hard, Lance made for this field. He plunged into the cane and surveyed his surroundings. As in the previous field, the cane was planted in straight rows about ten inches apart. He spied a narrow path about two rows inside the crop. It was scant cover, but he would be out of view and still able to move relatively quickly. Lance raced along the path, while behind him he heard the shouts of the men, who had now gained the beach. Although he could not see them, he knew the commander was ordering his men to search along the shore.

For fifteen minutes Lance raced along the path just inside the field. Then, his side aching and his breath ragged, he decided to plunge deeper into the cane. He made his way more slowly. Any sound of his pursuers had died away, but he resisted the temptation to peak out from the cane. Lance was startled as he looked down and saw a huge ant dragging an even larger spider across the path at his feet. Gathering himself, he stepped over the insects and kept sneaking through the stalks, trying to avoid moving them unnecessarily as he passed.

Finally Lance reached the end of the second field. In front of him lay an adobe farmhouse with a couple of outbuildings. There was no sign of people. Lance emerged from the cane and skirted along the rickety old fence that bordered the property. It provided little cover since there were wide spaces between the slats, so Lance broke into a run again. He had not seen his pursuers for quite some time, but the town was small and he knew his chances of evading them were low. Finally he came to a tall berm of sand covered with weeds that angled away from the shore. He hurried to the opposite side of the berm, hoping it would keep him hidden.

Half an hour later Lance reached a dirt road at the base of a hill. He was completely exhausted. He stealthily scanned the road, which led from the town down to the beach. Off to his right an old truck and a car of the same vintage approached, and townsfolk strolled along the sides of the road in both directions. Lance studied the hill, which rose precipitously upward, and instantly concluded that it was impassible. As nonchalantly as possible, Lance approached the road and followed it toward the sea, its breakers visible about a half-mile ahead.

The road petered out at the shore and was replaced by sand. Lance froze as he spied movement to his left along the beach. He hit the ground and crept forward on his belly until he could see along the shore. Several small groups of people were beachcombing in the distance. He didn't see the men who had chased him into the sugarcane.

Lance hesitated. He looked back down the road, and now two vehicles were headed in his direction. One could be the jeep he had seen parked by the police station, but at this distance he could not be sure. He certainly was not going to take the chance. The tall hill rose in front of him on the opposite side of the road. Lance looked in vain for a place where he might be able to scramble up the smooth sandstone. Even if he could make it up the slope, he would be exposed for at least fifteen minutes. Lance stared back down the road. The jeep had parked at the side of the road less than two blocks from where he hid, an excellent vantage point in all directions. No doubt the driver had been posted as a lookout to block him from returning to town.

To his right the ricketiest old pickup Lance had ever seen turned onto the road and rapidly headed his way, kicking up a cloud of dust. The truck approached the point where the jeep sat. Lance steeled himself. The jeep disappeared in the cloud of dust. It was now or never. Lance dashed toward the ocean. He looked back. The dust created by the truck was rapidly dissipating. Any second now he would be spotted. He dropped to the sand and crawled toward the waves. He looked back several times, but the jeep had not moved. At last Lance reached the water and slithered in. He waded in deeper on his hands and knees with his nose just above the water. He dared a quick look back along the road—still no movement from the jeep. He had avoided detection so far.

Resisting the temptation to leave the water and to flee on land, Lance stuck close to the hill's steep bank, which formed a point that tapered far out into the ocean. For the next forty minutes Lance waded along this bank. Close by its side there were only a few spots where the water was over his head. The angle also meant the waves lapped at the bank's edges, so he did not have to contend with pounding breakers like those he could see all along the sandy beach.

Finally Lance rounded the point and was now completely out of view of the beach and of the small town. He felt more secure. Glancing backward, Lance judged that he had not attracted attention, so he pressed on.

When he reached the outermost limit of the point, the ocean floor became interspersed with boulders, and Lance had to be careful with his footing. More than once he struck his shins against submerged rocks, and the salt water stung where sharp edges broke the skin. He also struggled against the force of the waves that crashed against the point, which rose sharply from the ocean floor. But the water remained about chest deep, and Lance slowly pressed on. Finally he found a spot where the sea had eaten deep into the rock, forming a channel. At the end of the channel lay a secluded beach no more than fifteen feet across at its widest. Lance waded ashore and collapsed onto the sand, allowing the afternoon sun to dry his clothing and to warm his body. He closed his eyes and rested.

Once he regained his strength, Lance sat up and looked around. With a renewed sense of urgency, he splashed back into the sea and out of the tiny cove. He would need to reach a more secure shore before nightfall. Lance found that the sea had eaten several of these little coves into the tall banks. But most were rimmed by large boulders, so he was unable to cross them on the sand. He had to venture into deeper water to get around the boulders. He waded across the mouths of some of these coves, but because of the depth of the water, he often had to swim a short distance to get across. He also had to be careful that the increasingly violent waves did not smash him against the boulders. Still, he made fairly good time, sometimes swimming and on a few occasions wading to shore and walking across sandy coves. For the next several hours, Lance made his way along the coastline in this fashion.

The water deepened when he left the last little cove, and the unyielding cliff steepened to ninety degrees. The water was neck deep, and each wave lifted him. Lance was forced to swim against the waves or risk crashing against the rock face. For the first time drowning seemed a strong possibility because there was no way up the steep cliffs and the ocean floor deepened. Lance swam hard with his waterlogged clothing dragging him down. Tossed by the waves, he was forced to swim away from the shore, but the current helped him, and ever so slowly he was swept across the point. Lance hoped a gentle shore would welcome him on the other side of the point. But he could not think about that now. He had to swim with all his might to prevent the waves from smashing him against the rocky cliff. Lance could hear wave after wave explode in an angry white froth at the bottom of the cliff. At all costs he had to avoid this violence just yards behind him.

Finally just as the last of the sun was about to dip below the horizon and his strength was almost gone, Lance could again feel the ocean floor beneath him, and a long beach appeared around the final jagged edges of the point. He relaxed his aching arms and wearily waded toward the shore.

Though night had fallen and his muscles screamed for relief, Lance immediately made his way along the shore. The cool night air gradually eased his pain. As he walked, his clothes slowly dried and his salt-caked skin itched. Lance thought of San Sebastian, knowing his idyllic paradise was lost to him forever. He had to escape this area. No doubt authorities would be alerted to be on the lookout for a white man. Then it occurred to him. His suitcase with most of his bank cards was still in his room in San Sebastian. That represented a good chunk of his fortune, and now it was lost to him. His wallet still held the card for the Peruvian bank where he had a sizable portion of the loot. That would have to do. As the sky lightened in the east, Lance saw the lights of a village. He had walked through the night. He hurried on until he reached a dirt road and followed it away from the sea.

Half an hour later he happened upon a small motorcycle with a canopied wagon attached to the back at the side of the road. These moto-taxis were everywhere in Peru. He found the driver slouched on the bench in the back. Waking him, Lance got a coin from his pocket and motioned in the direction of the road. The driver, wide-eyed at the sudden appearance of this foreigner, wordlessly took the coin and fired up the bike.

Ten minutes later they arrived in the central square of a sizable town. Lance recognized the town as Casma, a neighboring village to San Sebastian. Lance thought for a second and then made a rash decision. "Take me to San Sebastian," he told the driver. He handed the driver a few more coins, and the driver swung the moto-taxi onto the highway.

In less than ten minutes, the moto-taxi covered the distance Lance had taken all night to negotiate. When they pulled into San Sebastian, Lance kept a sharp lookout for the men who had pursued him the day before. Staying hidden under the canopy of the moto-taxi, he directed the driver to his place. When the moto-taxi parked in front of the stairs leading up to his room, Lance did not move. *What an idiot I am!* he thought. *The police could easily have placed a sentry in the room, hoping I would return.* Finally Lance made his decision. He got out of the moto-taxi and asked the driver to wait. He crept up the stairs as quietly as possible. Summoning his courage, he inserted the key in the lock and opened the door. The place appeared vacant. Lance surveyed the room. It was in a state of chaos, his belongings strewn everywhere. The police had obviously searched the room for any clues he might have left behind. His suitcase sat in a corner. Lance opened it and examined the false bottom where he kept all his bank cards. It was still intact. Not bothering with anything else, he scooped up the suitcase and ran from the room.

Lance asked the driver to take him back to Casma. Wordlessly, the driver cranked the machine back to life and headed out to the highway. When they returned, Lance crawled from the back of the moto-taxi. Businesses were just beginning to open. Lance immediately turned into a small store and picked out a pair of jeans and a T-shirt. From his wallet he pulled a bill still damp from yesterday's swim and handed it to the twelve-year-old girl tending the store. She had been watching him curiously since he had entered. She stared intently at the bill but finally nodded and handed him his change. In his broken Spanish, Lance indicated that he wished to change clothes. At first confusion clouded her face, but then she pointed to the back of the store. She drew the curtain behind him, and he put on his new clothing, stuffing his damp clothing into the suitcase.

From there Lance walked to a bank on the opposite side of the square. He hoped his card had not been irreparably damaged by the salt water. He wiped the plastic with his fingers as best he could and slid it into a machine at the entrance of the bank. The machine whirred to life. Lance withdrew the maximum allowable limit and left.

He approached a man in a long-sleeved white shirt and black pants standing at the intersection and simply asked, "Bus?" The man immediately nodded and gave instructions in Spanish, pointing in the direction he should go. Lance understood little of what he said but smiled and replied, "Gracias." He went in the direction the man indicated and soon found a bus station. "A'l norte," Lance told the clerk. North seemed as good a direction as any. The woman rattled off a list of destinations, none of which Lance recognized. He repeated the last name as best he could, and she nodded. He showed her his damp identification and handed her the cash. She entered information from his card into her computer. Finally she printed his ticket, handed it to him, and waved him toward the exit. Lance boarded a bus parked outside with its motor running. The driver took his ticket, and Lance nervously walked down the narrow aisle until he found the seat number matching the ticket. He sat down beside a tiny lady, who scooped up her bags to give him room.

After what seemed like an eternity, the bus finally edged away from the curb. Out on the highway Lance made himself as comfortable as possible and soon fell asleep. He had not slept all night. With a start Lance woke up. The tiny lady had been replaced by a neatly dressed older gentleman, who was fast asleep beside him. The bus was still rumbling along the highway. Lance looked at his watch, but it had stopped. Lance tapped it and wound it, but the salt water had destroyed the mechanism. He got the attention of a man seated across the aisle. Lance motioned to his watch, and the man pulled back his sleeve. The watch said 2:15 p.m. Lance blinked. He had been asleep for five hours. He sat back and studied the landscape through a crack in the curtains. The terrain was much the same as it had been on the way to San Sebastian. He thought about the village that had been his home for the past months. Meanwhile, rocky desert dotted with shoulder-high shrubs flew by outside his window. Tall brown hills rose in the distance behind the flat desert floor. Lance strained to see if he could spot the ocean in the distance, but there was no sight of it. He soon lost interest in the unchanging landscape and drifted back to sleep.

When he awoke it had turned dark. Lance had probably noted the slowing speed in his subconscious, for now the bus was making its way through the outskirts of a city. Most of the passengers were stirring, obviously preparing for the stop ahead. They had drawn back the curtains, and Lance studied the buildings that whistled by his window. He searched for any sign of the name of this city, but to no avail. Finally the older man who slept beside him stirred, and Lance showed him his ticket. "Trujillo?" Lance asked. The man nodded. He pointed ahead and explained in a stream of Spanish, little of which Lance understood.

The bus soon pulled into the terminal, which had the name Trujillo painted in large blue letters on its side. Practically all the passengers rose and lined up to exit the bus. The elderly man nodded animatedly to Lance. "Trujillo," he said, smiling and pointing at Lance's ticket.

Lance nodded in understanding. "Gracias," he said and followed the crowd off the bus. Lance spotted a hotel close to the terminal and headed for it. Fifteen minutes later he was in a small room with a lumpy bed at its center. He showered gratefully, washing the brine that caked his skin with a trickle of cold water. Once again it appeared he had narrowly escaped the long arm of the law.

For the next week Lance strolled the streets of Trujillo. At first he had no idea of the city's layout and several times had to resort to flagging down a taxi to get back to his hotel after becoming completely lost. He didn't mind, however, because taxis were ridiculously cheap. Three soles, equivalent to about $1.20, would get him anywhere he wanted to go. He spent time in the city's central square where hundreds of taxis zoomed by, and it seemed each one honked its horn as it passed him, hoping to gain a fare. With the cacophony of all the taxis blowing their horns, Lance felt he had to leave or risk losing his sanity.

He explored Indian ruins in the vicinity, some more than a thousand years old. At such places he blended in perfectly with the many tourists. One day he caught a taxi to a village about fifteen minutes away on the seashore. The buildings in this quaint little village were a notch above what he had been used to seeing back in the city. This was obviously a tourist town. Lance spent hours on the long pier, watching the enormous waves rolling into shore. He also studied the fishermen, who paddled canoes made of reeds with high, rounded fronts. The boats seemed to knife effortlessly through the towering waves. Once they had made it through the surf, the men took out strings with hooks on the ends, attached some sort of bait, and fished. Lance was amazed at how frequently this rudimentary method yielded a catch. Just as the sun was setting, the reed boats returned one by one to the shore. Lance stretched and left the pier to catch a taxi back to his hotel.

By the end of the week Lance had made his decision. He had fallen in love with Trujillo. It could not match the raw beauty of San Sebastian, but he knew he could never go back there. But Trujillo was a lovely enough place, especially along the ocean. He also felt there would be safety in numbers, especially Caucasian numbers. Lance saw fellow whites every day, so he was not nearly the oddity he had been in San Sebastian. The city was large. The traffic bothered him somewhat, but if he found a place in a quiet neighborhood he would not have to put up with it that much.

CHAPTER 17

A t his desk a week after returning from Peru, Rob was busy scanning a long printout. He crossed out sections of the report and scribbled notes. The first day back to work he had requisitioned from the airlines a list of passengers from flights that arrived at more or less the same time he had arrived in Peru. He wanted the identity of the mysterious woman Lance Knight had met at the airport. Rob had been so focused on apprehending the felon that he had momentarily forgotten about the woman. He kicked himself for such a stupid mistake. The first duty of a police officer was to control all aspects of a scene. Overlooking the woman was bad police work. Now he was rectifying that error.

Two hours later Rob had the identity of the woman narrowed down to two people. First, he had crossed off all male passengers from the list. After that, through cross-referencing, he had crossed off all women who had been traveling with a partner. Next, he had examined the ages of the remaining women, eliminating anyone older than fifty and younger than twenty. This had left nineteen women. Rob had then checked where each of these women lived. Only four were Canadian. The rest were American, Peruvian, or European. Since there was no record of Lance having traveled anywhere but on brief excursions to the States, the woman more than likely was Canadian. Of the four Canadians, two happened to reside in British Columbia—a Jennifer Robinson and a Toby Mantle. Rob quickly scribbled their names and addresses and left the office.

When Jen answered the door, Rob watched her closely for a reaction.

"Yes," she said. Rob stood there for a second or two. She stared at him, waiting for a response, and then suddenly her eyes grew wide and she let out an involuntary gasp.

"I see you recognize me," Rob said quickly.

Jen kept her voice as neutral as possible. "Yes," she said simply.

"I'm Detective Passaglia with the Vancouver Police Department. May I come in?"

Jen hesitated and then swung the door open and stepped back.

"We need to know where he is, Mrs. Robinson," Rob said once he was seated on the couch.

Jen sat in the large cushioned chair opposite him and looked Rob in the eye. "I'm sorry, but I don't think I could help you even if I knew."

"And why is that?"

"I think I love him."

"Hm. Did he happen to tell you what he did?"

It was obvious that Jen was wary of this question since she now avoided eye contact. Finally she shrugged her shoulders.

"He's wanted for bank robbery, Mrs. Robinson. Forgive me if I'm stepping out of line, but you don't want to get involved with this person. We *will* get him, you know," Rob said. "We always do. Save yourself some heartache and distance yourself from him now."

"I'm not sure I can do that," Jen said, her voice cracking.

"Well, there is the other thing."

"What's that?"

"Now that you've been informed by a duly appointed representative of the law of the charges against him, you are obligated to report anything you know to the proper authorities. Failure to do so amounts to aiding and abetting a fugitive. You could be charged, Mrs. Robinson."

Tears came to Jen's eyes and slowly slid down her cheeks. She gave an involuntary sob.

Rob rose from the sofa. "I'm very sorry, Mrs. Robinson. Lance Knight has unfairly involved you in something you had nothing to do with. If you know where he is, you should tell me now."

Jen rose from her seat, sobbing quietly.

Rob moved to the door. "Please promise me you'll think very seriously about what I've said," he told Jen, handing her his card. "If you know anything you can contact me at this number."

"I will," Jen said, wiping tears from her eyes.

"I'm sorry, Mrs. Robinson," he said and left the house.

Walking down the steps, Rob shook his head. This was a part of the job he hated. He had clearly upset the lady, and he felt sorry for her because of the predicament she was in. Yet he was doing his job. He hoped she would come to her senses and tell him what she knew, but he wasn't going to hold his breath. He knew that he had rattled the cage and that when Lance heard about it he might do something rash or say something that would reveal his whereabouts.

As soon as Rob returned to his office, he picked up the phone and arranged a wiretap on the phone of Jennifer Robinson.

········◆········

Lance decided to find a place to rent. He bought the local paper and began circling ads that peaked his interest. When he visited one of the condos in town, he ran into a younger man who was a realtor. Lance soon discovered Pedro could speak a little broken English. From that day on, the realtor would pick him up at his hotel, and they would drive from one property to another. Lance liked the convenience of the city but was drawn back to the seashore he had visited earlier. Finally, at the end of the second week, he settled on a small house at the end of a row of houses just off of the long pier in the little town just outside of Trujillo.

He had immediately fallen in love with it. The first time Pedro showed him the place, he did not have a key with him, so Lance could only circle the house, looking through the windows. It was obviously a new home. In fact, pails of paint still sat in the living room along with brushes and paint trays. The floor was constructed of parquet wood. The house had ample space, with three bedrooms, three baths, and even a servants quarters just off the kitchen. In the distance Lance could see the long pier he had visited a week or so earlier.

The place was built by a couple about six months before, Pedro explained. But then the husband was transferred to southern Peru, so they never had the opportunity to move in. After a brief look at the ample yard and the exterior of the house, Pedro and Lance moved on to see a few other houses in the area, but by the end of the afternoon Lance announced he wanted to check out the inside of the vacant house on the beach.

The sale happened very quickly. Pedro made the arrangements for the key, and they returned to the house the following afternoon. Lance carefully surveyed the rooms, especially those on the second floor that he could not see through the windows the previous day. The longer he looked at the house, the more certain he was that this was the place for him. He nodded at Pedro and simply said, "I'll take it." Lance agreed to the asking price, which he saw as an incredible bargain. He didn't haggle. A house like this in Canada would have cost several times the amount Pedro quoted.

Pedro made the arrangements with the sellers by fax and concluded all of the legalities, which Lance ignored. The only thing that mattered to him was that two weeks later everything had been taken care of and Pedro was handing him the keys.

Lance checked out of the hotel he had been living in for almost a month and spent the first night in his new home. There was no furniture in the place. He spread out his sleeping bag and bunched up clothing for a pillow on a ledge not quite big enough for him in the living room. Though the cement was cold and hard, he slept like a baby with the soothing sound of the distant surf in his ear.

He woke the next morning just after the sun had risen. Lance climbed the stairs to the flat roof and sat with his legs dangling over the edge, gazing at the ebb and flow of the waves. When the sun's heat began to make him uncomfortable, he went below, washed and shaved, and headed to the spot where taxi vans picked up passengers heading for the city center.

Lance went to a bank, withdrew a substantial amount of cash, and spent the morning shopping for furniture. He went first to one of the bigger chains and studied the store's large selection. By early afternoon he was browsing small family stores. Finally late in the afternoon he discovered a family business on the edge of town that made its own furniture. The furniture factory was adjacent to the store. Lance was shown into the factory where he examined several styles of furniture at various stages of completion. All of the furniture was made of cedar, and Lance fell in love with the aroma. He selected a large wardrobe that would serve nicely to hold all his clothing. He chose two queen beds that matched the stain of the wardrobe and arranged for delivery the next day.

The following day Lance shopped for bed linen and throw cushions for the ledge that had served as his bed for the last two nights. In the afternoon he purchased kitchen appliances and a patio set that included a large umbrella that he would place on the flat roof from which he loved to watch the ocean.

By week's end he had his new home fully furnished. Lance strolled through his home and studied each room, nodding in satisfaction as he surveyed the choices he had made. If this was not his dream home, he doubted he could come any closer. Each day he followed the routine of rising early in the morning and having coffee and a small breakfast up on the roof. He spent most of the morning there now that the umbrella shaded him from the sun. In the afternoon Lance would stroll along the beach for miles, taking in the beauty of the brilliant green sea beneath the blue sky with the occasional fluffy cloud floating far out from shore. In the early afternoon he would go to the market and purchase food for lunch, supper, and the next day's breakfast. He often chose fish caught that very morning to go with potatoes and vegetables. From the market he would walk back to the house and immediately cook what he had selected.

Lance had purchased cable and a large TV that he would watch for a while in the evenings. He found it increasingly easy to follow the plots of the popular Spanish-language melodramas. He stowed the umbrella and covered the patio set each evening before retiring for the night. He had learned the hard way that the wind often picked up at night, and one morning he had had to retrieve the umbrella from the water's edge.

One morning Lance was on the beach engaged in one of his favorite activities: people watching. He often stopped on his walks and observed the natives. He would see boisterous and energetic youths playing in the waves and shouting to each other. Or he would stop and watch when a crowd gathered. At the center a woman usually sat beside a reed mat with the morning's catch spread on it. People shouted, bargaining for the choicest pieces and pointing to one fish or another. The woman efficiently gutted and cut the fish, wrapping the pieces in newspaper and handing them to her customers, who took the packages and gave her money in exchange. Lance also noticed that a few elderly white couples resided in the vicinity. They loved to chat with him, but he was uncomfortable sharing too much information about his life. He kept the conversations light and would make excuses to keep the chats brief.

One morning Lance happened upon a little girl who was cautiously edging her way toward the water. As each wave receded she would venture as far as she could on the dampened sand toward the water, and then as the next wave came crashing in, she would turn, shrieking and giggling, running from the wave that chased her onto shore. At a distance from the water her mother stood watching her carefully. Occasionally she called to her daughter in a commanding tone, but the girl largely ignored her as she played tag with the waves.

Lance smiled at the mother as he passed and said good morning. She smiled and greeted him in return. He walked on several paces and at a discreet distance watched the small girl playing in the waves. The child would make her way toward the waves and then dash away at the last possible second. The mother continued to worry over her from the sand.

As Lance watched, the child gradually moved along the shore toward where he stood. The mother followed along from farther up on the shore. Eventually she ended up just a few yards from Lance, and they exchanged another smile.

"How old is your daughter?" Lance asked in Spanish.

"She is just four and is very mischievous," the mother said, smiling proudly.

"She is enjoying herself. Not a care in the world," Lance said.

"Yes, that's true. The care is for her mother," she said.

Lance laughed. "Do you live nearby?" he asked.

"Yes. We have a house on the beach past the pier," she said, pointing in that direction. "And you, what country are you from?"

"I'm from Canada," Lance said. He saw no reason to lie to this friendly woman.

"You speak very good Spanish. And how much longer do you have here in Peru?"

"Oh, I've bought a house," Lance said. "It's that yellow one." He pointed toward where it sat. "I plan to live here."

"That is a very nice house," she said.

For the next half-hour the two of them chatted as they watched the girl play. Then the woman called to her daughter with finality, and the girl reluctantly joined her mother. The woman took clothing from the bag she carried and rapidly changed the girl from her damp outfit.

"Welcome to Peru. I hope you enjoy our country. Adios," she said. Taking her daughter's hand, she left the beach.

Lance felt he would never tire of this idyllic life, but after two weeks he stared restlessly at the home he had made for himself. Something was missing, and he did not know what it was. Finally he decided he needed to share his home with someone. Over the past month Lance had maintained contact with Jen with sporadic phone calls. He was always careful to make these calls from the city, never from his house phone. Jen had been somewhat cool toward him the last time he had called. She finally admitted that the police had visited her and told him what the detective had said.

That afternoon Lance decided to call Barb again. He had avoided calling her because of the cool reception she always gave him. But today the restlessness and loneliness he felt made him travel to the city center to get in touch with her.

He entered an international calling center and handed the clerk cash. The clerk pointed Lance to a booth, and Lance dialed the number that had been his for many years.

As the dial tone sounded, Lance's heart began to race. He was nervous about talking to Barb. He hadn't spoken with her in almost two months. He hoped he would be able to rebuild the relationship he had so foolishly squandered. Yet she had been so cold each time he had called. The pain she felt was almost palpable.

"Hello?"

"Hi, Barb. It's Lance."

There was a moment's silence. "Hello," she said. That Barb had said hello seemed like a thawing to Lance.

"How is everyone?" he asked, not quite knowing what to say.

"Oh, they all seem to be fine," she responded.

"Listen, Barb, I know we've been over this before, but I've bought a place—brand new, new furniture. I just wish you'd change your mind and come down here. I know …"

"I'm seeing someone, Lance," she interrupted.

The sentence Lance had been constructing stopped and was gone, and his mind clicked into overdrive. He reviewed the foolish bank robbery that had cost him his family. He thought of the many years he and Barb had dedicated to each other. He thought of Jen and of the fact that he was falling in love with her. And even though he had been intimate with Jen on a number of occasions, what his wife had just told him felt like a knife to the heart.

The loss he had felt over the past several months once more stared him in the face. But now the finality of the loss was clear to him. He recalled what Barb had told him in the jail cell: "You're dead to me." And now another man would be enjoying Barb's company and Barb's body in a way only he had the right to. His role in the family had been completely eliminated. Lance stood staring into space in the booth. He was unable to form any kind of coherent thought and hung up the phone. After a long time he finally swung the door open and slowly left the cabina.

Lance walked for miles, paying no attention to where he was or where he was going. Barb's revelation had stung him. How foolishly he had acted, he told himself. He had known long before that his life with Barb had probably ended, but now that this reality had been confirmed, he was shocked.

"What are you going to do?" he asked himself out loud. "Give up?" Anyone observing this foreigner strolling through their barrio would no doubt have thought how strange he was, walking aimlessly, talking to no one. But at that moment Lance was entirely self-absorbed, and if he was getting strange looks, he would not notice.

"After four days of hell in the forest, after being beaten by crooked cops, after being shot at in a cane field and chased into the sea, is that what you're going to do, give up?" he asked. Finally after an hour Lance looked around him, not knowing exactly where he was. He reversed direction and searched for something familiar. Finally he spotted a cab on a nearby street and waved at it. The driver spotted him and made a sharp U-turn toward him.

Lance climbed into the cab and asked to be taken to the beach where he lived. The trip to the small beach community took more than a half-hour. Lance asked the driver to drop him off at the market. Lance climbed out of the cab and numbly resumed his normal routine. He picked up clams and mussels at one booth and then bought sauce at a second booth. A woman ladled the sauce into a plastic bag, tied it tightly, and handed it to him. He got potatoes and asparagus at another booth and began his trek home.

Once in the house Lance immediately began to cook. Forty-five minutes later he was on the roof where he ate what he had prepared and mindlessly stared out to sea. When he had finished his meal, he went down to the kitchen, feeling a little more alive, and immediately washed the plate and the cookware he had used.

For the next few days Lance busied himself with the minutia of daily life. He gradually recovered from the shock of the news he had received from Barb and fortified himself to push on. He finally resolved to return to the city center where he might treat himself to a meal at a nice restaurant or take in a movie at a theater he had spotted.

That afternoon Lance was in the city center in search of a restaurant. As he walked, he spotted a sign above a door that identified the establishment as a language school. On the window was a sheet of paper advertising English classes. Without thinking, Lance opened the door and walked inside. Seated at a desk was a young lady writing busily. She looked up and smiled when he approached.

"Hablas Ingles? Do you speak English?" Lance asked her.

She shook her head.

Lance switched to Spanish. "I noticed from your sign in the window that you offer English classes. Being from Canada, I wondered if you require instructors."

"Do you have a résumé, señor?" she asked.

"No, I don't," Lance said. "Actually I've never taught anything in my life." He asked her for a piece of paper and wrote down his name and phone number. "I'm not a teacher, but I do know English. I might be interested in teaching a few classes a week. If you're interested, you can call me at this number."

The woman thanked him, and Lance left to resume his search for a restaurant. After a leisurely meal accompanied by a couple of beers, he went to the theater and saw a movie. It was a Disney cartoon completely in Spanish with no subtitles, making it particularly difficult for him to follow. Lance got the gist of it but knew he had not understood some of the jokes. The audience laughed several times, and Lance had no idea why. He flagged a taxi and returned to his house. Night had fallen, and he spent time at his favorite perch, looking at the stars and listening to the invisible surf from his rooftop.

The following day Lance returned to the city. He had become

restless, and the thought of spending the entire day by himself made him uncomfortable. After just a month in his place, he found he was spending less and less time there. After window shopping along one of the main streets for a few hours, Lance returned to the cabina where he had called Barb the previous week. He thought about calling Jen. They had not spoken in more than two weeks. With the time difference he reckoned Jen would probably have returned home from work. Lance had called her every two weeks or so since she had returned to Canada. The conversations had been light, and it seemed she always brightened when she found he was on the line.

The one exception had been the call he had placed after Rob's visit to her. Lance had listened quietly as Jen recounted what the detective had said. Lance had tried to reassure her, but there was little he could say to contradict the warning Rob had issued. Now that he knew the detective knew about Jen, Lance had resolved to renew his caution, saying nothing that might provide a clue to his whereabouts if anyone had bugged her line. As he picked up the phone he could not escape the feeling he was calling her on the rebound. This was the first time he had called Jen since his call to Barb. He knew Jen she did not deserve to play second fiddle to anyone. Lance had been flipping like a fish on a hot skillet between his former life with Barb and his growing relationship with Jen, and he knew it. This wasn't fair to her, and he hated himself for it.

She picked up on the second ring and as always greeted him warmly. Lance had described the house he had bought in a previous conversation, carefully omitting any details about its location.

"I've done quite a bit with the place, Jen. You should see it." He described the furniture he had bought and how he loved to sit on the roof. He did not mention that he watched the surf in the mornings. Such details would give too much away. He asked about her life, and Jen talked about her job and Micky's activities at school.

They had chatted for fifteen minutes when suddenly Jen asked, "What's wrong, Lance?"

"What do you mean?"

"I don't know. You just seem a little ... distracted for some reason."

Lance hesitated. "To tell you the truth," he said, "I'm going a little stir crazy. I'm lonely, Jen. I know I've told you this before, but if you would consider coming back, we could try to set up a life here."

"I don't know, Lance."

"Look, I know I put you through hell the last time with everything that happened, but could you give it another chance?"

"I'm not sure I can do that to Micky. She's happy at school, and she's got her friends. How can I ask her to sacrifice that?"

"I know, but I think she could be happy here. I can give the two of you whatever you need. You know money is no object, Jen."

"That's not it, and you know it. It just seems incredibly selfish to ask her to do this."

"Is she home? Let me talk to her. We can ask her. I need you two."

"I don't know, Lance."

"Just let me talk to her. No pressure."

There was silence on the line as Jen considered. Finally Lance could hear her calling, "Micky, it's Lance. He wants to talk to you."

After several seconds Micky came on the line with a tentative hello.

Lance was happy to hear her voice. It had been months since he had talked to her.

"Hi, Micky. How are you?"

"Fine," she answered.

"Micky, I've got an important question to ask you. I want you and your mom to come live with me."

"Oh," she said.

"What do you think? Do you think you would like to do that?"

"I don't know."

"Listen, Micky, I'm not going to lie to you. It would be really difficult for you at first. You'd have to learn Spanish, but after a while you would find new friends, and it would be like you'd been here all your life. There's a beautiful private school here. I hear it's got a swimming pool, tennis courts, the works. Think about it, Micky. That's all I ask. You don't have to say anything right now. I just really miss you guys."

"Do you have your boat?"

"No, but I can buy another one, and we'll go to the sea and I'll take you fishing just like before."

"That was fun," she said, her voice brightening for the first time.

"Pass me back to your mom, okay? I'm not pressuring you, Micky. Just think about it, okay?"

"Okay," she said and then said something inaudible to her mom as she passed her the phone.

Lance and Jen talked for a few more minutes and then said their good-byes. Though nothing had been settled, Lance felt strangely uplifted by the conversation. He immediately caught a cab and returned home.

When he got home the phone was ringing. Curious, Lance picked up the receiver. This was the first incoming call he had received in all the time he had been in his home.

"Hello."

"Hello. Señor Johnson?"

Lance was confused for an instant and then remembered this had been his pseudonym over the past months. "Yes?" he answered cautiously.

"This is Señor Montoya," the man said in passable English. "I am the director of the Sunshine Language Academy. Are you the gentleman who stopped by yesterday?"

"Oh, yes. I did stop in. That's right."

"My secretary tells me you might be interested in teaching English classes."

"Well yes. I have recently retired and am living out in El Bayo. I thought I might like to do some teaching."

"Could you come to see me at eleven tomorrow morning?"

The following morning Lance entered the academy promptly at eleven and was ushered into the director's office by the lady he had met on the previous visit. The director started the conversation in Spanish. They engaged in small talk, chatting about the weather and places of interest in and around the city. It became obvious to Lance that Señor Montoya was gauging his proficiency in Spanish. Finally the director made his decision.

"Señor Johnson, I believe we may be able to use your services. I have an intermediate class that will be starting next week. I understand you have not any experience teaching, but our materials are clearly laid out, and it should not be too difficult for you to acclimate yourself to the classes."

By the time Lance left the office an hour later everything had been settled. He was to start teaching the following Monday. The classes were Mondays, Wednesdays, and Fridays from 7 to 9 p.m. The director had told him how much he would be paid. To Lance, it seemed like a pittance, but he readily agreed to the wage. He had been given the course materials and a tentative class list.

"Please go over these," the director had said, "and be well prepared for your first lesson."

For the next few days Lance dedicated himself to the materials, and by the time Monday evening rolled around he knew them backward and forward. This did nothing, however, to allay his fears as he walked into the classroom. A dozen students smiled up at him from their desks as he entered. Lance was nervous as he started the lesson, but after a bit of fumbling, he found he was beginning to enjoy himself. The adult students eagerly participated in the activities he had planned. Their accents were atrocious; in fact, Lance had difficulty understanding a number of them. But he patiently persisted, and before he realized it the two hours had sped by. The students rose smiling and bid him good night before exiting. As Lance was gathering his papers from the lectern the lone remaining woman approached him.

"Hello, Señor. Do you remember me?"

Lance studied her carefully. Suddenly his face lit up in recognition. It was the lady whose daughter he had watched playing in the waves.

"Yes, yes, of course. How is your daughter?"

"Oh, she is an angel. This angel has a bit of the devil in her, but I love her very much."

"Of course you do," Lance said with a smile.

Lance was pleased with his first week of classes. The students were dedicated, and they laughed happily at the mistakes they made. Lance was sure he saw improvement in almost everyone after only three sessions. For the next two weeks he busied himself preparing for the classes, and he looked forward to them very much.

In the beginning, Lance stuck closely to the lesson plans, but he soon gained enough confidence to take risks and go off script. Many of these attempts flopped magnificently, but occasionally some of his ideas worked out beautifully and the students benefited. He had noticed, for instance, that the students had an awful time pronouncing the *th* sound. No matter how many times he tried to teach them, they couldn't produce the sound consistently. One night, however, he brought a mirror into class. First, he produced the *th* sound using a number of English words. He pointed out to the students that they could see his tongue between his teeth when he made the sound. To confirm this, he moved around the classroom and gave each student a close-up view of his mouth when he made the sound. Then he passed the mirror around the classroom and asked the students to look in the mirror as they said some of the words he provided. It was amazing. Almost all of the students pronounced the words perfectly.

Lance called Jen and babbled happily about the classes he was teaching. They laughed about some of the outrageous things his students had said.

"This is good for you," she said.

Lance became serious. "Yes, it really is. But I still miss you terribly, Jen."

"I miss you too, Lance. I love it when you call."

"Have you thought about what we talked about?"

"Every day!"

"That's good. I hope you'll come."

As the weeks passed, with his part-time job and his daily routine around the house, Lance seemed to be settling in. He was amazed when he realized he had now been in Peru for more than six months. Despite the scare he had suffered in Lima a few months earlier, he was feeling more secure. He wasn't looking behind him quite so often. Though he sometimes felt lonely living in a foreign country by himself and dealing with an unfamiliar language and customs, he was beginning to enjoy a comfortable lifestyle. He was gaining proficiency in Spanish, and the different ways of doing things in this society no longer grated on him. The feeling of being a fugitive was rapidly fading. The threat seemed to be gone forever, and the possibility that he could make a new life in this country seemed more real. Lance chastised himself. *This is not a healthy way of thinking,* he told himself. *It takes only one mistake. I got lucky once, but the next time I screw up it will be for good.*

After the final class in the second week, Lance caught a cab outside the academy as was his custom and started off. As the cab approached a bus stop, he spied the lady from his class whom he had met on the beach. He directed the driver to pull over and unrolled his window. "Margot," he called.

She looked up surprised and smiled when she recognized him.

"Hop in. We're going the same way. We can share the cab."

She hesitated for an instant and then climbed in beside him. When they reached El Bayo, he had the cabby drop Margot at her place and then proceeded to his.

At the end of the next class he told Margot that he would soon have his things gathered and that if she waited she could again share the cab. She agreed and from that night on she accompanied him in the cab after every class. It did not take long for them to become comfortable with each other. They would chat happily, sometimes in Spanish but usually in English. Lance believed the extra half-hour or so they had together in the cab was helping her to become his most improved student.

One evening Margot said that Saturday was her birthday and that she was planning a party. A few friends would be coming by, and she wondered if he would like to come. She appeared to be delighted when Lance agreed.

On Saturday evening he arrived with a bottle of wine in hand. The other guests had already arrived. The music was playing loudly, and a few people were dancing. Others sat on white plastic chairs drinking beer from plastic cups, which they refilled often from a large container being passed around. Margot greeted Lance at the door and found him a seat. She introduced him to her husband and to the other guests. Lance soon relaxed and even danced with Margot and some of the other women. He spent a lot of time chatting with Margot's husband, Jorge. He spoke only broken English, but they managed to communicate, and Lance decided he liked him very much.

Though Margot and Jorge lived on the same street as Lance, their place was much smaller than his. It consisted of two rooms. A much larger room that served as both kitchen and dining room had its sparse furnishings pushed to the side on this night to allow space for dancing. The smaller room at the back was separated from the main room by a curtain. Little Lucia had tired, and her father carted her off to bed. Despite the loud music, she fell fast asleep in the back room.

The party went on into the small hours of the morning, and Lance was the last guest to leave. He thanked Jorge and Margot for a lovely evening and strolled home contentedly in the cool air. He flopped onto his bed and fell asleep instantly. Lance awoke late the next morning or afternoon—he wasn't sure which—with a pounding headache.

Lance and Margot continued to share the cab. Sometimes Lance would stop into her house to visit her and Jorge or to play with Lucia if she were still up.

A few weeks later as the term was coming to an end, he and Margot were riding home in the cab. They were laughing and chatting as usual when suddenly Margot became serious.

"You know, you are a very good teacher. I have enjoyed your classes very much and will be disappointed when they end."

"Thank you, Margot. That means a lot to me. You, of course, are my favorite student and my best student." He could tell even in the darkness of the cab that she blushed.

"I have an important question to ask you," Margot said suddenly.

Lance looked at her with concern. "What is it?"

She searched his eyes and then reached out and took his hand. Lance was taken aback. In all the time he had known her, she had never done anything so forward.

"Jorge and I have been talking. We want to ask if you would consider being Lucia's godfather. We would be very honored if you would do this."

"No, the honor is mine. I'd be proud to be her godfather."

"Oh, that's wonderful," Margot said, beaming. "I'll tell you when the baptism is. You, of course, must participate in the ceremony."

The next evening Lance appeared at their doorstep unannounced with a taxi waiting on the street. "Come on," he told Margot and Jorge. "We're going to celebrate." He refused to answer their repeated questions and hustled them to the cab. They traveled into the city, and following Lance's instructions, the driver stopped at the most expensive restaurant in the area. They ate luxuriously. Lance was in an experimental mood and ordered guinea pig. Lucia giggled delightedly at the faces he made as he tried his first bite. Margot and Jorge laughed until tears ran down their faces.

A couple of weeks after classes ended, Lance made one of his regular phone calls to Jen. They chatted animatedly for the first few minutes about some of the things that had been happening in their lives. This was frustrating for Jen because she was completely open about her life while Lance was cautious and avoided details about his life. She was sure he occasionally lied about specifics such as names and places. Though she was very interested in knowing about him, the image was always fuzzy and he seemed inscrutable. Since his appeal for Jen and Micky to join him in Peru, Lance had not brought up the topic again.

Lance described a shopping trip he had made to Lima. Apparently it was the responsibility of the prospective godfather to buy the baptismal dress and accoutrements. The trip had been a confusing adventure, but thanks to a particularly resourceful taxi driver, he had found a district with a number of stores specializing in that sort of thing. Lance took his responsibility seriously and spent several hours walking from store to store looking at gowns in Lucia's size. Eventually he narrowed them down to a few that he particularly liked. He described how he had walked back and forth between the last few shops, annoying at least one of the shop owners. Finally he had chosen a pure white gown with a lace headpiece. When he had gotten home with his purchases, he had gone straight to Jorge and Margot's house. Margot had put the dress on Lucia.

"She is positively angelic in it," Lance bubbled into the phone. His excitement about the upcoming baptism was obvious.

In his next phone call to Jen, Lance was again talking excitedly about the event when suddenly she said, "Lance, we'll come."

"What?" he said.

"I said we want to come be with you."

"Really?" he said. "What about Micky?"

"She misses you too, Lance. We had a long talk last night, and she says she wants us to be together. We both love you and we want us to be a family, so we're going to go for it, no matter what happens."

"Oh Jen, that's the best news I've ever heard. When can you come?"

"I'll give my notice at work tomorrow if that's what you want."

Lance thought hard. "Just wait," he finally said. "I need to think about this. Get packed and be ready to go. You'll receive an email from me."

Before they said good-bye, he scribbled down the details he would need—their passport numbers and address. "Check your email every day," he said and hung up.

CHAPTER 18

Rob had long since returned to his regular duties with the Vancouver Police Department. The pace was hectic, and he approached each case with vigor and intelligence. Through hard work he continued to rack up an impressive number of solved cases, some of which had been incredibly complex. He had astounded his colleagues on some occasions. His superior, Captain Harding, knew he would soon lose him. The department brass had noticed Rob's work.

Every detective who has been on the job for any length of time has one case that haunts him. Ask any retired officer years after the fact and he will be able to describe that case in surprising detail, as if it happened yesterday. For Rob that case was the one involving Lance Knight. It had been relegated to the cold case file, but for Rob it would never die. In his heart he knew it was not over. He still felt frustration whenever he thought about it. He had come so close to apprehending this felon more than once and even had him in custody in Peru. If it had not been for the total incompetence of a couple of cops in Peru, the guy would now be behind bars where he belonged.

But Rob was not the type of person to give up. Why should this man be allowed to live a life of luxury with money he had not earned? Everyone else struggled to make ends meet. Rob thought it was an insult to society for Lance Knight to be on the loose. He didn't know how it would happen, but he knew in his heart that one day he would see him pay for the crimes he had committed.

Despite Captain Harding's order to remove the wiretap on Barb Knight's line, Rob had been able to hide that tap and one on Jen

Robinson in a maze of paperwork and to fund the taps through creative accounting. On Thursdays Rob would stay late at the office making notes on every detail he could glean from Lance's calls. Lance was obviously careful about what he said on the phone, but Rob concluded that he had probably remained in Peru and was living somewhere on the coast. Lance had not said that, but this was a reasonable conclusion based on portions of his conversations. When he learned that Lance was teaching at a language school, Rob had generated a list of all the language schools in Peru. Checking a map, he had meticulously crossed off any school that was not located near the coast. The list still numbered in the hundreds. Rob was tempted to fling the papers in the garbage, but finally he had sighed and had begun the arduous task of contacting the schools and inquiring whether they employed a gringo matching Lance's description. So far his efforts had been fruitless.

Two weeks earlier Rob had finally decided to remove the tap on Barb Knight. He had learned that she was developing a new relationship, and the calls from Lance had ended.

On this Thursday night, Rob was zipping through all the calls made to Jen Robinson's home before he stopped at one placed by Lance a few days earlier. After a long day, he sat bored with a paper in front of him and pen in hand, making note of any new detail he could glean from the conversation. He sat bolt upright when he heard Jen's announcement.

Rob stopped the tape and turned to his computer. He logged on to her account, a relatively easy thing to do with the technological resources at his disposal. Lance had told Jen to check her email nightly. Rob scrolled through the messages. Nothing! Well, if she was checking her emails nightly, he would do the same. Rob shut down the computer and put on his coat. It looked like he could call it an early night. He glanced at his watch as he left the office. It was only a few minutes past nine.

Two days later Rob was eating a sandwich at his desk scrolling through Jen's emails when he got a hit. Continental Airlines had sent an electronic itinerary for two tickets on July 15, just three days away. Rob immediately picked up the phone and booked a flight to Lima for July 14. He could not risk being on Jen's flight, for she would surely recognize him. He gritted his teeth when he heard what it would cost him. He reluctantly gave the girl on the line his credit card number. Since this was a cold case, the expense had to come out of his own pocket. He hung up the phone and walked to Captain Harding's office.

The captain was going through a stack of paperwork when Rob walked in.

"I'm going to need a week off," Rob announced.

"What? Now? Aren't you in court on Friday?" the captain asked.

"I'll brief Bill on the case. He can handle it."

Captain Harding looked at Rob suspiciously. "What's going on that you suddenly need this time off?" he asked.

"My uncle back east died, and I'm going to the funeral," Rob said, lying effortlessly. "I've got plenty of time banked, and you yourself ordered me to start using it. So I'm using it."

"That's true. Other than that fiasco in Peru, you haven't had a vacation in years. It was on my agenda to talk to you about that anyway. You never told me you had family back east, though." He stared pointedly at Rob for a few seconds and finally said, "Okay, we'll see you in a week. My condolences!" He could not keep a touch of cynicism from his voice on this last part. "Now let me get this paperwork done." He immediately picked up the top sheet from the stack and was already signing forms when Rob turned and left the office.

As Rob left the office Captain Harding looked up and stared thoughtfully after him. He gave his head a single shake and returned to his work.

When Rob got back to his office he returned to Jen's email. A new message had arrived. He didn't recognize the sender, so he opened it. The message read: "Reservations at El Ejecutivo, 836 Avenida Puerto Largo, Lima."

Rob took out his leather day planner and searched in the back for a phone number. He knew he had an ally in Peru who wanted Lance Knight as much as he did. He found the number and placed a call to the Lima Police Department's head detective. After two rings, a voice came on the line in a no-nonsense tone.

"Diga!"

"Detective Gonzalez, it's Detective Passaglia from Canada calling."

"Señor Passaglia," Raiz said, "to what do I owe this honor?" His voice lightened.

"Lance Knight has finally surfaced, and I'm going to need your help."

"Very well! How can I be of service?"

"His girlfriend has decided to go to Peru to be with him. I have her flight number and the hotel she will be staying at. I want men on her at all times, and if he shows up I want him arrested."

"Señor Passaglia, you can expect the full cooperation of our police department. Give me the details, and as soon as I am off the phone with you, I will see to it that what you ask will be arranged. I have just the pair in mind to take on this task," he said with a chuckle.

"Not those two yoyos who beat up Knight? I was hoping you had some men who inspired a degree of confidence."

"I assure you, Señor Passaglia, that since that episode I have taken steps to teach these men some discipline. They have been model officers. They will not fail us. Besides, I can think of nothing more fitting than to place those two on an around-the-clock stakeout."

It was Rob's turn to chuckle. "All right, Raiz. I'm sure you know what is best."

"Thank you, Detective Passaglia. Now if that is all, I have some things to arrange."

"Oh, one more thing," Rob said. "I will be on a flight two days from now. That is a day before the girls arrive. I can get you up to speed on any new developments at that time."

Rob waited for a reply. He knew this would be the most delicate part. Finally Raiz sighed. "You and I, señor, have had this conversation before. I must point out again that you have no jurisdiction in this country and that your presence will only complicate my job."

"Look, Raiz, you owe me. After your men allowed Lance Knight to slip through your fingers not once but twice, I think I'm entitled to a little leeway here. I will be there strictly as an observer. I will take no active role."

The pause was palpable. Finally Raiz said, "Very well, Detective Passaglia, but you must guarantee your cooperation. You must obey my every command. If not, your involvement will be terminated."

"Of course," Rob said quickly. "So here it is. Three days from now at midnight, a flight will arrive at Chavez airport with this woman and her daughter on it. I will fax passport photos of both of them so your men can spot them when they meet the flight."

· · ●●●◆●●● · ·

"Midnight!" Detective Lopez exclaimed. "That is impossible. It is my son's birthday the next day, and our family will be celebrating." Raiz glared at him and Detective Ramirez. "If it was not for you two idiots, Lance Knight would now be in a jail in Canada. You are to follow the woman and her daughter from the airport. They have reservations at El Ejecutivo. If they deviate from this plan or do anything at all suspicious, you are to call me. And if you lose her, you'll both be working in a shoe store somewhere. Have I made myself clear?" His voice had risen steadily in volume and irritation as he spoke.

"Si, señor," Lopez said. The two men rose from their seats and returned dejectedly to their desks.

At 8 a.m. three days later, Rob and Raiz pulled up outside of the Hotel El Ejecutivo in an older-model Toyota Corolla. Just ahead of them in another vehicle sat Lopez and Ramirez. Raiz got out of the car and Rob followed. Having spotted their superior approaching, the two men stirred and Ramirez unrolled the window.

"Have you seen them this morning?" Raiz asked. Ramirez responded. Rob listened but did not understand a word.

Turning to Rob, Raiz said, "They followed the woman and her daughter from the airport last night. They checked in at about 1 a.m., and they have not come out since. I believe, Detective Passaglia, that I will allow these two fools to go home and get some sleep. You and I will take it from here." Raiz spoke to the two, and he and Rob returned to their car as the other vehicle pulled away from the curb.

An hour and a half passed before Jen and Micky emerged from the hotel. They turned in the opposite direction from where the detectives were parked. Raiz waited until they were near the end of the block and got out of the car with Rob discreetly trailing him.

When Jen and Micky turned left at the corner, Raiz hurried after them. He crossed at the intersection and could see them a half-block away. He followed them from the opposite side of the street. They made no effort to check behind them, so he closed the distance. They quickly ducked into a small store, but soon came out and turned left onto the sidewalk. Raiz waited until they had crossed the street and then walked at a leisurely pace to the corner they had just left. He and Rob were now on the bustling Avenida Puerto Largo, so the two were able to tail them, easily blending in with the crowds strolling the sidewalks.

After walking two blocks, they spied the girls enter the Agencias de Viaje travel agency, so the detectives crossed the street, sat at a sidewalk café, and ordered coffee. Ten minutes later Rob saw Jen and Micky leave the travel agency and turn back in the direction they had come. From his seat he followed their progress, and when Raiz saw them turn back in the direction of the hotel, he paid for the coffees and they crossed the street, entering the agency the girls had just left.

The small office had a large picture window fronting onto the avenida. Posters advertising exotic destinations adorned the walls. Two young ladies seated at desks were busy on the phones. Raiz approached one of the desks, took out his wallet, and flashed his police badge. Immediately a worried expression clouded the girl's face, and she hurriedly ended her call. Raiz questioned her briefly and then motioned for Rob to follow as he exited the agency.

"They picked up two airline tickets that had been purchased by a Señor Smith. They will be flying to Chiclayo at seven tonight. I have purchased a ticket for that same flight."

"You purchased only one ticket?" Rob asked acidly. "We agreed that I would be involved in all of this as an observer."

"Relax, Señor," Raiz said. "You told me that you had questioned this lady. It would be most unwise for you to be on that flight. I will make arrangements for you to take an earlier flight. Now please excuse me. I must make some calls. I will have a team from the Chiclayo detachment pick you up. You can be at the airport when the ladies arrive."

Raiz took out his cell phone and barked out commands. As the pair headed back toward the hotel, Rob could see the girls almost two blocks away headed for their hotel.

When Raiz pocketed his cell, Rob asked him about Chiclayo and learned it was a city in the far north of the country about a six-hour drive from the frontier with Ecuador. It was a medium-size city by Peruvian standards and was nestled on the coast. Fishing and agriculture were its principal industries.

When the detectives reached the hotel, they got in their car and resumed their vigil. Less than an hour later a vehicle pulled up behind them. A man got out and strode up to their car.

"You will go with the officer," Raiz told Rob. "He will take you to the airport and see that you make the flight to Chiclayo. I will stay here just in case Knight makes any attempt to approach this hotel."

Rob left with the officer, who raced through the busy streets of Lima at an incredible speed. After an hour of clutching his seat, Rob spotted an airport sign. When they arrived, Rob and the officer rushed into the terminal. At the ticketing counter, they approached a man dressed in the airline colors. His companion issued curt instructions to the man. From there, Rob was ushered through the gates and onto a plane. They had obviously been waiting for him, because as soon as he was seated the plane's doors were closed.

The flight took only an hour. Rob spent the time looking out the window. Heavy cloud cover blanketed the coast, but off to the east he could see the snow-covered Andes above the clouds in bright sunshine.

After landing, Rob walked on the tarmac to the terminal with the other passengers. This was a very small airport. He passed through the baggage claim area and saw a small crowd awaiting the arriving passengers. He spotted a sign with his name on it held up by a plainclothes officer. Rob approached him and introduced himself. The man greeted him in broken English and led him out to the parking lot. There he was introduced to the team assigned to this operation. There were six men in two vehicles. It seemed that only the man who had greeted him at the baggage area could speak any English, so Rob waited quietly in one of the vehicles for the next few hours.

When the flight they were waiting for finally landed, Rob spotted Jen and Micky walking across the tarmac. About ten passengers behind Jen and Micky he saw Raiz walking unobtrusively. Once in the terminal, Raiz stationed himself on the far side of the luggage conveyor so he could watch the two without being noticed. Rob saw Jen studying a cell phone, and then the girls exited the area without claiming any baggage. *Knight has somehow managed to get her a cell phone, and he's making contact with them. It won't be long now,* Rob thought.

Raiz hurried after them. Rob quickly moved back to where the team waited and got in one of the vehicles. Moments later Raiz joined them. Raiz quickly greeted the members of the team, and then all of them turned their attention to the terminal exit. Soon, Jen and Micky exited the terminal and climbed into a cab. They each wore a bright-red knitted cap and ponchos of the same color. The officers pulled away from the curb, following the taxi a half-block behind. Following so close was risky, but in the heavy traffic around the airport they had little choice.

Darkness had fallen by the time the flight had arrived. It was now eight in the evening. The cab arrived at a huge market. A canvas sign strung across the street announced the place as the Mercado Modelo. Rob was surprised that despite the lateness of the evening, the place was still crowded with people and the many kiosks were all still open.

He saw Jen exit the cab and hand the driver a handful of change. The driver studied it momentarily and nodded. Micky got out of the cab, and she and her mother stood in front of a small shoe kiosk and surveyed their surroundings. The Mercado Modelo was obviously a center of commerce. A line of kiosks of various descriptions lined the sidewalk where the girls stood. There were yet more kiosks on the opposite side of the street. People moved slowly among them, eyeing the merchandise for sale. A narrow, dimly lit lane led inside the market with row upon row of kiosks as far as Rob could see. The market seemed to span at least a city block. The strings of incandescent lights barely illuminated the labyrinth of shops inside. Suddenly Rob saw Jen jump and pull out her cell phone.

The police had stopped their cars on the street and had watched the cab stop and unload its passengers. They had watched as the girls stood on the sidewalk looking around. Finally horns began honking, so Rob and the other men got out of the cars and huddled on the sidewalk, watching the girls as unobtrusively as possible. They saw Jen pocket the phone and lead her daughter into the market. The men raced to the entrance, gathered there, and looked inside. Rob immediately spotted the girls' red caps bobbing in the crowd.

Raiz hurriedly organized his group. He sent two men on the run in opposite directions. They were to man the street corners on the far ends of the market, waiting for the pair to emerge. If Lance was with them, an officer would immediately descend and apprehend him.

Raiz directed a third man to the lane to the left of the one where they stood and sent Rob to the lane to the right. With everything set, the men entered the market with Raiz trailing the girls, who were still clearly visible about sixty feet ahead. The men followed slowly.

To Rob the market was a complete maze. The lanes seemed to stretch on without end, and every twenty or thirty feet they were intersected by perpendicular lanes. These lanes also seemed to disappear into the darkness in both directions. The kiosks displayed every imaginable type of merchandise. Some were dedicated to backpacks and purses, others to fruits and vegetables. Others might sell hats, T-shirts, or hardware including locks and keys. Still others sold a myriad of items. Rob saw no comprehensible system here.

The officers followed the girls at a distance. At each lane intersection they paused until they were in sight of each other. They gave each other brief nods and then moved forward. If the pair switched lanes, as they often did, Raiz would slide over to that lane, and Rob and the other man took up their positions to the right and left of Raiz. No matter which way the girls turned, they were out of sight for only an instant before a member of the team picked them up again. The trap was set, Rob thought. This had to be the place where Lance had planned to meet them. It didn't matter which way he came. With the network the police had hurriedly organized, he would be spotted well before he could reach the girls.

Heading deeper and deeper into the bowels of the market, the men followed the pair as discreetly as possible. They tried to appear as if they were examining merchandise, but their attention never wavered from their objective.

The girls turned right. Raiz hurried to the next intersection and moved one lane to the right just as Rob followed suit. "Did you see them?" he asked Rob. When Rob shook his head, Raiz looked toward the police officer to his left, who also shook his head. He motioned for Rob to take the next lane over and advanced quickly to where he had last spotted the girls.

In a few seconds Rob arrived at the spot. From where he stood lanes ran in four directions. A number of shoppers were immediately ahead of him. A Peruvian man strolled with his arm around his rather plump wife. To his right, shoppers moved among the kiosks. A mother and her daughter, both obviously Peruvian, walked hand in hand away from him. He spun in all four directions. There was no sign of the girls. He quickly checked the adjacent lanes. Still no sign of them. Rob motioned frantically for Raiz and the other man to join him. "Did you see them?" he shouted when they had congregated. Both shook their heads. Jen and Micky had simply disappeared. How was that possible? Rob waved Raiz to the left, and Raiz and his partner raced off in opposite directions.

Rob hurried through the market, stopping briefly at each lane crossing to see if he could spot the girls. There was no trace of them. He continued to advance until finally he emerged from the market onto the street.

To his left he saw one of the officers who had been standing post at the street corner. "Hey!" Rob shouted and then issued a shrill whistle. The man turned his gaze toward the sound. Rob motioned toward his eyes. The man shook his head.

Rob returned into the market, retracing his steps and keeping a sharp lookout for Jen and Micky. Finally he arrived back at the intersection where the three of them had gathered just a minute ago. He stood and waited, not knowing where Raiz and the other man had gone or when or if they would return. He surveyed his surroundings carefully and then he spotted something.

Inside a small kiosk selling sporting goods next to where he stood was a large cardboard box filled with soccer balls. Lance reached into the box and pulled out two red knit caps. He was still staring at the caps when Raiz and his partner arrived out of breath. Raiz looked at the caps. The kiosk was manned by an older woman and a younger man who were staring at the trio in consternation. Raiz turned to them and shouted in rapid Spanish.

"Did you see two white females here?" he asked.

Immediately the pair began nodding and pointing. Rob did not understand what they were saying, but he noted that the woman pointed in one direction while the man pointed in another. This caused a heated exchange between the two of them over which direction the girls had taken. Rob turned to Raiz for an explanation. The Peruvian detective had a confused look on his face. Suddenly without a word he turned and raced down one of the lanes. Rob and the other man followed as quickly as they could. Finally they emerged onto the street. Raiz was looking in both directions. Rob spotted the two officers who had been stationed at opposite street corners moving quickly toward them. Neither had seen any sign of the girls.

· · ●●●●◆●●●●· ·

Lance waited in a newer-model sedan on the outskirts of Chiclayo. He tapped on the steering wheel. Then he turned on the radio and scanned the stations. His nervousness was palpable. He had planned this day down to the minutest detail. He was reminded of his plan to rob the bank. If this plan failed, however, the personal costs would be even greater. What good would all the money in the world be if he couldn't be with the ones he loved? Lance had learned that lesson all too well.

Suddenly a vehicle pulled up behind him. He watched apprehensively in the rearview mirror. Four people piled out of the vehicle and raced toward his. And then they were climbing into his car, hugging and kissing him. Jen and Micky had made it. Everyone was laughing and crying. As Lance pulled onto the highway, everyone was excitedly reliving the recent escapade. When Jen had brought the phone to her ear at the entrance to the market, she heard Lance say, "Enter the market now. Go two lanes in, turn right one lane, and continue in two lanes. Just repeat the pattern. Do you understand?"

Jen's heart had raced as she processed the information. She had no idea what was happening. "Yes," she said finally.

"Go now and go slow," he said. "Keep to the pattern. Two ahead, one to the right." Then the line was dead.

Fearfully she had taken Micky's hand and they had entered the market. The dark lanes had done little to allay their fears, but Jen had concentrated on the course she was to take. She did not want to lose count of the lanes she crossed or to deviate in any way from the instructions Lance had given her. Despite that, she could not help but search for him with each lane she passed as they moved deeper and deeper into the market through the crowds. "I was so scared," Jen said. "I kept looking for you, but you were nowhere to be seen."

Finally she had taken a right and was passing a kiosk laden with sporting goods when a Peruvian woman had suddenly blocked their path. A male had approached from behind and had whisked off their caps. Startled, Jen had looked up at the man. He was smiling.

"Lance is waiting," he had said. He had stuffed the caps deep into a box of soccer balls. "Put this on quickly," he had said, handing Jen a heavy woolen coat commonly worn by the country folk of the area. As fast as she could, she had put on the coat while the man had fitted a long, dark-haired wig over her fair hair. The woman had slipped a black jacket on Micky and had placed a similar wig on her. The woman and the man inside the booth had stared wide-eyed at what was transpiring.

Seconds later the man had put his arm around Jen and had guided her into the lane, while the woman had taken Micky's hand and had firmly led her in a different direction. "I almost lost it when I saw Micky disappearing in the opposite direction," Jen said. At one point Jorge had gently turned her toward a stand of fruit and had picked up a mango. He had leaned her forward with his hand on her back in such a way that the wig had covered her white face. Just then, a man had raced past. When the man had disappeared they had continued toward the exit.

"That was lucky," Jorge said with a laugh from the back seat where he sat with Margot. "I saw him coming at the last second and just reacted."

Meanwhile, the woman had led Micky in the opposite direction through the maze. "I was afraid I was being kidnapped," Micky said, "but Margot smiled at me and calmed me down. At one point she told me, 'Don't worry, be happy.' That made me laugh. After that I was okay."

They had woven their way through the market at a leisurely pace and had soon reached the street. Margot had motioned for her to wait. Standing on the curb, she had waved her hands and a taxi had pulled up seconds later. The woman had then returned for Micky. "Put your hands over your face and pretend you are crying," she had whispered. Micky had done so and had let the lady usher her into the back seat of the cab.

"Just before I got in the cab I took a quick look around. Just a few meters away from us a man who was obviously a plainclothes police officer was standing guard at the corner. He didn't even notice us," Margot said.

The taxi had turned left in front of the officer. The man had stared right into the cab but had noticed nothing unusual. The cab had proceeded slowly down the street bordering the market.

Following Margot's instructions, the driver had suddenly pulled over and stopped. Margot had swung the door open, and Jen in her heavy coat and wig had crowded into the back seat, followed by Jorge. He had quickly given instructions to the driver, who had pulled away once more and had taken a right at the next intersection. Another plainclothes officer had stood at this intersection, but Jorge's body crowded against the window had prevented him from examining the other passengers in the vehicle.

Fifteen minutes later the taxi had pulled up behind Lance's car and the reunion was complete. Margot told her part of the story in nearly flawless English, which made Lance proud.

Once they were underway, Lance said, "I want to introduce my good friends Jorge and Margot. Without their help I never could have pulled this off. I'll never forget that. I approached them over a week ago and told them I had a problem. They said they would help me, no questions asked. I made a lot of strange requests, but they've done everything I asked."

Jen struggled out of the coat and for the first time examined it closely. The inside was lined with stuffed pillows about the size of bean bags. "Margot put that together," Lance said. I must say it does nothing for your figure." Jen laughed and gave him a playful whack.

They soon left the city and turned onto the Pan-American Highway. They continued to chat excitedly about their adventure as Lance headed south. He listened carefully and laughed along with them. After traveling to Lima to make the arrangements there, he had returned with Margot and Jorge to Chiclayo three days earlier. They had rehearsed the plan endlessly since arriving in the city. Everything seemed to be ready, but their careful preparations had done nothing to ease the lump in Lance's throat as he waited alone in the car he had rented in Trujillo.

The back seat grew silent and heavy breathing indicated they had all fallen asleep as Lance drove toward Trujillo. Jen reached over and took his hand, giving it a squeeze. They drove for the next three hours. At one-thirty in the morning, Lance slowed as they approached a glow in the sky. Jen concluded a fairly large city lay ahead.

Before entering the city, Lance turned left at a traffic circle. Half an hour later he pulled over and roused Jorge and Margot, who were dozing in the back seat. They sleepily climbed out of the car. As the car doors swung open, Jen could hear waves breaking onto the shore. Lance jumped out of the driver's seat and walked quickly to the other side of the vehicle. He gave Margot a huge hug and kissed her cheek. He then turned to Jorge and embraced him. Shaking his hand, Lance said, "I don't know how to thank you both. You've given me my life. I'll never be able to repay you for what you've done." He hugged them again, and then they disappeared into their house.

A minute later Lance pulled up beside his house. With pride he opened the door, and Jen and Micky walked in. Smiling contentedly, they surveyed the place. Lance showed Micky to her bedroom and gave her a goodnight hug. Then he led Jen to their bedroom. At last they fell asleep in each other's arms.

EPILOGUE

Two years later

A Caucasian couple and their beautiful teenage daughter sat at an outdoor table at a seaside restaurant on the Peruvian coast. Joining them was a dark-haired, dark-skinned girl. The two girls chatted and giggled while the couple lounged comfortably. They laughed at the girls' antics. Sitting in the middle of the table was an enormous plate of ceviche, a combination of seafood, diced tomatoes, onions, and corn.

The gathering at the restaurant had become a weekly ritual for the family. The restaurant owners had gotten to know them well and were disappointed if on occasion the family did not show.

The morning after the episode in the market, Lance and Jen had woken late and had made slow, sweet love to each other before preparing a breakfast. The three of them had enjoyed a quiet meal on the roof, and Jen and Micky had taken in the beauty of the scenery from their perch.

In the following weeks Jen had added her own touches to their home, and Micky had done the same in her bedroom. The place came as close as humanly possible to being their dream home. As promised, Lance had bought a boat and the three of them went fishing at least once a week.

Jen usually joined Lance on his walks. They strolled slowly hand in hand, occasionally stopping to beachcomb. They would usually return home early in the afternoon after shopping at the local market for the day's provisions. After the meal they often made love before Micky returned home from school.

Lance resumed teaching English classes at the school. As his Spanish improved he took on some of the introductory classes as well. This had been difficult at first, but now these had become his favorite classes. The students were so eager to learn, and he found their rapid progress highly rewarding.

The baptism of Lucia took place two months after the market escapade. One month before the baptism, Margot had invited Jen to a café. During the visit Jen started to suspect something was wrong. Margot seemed more serious than usual. Then Margot asked her, "Would you consider being Lucia's comadre?" The question took Jen totally by surprise, but after she recovered, she accepted. On the day of the baptism Lucia looked positively radiant. Lance and Jen performed their roles in the ceremony, holding her while the priest administered the water. Micky looked on delightedly. Margot and Jorge played the parts of the proud parents perfectly. They took photo after photo of the ceremony and then invited everyone for a supper at a tiny hall near the seashore.

The two families often got together. Lucia loved it when they did, because Lance would often take her out to the beach to play with her in the waves. Micky became attached to Lucia as well and often played with them when they went. Lance delivered Lucia back to her mother sopping wet so often that Margot finally got in the habit of bringing Lucia's bathing suit just in case.

In the beginning, Micky had great difficulty adjusting to her new surroundings. Jen and Lance had enrolled her in an elite private school in the city, and Micky absolutely hated it. The stares of the other students bothered her immensely. They made her feel like some kind of a freak. She was also very lonely. The language barrier meant she had no friends. To compensate, she began to spend her evenings chatting online with her friends back in Canada. She dreamed of returning home but would never talk about it. She turned moody and irritable and had several bitter arguments with her mother.

Micky's bad attitude bothered Jen, but she understood what her daughter was going through. Jen started to suspect she had made a mistake in coming to Peru. The situation began to create tension in her relationship with Lance. The two of them argued more frequently. Jen wanted to protect her daughter from the pain she was feeling but didn't know how, and that made Micky increasingly uncommunicative.

All of this changed rather dramatically. At the school, the one subject in which Micky excelled was, of course, English. The class was one of the school's prerequisites, and she was not exempted from the requirement. Unsurprisingly, Micky had the highest marks in the class. One day a girl who was having particular difficulty with the class shyly approached Micky and asked if she would help her. Micky froze. This was one of the few times she had been approached by any of her classmates. Finally Micky shrugged and invited the girl to her place after school.

Jen and Lance were astounded that afternoon when the girls showed up at the house together. The girls immediately retired to Micky's bedroom. Jen and Lance were delighted by the sounds of giggling and even uproarious laughter. The girls switched between Spanish and English all afternoon. Jen and Lance invited Karina for supper, and after a phone call to her parents, she accepted. The girls laughed at their mistakes in each other's languages, and before long any reticence they had with each other disappeared in gales of laughter.

The next night Micky was invited to Karina's place. They helped each other with their homework, and Micky provided private English tutoring. From then on, the girls were inseparable. When their classmates saw the relationship developing, one by one they began to accept Micky.

Finally a girl tentatively raised her hand one day and asked if the students could use Micky as a model during the pronunciation phase of the English class. The teacher may have felt somewhat threatened by the suggestion, but she could not deny the logic of the idea. Micky was elevated to the status of virtual assistant teacher. She even coached her teacher from time to time.

During the next year Micky became aware that several boys had developed crushes on her. She and Karina giggled about some of the things they had overheard the boys saying and teased each other about the boys they liked.

Thanks to Karina, Micky's Spanish improved exponentially, and Karina's marks in English were now the highest in the class— next to Micky's, of course. Micky's proficiency in Spanish was amply demonstrated when a waitress at the beachfront restaurant approached the table and said something to the guests. Jen and Lance looked at each other in confusion. Micky immediately translated.

For Rob, the episode in Chiclayo had been a bitter disappointment. Lance had slipped through his fingers yet again, and the costs of this useless undertaking grated on him.

With Jen's disappearance, Rob had lost his last remaining source of information on Lance. The one consolation was that he no longer had to cover up an unauthorized wiretap. That winter he was promoted to captain and was transferred to Kelowna to head up the investigative unit there. Despite the promotion, life in Kelowna was less hectic than in Vancouver. Rob took up hiking in the summer months and skiing in the winter. When on occasion he ran into his colleagues from the Vancouver department they always commented on how much younger and worry-free he appeared. He still called Detective Raiz in Lima every six months or so. They chatted amicably about their lives, but Raiz never had anything new to report on Lance Knight.

After two years, Lance worried less about someday being discovered. He gradually relaxed his cautious approach, but Jen noticed he was still on guard whenever he met new people. As they attempted to get to know him, he could not help but hold back. This meant their circle of friends was small. If not for Jorge and Margot, who included them in many of their social and family activities, Jen would no doubt have died of boredom. Lance realized that although he had enough money to live comfortably in Peru for the rest of his life, he would never be completely free.